Another Sunday

CYNTHIA STRAUFF

ISBN: 978-1-4834-3817-7 (sc)
ISBN: 978-1-4834-3816-0 (e)

Library of Congress Control Number: 2015915032

Lulu Publishing Services rev. date: 11/12/2015

Dedication

For Jane Grissom Cole,
without whom…..
and for
Celeste.
I hope I got it right.

She was educated upon the premise that she would be protected from the gross events that life might thrust her way….she had no other duty than to be a graceful and accomplished accessory to that protection, since she belonged to a social and economic class to which protection was an almost sacred obligation.

Stoner, John Williams

ANOTHER SUNDAY

PART I

December 24, 1901
These Will Marry
...William Strauff, 1108 East North Avenue, and Miss Celeste Wells, 1123 East North Avenue

Baltimore Sun
December 25, 1901
SLIP AWAY AND MARRY
Parents of the Bride Say she is Under Age
   Miss Celeste Wells, the youngest daughter of Mr. and Mrs. George W. Wells, 1123 East North Avenue, went to Towson Monday afternoon and was married to Mr. William Strauff, 1108 East North Avenue. The parents of the bride knew nothing of the marriage until 4 o'clock yesterday afternoon, while the parents of the groom received the news only about 12 hours earlier.
   Mr. Strauff and Miss Wells procured the marriage license at the County Clerk's office in Towson, and went direct to the parsonage of Trinity Protestant Episcopal Church, where they were married by the

rector, Rev. W.W. H. Powers. In the application for the license the groom's age was given as 24 and that of the bride as 17.

Mr. and Mrs. Strauff will reside at the Stafford for two weeks or more, when they will leave for Denver, Col.

Mr. and Mrs. Wells express great dissatisfaction over their daughter's act. Mrs. Wells said last night that her daughter would not be 17 years old until February, and that she was in the graduating class of the Eastern Female High School. She said she had no objection to the match except the extreme youth of her daughter.

The groom is the son of Mr. and Mrs. August Strauff, and is said to be 22 years old.

One _____

Celeste knew about it from her girlfriends. They whispered and giggled about a visit from their friend, the curse. Her mother, Annie, had talked to her, told her what to expect. She told Celeste that it meant she was becoming a woman, that she should rest during these times, and certainly sit out of gymnastics class.

So, Celeste realized, this was why that group of girls strolled past the gymnasium to sit in the library, looking smug, womanly.

But talk of babies. No. Annie didn't think it proper, yet. Not until Celeste was ready to be married.

When Celeste learned about babies, and, even better, about The Act, she squealed right along with her classmates, her friends, that group of four who did everything together. Celeste, Margaret, Irene and Elizabeth, always in concert, gossiping, laughing, plotting, certainly not studying. They met each morning at the main entrance to Eastern High School, Celeste and Irene coming south from North Avenue, Margaret walking the two blocks from her home on Aisquith Street, and Elizabeth, with the longest trek, from Broadway. When Elizabeth ran late, her father's carriage delivered her. She would jump out to greet her friends before the horse came to a full stop, without a backward glance to the driver. None were burdened with piles of books, but carried just one or two, bound with a leather strap, enough to keep their parents' questions to a minimum.

When Margaret started to bleed, the others were congratulatory. And jealous. Celeste told Annie as soon as she walked in the door after school. "Oh, Mama, Margaret is a woman!" Annie blushed. The next day, Annie prepared a stack of sanitary rags for Celeste. She brought them to her bedroom, and instructed her on their care. They needed

1

to be soaked, only in cold water, then boiled, and washed every day before hanging them on the lines in the back of the basement. She was not to expect the housekeeper to do this; Meg had enough to do. And she was never to mention her monthlies to anyone.

Celeste placed the stack of cloths in the middle drawer of her bureau, under her lace-edged combinations. She tied the packet with a narrow, foam-green grosgrain ribbon and waited to become a woman. Margaret had been the first, then Irene, then Elizabeth. But for Celeste, nothing. She thought about lying to them. Some days she wore the thick pads, held in place with an elastic belt and safety pins, just in case. Still nothing. She decided that it was too uncomfortable to continue; wearing the equipment did nothing to make it happen. When her friends sat out gym class, when they walked with that special "adult" walk, Celeste fumed.

That April, two months after her sixteenth birthday, she found the rust-colored stain. "I am a woman," she crowed to herself. Lining her combinations with toilet tissue, she rushed from the stall to tell her friends.

She arrived for history class early and, eyes lowered, told Mr. Collins that she needed to leave school for the day. She offered no explanation. She didn't need to. Collins dismissed her with a rushed approval. She left, affecting the regal gait she had practiced for months.

She walked the eight blocks from school to home, slowly, sedately, posture erect. But she skipped the last half-block and bounded up the four front steps two-by-two. She paused before ringing the bell, altering her pace and her demeanor. When Meg came to the door Celeste greeted her with a smile. "I am a woman," she announced, and twirled into the vestibule. Meg raised her eyebrow, the right one, and, shaking her head, went back to the kitchen.

"I am a woman," Celeste sang as she walked into the house. She raced up the stairs to her room, her bureau. She knew exactly what to do.

Minutes later, she descended the stairs primly, imagining a book resting atop her head. Annie stood in the doorway of the front room, her mending left in the chair. "I am a woman," Celeste announced.

"I gathered," Annie responded, watching Celeste, standing erect, no longer displaying the pose of a child wanting to be hugged. She really is a woman, Annie thought. Too soon. Too beautiful. Too certain.

Two _____

She told no one. She wasn't sure. It was almost three weeks late, but it had been late before. In fact, she had had only two monthlies in the eight months since that day in April. But before she hadn't had to worry. Now she did. One time, she thought. Surely not.

If she and her girlfriends hadn't talked, hadn't whispered, hadn't giggled about The Act, Celeste would have been unconcerned. If not for a classmate, Edna, no longer at school. Consumption, her brother said. But her girlfriends nodded knowingly, firm in their beliefs that this was not the case. It was certainly more interesting, more fun, to speculate than to take him at his word. Whatever the situation, when Edna returned to Eastern High School, if she returned, life would not be the same for her. Consumption-cured or not, Edna was ruined. That Celeste knew for sure.

Celeste told Annie about her. "Edna's not been at school for weeks. Margaret told us her brother said it was consumption. But she didn't look very sick to us." Annie was silent, returning her attention to her tapestry, concentrating, not looking at Celeste.

Now it was Celeste who waited, and thought. And thought again. She tried to remember a book she had read, *Story of a Coquette*, by Charlotte Braeme, her favorite author. Had there been someone with her predicament? Her possible predicament.

She stood at her bedroom window and looked out at the grey December day, not noticing the wreaths decorating the doors across the wide street.

She had only one choice. Marry Willie. And why not? He was handsome; his family was rich. He was a gentleman. Well, not too much of a gentleman. Celeste took pleasure, even pride, in that. She had made him shed those scruples he held so firmly, so righteously. It had been fun; she had won him over.

But now this.

She hadn't seen him since that afternoon, that exquisite, clear, crisp November Saturday. He had sent her letters. A liveried driver had delivered a silver bracelet, with a note included, a few days ago. Celeste's sister, Eva, had answered the door and handed the package to Celeste without a word, though her expression shouted disapproval. The two sisters lived their lives in parallel, strangers sharing the same house.

The old stick, Celeste thought, an old biddy at twenty, nothing but a blue-stocking, always studying something or other, walking the ten blocks each day to The Methodist Women's College on St. Paul Street to be with a lot of other dried-up old sticks.

But Eva had said nothing to Annie. At least she's not a snitch, Celeste thought.

Willie had been calling on Celeste since school began, finally succumbing to her summertime sashays up and down North Avenue, sometimes with her friends, sometimes alone, but always with a parasol. All the girls knew of Willie, shy, self-effacing, his delicate build, a combination of pure and sensual, made him the topic of many giggling conversations. It had emboldened the more intrepid of Celeste's coterie to take daring steps to attract his attention. Elizabeth, who had spent many summer hours visiting Celeste, was the leader; Celeste was right behind. Willie didn't appear to have a sweetheart or to be courting anyone. It was hard to tell. They all knew of the Strauffs, but none actually knew them.

Celeste, sometimes with Elizabeth at her side, would stand at her bedroom window, and if she angled her head just right, she could see the front door of his townhouse, a block away on the north side of the street. The girls were seldom rewarded with a view of Willie. He left early each morning with his father and returned in late afternoon. They spied his comings and goings only on weekends. They could only guess where he'd been.

Late one summer Saturday morning, as they passed his door, he emerged. Freshly shaven, elegant in his starched collar, they recognized the subtle scent of Bay Rum, the same cologne Celeste's father wore when he left the house for his job at the United and Electric Railway.

Willie greeted Celeste. He had seen her in the neighborhood. Everyone knew of Celeste. Many called her The Belle of Broadway, Baltimore's tree-lined promenade that ended at North Avenue, just east of Celeste's home. He hardly noticed Elizabeth. Then, remembering his manners, which were never far from his mind, he greeted her as well.

Celeste stepped toward him. "I've seen you so often, but I don't think we've formally met. I'm Celeste Wells, and I live across the street. This is my friend, Elizabeth Burton. We attend Eastern." Celeste added this, hoping that her bold introduction would convey a sense of sophistication and worldliness to this handsome, gallant fellow.

Willie stood, trying to think of something to say to this vision, so assured, such a contrast to his stammering, shy ways. He said nothing, and eyes cast downward, smiled a greeting.

"It is nice to finally meet you," Celeste continued. "I wouldn't say no if you choose to call on me. You do know where I live, don't you?" She couldn't stifle her giggle. Elizabeth hid her smile behind her gloved hand.

"I do know where you live, and if your parents wouldn't mind, I would like very much to call on you," Willie responded, spilling out more words than he thought he could manage, this time with no stammer, no hesitation, although he felt the heat rise in his cheeks.

"Lovely," Celeste answered, and the two girls twirled their parasols as they turned up the street, swaying in unison. They erupted into giggles before they reached the end of the block.

Elizabeth turned to Celeste. "What will you say when he calls? What will you tell your mother?"

"Oh, Elizabeth, he's so handsome. He's such a gentleman. He's so rich. What could she possibly say? After all, I am sixteen. And she better not push Eva at him, even though they're just about the same age. Not that she'd look up from her books to see what was right in front of her."

The next week, Willie, smelling of Ivory Soap and Bay Rum, called at the Wells' house. He charmed Annie, as Celeste knew he would, his shyness speaking to Annie's own. He was polite and serious with George, Celeste's quiet, scholarly father. Willie seemed to them an earnest counterbalance to Celeste's giddiness. They hoped he would be a good influence, though they had some concern about the age difference. They knew Willie was older, but he showed such a solemn timidity that their worries were contained. Maybe, they considered, that's how Germans raise their boys.

*Three*_____

For three consecutive weekend afternoons Willie and Celeste spent time together in her family's front room, Meg serving tea and cookies, Annie bustling in and out, gathering her needlework, keeping an eye on Celeste. Annie knew Willie was a shy one; she was less sure of her younger daughter.

The following week, having proved himself trustworthy, Willie, with Celeste by his side, headed south on North Avenue. Just three blocks south of the Wells' home, Green Mount Cemetery proved a luxuriant location. The garden cemetery, with its quiet, tree-lined, winding paths, was a fashionable scene for courting young men and women. Towering oaks, maples, walnuts, and lindens supplied shade in summer; in autumn, they provided color, especially the ginkgos with their brilliant yellow. The grassy knolls, shaded dells, and monuments and statues added a sense of history to the setting. It was here that the couple spent their first time alone, unchaperoned. Green Mount Cemetery became *their* place.

On the afternoon of their second outing, the weather proved delightful; the morning chill had melted into a golden warmth. Celeste and Willie ambled down gravel paths. Willie took Celeste's arm; Celeste leaned her body into his. The cemetery was crowded with others enjoying what may have been the last inviting weekend before the arrival of bitter November winds. Families visited graves, old men and women sat on the benches enjoying the day, young lovers strolled hand-in-hand down winding lanes.

Celeste led Willie to a secluded trail to the left. As they passed a stolid granite mausoleum, Celeste pulled Willie to its entrance. She knew Green Mount Cemetery; her grandparents, her uncle, her older sister were buried here and her parents visited often, every holiday and birthday, every anniversary of their deaths. The Snyder mausoleum was off a path that ran parallel to the Wells' plot.

"Willie, let's go in here. I want to show you something." Willie watched as Celeste skipped ahead.

"Isn't it locked? What's in there?"

Celeste hopped back to lead him to the door of the granite edifice. "Wait. Just watch." She laughed as she pulled the iron bar up and to the side, then pushed open the thick dark wooden door. She grabbed Willie's hand and pulled him in.

"I found this secret space when I was a little girl. Mama and Papa would be at the graves, they'd forget about me. I'd come in here just to be wicked. When they noticed that I was gone, when I knew that they were searching for me, I'd pop out from behind that tree over to the side. They never found my hiding place! And now I've shown it to you. So, don't you think that you are special?" Celeste teased Willie. She loved to see him blush and stammer. He was enamored with her; she knew that. And Willie was just so handsome.

His eyes are hazel, she noted, and bit her lower lip as she smiled. She knew from practicing in front of the mirror that it made her look especially fetching. She leaned in and kissed him, on the lips. She thought that he would blush and bluster, that she would laugh and then kiss him again.

But instead he pulled her close, his lips pressed to her cheek. Celeste had read about this in her Charlotte Braeme books. Now she knew what it meant to swoon. She let her body go limp against his as she heard him moan. She held him tight, knowing that she loved him more than anything. They clung to each other, saying nothing. She wondered if this were The Act. There was no one whom she could ask. It was, she decided, nothing like what she and her girlfriends had imagined it to be.

"Oh my God. Oh my God. I am so sorry. Celeste, I am so sorry." Willie's voice sounded as if he were far away. She opened her eyes.

"Don't be sorry. I love you, Willie. I love you."

He took her hand and kissed her fingers. "You are everything to me, Celeste. Everything." He tried to pull away, but Celeste held

8

him tight. His face was pressed against hers. She felt his tears and wondered why. All she wanted to do was sing.

Finally, clothes adjusted, they left the mausoleum. The sun had moved behind a cloud. Willie walked Celeste home. At the vestibule, he greeted Meg. He kissed Celeste's hand, this time in front of the maid.

He turned and walked the one block south to his home. His father, August, sat in the front room, reading an issue of *Berliner Abendblatt* dated three weeks earlier. A pince-nez perched on the end of his nose, August held a black fountain pen in his right hand, ready to check any article he thought would be of interest to his Baltimore readers. A stack of unread issues lay beside him, heavy black Gothic lettering visible in the glow of the three gas lamps that kept the room bright in the afternoon gloaming.

His mother, Paulina, sat at the dining room table, putting the finishing touches to the mock-up of the following week's issue of *Der Bayerische Volkenblatt*, the newspaper August published. Her short, buxom figure was encased in black bombazine. Though she had completed her year of mourning for her mother-in-law, she wanted to get some more wear from it, so expensive had it proved. Her shoes sat at the side of the chair, and she wiggled her feet to loosen the black lisle hose that had tightened around her toes.

Clara, Willie's sister, older than he by fifteen months, sat at the piano, reviewing the Schumann Sonata No. 2 she was scheduled to perform for the Baltimore Music Academy later that month. August and Paulina were accustomed to her playing; the sound of her deft touch did not intrude upon their work.

Hanne, the housekeeper who had been with them since Willie and Clara were babies, was in the basement kitchen preparing the Sunday evening meal.

Willie greeted the three and went up the stairs to his room. Before he could close his door, to be alone, to try to make sense of what he had done, Clara appeared. She entered and closed the door quietly behind her.

"Don't get involved with her, Willie. It's not a good idea. She is not good for you."

He was silent.

"We know that you are seeing the Wells girl. She's too young for you. She's not serious, Willie. She will only bring you heartbreak. I'm your sister. I know what's best for you. Stop seeing her, for your own good."

"It's too late," he breathed.

"I don't know what you mean by that. But do not think that this will go down well. *Vati* doesn't suspect, but *Mutti* knows that something is going on. Break it off before you have to talk to them." Clara turned and walked out of the room. Before long he heard the notes of the piano once again.

He walked to his desk and stared out the window. His view was the alleyway, but in his mind he saw the mausoleum, felt Celeste. He closed his eyes and relived those brief moments. He turned and sat down at his desk, head in his hands.

Willie did not appear when, an hour later, the family gathered for dinner.

"Go get your brother," August said to Clara. "Hanne is ready to serve. We will not hold her up. Tell him that we expect him immediately. He can go back to his drawings later." August removed his napkin from the ring and spread it on his lap. Paulina followed suit. Hanne stood by the dumbwaiter, ready to bring out the bowls and platters.

A minute later Clara returned to the dining room and asked Hanne to take him his dinner on a tray. Paulina nodded to Hanne to begin serving the meal. August shook his head and started his dinner without comment.

Four

Dearest Celeste,

I think about you day and night. I close my eyes and see your face, your eyes, and your teasing smile. I am besotted with you, my darling one. So besotted that I feel that I cannot control my actions toward you, a sweetheart who must be revered and respected.

I know of no other course than for us to take some time apart. My heart aches every moment; I can think of nothing and no one but you. Can we at least write to one another? Please answer my letter and tell me that you forgive the unforgiveable. You have my heart.

Always,
Willie

Dear Celeste,

I have not heard back from you. Please tell me that you forgive me, that there is a chance that we might see each other once more, that you know me to be more than a craven fool. If I am a fool, it is for love of you.

You hold my heart. Please let me hear from you.

All my love, forever,
Willie

Dearest Celeste, please accept this bracelet as a token of my love for the most beautiful girl in Baltimore. You truly are the Belle of Broadway. I think of you every moment. Please let me hear from you.

All my love, forever,
Willie

*Five*_____

Willie took his breakfast with the family that Tuesday morning. Hanne was not there to serve. She was in the basement kitchen, preparing for the evening's special dinner. The mixed scents of sugar and butter and sauerkraut wafted up the stairs. August had left for the office early. It would close at noon, in observance of Christmas Eve. Willie was not needed that day.

He returned to his room to finish dressing. He attached the linene collar to his stiffly starched and ironed shirt, and put into place the heavy gold cufflinks presented to him by August on his 21st birthday. This was to be a day to be remembered.

Celeste's letter had arrived the previous Thursday, placed on the silver tray in the vestibule, her child-like scrawl telegraphing to all who passed just who it was from. Clara handed it to him when he walked in the door. "Willie, don't get involved with that girl. Just don't."

Willie ignored her and walked up the stairs to his room.

> *Dearest Willie,*
> *I need to see you. Please come.*
> *Your,*
> *Celeste*

He stared at the note, deciding what to do next. Then he folded it, put it in the breast pocket of his jacket and left the house. Clara was busy at the piano; August was reading a November issue of *Der Stutgarter Nachricten*; Paulina, at the dining room table, was clipping the articles August had circled for inclusion in the next issue of the paper. No one noticed Willie's exit. It was still early enough to call on Celeste, he thought.

Willie crossed the street; lights shone in every window of her house. He thought it looked inviting. He rang the bell. Meg answered and went to get Annie. Such a nice boy, she thought, so well-mannered. He remained in the vestibule. Annie smoothed her hair as she came to the door

"I'd like to c-call on C-c-celeste, Mrs. W-w-ells," Willie said. His heightened stammer made Annie want to take him into her arms.

Willie waited in the hallway while Annie ascended the stairs. A few minutes later, Celeste came into his view, her blond hair scooped up in what would appear to the uninitiated to be a careless bun. She adjusted the pale blue cameo that she had placed at her neck. Once she reached the landing, she put her hands to her sides, clenched and unclenched her fists, willed herself to smile, to act as if she were at ease.

"Mama, can we use the front room?" she asked. Annie agreed, wondering about this unannounced visit. Willie saw that Celeste wore the silver bracelet.

Annie pulled the room's pocket doors together, leaving them open the six inches she deemed decorous. She stood by the door, considering whether to stay. Then, pulling herself up to her full height, she decided to give them some privacy. She walked quickly to the back of the house, not giving herself the opportunity to change her mind.

The couple had moved to the sofa. Celeste took hold of Willie's hands. He brought her fingertips to his lips. "Willie, I think that we should marry." And she fixed him with a stare, her eyes filled with tears. She lowered her face against his chest. "I'm late."

Willie wondered if he had heard her correctly. He felt her tremble against him.

"No one must know. Please Willie."

He lifted her face so that she could see him; their knees touched. "I'll never let you down, Celeste. I'll make all the arrangements. Don't worry about this. It will be our secret, just the two of us. We'll be together. It will be fine." He laughed, "It will be more than fine. It will be perfect. I love you and now we'll be together. I'll make the arrangements."

Celeste closed her eyes and put her arms around his neck, "I knew you would. I knew you were a gentleman." Then she stood, placed her hands on her hips.

"You need to go now. I've got school tomorrow and need to finish reading a chapter for history class. And I love you." She smiled while allowing him to kiss her. He felt her teeth. I love this, he thought.

All will be well, she thought. Willie is a gentleman. He will do the right thing.

Six

Willie reviewed his "needs to be done" list as he looked at his reflection on the morning of Christmas Eve. This time tomorrow I will be a husband. I will be an adult. I will be respected, he thought.

He had made reservations at the Stafford Hotel. He had talked to Charles Steiff, an old schoolmate whose father owned a jewelry business. Steiff had suggested the wide gold band. It would be ready and was waiting for them.

Since he lived on the north side of North Avenue, he knew that they would have to journey to Towson for their marriage license. He had hired a carriage to take them on this Christmas Eve adventure. The Episcopal Church was close enough that they could walk from the Courthouse. The driver would wait for them, and then take them back home. Only it wouldn't be home anymore, he thought. We are starting our new life. This will show *Vati*. This will show *Vati* that I am a man, a proper man, a proper husband.

Willie stared at his reflection: shoes polished, suspenders snapped, vest buttoned, shirt and collar perfect, hair oiled and combed. He was satisfied that he looked like a proper husband. He headed down the steps. He wanted to be outside waiting when the carriage arrived.

Clara, wearing the red bathrobe with white piping she had since her high school days, met him at the landing Her brown hair was still swathed in the paper wrappers she slept in to give it a bit of wave.

"And just what is that outside? Where are you going?"

Willie eased into his black overcoat, cashmere, and adjusted his maroon neck scarf. "I'm taking Celeste downtown to look at the store windows, and then we're having a holiday lunch at Marconi's. Does that meet with your approval?" Both he and Clara were surprised at the secure and sarcastic tone in his response. As he pulled on his grey gloves he thought, maybe I am a proper man.

"You are asking for trouble, Willie. I beg you to stop this nonsense. Where did you get the money for the carriage? Such an extravagance. You better hope that *Vati* doesn't find out. When will you be back? You know that tonight's dinner is special, and then we go to midnight mass. Don't you dare miss this.

"Such nonsense. She is a child, Willie. And you're not much better." Clara turned on her heel and marched to the back of the house, black silk skirt swaying, her limp imperceptible. Willie strode out the front door and down the steps.

The driver jumped from his perch to open the carriage door. As Willie entered, he said, "Our first stop is just across the street. And we have you for the whole day, correct?"

Seven ————————————————

Celeste stood at the front window, nervously hopping from one foot to the other. She saw the carriage stop, and as Willie stepped onto the sidewalk, she ran to the door to greet him. Even in his nervousness, Willie inhaled sharply when he saw her. She stood in the doorway, wearing a high-necked, long-sleeved lace blouse, the color of soft candlelight. She was taller than most girls, so the black, red and green tartan taffeta skirt, bought for holiday parties the year before, allowed a glimpse of her ankles as she ran to him. Low-cut black patent-leather French-heeled shoes shone on her narrow feet, and black stockings, the sheerest she could find, filched from Eva's bureau, completed her outfit. Her hair hung loose in the back, tied with a black velvet ribbon, wider than the ones she normally wore.

Though the wind was biting, she thought her maroon wool coat not nearly festive enough for the occasion. She wore a waist-length jacket, black velvet, also Eva's. It fitted tightly, her bosom always fuller than her older sister's. She added a small chinchilla muff, a February gift from her parents for her 16th birthday.

Annie followed Celeste to the door. Willie greeted the Celeste's mother and wished her a Merry Christmas. Celeste and Willie had agreed upon the story they would tell their parents. Celeste said that they would be back by dinnertime.

She skipped down the steps toward the waiting carriage and started to clamber in. Remembering her dignity, she stopped and waited for the driver to help her. Willie slid in beside her. She waited to be kissed. He took her hand and drew it to his lips.

She turned to face him. "This is the happiest day of my life, Willie. Really." And she leaned against him. He put his arm around her and whispered, "We have a stop to make."

Celeste's heart lurched. "Where are we going?" The carriage turned south from North Avenue, not the route to Towson. Celeste swallowed and looked straight ahead. She closed her eyes and took a deep breath.

"Not to worry," Willie said. "This is a good surprise." She settled back into the seat, but her breathing remained shallow. She watched streets pass, trying to trust Willie. The horse trotted down Charles Street, passing the commanding Belvedere Hotel on the left. When the carriage entered Mt. Vernon Place, Willie pointed out the Stafford Hotel, newly opened and majestic with its brown Roman brick. The horse kept a lively gait, the streets almost empty this Christmas Eve morning.

As they approached Saratoga Street, Celeste saw The Old St. Paul's Episcopal Church to her left. Maybe we will be married there, she thought. But the carriage veered to the west and Old St. Paul's was left in the background. Celeste tugged at her gloves, pulled the handkerchief from the pocket inside her muff.

The carriage stopped in front of a small shop on Liberty Street, The Baltimore Sterling Silver Company. Willie turned to her, "You have to have a wedding ring. I called ahead. They know we need it right away. All you have to do is make sure that it's the right size."

"Oh, Willie, I knew you'd take care of me." Celeste threw her arms around him. Willie blushed, afraid that the driver could see them, fearful of what he might assume of Celeste's character and reputation. Extricating himself from her clasp, Willie patted her hand, and hopped from his side to open the carriage door for her. He told the driver that they'd be just be a few minutes. Celeste giggled as she stepped from the carriage. Willie looked long at her ankle clad in the black stocking as her skirt caught briefly on the door handle.

Celeste took his hand and skipped into the store; he followed sedately behind her, slowing her pace. She is a child, he thought. But I will do the right thing. Everything will be fine. Yes, everything will be fine.

The ring was perfect, she said, as they continued their journey north to the Towson courthouse to apply for their marriage license. When they arrived, Willie told the carriage driver where to meet them, telling him to be there at two p.m.

Celeste clasped Willie's hand as they mounted the stairs of the four-story granite building. Within minutes, the clerk had transcribed the particulars in an elegant script, holding the long, thin, wooden pen in his ink-stained fingers, dipping it into the black inkwell, twice for each line.

Celeste lied about her age. "I am eighteen," she said in response to his question. "Nineteen in February."

Willie gave his age as twenty-three. He was the man, who would, and did, take care of things

Celeste kissed Willie when he took the document from the clerk. Willie blushed and immediately felt his erection. He blushed even more and turned away. Celeste had no idea why.

Trinity Episcopal Church was three blocks from the courthouse, on Allegheny Avenue. Willie had located it as part of his planning for the day and had talked to the priest there about their situation. He was surprised at the cleric's kind response, so different from the stern Catholic priests of his childhood.

The couple walked sedately, Celeste practicing what she considered to be the gait of a married woman. Willie's overcoat hung open. He didn't notice the cold.

Nearing the church, the couple saw finely outfitted ladies, members of the Episcopal Church Women, bustling in and out carrying white poinsettias. Entering the narthex Celeste noticed the white flowers tightly enclosing the altar, only a narrow aisle for the priests to navigate left open.

The women glanced at the young couple, saw their tentative steps. One kind soul asked if they needed help. She didn't recognize them, but they looked like Episcopalians to her.

"We're looking for Father Powers." Willie worked hard to make his voice strong.

"I'm sure that The Reverend is in the rectory," the woman said, shifting a top-heavy poinsettia to her right hand. With her left, she pointed to the grey granite house next to the church. An unadorned green wreath hung on its front door. "Most likely he's preparing for tonight's services." She paused. "Is he expecting you?"

Celeste jumped in. "Oh, yes. He's going to marry us." She looked down to adjust the pearl buttons on the ivory kid gloves she had quietly lifted from her mother's glove drawer.

The woman purposefully kept her smile, a welcoming one, she hoped. She wondered about the family of this finely-outfitted, refined-looking couple. No proper wedding? Something afoot, if not amiss, she thought, and was grateful that she, and not some of the other ECW members, had been the one to approach them. She watched them, a sweet, young couple, the groom serious beyond his years, the bride an innocent child.

Celeste glowed. Christmas Eve, she thought, and I will be married. Willie was silent. Celeste didn't notice.

"Would you be our witness?" Celeste asked. The woman looked startled, as did Willie.

Smiling, the woman replied, "I would be delighted. Let me get some flowers for you to carry." She turned back to the church.

The couple walked to the rectory door, Celeste carrying a bouquet of greenery with two white poinsettia blooms in the center. The woman had wrapped it in a starched white linen communion veil that she took from the drawer containing the fair linens. No better use for it, she thought, though she made sure that none of the others saw her remove it.

Willie rang the bell. As they waited, he felt in his pocket for the ring.

Eight_____

They left the rectory and Willie saw that, right on time, the carriage was waiting. The woman kissed Celeste as the couple got into the carriage.

"Oh, I'll never forget you and your kindness," Celeste said. "And Merry Christmas!" Willie added a quiet word of thanks to her as well.

He addressed the driver, "Please take us back to North Avenue, 1123." The driver folded the penknife he had been using to clean his fingernails and tipped his hat as he closed the door behind Willie. "Some kind of ceremony?" he asked.

Willie answered softly, "Yes. A wedding, ours."

"Well, congratulations are in order. I never did a drive to no one's wedding before. And on Christmas Eve. You are a lucky bunch," and he stuck out his hand to Willie.

Embarrassed, Willie shook it. "Thank you. Thank you very much."

The couple was quiet on the drive down York Road, Celeste uncharacteristically so. Each was engrossed in his own thoughts. Celeste studied her new ring and regretted that she hadn't filed her nails more carefully. Willie was unaware of the continual tapping of his foot. His thoughts ricocheted between the delight of imagining their wedding night and the dread of telling August and Clara. Neither talked about how they would tell their parents.

As the carriage crossed 25th Street, Willie turned to Celeste. "I think it best if we told your parents together. Then, while you gather your things, I can go and talk to mine. I think it would be better if I did that alone. Then I'll come and get you and we can start our new life." Willie smiled and took Celeste's hand.

"Are you nervous about telling them?" he asked.

22

"Oh, they will love you, Willie, almost as much as I do. And you will be there to tell them. You'll be there to take care of me. I love you so much. How could they not be happy for me, for us?"

Willie kissed the top of her head and breathed in the scent of her hair, her ribbons. No worry, he thought, how could they not be happy? He smiled, closed his eyes. Celeste sat snug against him, for the rest of the journey.

He felt the carriage stop and Celeste spring away, her hand on the door handle before the driver could reach her. "Come on, Willie. Let's go in," Celeste bubbled. Willie scrambled from the cab and paid the driver, including a generous holiday tip.

"Thank you, sir, Merry Christmas. And congratulations. This is one I'll tell the wife, for sure." He tipped his hat, stepped high to his seat. Horse and driver headed home, the horse to his barn, the driver to his family, both anticipating their holiday dinners.

Celeste rang the bell. When Meg answered, Celeste hugged her as she called, "Mama, Papa, Eva, we have some news." Willie stood behind her. The household gathered in the vestibule, Annie anticipating an engagement announcement, George the same. Meg edged out of the way to give the family some room in the crowded space, but remained close enough to hear what was being said.

Holding up her left hand, Celeste exclaimed, "We're married!" and twirled around to kiss Willie. Willie gently disengaged her and, facing her parents, said, "I know this is sudden. I know you m-m-must be d-disappointed. It was my idea. Please don't b-blame Celeste. I want you to know that I will take care of her. N-no n-need to worry. I will make a good h-home for h-her." He stopped, breathless from the effort of his speech, realizing then that he should have prepared something more substantive, more husbandly.

His words were met with silence. Meg stood, not willing to miss a word of the exchange. Eva reached for her father's hand and led him into the hallway. Annie followed. Celeste and Willie remained in the vestibule.

"Well, aren't you happy for me? For us?" Celeste said, tears coming to her eyes. Willie stood straight, his hands clasped behind his back, awaiting a response from his new in-laws.

Annie was the first to speak. "Celeste, you are so young. You haven't even graduated from high school. You hardly know one another."

George spoke, a sternness in his voice that was new to Willie. "Young man, do you know how old Celeste is? Do you know that she is still sixteen? A child? We will have to consider getting this annulled. Where did this happen? How could you have done this without our permission, or without even letting us know?"

"I know that, sir," Willie started to speak. But Celeste interrupted him. "Papa, we are in love. We want to be together. There was no reason to wait. It was so exciting."

Willie interrupted. "I know this is a disappointment to you, sir. But I will make it up to you, I promise you that."

Eva stood in the background, observing, saying nothing. Finally, she asked, "And where will you live?"

Celeste jumped in, "Oh Willie's taking care of everything. We'll stay at the Stafford until he goes to Denver for the paper. I'll go with him. That will be our honeymoon. We'll find a place to live when we get back home. It will be the most exciting honeymoon anyone ever has had! Oh, please be happy for us. We want everyone to be happy."

Annie pursed her lips. "Willie, does your family know about this?" already knowing the answer.

"We wanted to tell you first. If it's all right, we were hoping that Celeste could stay here and prepare her things while I go and tell them. I think it better if I did this by myself."

Annie and George exchanged a look. This time it was Eva who pursed her lips.

Annie faced her daughter. "I just don't know what to say. Celeste, you have always been so strong-willed, so sure of yourself. I wish you had come to us. I wish you would have at least waited until you graduated. That wouldn't have been too much to ask." George's fists and jaw were clenched tight.

Seeing her father, Eva jumped in. "Willie, if you need to talk to your parents, then you'd better get on with it. I can help Celeste pack, if that is what Mama and Papa allow."

George nodded his assent. Celeste crossed the hallway to kiss her father. "Thank you, Papa. I knew you'd want me to be happy."

"Mr. and Mrs. Wells, thank you. I promise that I will take care of her, that I will be a proper husband." He reached to shake George's hand. After a hesitation that both of them noticed, George clasped it. Annie stepped closer and kissed him goodbye. To Celeste Willie said, "I'll be back before you know it." And he kissed her, on the cheek, and left the house.

Celeste headed for the steps, "Come on, Eva. Will you help me pack? Mama, will you come? Papa, I love you. Please be happy for us."

Eva followed Celeste to her room. George and Annie remained in the hallway. Meg scurried toward the kitchen, but remained on the top step where she could hear their conversation.

"What should we do? What can we do?" Annie asked her husband. "Should we try to have it annulled?"

George shook his head. After a moment he responded, "She's always been so headstrong. If we did that, most likely she would run away. And he is a nice, decent boy. I don't think that he will harm her. It's just that he is a boy, and, really, we don't know him. She doesn't know him, and he certainly doesn't know her. We've never even met the Strauffs. And what does the boy do? He works for his father, but he seems such a gentle, tender soul, I'm sure he's under his thumb."

"The mother seems a decent sort. And isn't the daughter some kind of musical prodigy?" Annie said. "Celeste said that Willie is going to Denver for the paper. That must mean that he has some position, that August Strauff has some confidence in him. And he is a nice boy; you've got to give him that. He could be a good influence on Celeste, help her not to be so self-centered, help her to grow up. Maybe once we get used to it, it won't be so bad. It's just that it's such a shock. I had no idea, no idea. He didn't, he doesn't, seem like the kind of boy to go off and do this kind of thing."

"He can't be a boy any longer, Annie. That's what we have to worry about."

Disappointed with the pace of the conversation, Meg descended the steps to the kitchen. It appeared that high drama was not going to take place.

Upstairs, Celeste pulled clothes from her wardrobe and bureau drawers and flung them onto her bed. "Do you have a suitcase?" Eva asked.

Celeste stopped. "I never thought of that. Maybe I could use one of the wicker hampers that we take with us when we go to the ocean. Do you think that would work?"

"You can't take a hamper to the Stafford, Celeste. Let me get my luggage. You can borrow it. And I do mean borrow. And I want my jacket back too." Eva went to the box room and returned with three pieces of dark blue Lady Baltimore luggage: suitcase, hat box, and train case. "You don't need to fill all these right now. If you need more, you can just come back. Meanwhile, take what you think you'll need for the next few days."

Eva's offer surprised Celeste. Maybe now that I'm a woman, Eva will treat me with some respect, she thought. "Thank you, Eva. You are so nice to do this. Please take care of Mama and Papa. Don't let them worry about me."

Eva stood beside the bed, watched Celeste as she tossed her clothes into the valise. She saw a child playing at being an adult. Eva hadn't experienced much of the world, but she had read enough that she feared for her sister.

"Don't worry, Lestie," Eva said, using the nickname that she hadn't used since they were children. "It will all turn out for the best."

Suitcase and train case packed, the two sisters returned to the front room to sit with George and Annie to wait for Willie. The room was filled with the scent of the pine Christmas tree. All were silent.

Finally, Celeste said, "Can we open our presents now?"

Nine————————————————————

Willie didn't need to use his key; the front door was unlocked. Kitchen smells wafted from the floor below, sauerkraut, spices from mincemeat pies, pumpkin, cloves, cinnamon. The front hallway was steamy from cooking.

He came in quietly, unsure of what he would say, how he would say it, but certain of his task, his duty to his new wife. The family was gathered in the front room, August in his chair beside the fire, Paulina in the crimson damask chair that sat in the bay window, Clara in the middle of the navy brocade sofa, music scores of Brahms and Haydn spread out around her. Sounds of Fritz Kreisler's violin came from the gramophone.

"It's about time." Clara's words greeted him before he entered the room. She saw that his face was wet with perspiration and worried that he was sick again. So much family energy expended worrying about Willie and his health, she thought.

"That must have been some lunch," Clara said. Paulina was busy wrapping a last minute gift, attaching a dried wishbone with a thin, red ribbon, laced at the edges. The sounds of *Liebesliede* filled the room. August read, *The Baltimore Sun.* Paulina put down her scissors; August lowered the paper. All awaited Willie's explanation.

"I have something to tell you," Willie began. He felt his heart race, his mouth dry, that familiar fainting feeling. He reached out to steady himself and continued, "Celeste and I were married this morning. We will be staying at the Stafford until we leave for Denver."

The family was silent. Willie saw shock, disbelief in the faces of Paulina and Clara. When he looked toward his father, he saw disgust.

"I know this is a surprise to you. I wish it could have been otherwise, but we felt that it was the right thing to do. I love her very much and know that she will make me happy. I only hope that I can bring happiness to her as well."

Willie waited for their response. None came.

After a time, August spoke. "How do you intend to support yourself and this girl?"

"I make a good salary at the paper. We can live on that."

August stood. "You make nothing. Do you realize that? Your salary is a pittance. It is enough for you, living in this house, having all your needs taken care of, being coddled like a child. But you want to be a man? You want to have a wife? You need to be in a position to support her. And, young man, you are not in that position."

Clara gathered her music and sat, her hands folded in her lap.

August strode toward Willie. "Do her parents know about this? How old is this girl, anyway?"

Willie forced himself not to back away from his father. He had known that the confrontation would be dreadful, whatever he said. He had prepared himself to accept whatever came. He opened his mouth to speak.

Paulina placed her hands on the arms of her chair, addressed her son. "Where were you married? Who married you? What priest? It was a priest, wasn't it? It was a Catholic ceremony, wasn't it?"

Willie steeled himself. "We were married in the Episcopal Church. That's almost Catholic. Celeste is Episcopalian."

"Oh my God," Paulina cried. "The scandal. What will people think? You are excommunicated from the church, Willie. Do you know that?" She struggled to catch her breath.

"Not to worry," Clara interjected. "If they weren't married by a priest, they aren't really married. We can have it annulled." She rose and went to her mother's chair.

Willie remained standing in the doorway. "You will do no such thing. I am an adult. This is why we kept it a secret. I don't expect your blessing, but I d-do exp-p-pect your g-good wishes. Celeste is part of our family now. And I need to get b-back to h-h-her."

Willie walked into the room, posture erect. He inhaled deeply before he spoke. "She is part of our family now. P-please accept her. P-please be k-kind to her, to me."

Clara stepped toward him. "You have ruined this holiday for us, Willie. Not only this year, but every year, this will be what we remember."

"Clara, enough," August said. He turned toward his son. "Where is she, your bride? What do you intend to do now?"

Willie told his father of his plans. August replied, "You go to your bride. But you come to work on Thursday. We will work something out."

"I want to take Celeste with me when I go to Denver. I will pay for that."

"Yes, you will. What's done is done. We will make the best of it, Lina. Clara, stay out of this. This is between your brother and this girl." August's accent was heavier now, telegraphing his anger. Willie recognized it.

Turning to Willie, he said, "Tell me the truth. What is the reason for the secrecy, for the rush? What do we need to know?"

"We love each other. We knew that we would meet with nothing but opposition. We are adults. We made our own decision. That is what you need to know, nothing more."

Clara went to her father, her limp more pronounced this afternoon, "*Vati*, don't let him go. We can have the marriage annulled. They really aren't married if a priest didn't do it."

"Clara, I said enough. Let the boy be. Let him be a man. Let him make at least one decision for himself." August fixed his stare on Willie. "You have done this. You must now learn what it is to stand firm. I will not indulge you. You will continue to earn the same salary, no more. And you and that girl will learn what the world is like.

"It is not an easy place. You will not have an easy life. Now, go. We talk at the office on Thursday. Do not be late."

Paulina stood. "What about Christmas dinner? You won't be here for Christmas dinner?" She put her hand over her mouth when she saw Willie shake his head.

"I will be with Celeste. We will spend the day together, the two of us."

August walked to his son and placed a hand on his shoulder. "Willie, be with us tomorrow. Bring Celeste so that *Mutti* and I can meet her," his words more gentle than his son could remember hearing. "Do that for your mother, I promise you that we will welcome your wife. Do this for your mother."

Without answering, Willie turned toward the stairs to his room. Clara followed him. "You are a fool, Willie. There is still time to get out of this insane predicament. Let us annul this disaster. It will be best for both of you. You will never be able to support her, Willie. Don't you understand that? You belong here with us. We are your family, not her, not that capricious child. She will bring you nothing but heartache. Let us help you. I am begging you, Willie."

"Clara, come down here," August's words rang out.

Willie retrieved his suitcase from where he had placed it under the bed the night before. "Enough, Clara. Just enough. Let me be. Let me leave this house. You can't control my life. Please leave me in peace. Please wish the best for me."

Without responding, Clara turned and left.

A few minutes later Willie returned to the front room. Clara was not there. He walked to the window and leaned down to kiss his mother. To his father he said, "We will come tomorrow, *Vati*."

Hanne stood by the door, watching. She opened the door as Willie left. *"Fröhliche Weihnachten, Herr Willie,"* she said.

Willie responded, *"Fröhliche Weihnachten, Hanne.* Merry Christmas."

Ten

Willie walked east to the Wells' house, crossing the wide median mid-block. His valise felt light. He thought it matched his heart. He had stood up for himself, for his wife. He had faced Clara. His father's wrath had not been as dreadful as he had imagined. Clara was the tough one. He could talk to his mother later, when they were by themselves.

Celeste, watching from her bedroom, saw him leave the house. She bounded downstairs to open the door and threw herself into his arms. Annie and George sat together on the sofa in the front room. Willie left his suitcase in the vestibule and went to them.

"I've told them, my parents, I mean," he said. Then, turning to Celeste, he said, "We should be on our way."

"How will you get there?" This from George. "There are no carriages available now, this late on Christmas Eve. You'll have to take a trolley. They're running a light schedule today, but they're running." George knew the schedule of every trolley car in Baltimore. It wasn't part of his job at the Railway Company, but he liked the symmetry of counting off routes, car numbers and times. "You'll be able to pick up the #7 Broadway, and then transfer to the #43 up Madison. That should leave you close to The Stafford."

Celeste frowned at the idea of arriving at her honeymoon hotel by trolley, but she knew her father was right. She sighed while Willie picked up her valise. She would carry her train case.

"Thank you, Mr. and Mrs. Wells. I know this day has been a shock for you. I will take care of Celeste. I will make her happy." He put down the bags to receive Annie's embrace and George's handshake. This time there was no hesitation.

The couple walked to Broadway, Willie burdened with the valises, Celeste holding his arm while she smiled, at him, at herself, at her new life.

Eleven_____

Celeste watched as Willie signed the register, Willie embarrassed by her giggles. But he smiled to himself, and added a flourish as he signed their names, Mr. and Mrs. Strauff. The bellboy took their luggage and after Willie had the desk clerk make their reservation for dinner in the hotel's Anne Arundel Room, they entered the mirrored elevator. Celeste touched its velvet cushions, but did not sit down. The lanky elevator operator, wearing a uniform of navy and maroon that could have used a pressing, opened the wire gate, then the brass doors at the sixth floor, and tipped his hat as they exited. The couple walked hand-in-hand to their room. When they arrived, they saw that their suitcases had been placed on the luggage racks at the bottom of the double bed.

Celeste ran to the window and called to Willie, "Come, look. We have a view of Mt. Vernon Place. There's the monument, if you tilt your head to the left." Willie came near. His arms went around her waist. She turned, and they shared a first long kiss as husband and wife.

Willie searched for his voice. "It's been a long day. It's probably best that we have an early dinner. Then we can come back to our room and--"

Celeste interrupted him, "Oh, yes, an early dinner, Willie. Shall we go down now?"

Willie moved to the basin to wash his hands. His face was flushed and he struggled not to stammer. "Y-yes. Let's go. You are beautiful, my lovely Celeste."

"I know." And she smiled.

They sat at a table for two in the near-deserted dining room. Stiff white linen covered the table, with its heavy monogrammed silver.

"S," for Strauff, Celeste thought, as she used the fish fork for her shrimp cocktail, served in the silver bowl that rested atop a larger one brimming with ice chips. She pressed the heavy linen napkin to her lips. Prime rib, baked potato, and champagne, the last of which, the waiter informed them, was compliments of the house. The desk clerk must have suspected. The couple didn't wait for dessert. The waiters cleared their places, obviously glad for an early Christmas Eve closing.

Willie felt a bit giddy. The champagne, he thought. Celeste was lightheaded and delighted, the mix of champagne and excitement. She didn't wonder why.

Once in their room even Willie laughed as they set about unpacking their suitcases. One of the shared bathrooms for the floor was just outside their door. Willie asked if Celeste preferred that he change there. Celeste, suddenly shy, agreed. While he was out of the room, she looked at the nightgown she had packed. It was the best one she had, but still had the look of a schoolgirl, which, she realized, she had been until that morning. White, beribboned, a smattering of lace, it would have to do for her wedding night. But she wasn't pleased.

Willie returned, wearing his camel-colored wool robe over white-on-white striped pajamas still crisp from Hanne's iron. Celeste stood in her gown.

"You are beautiful, my dear sweet one," he said.

"And you are handsome, my dear sweet one." Celeste laughed as she answered. Willie stepped toward her. They both laughed as he struggled with the drawstring of his trousers. And soon, their marriage was consummated, with joy, with laughter, with lust, and not a small amount of love.

Willie felt the length of Celeste's long body against his, her legs white, sturdy. I am all bones, he thought, and held her even tighter.

Celeste inhaled the scent of Bay Rum. "I knew you would take care of me, Willie. I love you. I love this. I love being married."

They didn't talk of their future; they didn't talk of the day. They didn't talk. Willie was beyond words. He was not above actions, however, and Celeste was the recipient of his husbandly duty three more times that night.

Twelve ————————————————————

December 25, 1901

Dear Elizabeth,

You will never guess what I'm going to tell you. Or maybe you can if you looked at the envelop. Did you see the return address? The Stafford Hotel! Did you notice the name? Celeste Strauff!

Yes, that's me! I'm married!

Willie and I eloped yesterday. Isn't that the most exciting thing your friend has ever done? We told our parents after we did it. They were livid! But, you see, we are in love and just couldn't wait to be together.

I have a ring. Willie bought it for me. It is beautiful. I didn't have time to gather a trousseau, but Willie said that I could buy one when we are in Denver. Yes, Denver, Colorado. We are leaving in a few weeks. Willie has business there, and I am to accompany him as his wife. It takes days to get there on the train, and there are mountains like the ones in Europe. To think, I'll be seeing all that geography that Mr. Dencil droned on about. You be sure to tell him. I'll send postcards and you can take them to school to show everyone.

Well, I wanted to be sure that you were the very first person after the family that I told. And you are!

I must close, as we are getting ready to visit the Strauffs for Christmas dinner. They were furious, especially that old stick, Clara. I'm sure she already had one of her musical friends picked out for Willie. Mrs. Strauff, should I call her Mama?, cried. And I guess we'll not be able to call August

35

"that old Kraut" anymore, since he's my new father!! I will need to make sure I look my most innocent, and I will try hard to make an impression so that they like me.

Mama and Papa were sad, but Eva loaned me her luggage, and I wore her jacket, the black velvet one, which I do not intend to give back to her. Don't you think it should be mine now, to remember what I wore to marry Willie?

Now, a favor. Will you go through my things at school and bring anything that you think I'll want to my house? Well, not really my house anymore. Don't bother with any books. I am through with schoolwork. No more studying for me. I am a wife now!

So just drop them at Mama's. We don't know where we'll be living yet. We'll do all that when we get back from Denver. Then I'll invite you over for tea.

Be sure to tell all the girls. Mama cried, like Mrs. Strauff, Willie's mother. I need to differentiate now that I am Mrs. Strauff too. Maybe all mothers cry when their children marry.

Thanks ever so much. I can't wait to see you.

Your married best friend,
Celeste

Thirteen———————————————

The doorman called the carriage for them. Willie worked to maintain a serious demeanor, though he felt giddy with happiness. Celeste felt both self-conscious and grand. The couple stepped into the carriage that would take them to North Avenue, to Christmas dinner with the Strauffs. Willie was too exhilarated from the activities of the night before and that morning to feel nervous. He believed that he would never stammer again. He was a man; he was certain of that.

His resolve wavered, but did not desert him, as the carriage halted before 1108. The driver helped Celeste down the final step. Willie paid and made arrangements for him to return at five o'clock that evening. Unsure of their reception, Willie wanted to insure that their time at the house was limited.

Hanne greeted them at the door. Willie introduced Celeste. "Happy to meet you, Mrs. Strauff," she said. Hanne curtsied, something that she never did. Celeste smiled, delighted to be called by her new name. Willie led Celeste into the front room, where the family was gathered. All were dressed for the holiday, August in his finest Lebow Brothers' suit, Paulina, fully corseted and uncomfortable in navy silk and diamond earrings, and Clara in a serviceable brown wool skirt, a white lace blouse, a concession to the holiday, along with her black kid boots that made it even more difficult for her to walk without a cane. They had made their family visits earlier that day and were now officially "at home."

"A reporter came to the house yesterday before we left for church." August greeted his son and his new wife with these stern words. "News of your marriage was in this morning's paper." August stood. "We can only hope that not many found time to read the paper on Christmas

Day." Paulina remained in her chair, a lace-edged handkerchief pressed to her nose. Clara sat in the window seat.

Willie led Celeste to the middle of the room. "This is Celeste, my wife." He smiled as he delivered her title.

"I am happy to be part of your family," she said, and gave them what she intended to be a shy smile.

August went to her, eyeing her as he would a typeset sheet of his newspaper. "Yes," he nodded.

Celeste walked to Paulina, who rose, as did Clara. Willie introduced them:

"And this is my mother, Paulina. And this is Clara." Paulina rose to embrace Celeste. Both of them stiffened as their bodies touched. Clara stood a few steps behind Paulina. She said nothing.

"Would you like some sherry?" Paulina said.

Though not fully recovered from the effects of last evening's champagne and their wedding night, the couple accepted. The newly constituted family sat, struggling for words that would forge a new bond with the stranger in their midst. Finally, Willie rose. "A toast to Celeste, our newest Strauff."

An awkward silence followed, a hesitation before glasses were raised. "*Prost!*" Paulina said. All raised their glasses, Clara slower than the rest. Paulina left to attend to the dining room.

"I'm not happy about the publicity. Celeste, they contacted your parents as well. Not a good situation; not in good taste, not a good start," August said.

"No sir," Celeste responded, eyes lowered. Willie did not come to her rescue. Celeste noticed, but decided not to think about it.

Hanne announced dinner and the group went to the dining room to begin their first meal together. Celeste eyes went to the dark mahogany sideboard topped with an ornate silver service, to the gas-lit sconces, then, above the table, to the crystal chandelier. She touched the starched lace tablecloth. Just like home, she thought. Just like my home.

She commented on the turkey, sauerkraut, dressing. "This is just what we have at Christmas too," she said. "It smells just like Christmas."

The family avoided questions about the future; talk centered on August's newspaper and relatives who remained in Germany.

After the mince and pumpkin pies were cleared, Willie made the farewells for him and Celeste. "I'm glad we came, *Mutti*. You are looking well. We will visit again, soon. And you will come visit us once we get settled in our new place, after we return from our trip."

"Thank you, Mr. Strauff," Celeste added, "Mrs. Strauff, Clara. I look forward to being part of your family." Willie shook August's hand, kissed Paulina on the cheek, nodded to Clara. Hanne helped the couple on with their coats, this day Celeste wore her maroon wool, and they left the house. Their carriage was parked by the door. Celeste looked up the street at her own house, wondering what Eva, George, Annie were doing then.

"Can we stop in, just to say hello. It is Christmas, Willie."

At a signal from Willie, the driver turned crossed the street and headed east. Once in front of her house, Celeste longed to be a child again, to be back with Annie and George, beloved beyond question, removed from having to cope with the Strauffs. But she knew a happy front was required. She took Willie's hand as they went up the front steps to ring the bell.

Meg answered the door and whisked them into the hallway. "Oh, here is the young couple," she said. "Your parents will be so pleased to see you, a Christmas gift for all of us."

The couple saw the family seated at the dining room table, their meal almost concluded, the house filled with identical aromas of holiday dinner as the one they had left. Annie left the table to greet them. "Oh, come, sit, have something to eat. This is a wonderful surprise for us." She led them to the table. Willie took the chair beside Eva. When George got up to kiss Celeste, she followed him to his seat and settled on his lap.

"Reporters came, I heard," she said to her mother.

"Yes. It was late afternoon. I didn't know what to do except answer their questions as best I could. I didn't think your elopement would be such news," Annie said.

Eva interjected, "I'm sure it wouldn't have been except for Willie's father. I wonder if he'll put it in his paper. They got some of it wrong, you know."

"I doubt that my father will report on it," Willie said with a nervous laugh. Eva chuckled, more heartily than she intended. George raised an eyebrow. Annie reached over and patted Willie's hand. Meg stood in the doorway, ready to serve the young couple, and ready to glean any fresh information she could garner.

"Have some pie, some coffee," Annie said.

"Our carriage is waiting, so we can't stay long," Willie said, "but I will have a piece of that mince pie."

"And take a piece to give the driver," Annie said, and directed Meg to wrap two pieces in waxed paper.

Dessert finished, the couple stood to leave. Celeste kissed both her parents. She leaned to kiss Eva, but was stopped by Eva's comment. "I want my jacket back."

"Oh Eva, you are such a tease," Celeste said. She had no intention of returning the jacket.

Willie shook George's hand; Annie kissed him on the cheek; Eva allowed him to shake her hand, and the couple went out into the dark Baltimore night.

Fourteen————————————————————

Paulina had watched as Willie helped Celeste into the carriage. It turned north, toward the Wells's house. She replayed the scene that had occurred minutes before, Willie struggling to stand tall, to be firm, to stand up to his father, to Clara.

Oh, Willie, my boy, Paulina thought, what have you done? *Ach*, you have learned nothing. Trying to be someone you aren't, trying to please someone you can never please. Instead, you just looked like a weak, struggling boy. If only you had just a bit more backbone.

Where did all this softness come from? Paulina believed that she was at fault and sensed that August judged her for it. He had remained silent, but she saw it in his eyes.

Willie had had been sickly all his life. And it didn't help that Clara had been born just fifteen months before him. She had come into the world red, screeching before she was even completely separate from Paulina's body, so anxious was she to get started, to get on with life, to take on the world. Clara, always bright, walking early, talking early, at first a gibberish of German and English.

August had decreed that only English was to be spoken in the house, even the servants, though when he was away they spoke German. August and his "English only" pronouncement, Paulina thought. Easier for him, of course. He had forgotten that his early years in London with his family made speaking English less demanding, not the indecipherable mishmash that she found it to be. She could speak it, she had to, but spelling and pronunciation, plagued her. She always carried a dictionary, but many times she could not find the word.

"How can you find it in the dictionary if you don't know how to spell it?" she would ask August. "You can only learn how *not* to spell

41

it". August would laugh and hold her close, at least in the early days. Now she had her notebook. She wrote down those English words she considered crazy, those with impossible pronunciations, and practiced, memorized, one or two challenges every day.

But Clara, of course, she listened, she learned. When August heard Clara lisp German words, he cautioned, "English, *liebchen*, English," and would give her the English word, August always working on his own vocabulary, trying to be American first, German second. Such tenderness he showed Clara. And she, such a quick study, even as a toddler, English to him and me, German with the servants.

Paulina realized then that she had always been intimidated by Clara, even when her daughter was a child. Clara was a reader, first books in English, then asking for ones in German. By this time, August, infatuated, agreed to any of her requests.

Paulina closed her eyes and pictured Willie, quiet, shy Willie. So different from his sister. Paulina had known from the first that life would not prove easy for him.

*Fifteen*_____

August returned to the front room and saw Paulina at the window. He knew her thoughts, what was in her heart. He was alone with his, sharing his feelings of anger and sadness and fear with no one.

When Willie was born, he had envisioned a son who would have everything that he had longed for, a son to take what a father could give and make even more of it. August reviewed his life, his story, the one he recounted at those awards ceremonies: I came here with nothing. I worked in a saloon. I was a barber. Finally I found a job as the lithographer I was trained to be. Then I bought the newspaper I worked for and I made it successful.

By God, he thought, I own a newspaper. I am somebody, not just another Kraut off the boat. I did that on my own.

Through the years and countless retelling, August had first omitted, then forgotten, the help he had received from his uncles, who had arrived a generation earlier, who provided a home for him when he arrived in Baltimore. August now viewed these men through a veil of shame, they with their heavy accents and beer-hall mentality, his cousins content to replicate the lives of their parents.

August studied the Oriental rug, recently purchased, its pattern faintly discernible in the deep blues, reds and purples. I had ideas, he thought. Articles in this paper for Germans; what was happening in the German community here, in Washington, in Philadelphia, back in Germany, our news. I knew that I couldn't compete with the Baltimore papers, *The Sun*, *The News*, *The American*, but I could offer a touch of the old country in this new country. A paper for Germans in America, stories of their successes, stories of their becoming American, being respected by Americans, yet keeping a touch of home.

We made it happen, Lina and I, she writing the articles, the babies clamoring around her. People loved the paper, were keen on seeing their names in print, their activities reported. All these new Germans who came to America, they wanted to see how successful Germans lived, where they lived, the schools their children attended, where they vacationed. We gave them all that. And now the Germans in Denver, in Texas, wanting to meet with me about publishing the paper there. Those big shots want to meet with me, who came to this country with nothing.

August pictured Willie, unassuming, tentative, forever catching, smoothing back that forelock of chestnut hair between his second and third fingers, such a nervous gesture.

August had made the decision to send Willie west to negotiate the paper's expansion, a chance to prove himself, optimistic that Willie's sincere demeanor would convince publishers in Denver, Austin, and those western territories to make a deal. He wanted that success to build Willie's confidence and character. He was taking a chance. The acid in August's stomach released as he pondered the risk of his decision. But he was doing this for his son, giving him a chance to succeed.

And now the boy had done this, brought this child, this girl, into his life, into theirs. A sad excuse for a son, August thought. He looked at Paulina, still at the window, and walked out of the room.

Sixteen————————————

The Stafford Hotel
Baltimore, Maryland
December 26, 1901

Dear Elizabeth,

Well, I wanted to write to you and tell you about meeting Willie's family. We went there on Christmas Day, for dinner. You should see the inside, three gold canes, three! in the vestibule. There are pictures everywhere. I don't just mean pictures; I mean paintings, oil paintings! The walls are covered. I asked Willie about it later. He said that his parents, and sometimes he and Clara too, go to Europe just about every summer and that his parents, and Clara, come home laden with things — paintings, ornaments, fabrics.

Mr. Strauff meets with newspaper people there; Mrs. Strauff visits with family — she has cousins everywhere in Germany, and Clara travels all over the place. Willie told me that when he was there he was just a vagabond, but he and Clara can speak real French, not like our attempts at school with Mme. Bassler.

Clara's been to Paris, to Italy, meeting musicians. It seems that she is quite an accomplished pianist, although you certainly wouldn't know it to look at her. She was decidedly unfriendly when I was there. Her piano is huge and dominates the front room. I think it may be a grand piano, but it seems a little smaller than the ones I've seen. She had some kind of problem when she was younger, so now her knees hurt her all the time, although she didn't say a word about it. She walks

45

with a limp, and I can tell that she's trying to hide it. I saw her looking at my clothes. She could learn a lesson or two about dressing. She looks frumpy, I'd say.

Mr. Strauff was better, though a bit huffy about the newspaper article. Did you see it? If you still have the Sun Paper, will you save it for me? It's the first time my name has ever been in the paper, except for a few parties I went too, but that really doesn't count, does it? This was about me – and Willie, of course. I wonder if I will be famous.

The Strauffs ate the same food for Christmas as we do, so there aren't many differences there. And the dining room looked just like ours. It's the middle room, just like at my house – or I should say my old house!

They even have a gramophone, like yours! It was playing when we got there. Classical – that's what they like. That's what Clara plays. But when we get our own home, I'll ask Willie to get one, and we will have happy music, only happy, and dance every night. You know, he and I have never danced. But we will once we get to Denver.

Mrs. Strauff was very quiet, sort of a homey lady. But I think she was feeling sad about losing Willie to me. Well, once we get our own house, I will invite them all over for a visit. We will get to know one another better. I think that Clara is the boss of the house. Willie said that his father commanded that they speak only English in the house, so they all do that when he is there, even Hanne, their maid. But it is German, German, German, once he leaves for work. Mr. Strauff speaks with an accent, but his vocabulary seems very educated. I only heard Mrs. Strauff say a few words, and her voice is so soft, it is hard to tell.

Willie and I are leaving for Denver in a few days. I need to go home and get some more clothes. I am taking a trunk with me. It won't be full when I leave, but I want it to be full – my wedding trousseau—when we get home again.

Oh, I miss you and want to see you. These letters just aren't the same. Do write to me. I want your letter to be my first piece of mail with my new name, Mrs. William Strauff. And it will be from my very best, dearest friend. Once we get settled, you must come for a visit. We will have a real tea!

Oh my, what a long letter this is. I will write you from the train. Be sure to tell the girls and the teachers that I am married, and will NOT be back to school. You can tell everyone that I love being married, if you know what I mean.

Love,
Celeste

Seventeen————————————————————

Willie had spent his days working at the paper, listening to his father, learning the vocabulary of publishing, of advertising. He understood the importance of his trip to Denver. The increased circulation to these new areas in the west would enhance the paper's, and the Strauffs', reputation. Germans moving there wanted news of home, of "the old country," exactly what *Der Bayerishce Wolkenblatt* provided. August had made the initial contacts; Willie only needed to follow up.

The day after Christmas, Willie's first day back at work. He had kissed Celeste goodbye, she still deep beneath the blankets of their double bed at The Stafford. He pictured her as he waited at the corner of Charles and Biddle Streets for the streetcar that would take him to Front Street and the newspaper.

He opened the heavy brass entry doors to the paper's offices, saw his father seated at his desk. He knew that August was focused on finances.

As he walked to his desk, he saw that August had placed articles from various German papers there. Willie's job was to review and rewrite them for placement in the paper, arranged them by geographic area. August had subscriptions to all the large German dailies and the weekly papers of the country's smaller cities. He circled those articles he wanted included. It was a way that the German community in Baltimore kept current of happenings in the old country. Paulina painstakingly cut the articles out, pasted them on heavy card stock, and sorted them by area, noting the byline of each article. August chose those he believed to be of interest, and, calling on his training in linotype, estimated their position in the newspaper. Willie prepared the articles, readying them to be typeset. Paulina would take over his duties while was Willie in Denver, much as she did in the early days.

August came to the door of his office and called, "Willie, come in. I'd like to talk to you."

Willie faced his father, forced himself to meet August's eyes. He was surprised. He saw neither anger nor the usual disappointment that had become part of August's gaze whenever he looked at his son.

"What do you intend to do with your life now, *John*?" August's voice was low, soft. This was not the August Willie knew, the August he feared. He wanted to meet his father's gaze; he wanted to speak forcefully. He wanted to be a man. He wanted not to stammer.

"I was hoping to have some time off so that Celeste and I can look for a place to live before I leave for Denver. I want to take Celeste with me when I g-g-go."

"Do you have money for a house? Do you have money to furnish a house? Can that child take care of a home? Does she know what to do? Does she know how to cook? To clean?" August walked back to his desk, cleared his throat.

"Willie, I will not belabor how disappointed we all are with this escapade of yours. I'm sure that the Wells feel the same way. But what is done is done. You are now a married man, and you must assume the responsibilities that go with that position."

Willie started to speak. "I intend--"

August stopped him. "Let me finish. You have no idea how much money it takes to maintain a household. Celeste, I am sure, has no idea how to run a house. You were both raised with servants doing the most of the work. Do you think, on your salary, that you can afford a servant? You are both children. Do you think that I will support you? Because if you do, you labor under a mis-, a mis-" August searched for the English word. "You are wrong.

"You know nothing about the finances of the paper. But now I will tell you the truth, the naked truth as they say here." August cleared his throat once again.

"We are less than successful, but we must always look like we're doing well to those we come in contact with. The advertisers will pay only if they think that the paper is thriving. It takes money to look successful, Willie. Your trips to Europe, the house, the society we move in, Clara's friends. This all takes money.

"We pay the printers, the distributors, the janitors first. Then we take whatever is left over. Our advertisers are our bread and butter. And we need more of them if we are to expand. That is why the trip to Denver is important, Willie. You have the opportunity to expand the paper. I am trusting you with this, and you must concentrate on the reason that you are going west. It is not a honeymoon.

"You make a very small salary. That is all that I can afford to pay you. You must know that you cannot support a wife, cannot support a household. You must be honest with that girl."

August continued, his gaze holding Willie's. "You have much to think about. You have made a dreadful mistake, and you must decide how you are going to live with it. I will support this marriage as best I can, Willie, but it will not be easy, for you or for her."

Willie nodded.

"I am not saying this to be harsh, Willie. Now that you are married, I am talking to you like an adult, like a partner in this business. There is no need for me to hide things from you.

"I will be blunt. I know of no other choice than your coming to live with us. You and Celeste can take Clara's room. It is large, and the third floor will give you at least some privacy. Hanne's room is there, but that is the best that I can offer."

Willie started to speak, but August silenced him.

"There is one more thing. Your mother is distraught that you were not married by a priest, a Catholic priest. You know how important this is to her. That you and that girl married outside the church has wounded her as much as the marriage itself.

"Now I won't listen to Clara and her ravings about having the marriage annulled. What's done is done. But, before you come to live in my house, I want you married by a priest. Your mother and I will arrange it. It can be a private affair."

Finally Willie managed to say a few words. "I don't know what Celeste will think, *Vati*. I'm not sure that she will do it."

August stood. "Then this will be your first act as a husband. This is something that must be done before you come into my house. You will do this for your mother. Is that understood?"

August walked Willie to the door. "It is the only way, Willie. It is the only way you can take care of your wife. You went into this act as two children. Now you must act as adults."

August stepped back into his office and closed the door. Willie walked to his desk. The lithographer stood by the window, setting type.is hi

Eighteen

A carriage waited at The Stafford entrance to take them to Camden Station. The bellman loaded the trunk and suitcases, hat boxes. Celeste kept her train case with her.

She had spent the holiday season visiting relatives, seeing her girlfriends, acquiring a leather traveling trunk from Tuerke's, and her own set of Lady Baltimore luggage. She had returned Eva's to her, though the black velvet jacket was safely wrapped and packed at the bottom of the new trunk, ready to wear once they arrived in Denver. She was sure that there would be dinners and parties to attend.

The couple stepped into the carriage. Their first two weeks of marriage had been a fairy-tale for Celeste. She was in love; Willie treated her tenderly; her friends were impressed, and, even better, jealous. She had snared the handsome Willie. She resolved to ignore any memory of that second marriage ceremony. Willie had asked her so sweetly, tried to make her understand how important it was to his mother.

August had made the proper contacts with the diocese, dispensation in hand for Willie's transgression of marrying someone who was not Catholic. August cautioned the couple to say nothing about the Episcopal ceremony.

On Monday, December 30, Willie and Celeste, accompanied by August and Paulina and Clara, journeyed to Saratoga Street, to the rectory of St. Alphonsus Catholic Church, where they were married, for the second time, by Father Ademar Schneibel. Thus assured of their being properly in a state of grace, Paulina welcomed her daughter-in-law into the family with a kiss that was almost genuine. Clara, wearing the same brown skirt that she had worn on Christmas Eve, signed the registry as a witness. She had worn her comfortable shoes.

August escorted the group to Marconi's, the same restaurant where the couple were to have lunched the day that they went to Towson.

Celeste hoped that this would make things easier for Willie, at his work, with his parents. Once she agreed, Willie didn't mention it. She knew that he viewed it as his failure. He hadn't stood up for her, for them; he had caved in to his parents' wishes. She would not allow herself to be disappointed in him; she would not allow a shadow in their lives. Agreeing to this ceremony would show him how much she loved him. She didn't tell her parents; they were warming to Willie and she didn't want to do anything to change their feelings about him.

Nights had continued to be bliss for Celeste and exuberance for Willie. In that room overlooking Mt. Vernon Place, his stammer, his inhibitions, his reserve vanished. Both were sure that those joy-filled times would last forever. Celeste's profusion of lace and stockings and pantalettes, strewn throughout the room, filled Willie with delight. Such disorder, he thought, such abandon, so different from his narrow, neat, proscribed life before the ebullient Celeste.

Relieved that she agreed to his request about the Catholic marriage, Willie felt a surge of hope that his love was reciprocated, that they would be able to work out anything they might encounter.

But the conversation with August stayed with him. He knew that his father was right. He and Celeste had had a splendid few weeks, living at The Stafford, dining at the finest restaurants. Celeste delighted in signing her new name to the receipts as she gathered her trousseau, prepared for her honeymoon.

August had agreed to pay their expenses on their journey, a reward for the ceremony at St. Alphonsus, not quite a peace offering to the couple. But, when they returned, Willie knew that there was no money for a house, not even to rent. He was not in a position to offer Celeste a proper home.

Checking out of The Stafford, Willie put the receipt for their stay in his pocket. August would pay for that. He looked down at the bills from the dress shops Celeste had visited. One more thing he would have to confront.

He put his foot on the top step of the carriage, then settled himself beside his bride. The carriage headed south, toward Pratt Street.

Nineteen

Celeste sat primly, gloved hands grasping her train case. They were going to Denver. She knew no one who had ventured so far west. She thought of the stories she'd tell her friends when they returned.

She stared out the carriage window, remembering the past two weeks. Such a whirlwind, and Willie handling it all, treating her like she was a grown-up. Well, she thought, I am a grown-up. I am a married woman, and I am going to Denver for my honeymoon.

The carriage made its way down Charles Street turning west at the harbor. She looked out at the ships crowded one beside the other, some anchored far out in the brackish water. Maybe one day Willie will take me to Europe, she thought. She pictured them waltzing in Vienna, and suddenly realized that she and Willie had not yet danced together. That would change when they got to Denver. She smiled to herself. Mr. and Mrs. Strauff will dance!

Seated beside her, Willie studied the warehouses, in early afternoon almost empty of their wares, the fish, fruits and vegetables offloaded to the piers early that morning, before sun-up. The harbor looked bleak, the water an ominous grey, the sun hidden behind clouds.

As the carriage turned onto Howard Street, the sun broke through. Willie saw Camden Station ahead. He had said nothing to Celeste of his conversation with August. August was paying for this trip; August was offering them a home; August was his employer, August was his father. Willie would talk to Celeste, he would *tell* Celeste, when they got to Denver.

He looked over and reached for her hand, brought it to his lips with a gentle, a silent, kiss. She was so bright, so hopeful. He didn't want to spoil that light that touched him, that made his life different, meaningful. Celeste smoothed back the errant lock of brown hair that always seemed to find its way down Willie's forehead. She liked it; she thought that it gave just a glimmer of rakishness to Willie's serious demeanor. She leaned back in her seat. Willie knew that was her signal for him to kiss her properly. He did so, but kept in mind that they were fast approaching the station.

The driver pulled the horse to a stop and jumped down to open the door for Celeste. She stood on the running board, posture erect, to look at the station. She wanted to be sure to remember this moment, the first moment of her *real* honeymoon. She put her foot, shod in a newly-purchased wine-colored leather boot, down purposefully and turned as Willie followed her from the carriage. He stood a bit taller as he took her arm, and directed the redcaps to deliver their luggage to the baggage car. Willie had reserved a drawing room in the sleeper car through to St. Louis, the first leg of their journey. It sat on a secondary rail, waiting for the B & O Train Number 1 from New York.

The couple found their compartment; Celeste placed her train case on the velvet sofa. "Willie, this is just like a book. I can't believe we're going West. Do you think we'll see Indians?"

"Oh, I think there will be time to see Indians, and buffalo, maybe even Wild Bill's show. But now I want to show you something. We have time. Come across the street." He took Celeste's hand and pulled her across Camden Street. As long as her legs were, she still had trouble keeping up with Willie's pace. They stood across from the terminal.

"Look at that building. Isn't it one of the most beautiful you've ever seen?" he asked.

Celeste stood, quiet, then looked at Willie, not quite understanding what he was asking.

"The architecture is called Italianate" he continued. "You can see that by the windows. And see that middle tower? That's a belvedere tower. A belvedere is a place where you can look out. So when it was built, you could climb the tower steps and look all over Baltimore, the harbor to the south, past the Washington Monument to the north."

Celeste watched her husband more closely than the building he described. He is just so handsome, she thought.

"And Abraham Lincoln came here, several times," Willie continued, "once on the way to his inauguration, then again on his way to Gettysburg. He wrote his Gettysburg address here, right here in Baltimore, right in this station. Of course, when he was here just the central part existed. They added the two wing sections after the civil war."

Celeste interrupted, "Willie, you sound just like Mr. Wilford. You should be a teacher. How do you know all these things?" Celeste was impressed with his knowledge, though she wasn't so pleased to be lectured to. This was her honeymoon, after all, not a history lesson.

"It's just something I'm interested in. And I've had no one to share it with. Until now," and, once again, Willie brought Celeste's fingers to his lips.

Celeste grinned and looked toward the right. Not only was Willie handsome and rich, she thought. He was smart!

Back in the sleeper car, Willie stood on the platform and watched as the train backed into the coupling to attach the car to the main train. He had been fascinated with trains, with architecture, since he was a boy. While August supposed him to be struggling with homework assigned by the Christian Brothers, he spent hours at the small wooden desk in his room sketching his ideas for grand buildings, some of which just happened to be train terminals. The trip west offered him a chance to see firsthand what he had seen only in newspapers and magazines. And now he could share this with Celeste.

They entered their compartment. Celeste knelt on the red velvet sofa and looked out the window. "We'll be able to see everything, won't we? We won't even have to leave our room."

Willie sat on one of the two matching chairs and unpacked two of the books he had brought with him. "We can do anything we want, my sweet."

Celeste came to him and sat on his lap. He touched her hair and pulled her close.

When the train arrived at the New Jersey Avenue Station in Washington, Willie jumped up, unceremoniously dumping Celeste to the floor. She looked up at him. They both chuckled.

"I want you to see this station. It was where Lincoln was sworn in as President. I want you to see it now, because plans are underway to construct a major terminal to replace the different ones here, so this may be torn down soon."

He led her through the station's grand hall, past the ladies' and gentlemen's saloons on either side, to New Jersey Avenue. Celeste had to run to keep up with him as he walked across the street for a better view. "Look up," he said, "that's another example of Italianate architecture. See the belvedere tower, just like Camden Station's. It will be sad to see this piece of history go. Progress always destroys as much as it gives us."

"Willie, that's very philosophical," Celeste said, proud to use such a fancy word. She wanted Willie to know that she was smart too.

They heard the train whistle and hurried back to their car.

A new dining car was attached at Hancock, and they had an early dinner as the train approached Cumberland, Maryland. It was dark when they finished their after-dinner drinks, Willie a cognac, Celeste crème de menthe, and they soon returned to their room. The porter had turned down the beds, but they only used one.

Early the next morning, Willie woke Celeste. "Come, let's have an early breakfast so that we can use the stopover time in Cincinnati to look at the station." Willie stood before the mirror, placing his diamond tie tack directly in the center of his wine-colored tie. He thought it provided a fine contrast to his navy-blue suit and vest and his white cotton shirt.

Celeste pulled herself into a sitting position. "Oh, Willie, you're dressed already." She yawned and leaned back on her pillow. "Do we have to look at *every* station?"

"Not every one, just the ones you'll want to remember," he replied, and sat down next to her. Even after a night in a shared narrow bed she looked beautiful, Willie thought, looking at her blond hair, tousled but not tangled.

Celeste beamed. She knew she had this power over Willie. "You go on; I'll meet you in the dining car."

"Now you know it's a new one they just put on at Chillicothe."

"Willie, just go. I don't need to know every detail."

"This will be the last station I'll make you look at until we get to St. Louis. They have double-railed tracks here. It's a nightmare for the switchmen. Really, you must see this. I won't even make you go outside to see the station. It's not really a significant structure, but you've got to see these double tracks. The outer set is broad-gauged, the inner ones are standard. This is the only example that I know of in the whole country, and it can't last much longer."

Celeste, arranging her hair and tying the pale blue ribbons on her chemise, half-listened to her husband's description. She arranged her white shirtwaist, fixing the blue cameo at the neck, and pulled on her navy serge skirt. She looked at Willie. "How in the world do you know all this?

He didn't answer. He was focused on her stocking-clad ankles as she fastened the buttons on her boots. He took her his hand as they went to the dining car.

Twenty————————————

Their study of Cincinnati's Baymiller Station, complete with a view of the double-railed tracks, behind them, Celeste and Willie returned to their drawing room. He went to one of the chairs, and picked up a book. Celeste looked over. Ralph Waldo Emerson. Willie was reading Ralph Waldo Emerson when he didn't have to. She thought of her father. He read Emerson too.

"Do you like that?" she asked, and wondered if she should get a book to read. She had purchased several magazines when they were at Camden Station, and had already looked through the newest issue of *Harper's Bazaar*. Maybe it would have been better to have brought a book, she thought.

Willie put down *Compensation, Reliance, and Other Essays* and sat beside her on the sofa. "I do like it, but I must confess that I brought it so that you would think me intelligent."

Celeste smiled so widely that her molars showed. "Oh, I do love you! I do." The magazine was forgotten and Mr. Emerson was left for later in the day.

Twenty-one

On the evening of the third day of their journey, The B and O Royal
Blue Train Number 1 pulled into the St. Louis Union Station at 6:45
p.m., just five minutes off schedule. Celeste was more than ready to
step on ground that wasn't moving. She knew Willie wasn't finished
with his guided tours of every train station from Baltimore to Denver,
but they were spending the night in St. Louis. They would have at
least a few hours in one place.

She took Willie's hand as he led her from the Midway, and noticed
to her right an expanse of tracks so wide that she couldn't see to the
end. Willie was certain tell her about them, and she was surprised to
find herself a bit interested.

"Over there is the largest single-span train shed ever built," he said.
"There are thirty-two tracks." Celeste nodded and, clutching Willie's
hand, looked up to take in the Midway's soaring glass ceiling, though
she could see nothing but the black night sky. Following behind,
skipping to keep up with his pace, she careened into him when he
stopped suddenly. His gaze was directly above their heads.

"Now you can't see because it's dark, but tomorrow morning you'll
be able to take a better look and see that the ceiling, I think that it's
about 140 feet high, all glass and steel. I used to imagine coming here,
Celeste. I would sit in my room and imagine all these stations, and
now here I am. And with you!"

Celeste thought she saw tears in his eyes, but then thought, no, not
my Willie. He's stronger than that.

He resumed his purposeful stride as they entered The Headhouse.
"Our hotel is here, but before we check in, there are things that you
must see. I've read about them. I can hardly believe that I'm going to

see them in real life." He laughed. "I'm pinching myself to make sure this isn't a dream."

Willie led Celeste into the Grand Hall, pointing out the sweeping archways, mosaics, and frescoes. They stopped before the station's main entranceway. "There it is, Celeste, the 'Allegorical Window.' That's Tiffany glass. See it? And the three women represent the main train stations when this station was built. New York, San Francisco, and, now, St. Louis. Just wait until we can see it tomorrow morning with the sunlight coming in." Willie stopped and turned. He put his arm around Celeste's waist.

She looked over at him. Rich, handsome, smart, and now this. And while she couldn't identify what she was feeling, she liked it. Maybe, she thought, it's love.

Twenty-two

Willie hurriedly checked into the hotel, but rather than going directly to their room, he told Celeste of a surprise he had arranged.

"I know that we won't be in St. Louis long enough for you to see the city, but there is one restaurant I've read about. I wired ahead for reservations, so they're expecting us." Celeste adjusted her chinchilla muff and saw her reflection in the mirrored wall. Her coat, she thought, was that of a schoolgirl, a situation she would remedy when they arrived in Denver.

She matched Willie's pace as he strode to the front of the station where carriages were parked waiting for fares. Willie went to the first carriage. "Tony Foust's," he said.

The driver hopped down to help Celeste into the cab. Willie started to give him the address, but he responded, "No need. Everybody knows where Foust's is," and the carriage headed to Olive Street.

Once at the restaurant, they were ushered in. They were expected. How nice, Celeste thought. We must be important.

They dined on sweetbreads resting on lobster patties, and shared a broiled lobster, the first time for Celeste. Willie manfully handled the hard red-boiled shells for both of them, feeding Celeste the butter-drenched morsels. They drank champagne. They laughed through the whole meal. He didn't care who saw them. Dinner ended with eggnog ice cream for Willie, Nesselrode pudding for Celeste. Willie gave the waiter a five dollar note and told him to keep the change.

The couple floated out of the restaurant and into a waiting carriage to return them to their hotel. Both felt wise, sophisticated, and pleasantly full. He had paid for the dinner with his own money, had not put it on August's account. That night Willie considered himself a proper husband.

Twenty-three _____

Willie roused Celeste early the next morning. Their train was scheduled to leave at 9:00 a.m. He worried as he looked over and noticed dark circles under her eyes. "Are you feeling all right?" he asked, a tentative manner replacing his newly-instituted husbandly bravado.

"I'm fine, just tired," Celeste replied. "Just give me a few minutes while you get dressed. I'll be myself by the time you get back. Would you ask room service to send up a pot of tea?"

Willie gently kissed the top of her head before he gathered his shaving brush and left the room. Celeste pinched her cheeks for color before she rose from her bed. Two glasses of water, two cups of strong tea, and she felt like herself once again. She dressed hurriedly, wearing the same outfit she wore the day before.

Forty minutes later the couple entered The Headhouse with time to spare. Celeste turned to Willie, "Don't you want to see the outside of the station?"

"I'm more worried about you. Maybe we should find our compartment on the sleeper car. We can see it on our way back."

"No, really, I feel fine. Let's go out and take a look." And this time, Celeste led her husband across the street so that they could have a better view of the building.

"Well, will you look at that," she exclaimed. "An eclectic mix of Romanesque styles. I do believe that Mr. Link modeled it after Carcassonne, a walled medieval city in southern France. What do you think?"

Willie stared at his bride. "How? What in the world?" And Celeste clapped her kid-gloved hands together and turned away. He touched

64

her shoulder and she twirled to face him. "Are you surprised that your wife knows about train stations and architecture?" she asked.

"Nothing would surprise me." He laughed and drew her toward him. He didn't care who saw.

"I found a brochure in the nightstand after you'd fallen asleep. I wanted you to be proud of me, Willie. I want you to think I'm smart too."

"You are wonderful to have done that. I didn't think that I could love you more, but I do. My heart feels like it will burst. Oh my dear, dear Celeste."

Twenty-four _____

The Missouri Pacific Train Number 3 left Union Station at 9:00 a.m. with Willie and Celeste seated in the dining car enjoying a leisurely breakfast. Their luggage had been delivered to their Pullman sleeping car.

When they returned to their car, Willie pulled a book from his suitcase and sat on the burgundy velvet sofa. Celeste sighed, riffled through the January issue of *Woman's Home Companion,* and flounced against the back of her chair. Willie appeared to be engrossed in his book. She exhaled noisily and flounced again, this time her sigh a bit louder and longer, her repositioning exercising a bit more bounce. The magazine landed on the table between them.

Willie looked up. "Are you bored? Would you like to walk to the observation car?"

During those morning hours spent in their drawing room, Celeste realized just how used to travel Willie was. He knew how to handle the interminable hours on a train moving across the country, hours broken up only by meals and walks from one car to the next. Their drawing room was comfortable, it was private, but it was also lonely. Celeste envied those who sat in the Pullman cars, able to talk to those on both sides of them. She forgot that those passengers had to sit up all night.

The train had added an observation car during the night; she and Willie made their way down the narrow corridors until they reached it. A high glass dome allowed the sun to shower the car with light. There were two levels of seats, the upper ones almost full.

"If we sit upstairs, you'll be able to get a better view. Let's do that," Willie suggested. He walked behind her as she mounted the stairs, he still entranced by the sight of her narrow foot in her maroon boot and by the swaying of her hips. He would talk to her; he would tell her about living with *Vati* and *Mutti*. But he would do that later, once they got settled in Denver. For right now, he thought, all I want to do is look at her, be with her, hold her close.

Celeste perched on the edge of a seat beside the window and took Willie's hand as he settled in beside her. She wanted to see all that could be seen. She had left her magazines in their drawing room. Willie said there was scenery, and she was determined to see it. The train sped through Kansas. Celeste looked over at Willie, now studying the notes from his father.

"I think I'll go back to our room," she told him. He looked over at her.

"Would you like me to come with you?" he asked. She shook her head, and, this time, she kissed his fingers.

"No. I think I'll take a little rest," she answered. "I think I've seen enough scenery for the day."

When she got to her room, she slipped off her boots, unbuttoned her skirt and lay on the sofa. Her thoughts went back to narrow bed on North Avenue, to her mother, her father, even to Eva. If she hadn't married Willie she would just be getting home from school, walking with her friends, laughing and talking with them. She would have known what was expected of her.

She understood that Willie loved her, realized that she was cherished, but, alone with her thoughts, she recognized that she was much too young to be a wife. She longed for one of the cloth dolls she had loved as a girl. Instead, she hugged the pillow tight to her chest. Now was not the time for tears.

Twenty-five——————————————

When Willie returned to their room he saw Celeste asleep on the sofa. He sat down on one of the chairs and watched her easy breathing, noticed the hairpins that remained as her hair loosened around her face. He stood to return to the observation car. He closed the door quietly; he did not want to disturb her innocent sleep.

A few hours later, Celeste joined him. Scenery, she thought, this is just scenery. She wondered what enchantment Willie saw in it, though the mountains of Colorado were impressive. But why was he so excited about it?

The train pulled into Denver's Union Station in the late afternoon of the following day. Willie, exhausted from five days of travel, did not even glance up as they found a carriage to take them to their hotel. "I know it is beautiful, Celeste, and I want to see it and show it to you, but I think it would be best if we went directly to the hotel. I must confirm the meetings with the men from the newspapers here, and I want to go over just what I am supposed to do. We also need to wire *Vati* that we arrived safely. I'll send one to your parents as well. I know they must be worried about you. Have you ever been away from them before?"

Willie turned to look at Celeste. He thought she might be homesick. Perhaps that was the reason that she was so quiet.

Celeste looked over at Willie, glad to forgo a train station lecture. His face looked grey. She wondered if he had lost weight. His clothes seemed to hang on him a bit.

They stood a few minutes, waiting their turn for a carriage. The brisk, cold air breathed new life into them

The carriage made the twelve block journey without a stop. When Willie caught sight of the Brown Palace Hotel, Celeste saw him gain new energy. "We made it. Here we are at the Brown Palace. I've never even seen pictures of it, just read about it. But wait until you see!"

Yes, Celeste thought, her Willie was back.

*Twenty-six*_____

Willie registered, now feeling quite comfortable signing "Mr. and Mrs. Strauff" on the register. He blanched when he saw that their room was five dollars a night. Then he remembered that August had arranged it. August wanted the Denver publishers to think, to know, that he and the paper were prosperous.

"Do you prefer the afternoon or the morning sun, sir?" the clerk asked. Willie was startled by this question, but thought it a nice touch. He gave a moment's consideration. "I think the morning sun would be best for us. Thank you." And so he was handed the heavy brass key to room 448.

Willie arranged for dinner to be delivered to their room. That evening, exhausted from their journey, Willie held Celeste in his arms until they both slept.

The next morning, they breakfasted early, in the Solarium, but not before Willie, now recovered from their travel ordeal, made sure to show Celeste the beauties of the finest, the most elegant, hotel in Denver. He took her outside, though the temperature was 25 degrees, to show her how the building was placed on the triangular plot at the corners of Broadway, Tremont and 17th Streets.

"Now see, this is Italian Renaissance architecture, and the builders used Colorado red granite for the exterior, along with some sandstone to make the red stand out.

"Look up!" He tilted her face toward the 7th floor. "See those medallions? There are twenty-six of them, and each depicts an animal that lives in the Rocky Mountains. Bear, mountain goat, elk, wolf, can you make them out?"

Celeste dutifully looked upward and agreed. She wasn't interested, but she loved this side of Willie, so passionate, so different from her father's and Eva's, quiet, scholarly way of keeping all that knowledge to themselves.

When they returned to the lobby, their faces were flushed with cold.

"Now we'll have a real chance to look at this lobby," he said to her. He lifted her hand to his lips. "You're cold," he said. "Here, let me warm you." He cupped her hands in his and blew on them. Celeste laughed. "I love you, Willie, I do love you."

She looked around the atrium lobby. Balconies rose eight stories, surrounded by cast iron railings with ornate grillwork panels. The smoking room and men's bar were to her left; a ladies' waiting room to her right. And the stores. I can shop without even leaving the hotel, she thought.

They reviewed their plans for the day. Willie would confirm his meetings with August's contacts; he would review his notes; he would practice his presentations; he would work on his nerves.

Celeste chattered. "You are not to worry. You will not stutter. Your father has trusted you with this task. He has enough confidence in you to assign this task. That is a good thing, a very good thing."

Willie listened. He recited to himself: "I will not let him down. I will prove to him that I am a man. I will go home successful."

Celeste's words interrupted his thoughts. "Now I think that the stores will just send the bills here, Willie, like they did at the Stafford. Is that all right?"

Willie nodded distractedly. He looked over at the blue-eyed, blonde beauty seated across the table from him. "Let's go back to our room for a while before we start our day."

Twenty-seven

Early the next morning, a searing pain bolted Willie awake. He rose shakily and walked toward the window. Four-thirty a.m. In four hours he would begin his round of meetings with the publishers. A wave of nausea came to him, so strong that he stumbled into the chair by the desk. I must get myself under control, he thought. I must not stutter. I must be confident. I must act like the publisher of a newspaper. He rose and walked unsteadily from the room to the bathroom down the hall.

When he returned a few minutes later, careful not to disturb Celeste, he lay on the bed, a washcloth drenched with cold water across his brow. He breathed deeply, working hard to combat the nausea.

As he turned his head to the window he realized that he must have slept. The sun was shining, a clear, crisp, cold day ahead. He turned his head, saw a lump under the covers, all but the very top of Celeste's head enveloped in the celadon green down comforter. He slid out of bed, wincing at the pain. At least, he thought, the nausea is gone.

He made his way down the hall to the bathroom once again, shaving there rather than in their room. He needed time to be alone, to prepare his thoughts. He dressed, the belt for his trousers now needing to be pulled a notch tighter. He carefully placed his tie pin, the diamond stud perfectly centered, and inserted the gold links into the cuffs of his shirt. When he looked in the mirror, he looked the part, he thought, of a prosperous young businessman. He pulled his shoulders back and stood tall.

He walked to the bed and leaned down to kiss Celeste goodbye. As he did, she lifted her head and saw that he was dressed.

"Oh, Willie, why didn't you wake me? I wanted to be with you as you prepared for your day. Let me dress and I can meet you in the breakfast room." She bounded out of bed.

"No, my sweetness. You stay here. I want to remember you nestled in these bedclothes. I need to review my notes anyway, so it would be best if I had some time alone. But you be thinking of me today. And as soon as my work is completed, I'll come back and tell you all about it."

Celeste kissed him, and jumped back into bed, pulling the covers around her. "You look so handsome, Willie. I would buy anything from you. Yes, I would!" And she reached up to give him a final hug before he left the room. He saw her roll over and, once again, all but the top of her head disappeared.

The waiter led him to a table by the window. He seated himself and spread the linen napkin in his lap. Outside businessmen walked briskly to their offices, their faces half-hidden by their neck scarves pulled tight against the morning winds. The bright sunlight eased Willie's headache, though the nausea returned. He decided to forgo his usual coffee.

"Could you bring me some English tea?" he asked. The waiter hesitated and then replied, "We do have American tea here, sir. But I can check if there is any English tea."

"Oh, no bother. Anything will do, really. And an order of dry toast, please."

"Would you like a menu, sir?"

"Just toast, please. And that tea as soon as you can get to it."

Willie looked around the room. Only a few tables were free; most were occupied by single diners, solitary businessmen hidden behind their newspapers. In the center of the room, at a table set for eight, four men studied a blueprint that was spread before them, plates, cups and saucers pushed to one side.

Willie finished his tea and, leaving his toast uneaten, stood, straightened his vest, pushed his hair back from his forehead, and walked to the lobby door and into a waiting carriage.

Twenty-eight ⸻

He decided to walk the seventeen blocks back to the Brown Palace. He wound his scarf tightly around his neck, pulled on his suede gloves. His feet felt the frigid pavement through the fine leather of his shoes. He wanted to be out in the air; he wanted to review his day before he returned to the hotel, to Celeste. He wanted time, needed time, to be by himself. He realized that, since his marriage, he had missed this private time, solitary spells where he could let his mind wander, where he could savor the silence in his life.

He thought of how much he loved Celeste, how he reveled in her youth, her enthusiasm, her lovemaking. That last was more than he had ever imagined. So unrestrained was she, so free. He smiled and decided that it was worth giving up some of that precious seclusion.

Willie tipped his hat to the doorman as he made his way to the entrance and headed straight to the bank of elevators. He would wire August later that evening. He wanted Celeste to be the first to know.

He opened the door to their room and stepped into a room filled with tissue paper, boxes, tea gowns, dresses, ribbons and laces. Celeste ran to him. "Oh, Willie. You're here. They just delivered these. But first I want to hear about you. Tell me everything, every minute. Don't leave a word out."

The chaos of the room left Willie's mind. He led Celeste to the sofa where they sat, knee to knee.

"I did it!" he exclaimed. "I got the deal! They're going to buy our issues and then package them with their paper. *Vati* thought that we would get their subscriber lists and then send individual copies. But this way, we send just one and the paper includes it with their editions.

I'll wire him tonight, but I wanted you to know first." He pushed his hair back from his forehead.

"I can't begin to tell you how this makes me feel," he continued. "I didn't stutter once, not even once." He laughed. "Tonight we celebrate. Tonight we dance!"

Celeste threw her arms around him. "Oh, Willie! And I have the perfect dress to wear."

Willie inhaled joy from the confusion of the room, the spontaneity of his bride. He would talk to her, he would. But not yet.

Twenty-nine —————————————

Dear Elizabeth,

I am writing to you from *The Brown Palace Hotel* in Denver! It is quite the place, the most luxurious hotel in the whole state of Denver. There is an atrium in the center (I learned that word from Willie) that goes up eight floors. The ballroom is on the top floor. I went up to see it, although it was empty at the time. It is all gold and glass, as nice as anything that we have in Baltimore.

The train ride here was long. It took days to get here. I lost track of time, all the sameness of the train ride. We spent the night in St. Louis, and it felt good to be off the train, although our train accommodations were luxurious too. We had a stateroom! I am feeling very grown up these days. I've even eaten lobster!

Willie works most days and I spend the time shopping for my trousseau. You should see it! Of course you will, when we return. I am looking forward to getting our house and becoming a real wife, although I am certainly now a real wife, if you know what I mean.

Now, let me tell you about my new clothes. I bought two wool walking costumes. One is bright red, with fur on the cuffs; I think it's mink. It is quite elegant. And the second one is more subdued, for those more formal occasions (now what would they be?). It is a grey pinstripe, and the stripes go up and down, naturally, except for the border on the skirt. There it has a deep panel at the hem cut across the grain. The jacket is a Zouave *style, close-cut. (Don't you love it that I'm learning all these fancy words? And won't Eva be jealous.)*

The suits will make quite an impression, let me tell you. I haven't bought any hats here, because they would take up so much room in my trunk, and I want to save all that for clothes. Today I am heading out to look at tea gowns. I think that I'll need at least three, don't you think? I brought two with me, but they are nowhere near enough. I can hardly wait to show you my new wardrobe.

Elizabeth, you would laugh if you could see the way that salesladies treat me, and the way that I act, like I am a grown-up and am used to buying all these things. It's a good thing that we read all those novels. I just pretend that I am the heroine in one of them. And sometimes it really does feel like I am in a book, a fairy tale, Elizabeth.

Remember that I told you that Willie and I had never danced. Well, now we have! He and I attended a tea dance in the hotel yesterday. And, yes, he does dance like a dream. He waltzed me around the room. And we danced to "When You Were Sweet Sixteen." I had forgotten for a while that I am sixteen, at least for another month. I felt like a princess, I really did. And he can do all the new dances. He loves ragtime, and now I do too. He showed me how to dance the cakewalk, the turkey trot. We danced to songs that I had never heard before. Do you know "I Never Trouble Trouble 'til Trouble Troubles Me?" or "Ain't Dat a Shame?" You should have seen us. In fact, everyone there left the dance floor until it was just us, and then they applauded. Isn't that the best?

See, we thought he was so shy, but there is a bit, more than a bit, of devilry in him. He just needed the right girl, and that is me!

Willie is just the sweetest thing, and he is so smart. Sometimes my head just spins at all he talks about. And he loves me! I can tell. And I really do think that I love him too.

Well, more later. We are coming home soon. I will write to you on the train and post the letter in St. Louis. It will be good to be home. I miss Mama and Papa, and I even think about Eva every once in a while. But mostly I am thinking about my new life, and working on how to be a proper wife.

See you soon, my dear friend. I miss you so much. I need to see you, to talk to you. Since we left, I have had no one to talk to except Willie. Tonight we are invited to a dinner at the home of one of the men Willie is working with. I am looking forward to that.

I miss you so much,

Your friend,
Celeste STRAUFF

Thirty———————————————————————

Willie's heart lurched and his bowels loosened. The wire in his hand read:

> *Sign nothing. I will telephone you at the hotel this afternoon. Be available. August Strauff*

He had expected a congratulatory return wire. But now this. Willie tried to understand his father's response. Why was he not elated? Why did he not see this as a victory for the paper, for Willie? He had sealed the deal. The paper would be published in Denver, an opening to the entire west. And now a telephone call, long-distance.

Thirty-one ————————————————————

August stood in his office, gazing out at Pratt Street, focusing on the almost-deserted fish market in the distance. He noticed a few cooks and housewives mingling there, haggling for bargains for the fish not yet selected by the grocers and restaurateurs. He held Willie's wire in his hand.

Had Willie lost the paper's chances? August's mind raced. How to find a way to undo Willie's blunder, how to construct an alternate solution. He could not afford to alienate the publishers in the West. They were the only way he knew to help the paper survive, his last hope, his last idea. He left the window and paced the length of his office.

He regretted his terse wire to Willie. August knew how his son would respond; he pictured Willie's face. He would make that up to him when he called. But first, he must work out a way to right this state of affairs.

An hour later, August placed the call. He knew Willie would be waiting.

The long-distance operator reached the Brown Palace. Their switchboard operator had been alerted, and transferred the call to Willie who waited in the telephone niche off the main lobby.

"*Vater*, I am here," he answered.

August began without hesitating. "Willie, my wire to you was abrupt, too brusque. I realized that I did not have all the facts before I responded. Tell me exactly what you agreed to."

August tried to soften his words to his son while holding down his temper and his dread that Willie may have made a mistake from which they could not recover.

"They liked the idea, *Vati*. You know that. And they were the ones who suggested including our issues with theirs. They had given this affiliation much thought."

"I have no doubt of that. Did it occur to you to question just why they were so enthusiastic? Did it occur to you to wonder just why they would be so anxious to help us? Did you think at all? Did you forget just who you were working for, whom you represent?"

August heard his harshness, but could not moderate it. He felt heat rise to his face.

"*Vati* --" Willie began.

"I gave you specific instructions, Willie. We discussed this. Did you even remember the parameters that we decided we could work with?"

Willie did not respond.

"Did you sign anything?"

Willie fought waves of nausea; he felt heat rise to his face; perspiration ran down his sides. He willed himself not to stutter.

"*Vati, Vater,*" he began. "Let me explain. I think that this arrangement could be a b-b-better one than the one w-we d-d-developed." He leaned back against the chair, waited for August's reply.

Hearing nothing, he continued, "We can either send one copy to them and they will re-set it and include it with a specific group of subscribers, or we can send batches matching their subscriber number." Willie realized that he had completed a thought without stuttering.

"They will give us their list of paid patrons, and pay for 400 newsstand editions. They will pay us, *Vati*, plus do the work of the distribution. That will save us the costs of mailing. We can still tell our advertisers that we reach that number of readers. We will have their names if they want proof."

Willie rested his elbows on the narrow shelf that held the telephone. He rested his head in his free hand. "So, you see, *Vati*, it does work out for us. We get the subscribers and the newsstand sales, without the newsprint and mailing costs. It will still show our banner and will be included as an extra section in the Denver paper. Now all that is left is negotiating a price"

Sitting more erect, he concluded, "I did get the agreement, *Vater*. I did get the deal."

August was surprised, pleased, though he remained a bit skeptical that Willie had done this, acted on his own, outside his own prescribed directive. Willie had negotiated an exchange that would benefit both parties. He had done it and it could just save the paper.

"Willie, well done. If what you say is true, I stand corrected." August rose from his desk, holding the phone in one hand and the earpiece in the other, and went to the window. This time he ignored the activity on the street below. Instead, he saw the face of his son. He inhaled deeply. He recognized a hope, albeit faint, that Willie would yet be a man.

"Let us spend a few minutes talking about pricing."

Thirty-two —————————————————

An hour later, Willie folded the morning paper to the page he had been reading and placed it on the table. He had left Celeste asleep in their room. He withdrew the slim, black leather calendar from his jacket and extracted a pearl pen-knife, a gift from his father the previous year when they had attended the Paris Exhibition. He unfolded the small scissors from its sheath and carefully cut out the ad which he then folded and placed in the calendar. The girly chorus at the Tabor Grand offered a matinee that afternoon, "The Devil's Auction." Willie stood, and nodding to the waiter, left for a final day of meetings with the publisher of the *Denver Review*.

He stepped out into the bracing mountain air, adjusting his scarf and pulling on his cashmere-lined leather gloves. He considered hiring a carriage to take him to the newspaper, but decided that a walk would give him a better sense of the city. He looked over at the wide streets, streetcar tracks running down the middle. They call them trams here, he remembered. He passed the Smith Watch Factory, with its sign indicating that it had been in business since 1857. He noted that Kipp's Grocery displayed its fruits and vegetables outside despite the cold. He narrowly missed being hit by a bicycle as he crossed the street for a better look at Meyer's Bakery.

Interesting architecture, he thought. Something like Baltimore, lots of dark, red brick. Very German-looking. Good for the newspaper. He'd mention that at his meeting.

That afternoon, his business with the publisher concluded over lunch at the Stockyard Saloon, Willie strode purposefully toward the music hall. He came upon a building of grand proportions. This should be an opera house, he thought, not a venue for girly shows. He imagined the building in its grander days. He purchased an orchestra seat, handing over a dollar bill and receiving seventy-five cents back.

Once inside, he looked up at the circular dome. He was surprised by the building's elegant stained glass windows, the cherry and Honduran mahogany moldings, and wondered if he had made an error. Perhaps "The Devil's Auction" was different from what he had assumed. He was prepared to see what the advertisement promised: "fox and foxie, new, bewildering scenic specialties, saucy girls, naked girls with horses; get your seats quick." The verbiage of vaudeville, not fine drama, Willie noted.

He put his coat over his arm and took his seat in the orchestra section He often went to burlesque shows in Baltimore, sometimes leaving work early, always the matinee, where he was less likely to be seen by anyone he knew. He was drawn to these productions, where girls paraded. But now that he had Celeste, who was so delightfully uninhibited, he thought that the pull of these shows would diminish. He had a wife; he should have no need for this type of coarse, vulgar entertainment.

Willie noticed the spittoons on both sides of the lobby entrance, in need of a good cleaning. Once in the auditorium, he studied the few patrons already seated. Shabby, he thought. The aroma of body odor and stale whiskey filled the air. Not a gentlemen's club. He made sure that he had a seat in a row by himself.

When the curtain rose, Willie saw that the show was primarily *tableau vivant*, interspersed with acts featuring exotic dancers. He had attended many *tableaux*, but none like he was seeing here. His experiences had been in the company of his parents and Clara's friends, amateur evening entertainments after dinners at their homes, always classical interpretations.

But here, naked women stood motionless, giving the audience abundant time to look upon them, time to savor their alabaster outlines. From his seat, Willie saw that they wore transparent body stockings, yet his excitement rose when the women turned slowly to give the audience a full frontal view. Rosy nipples had been painted on their suits, and Willie felt his mouth water. His penis pressed against his trousers. Celeste was beautiful, but he realized that these women roused something primal. He covered his lap with his coat and clutched his penis.

He was ashamed, but couldn't control his urge. He willed himself to resist, he, a proper husband, a gentleman. What kind of man am I, he thought. But he could not move his eyes from the rosy nipples that he knew were painted on, not real. He found himself panting, and was mortified by his response.

He had thought himself a man of the world, inured to such base reactions. He patronized the red light houses on George Street in Baltimore; he had visited to *La Folies Bergere* where the girls danced naked except for their feathered headdresses; he had been to *le Moulin Rouge*, where at the last show some of the cancan dancers shed their ruffled pantaloons. Willie knew about women; he knew about sex. But this was different. These tableaux, still as statues, the women standing with their arms at their sides, facing the audience, allowing their bodies to be viewed in sculptured stillness, roused him in a way that he'd not experienced. Painted though they were, Willie saw them as Grecian goddesses, untouchable women he longed to possess.

He pulled his handkerchief from his pocket, this time not noticing that the hotel laundry had not ironed it as smoothly as Hanne's work, and wiped his mouth. He held the white cloth, willing himself to return it to his pocket. But almost immediately he placed his hand underneath his coat, inside his trousers. His first touch brought him to orgasm. He stifled his moan. At the same time he was filled with repugnance at what he had done.

He adjusted his clothes and, head down, looking at no one, left his seat and the theatre. The performance was still in its first act.

Willie walked the fourteen blocks from the theatre to the Brown Palace, overcoat unbuttoned. He wanted to feel the cold air, wanted it to cool his forehead, his soul. His feet, clad in their thin-soled leather shoes, pounded the pavement. With each step he rebuked himself.

How could I have ended this day of triumph with such a vile act, he asked himself. Me, a married man; me, a businessman. I have no discipline; I have no moral rectitude; I am just what my father thinks I am. He knows. I am a worm.

He stopped at a corner, struggling to catch his breath. He buttoned his overcoat, and as he did so, realized that he had left his hat and gloves at the theatre. No matter; the cold was a just punishment.

Thirty-three———————

He circled the block three times before he could bring himself to face Celeste. He had good news to tell her. He must remember that. There was no need for her, for anyone, to know about his afternoon. They would attend a dinner hosted by the Denver publisher the next evening, and then, his work completed, they would begin their journey east, their journey home.

He told himself that he would tell her the truth about their finances, about moving back to stay with *Mutti* and *Vati*, with Clara. He would tell her how it was going to be.

As he walked, he rehearsed his words to her. He predicted her responses, her objections, and planned his replies. It was settled.

He slowed his pace. His stride became more secure. He straightened his shoulders; he was ready. He would tell her the news about the paper, then tell her about the house.

With his decision made, he did not anticipate the sudden lurch in his chest. He loved Celeste; he hoped that she loved him as well. What would she think, what would she do if he delivered an ultimatum? Perhaps he could sit with her and explain, explain about the money, explain about living with Paulina and August, at least until they got on their feet. She would understand that. They would go through this together. That would be the better plan.

The doorman tipped his hat as Willie approached the entrance. Willie nodded and went directly to the elevator. Celeste would be waiting, anxious to hear the news of the day.

When he reached their door, he knocked lightly as he put his key in the lock.

"Oh, Willie, I have been so worried. I've been thinking about you all day. Could you sense it? Tell me, how did it go?" She touched her lips with a fluttering gesture.

Willie stepped into the room, his eye immediately taking in the disarray. More dresses, gloves draped over the sofa, shoes strewn across the bed. He had anticipated talking with her in a calm and peaceful setting. Now all he saw was chaos and mayhem. His throat closed; he willed himself to be calm, composed, but the room's disorder caused him to respond in panic and anger.

"Celeste, how can you live in this mess? I can't even think straight. Do you do anything all day except shop?" His tone was sharp.

Celeste stepped back. Willie's demeanor, as much as his words, frightened her.

"Willie, why are you acting like this? Did today not go well? Please don't be cross with me. Please tell me you love me." She felt acid rise in her throat, and she turned toward the window waiting for him to come to her, to put his arms around her, to apologize, to hold her.

He remained where he was. "You'll have to send all these back. I can't afford them; you have no need for them. What kind of a life do you think we'll be leading? Who do you think you are? Who do you think I am?"

"Willie," she struggled for words. "What is wrong? Why are you treating me this way? I thought you loved--"

He interrupted. "Celeste, this is not about love. This is about real life." Willie heard his father's words, his father's voice come from him. "There is no money. Do you understand? There is no money. I have no money. I make almost nothing. My salary is just a living allowance."

He moved one of Celeste's chemises from a chair, started to fold it, then stopped and threw it onto the bed.

"Everything that I have has been given to me by my father. My clothes, my house, my earnings, everything. I have nothing of my own. I have nothing to give you." He put his hands to his face, pressing his temples, willing the pain in his head to stop.

"There won't be a house for us when we get back to Baltimore. We will live with my parents. That is the way it is going to be. Now you make arrangements for all these clothes to be returned. I don't know what you were thinking. You won't even be able to wear them in a month or so. Why have you bought them? What life did you think you would have?"

He stopped, horrified at the attack he had just delivered. She remained at the window, her back toward him. He saw her tremble, heard a sob catch in her throat. She turned to face him, her face wet. She wiped her nose with the back of her hand, the gesture of a child.

"What have I done, Willie? I don't understand why you are talking to me this way? What have I done? I don't even know who you are anymore."

She forced the words out, the pitch becoming higher, reedy, whiny, even to her ears the sound of an infant wailing. She stumbled to the dresser for a clean handkerchief. She held it to her face. She knew that her face would be red, swollen, ugly. She couldn't let Willie see her like this. She had to charm him. She had to make him love her again.

When she looked up she saw Willie's face, grey, wet with perspiration. His hands shook as he sunk to the bed, holding his head. He lowered his head between his knees, gasping for breath. Celeste leaned against the window, placed her head against the cool glass.

Willie's head pounded, a sick headache suddenly upon him, filling his mouth with acrid saliva. He put his hand to his throat, tried to swallow.

Celeste struggled to clear the piles of clothes, folding each of the dresses, placing them back in their boxes. Willie saw flashes of maroon, of grey, the wide white ribbons which once tied them. He started to rise and felt his knees buckle. Celeste did not go to him. Turning toward the bed, he willed himself to stand, raising himself with the strength in his arms.

He started toward her. At his approach she turned to face him. He took the grey tea gown from her hands and laid it on the bed. He took her hand tentatively. She let it rest in his. He led her to the bed and they sat, Celeste staring straight ahead. She felt that she was above the room, watching a scene where she had a starring role.

Willie turned to her and touched her hand to his lips. "This was supposed to be a wonderful day. I made the deal. I made *Vati* proud of me. I was a businessman. I didn't mean it to be this way, really I didn't. I wanted you to be proud of me, to think that I am, that I will be a good husband to you, a good father. And now I've ruined it. Oh, Celeste, I am sorry. I didn't mean to take it out on you. I knew I had to tell you, but I didn't know how. I should have told you earlier. I should have treated you better. You d-d-deserve b-b-better."

"I don't understand, Willie. What are you saying? What do you have to tell me? What have I done to make you so angry with me?"

He forced himself to look at her, forced himself to tell her the truth.

"You've done nothing to deserve this, Celeste. This is all my fault, all my doing. I should have told you from the beginning, but I was so proud of the way I handled our getting married, so proud of you, so proud that you were my wife. I couldn't bear to break the spell. And now I've done the worst. I've hurt you for no reason. And when you learn the truth, you're sure to hate me."

Celeste waited.

"I have no money. I am in no position to take a wife, to be a husband. All I have is what *Vati* chooses to give me. He is disappointed in me; I see that in his face every day.

"When we married, he told me that he would support my decision, our decision to marry. And he did that. Your agreeing to marry in a Catholic ceremony helped, it really did. I asked a big thing of you, but had I been truly courageous, I never would have allowed that. I should have put you first. A real man would have put his wife first."

Willie struggled to get his breath. "*Vati* said that we must move back with them, at least until the paper turns around and he can afford to give me a proper salary. I agreed to that, Celeste. I agreed without even talking to you about it. I should have told you. I cannot afford a home for us. I have no money. Everything I have comes from him.

"That's why I said what I did about the clothes. If I could take back my words I would."

"Willie, the clothes. Some of them have been fitted. They won't take them back. What should I do? Should I ask my father to buy them?"

He turned to look at her. "No. I spoke rashly. Keep those." He paused. "But can you return the others?"

She nodded, stood up and returned to folding the garments, inserting tissue paper between each garment. "I can call tomorrow. I'll tell them some excuse or another. I'll think of something." She didn't face him as she said this.

"What can I do to make this up to you? I will make it up to you, I promise."

"Just tell me the truth, Willie. I never thought you'd lie to me, never. I thought that you were, that we were, rich. Why didn't you tell me? Why did you let me think that? From the first time we met I thought that. And I thought that we would have a home. Now you tell me that we will live with your family. That will be my home, with your parents, with Clara? What kind of a life will that be for me, Willie? Have you thought about that?"

Celeste surprised herself with the strength of her words, her tone.

"I will make this up to you. I will. It will only be for a little while. This agreement with the Denver paper should make a big difference. *Vati* is proud of me, I know he is. He will believe in me now; he'll give me more responsibility, and a bigger salary. And if he doesn't, I'll find another job. I will, Celeste. I will."

He moved to embrace her. She allowed him to put his arms around her. They stood together, both shaken.

Finally, Willie broke the silence. "Let's order our dinner from room service. They can set up a table here. Let's just be alone, quiet, tonight."

He helped her clear the room. They stood at the window and looked out at 16th Street. A fine sleet covered the streets. They were silent as they watched as the sleet turned to snow.

That night Celeste went to her trunk. She pulled out the old stuffed dog she'd had since she was five years old. In bed, she held the dog close, her back to her husband. Willie reached out and put a gentle hand on her shoulder. She did not respond.

Willie lay awake, head throbbing, dinner heavy in his stomach. He knew he had harmed his marriage. He had harmed himself. He wondered if either could ever be made right.

Thirty-four———————————

Dear Elizabeth,

It is so nice to hear from you — and to receive letters addressed to "Mrs. Strauff" at the hotel. It makes me feel very grown up, which I am, of course.

You are good to be so studious and interested in school. I'm letting Willie be my teacher. It seems he knows everything about everything. He's always reading, books and newspapers, not magazines, and I have learned a lot about architecture. Maybe those trips to Europe got him interested. He's promised to take me there. I want to see Paris most of all.

You are going to so many parties. I hope I will be included, invited, when I return. But maybe now that I'm married it won't be the same. I must confide that I do miss my friends. It has been a bit lonely for me, with Willie working every day.

We've had a lovely time here, though. I've shopped, shopped, shopped during the days that I was on my own. Willie negotiated an arrangement between his paper and the one in Denver, a very important arrangement! We had dinner at the house of the publisher. It was very fancy, but all old people except me and Willie — very boring.

I have to tell you that the fashions here are way behind those in Baltimore, so I only bought a few things for my trousseau. My trunk will not come back full. But you will like my new tea gowns and suits, I think.

Also, some more news. Willie and I have decided to live with his parents for a while. I haven't told Mama and Papa yet, so don't let on that you know. We thought that we would save our money for a really big house – like the ones on Mt. Vernon Place – and not waste our money renting or buying a little house. This way, in a year or so we will really be set – a big house, servants, a way to really entertain. Like your parents do. And you will always be the guest of honor, my dear best friend, Elizabeth.

I am writing this on the train. We left Denver yesterday.

Willie took me to some shows. We saw Miss Mary Mannering in "Camille." We also saw "The Pride of Jennico." I don't remember who starred in it, but it was much more exciting than "Camille." Lots of sword-fighting and jumping around on the stage. Both were as good as anything that I've seen in Baltimore. Willie's promised to take me to New York to see real Broadway shows. I can hardly wait.

He found out that Miss Mannering was also there to star in "Janice Meredith," but that was scheduled for this week, so we weren't able to see it. "Janice Meredith" is based on a book, Willie told me, and he actually went to a store and bought it for me! I plan to have it completed by the time we get home to Baltimore. So if you saw us on the train, you would see two old married people just sitting and reading.

I can hardly wait to see you too. I will be in touch as soon as we get settled. The redcap said that he will mail this letter for me. I'm not sure exactly where I am, somewhere between Denver and St. Louis. So let me know what the postmark says.

Now I will say goodbye and find Willie. I am in our drawing room writing this; he is in the observation car (always) reading.

My birthday is almost here. I wonder what kind of celebration he will plan. You must help him remember and let him know how important it is to me. I'll be 17. Can you believe how old we are?

Much love from you devoted friend,
Celeste

Celeste stood, smoothed her skirt and headed for the observation car. Yes, she thought, those Denver clothes were not suited to me. Yes, next year we will buy a house on Mt. Vernon Place, or maybe Biddle Street, bigger, much bigger than the one the Strauffs live in.

She sealed the envelope and went to find the porter.

Thirty-five————————————————

Hanne placed the tureen in the middle of the table. Paulina ladled the pumpkin soup into bowls and handed them to August and Clara. Clara passed the basket filled with pumpernickel rolls. August sat at the head of the table. Gas sconces lit the dining room, their dim shadows reflected in the windows.

"Now there is something we must discuss," August said.

"August," Paulina said, her soup spoon raised. "Can it wait until after dinner?"

"Can what wait?" Clara said. "Oh, this has to be about Willie. It's about Willie, isn't it? What's he done now?"

August looked at his daughter. He wondered if she disliked Willie as much as it appeared. He had hoped that the antagonism would lessen as they became adults. Clara had her music, her friends; Willie had his work, his books. He knew that Clara thought Willie weak, a failure, not unlike his own view of his son. But Willie had proved himself in Denver. August sometimes worried that he hadn't been the best father to Willie, that he might have listened to Paulina's advice, treated Willie a bit more gently. He thought that his sternness would make a man of him. Perhaps Paulina had been right. Or maybe Paulina's softness had kept him a child.

If only Willie had been like Clara, he thought. I would have known how to act, what to do. But now I will help my son, help him get on his feet.

"Clara, Willie and Celeste will make their home with us for the time being. When they return from Denver, they will have the third floor front room."

Clara put down her spoon and looked her father squarely in the eye. "*Vati*, that is my room. You cannot give them my room. That has been my room forever. It belongs to me. You have no right to take that. I will not allow it."

Paulina looked down at her plate. She had anticipated such a response from Clara.

August focused on his daughter. "You won't allow it? How dare you speak that way to me? How dare you." Clara met his gaze. Both stared at the other; neither flinched.

"*Vati*, that is my room." Clara's voice softened. "You know how I love it. I've done nothing wrong, and you are punishing me. You are punishing me for Willie's foolishness. How can you?" Her tone hardened. "Why can't they stay in his room? He wanted that girl, why should I have to pay the price?"

August looked over at his daughter, her expression so like the one he often saw in his own mirror. He understood. She was right. But his mind was made up.

"Clara, we all must act together. Celeste is now part of Willie's life. You know that he cannot afford to live on his own. He made a success of this trip to Denver. We must reward him for that."

"And you are rewarding him by giving him something that belongs to me? How do you justify that, *Vati*? I always thought that you were a fair man, a just father. This is absolutely beyond the pale." Clara did not look at her mother. She knew that August's word was law in their house, and that, in any case, Paulina would support anything that gave the advantage to Willie.

August placed the starched white linen napkin beside his plate. "There will be no more discussion of this, Clara. I have made the decision. That room does not belong to you. This is my house, I make the decisions. Is that understood?"

Clara could not remember her father raising his voice to her. She had been the daughter he wanted; she had always acted to make him proud. And now this betrayal.

August continued. "The furniture will be moved tomorrow afternoon. You choose how you want it arranged. I think that it will all fit. Yes, it will be a bit crowded, but you won't have to give up any of your things."

Clara swallowed hard. She had never before been angry with him.

August realized how much her love, her admiration meant to him. *"Liebchen,"* he said softly, "I know this is hurtful to you. But I must do it, we must do it, for Willie. He needs us. You've always been the strong one; you can handle this."

"There is really nothing more to be said about this. He is bringing that girl into our house. Our lives will not be the same. Oh, yours will go on without a problem. You'll go to work every morning; everything will still be done for you. But *Mutti* and I will now have a stranger living in our home. When you made this decision did you even think about us?"

"Clara, that is quite enough. I will not have you being disrespectful in my home."

Paulina put her head in her hands. "Please, I cannot bear this. Willie and Celeste will live here, Clara. We will make the most of it, the best of it. And Celeste will have to fit into our lives. We will go on as before."

Clara looked over at her mother, surprised by her firm words. Yes, Celeste would have to fit into their lives. She would see to that.

Hanne stood in the doorway holding the platter of rouladen and roasted vegetables. She had heard. Another person in the household. More laundry, more ironing, more cooking, more shopping. No one considered her.

August looked over at Clara. "There's a new exhibit at the Metropolitan Museum. Perhaps we can arrange you to meet *Tante Anna* and spend a few days in New York."

Clara looked at her father and raised an eyebrow. Hanne removed the soup bowls and placed the platter on the table. This, Clara thought, is not over.

Thirty-six

Celeste looked out as the train pulled into Camden Station. Her honeymoon was over; she was to begin her real life as a wife. In someone else's house. But, no matter, she thought. Willie and I are saving money for a big house.

Willie looked over at his bride, and took her hand in his, brought her fingers to his lips. There had been no further mention of that night at the Brown Palace. Some of the dresses had been returned; most were in Celeste's trunk. She had worn a different, new outfit every day since that night. She was enchanting, he thought, and pushed away worries about how to pay for this wardrobe. He tried to keep his focus on his success in Denver.

Celeste had been the hit of the dinner their last evening there. She had charmed all the men; they had been taken with her guileless smile. They thought Willie had made quite a catch. The women were wiser.

Watching Celeste, Willie wondered how she would fill her days. She had been right in questioning him, in accusing him of not considering how his decision would impact her life. It all had been too sudden, too soon. He knew that. And now he had to make it right.

Celeste closed her eyes, willing herself to see this new phase of her life in a positive way. She thought of her mother, of Annie's deference to George. That seemed to have worked out. She opened her handbag and fingered the letter from Annie. She would tell her parents about where they would live when she saw them. She would have to work to keep Willie captivated, that she knew. So far, she thought, he was. Except for that one night, that one time. But that was behind them. Now they would start their real lives.

Willie put his arm around her as the train came to a stop. This would be the test, this day, this move back home. He pulled Celeste close, put his lips to her hair. He would take care of her. They would get on their feet and soon be able to live on their own. Celeste had been so accommodating about issues with his family, the Catholic marriage ceremony, now this. Yes, there was a mettle to her that he could learn from, emulate. And, so beautiful, so beautiful and full of life. More that he could learn from her.

They put on their coats, ready to face the cold. Celeste had traded her schoolgirl maroon coat for a new one, brown wool, fastened with black frogs and trimmed with black fur at the collar and cuffs. She had new black kid gloves to match, and a newly purchased black fur hat sat on the back of her head. She had made sure that a few floating blond curls showed around her face. She had returned the matching boots, and her feet were clad in the black patent-leather shoes she wore on the day of her wedding.

August had sent a carriage to meet the couple. "Wait here," Willie said. "I'll see if it's outside."

A moment later he returned. Celeste took his arm as they left the marble floors of Camden Station and entered the black phaeton, August's peace offering. It seemed that the flamboyant carriage with its yellow trim confirmed his tacit acknowledgement that this was a special occasion, a special day. Willie noted this; so did Celeste. Settled into the high seat, she leaned over and kissed him on the ear.

Twenty blocks later the carriage pulled in front of the house. Willie looked across the street to Green Mount Cemetery, a study in grey and black in winter, the few firs standing below a dreary January sky. Towering above the granite wall surrounding the cemetery, the branches of the oaks and catalpas and lindens formed a scherenschnitte against the sky. How ironic, he thought, a cemetery as metaphor for the beginning of our lives together. He felt a sick headache coming on as he turned and looked up at the front door.

The driver had stepped to the street, and he gave Willie a needed hand as he left the carriage. Willie turned to help Celeste, whose expression was no longer as joyful as on the ride there.

"It will be fine, Celeste. They are so lucky to have you in this family. Just give them time; they'll come to know it. I certainly do." He smiled at his bride, who, despite her fur hat and trimmed coat, looked like a little girl to him. He had married a girl. Yes, and he must take care of her.

Willie was watching the driver unloading the luggage when he heard the front door open. August stood in the doorway, hesitating whether to come down the four steps to the sidewalk or wait for the couple to come to him. Willie will have enough worries, he thought, and stepped toward the carriage.

"Welcome home, *mein gut sohn*." August shook Willie's hand. "And welcome, Celeste. I hope that you will find this your home."

Celeste waited for August to embrace her. When none was offered, she spoke. "Thank you, Mr. Strauff."

August turned to show the driver to the vestibule where the luggage was to be deposited. "Your mother has been waiting for you," he said. Celeste's heart leapt and she ran up to the front door. She realized that August had been talking to Willie when she saw Paulina's stout figure standing behind the pile of suitcases and the trunk.

"*Mutti*," Willie said and went to embrace his mother. Paulina held him tightly, then releasing him, noticed Celeste. The older woman gazed at her daughter-in-law, observing first her hat and coat. Celeste waited for her embrace. None came.

"How do you do, Mrs. Strauff," she finally said.

"Yes. Welcome to our home, Celeste," Paulina responded. "We will do our best to make this a pleasant stay for you." The four stood awkwardly in the narrow space. Willie took off his coat and hung it on the rack. He helped Celeste off with hers. There were four hooks. One was empty, and he placed it there. Clara was not home.

August led Willie, Celeste and Paulina to the front room. "I'm sure that you would like to freshen up after your journey. I am anxious to hear about it." He paused. "I should say that we are anxious to hear about it. Clara was sorry not to be here when you arrived. She is rehearsing for a recital and should be home by dinner time."

August adjusted his pince-nez and smoothed his mustache. "In the meantime, I do, we, have a surprise. Willie, I thought your room on the second floor too small for the two of you. And Clara has graciously consented to switch rooms with you so that you can have the large third-floor front room. It gets the first light in the morning and is a rather cheery space. Your furniture and closet contents have already been placed there, and, as another of our wedding gifts to you, we made arrangements for a new bed. That also is in place."

Willie blushed at the mention of the marriage bed. Celeste took his hand.

"Perhaps you would like to take Celeste upstairs and have a few minutes of privacy," August continued. "We will be in the front room. Come down when you are ready. I would like to talk to you, Willie, about our next steps in Denver. Your mother and Celeste can get to know one another."

Willie led Celeste up the narrow stairway. When they got to their new room, he took her into his arms. "This is the beginning of our life together, Celeste. This room, this bed. It's not so bad, is it?"

She put her face on his shoulder. "When can I see my mother?"

Thirty-seven _____

She heard the alarm clock in the distance. Hanne's, she thought, and rolled over against Willie. He turned and took her into his arms. Both lay there, each with their own thoughts.

Willie looked around the room, seeing the new furniture his father had purchased for him, for them. He must love me, he thought, to do this for me. Willie smiled thinking of the scene that must have taken place. And now he would soon rise and dress, take his breakfast, begin his day as a married man. He hugged Celeste tight to him.

She responded, though her thoughts were not the same as those of her husband. She was thinking of the softness of the featherbed, of the warmth of the down comforter, and wishing that she had her old pillow, so much firmer than the ones here. *Maybe I'll bring it back with mer. Today I'll see Mama; maybe even Papa would be at home. I'll arrange to have dinner with them, on a regular basis, at least once a week. I'm only across the street. And I'll bring the rest of my clothes home, the rest of my treasures.*

She put her arms around Willie, held him tight. With her face pressed against his, her eyes took in the room. *Maybe I'll buy a painting or two. That would make it more home, more mine. I'll get a book on that.*

A few minutes later, Willie whispered, "Time to arise, my sweet one. Breakfast is at 7:30. I'll use the bathroom first and then come back up to dress. Usually it is just *Vati* and *Mutti* and me; Clara sleeps in."

Celeste giggled. "At least on this first day, I won't have to face Clara first thing." She smiled to herself. *If Clara doesn't appear for breakfast every morning, perhaps I won't have to either.* She turned on her side, content with Willie holding her. She felt him slip out of bed; she'd get up when he returned.

August and Paulina were already seated at the table when the couple arrived in the dining room. The breakfast Hanne had prepared was laid on the sideboard.

August looked up from his newspaper. "We eat a simple breakfast during the week, Celeste," he said. "Please help yourself."

Paulina looked up from her notebook and nodded at Celeste. "Willie, how did you sleep? Are you recovered from your trip? I want to hear all about it, but maybe at dinner this evening when Clara is here."

Celeste looked over at Willie. He seemed happy, she thought, at ease. At home. Willie offered to bring her breakfast to her.

"No, I'll get it. Thank you." She went to the sideboard. A simple breakfast? she wondered. Eggs, meat, toast, oatmeal. She filled her plate. Paulina noticed.

"I'd like to see Mama and Papa today, and bring some of my things back with me. If that is all right with you," Celeste said.

"Of course," Paulina responded, not looking up from her notebook. Celeste waited, but nothing more was said, the scraping of forks on plates the only sound in the room.

A few minutes later, August put his paper down. "Willie, are you ready? The driver is coming at the regular time. We can go in together." August left to get his coat.

Willie rose from the table and headed for the stairs. Celeste watched him go. Her toast caught in her throat. She was now alone with Paulina.

"Our room is just lovely, Mrs. Strauff," Celeste began. "This is so nice of you to welcome me into your home. I promise that I will make Willie happy. I can see that you love him too." Her voice shook on this last sentence.

Paulina put her papers down and looked over at the young girl. She had been the same age when she married August. But such different circumstances. August was a go-getter, yes, that was the English word. He had no money, but everyone knew that he would be successful, at something. A barber during the day, he ran a saloon at night. He was a hard worker; he was ambitious. He had a house, rented, but it was his. They came back from their wedding to that house. He was younger than Willie, but he had been a man. No question about that.

And now, here she sat with Willie's wife, a girl. Paulina reached out and took Celeste's hand. She smiled. "You will be welcome here. You will be family. It will be all right, you'll see. I was your age when I married Willie's father. As long as you put him first in your life, you will be fine."

Celeste felt tears well up in her eyes. She lowered her eyes. "Thank you, Mrs. Strauff. May I help clear the table?"

Paulina looked at this girl, and saw her younger self, though not as pretty, trying to make a good impression, frightened. "No, Hanne takes care of that. What do you have planned for the day?" As soon as these words left her, Paulina remembered Celeste's earlier words.

"I'd like to see Mama, if that is all right with you," Celeste said.

"Dear Celeste. This is your home now. You come and go as you wish. No need to ask permission," Paulina replied. And hearing Clara's footsteps, Paulina picked up her notebook and pencil. Celeste knew that she was dismissed.

As Celeste stood to leave, Clara entered the dining room carrying the Czerny etudes she had been studying the night before. Celeste wished her good morning; Clara nodded.

She returned to her room to finish unpacking her trunk. She noticed how neatly Hanne had placed Willie's underclothes in the new bureau, ironed, stacked in neat rows of white, his socks rolled in three rows, placed light to dark. His shirts hung in the mahogany wardrobe, along with his suits, taking up most of the space. Hanne had placed each one an inch apart.

No room for me, Celeste thought, and then shook her head, willing that notion from her mind. She walked to the wardrobe and, gently, pushed his clothes to one side. She would need more hangers. She would buy the fancy wooden kind, like Willie had.

She unpacked her newly purchased lingerie and placed it in her side of the bureau. She would buy some scented drawer paper and sachets. She looked out the third floor window onto North Avenue.

The trees were bare, their limbs forming a pattern above the stone wall of Green Mount Cemetery. From her vantage point, she could see into it, see the benches, empty of visitors this cold morning, the caretaker making his rounds to remove tired Christmas wreaths and wilted flowers. She couldn't see as far as the Wells' plot. What a beautiful view I have, she thought. When spring comes I'll look out on a park as beautiful as New York's Central Park. How lucky I am to be on this side of North Avenue. She hummed as she finished her work, *I Ain't A-goin' to Weep No More*, a song that she and Willie had danced to in Denver. Her feet moved to the ragtime beat. Yes, this would be just fine, just fine until they had enough money to buy their own house, a really big house, bigger than this one.

An hour later she descended to the first floor, looking for Paulina. She found her in the front room, still working with her notebook.

"I'm going to Mama's now. Should I tell you when I go out?"

Clara sat at the piano. "No need to report to us, Celeste. Come and go as you wish, why should we c--."

Paulina interrupted. "Clara, please. Celeste, of course we're interested in where you are, where you go. We don't want to worry about you. But this is your home. No need to ask permission of us. Please give your parents our best wishes. We will talk about arranging a time for us to meet, to have dinner here soon."

Celeste went to the hallway and slipped into her coat, her new one. It had been moved to the hook that Willie used. "I'll be back in the afternoon. I'd like to make arrangements to bring my things here. Is there a time that will work better for you?"

"Let Willie help you with that when he gets home this evening. He usually arrives an hour or two before his father," Paulina said.

"Don't bring too much. There really is not much room up there," Clara added.

"Clara, please." Paulina closed her eyes.

Once on the street, Celeste looked across to her house. Now I must think of it as my parents' house, she thought, across the street and up one block. So anxious was she to see her mother again, she had to stop herself from skipping.

Her hand was on the doorknob when she realized, no, I must ring the bell. I am a married woman, now visiting my family. But Annie had been watching for Celeste, and when she saw her younger daughter approach, she swung the door open and scooped Celeste inside.

Celeste was surprised, and delighted, to experience such an outpouring of emotion from her stoic mother.

"I have missed you, my dear," Annie said, as she held her close.

"Oh, Mama," and Celeste felt warm tears on her face.

"Come, let's sit. Tell me about your trip; I loved your letters. They sounded so grown up," Annie said. "Tell me, are you happy?"

"I am happy, Mama. But I miss you. I miss Papa. I even miss Eva. But, Willie is wonderful, and our trip to Denver, our honeymoon was lovely. I bought so many new things, for my trousseau, and Willie says that he will pay for them, not you, since we were so naughty in running away to get married. And we will be living with the Strauffs for a while, while we save to buy a big house. That is what Willie wants. A house, bigger than the one he lives in. And he was a big success in Denver, with the publisher. We had dinner with them, served by a lot of servants, and we saw shows. I wore my new dresses. And we danced. Mama, Willie can dance! And we have our own room at the Strauffs, on the third floor, in the front, and I can see across to the park, well, the cemetery, but I'm calling it a park, and if I press my forehead to the glass and turn to the left, I can even see home, well, your house. I think it will be just wonderful, and now that I'm back home I can see you anytime I want and you can come to visit me. Mrs. Strauff says that she wants to have you and Papa to dinner. I'm not sure if she means Eva too, but maybe I can find that out."

Annie sat and watched her daughter. Still a child, she thought. Then she too remembered that she had been but a few months older than Celeste when she had married George. A few months older, but she, and George, so serious minded, so unlike this fairy-like creature facing her.

"I need to pack the rest of my things. Willie will come over when he gets home from work and take them to our new house."

Annie nodded, and was silent. She could think of nothing to say.

Thirty-eight _____

August preceded Willie as they entered. August nodded to Franz, who was setting type for the paper's next edition, then went immediately to his office; Willie stopped at his desk in the work room.

"Good trip, Willie?" Franz asked, although he knew the answer. He wanted to give Willie a chance to bring him good news. God knows, Franz thought, he's had little enough chance to do that. Willie, always nervous, brushing that lock of hair from his forehead, anxious, trying to please his father. Married now. Well, maybe that will make a man of him.

"A very good trip, Franz. It looks like we'll be distributed in Denver, and that's just the start."

"Well, welcome back. *Frau Strauff* was at your desk while you were away. It was like the old days while she was here. But now new days are upon us, *yah?*"

Willie nodded and sat down at his desk, pulling out his notes from the trip. The edition would be sent by week's end. A trial run they were calling it, to give them time to work out any snags. Franz would need to finish a mock-up by tomorrow noon.

Willie also knew that he could no longer put off talking to his father. Why, he thought, could this not be a complete victory? I've sabotaged *Vati's* approval? I will talk to him before day's end. But not now. This morning, this morning is for hurrahs and compliments.

Willie saw his father striding toward him. "Let's see what you have there, son. What are your ideas about how we start this off? What did you and the Denver tycoon decide?"

106

Franz observed that father had come to son, rather than August's summoning Willie to come to him as he usually did. Willie must have worked out quite an arrangement, the typesetter thought.

August pulled up a chair beside Willie's desk. Willie smiled. The morning was going to go just fine.

Thirty-nine———————————

That afternoon Willie stretched across his desk to turn on the bronze lamp. Franz had left for the day, his work done. Willie knew that there was not enough work to keep Franz busy. He sensed that August, remembering his own early days as a typesetter, felt a bond with Franz, kept him on because of that. But, unless they found more advertisers, and more subscribers, Franz's hours would have to be cut.

Willie thought that it was only a matter of time for him as well. He had to approach his father; he had to break the spell of his success.

He remembered the meeting with his father just a few weeks before. August had agreed to pay his and Celeste's expenses on this business trip. He had not agreed to provide Celeste with a trousseau. That was something that Willie had exuberantly offered. Swept up in the moment, he had imagined that he could provide for her, and provide for her in the way that she deserved.

He wanted to do that; he wanted to make up for the crude way he had treated her that afternoon in Denver. Neither had mentioned again, though it was never far from Willie's mind. He had failed. He had failed his wife. He had failed himself. And he was set to fail again, this time as a son. Some of the bills from the Denver stores had been waiting for him when he arrived at North Avenue. More were on the way. Willie knew of only one way to pay them. August.

He placed his hands flat on his desk, then stood and walked to August's office. His father was hidden behind *The New York Times*.

"*Vater*, may I see you for a moment," Willie said, entering the office.

August put down the paper, sensing that a difficulty was about to present itself. He raised his right eyebrow, inserted his pince-nez.

"What is it, Willie?" He tried to make his tone kind, but even he heard the edge in his voice.

Willie stood; he willed himself not to stammer. "It's not good, *Vati*, and I know that you will be disappointed in me. If I knew of any other option I would use that." Two sentences, no stammer. A good start, he thought. *Vati* respects strength.

He inhaled deeply and verbalized what he had rehearsed earlier in the day: "I know that you paid for the clothes that Celeste bought while we were at the Stafford. I want you to know how much I appreciate that. I also know that you are in our corner with Clara. And you have offered us a place to live. I don't know what we would have done without that kind offer."

August folded the newspaper and placed it on the corner of his desk.

Willie cleared his throat, pushed his hair from his forehead. "I acknowledge to you that I made a mistake in marrying so suddenly. It was unwise. You are right, I was not, am not, in a position to take a wife. You were right, *Vati*. You are right.

"You gave me a great opportunity when you sent me to Denver. I hope that you will be proud of my efforts. I want to make you proud --"

August interrupted. "What is it you need to ask me, Willie?" Both men heard the impatience in his voice, thought August had meant to sound kind. "Just say it."

Willie's prepared words were forgotten. "I talked to Celeste, believe me I did. But not until I realized how much money she had spent while we were there. She shopped every day, *Vati*, clothes, clothes, and more clothes. I made a terrible mistake and became very angry. I spoke callously and unkindly to her. I told her that she had to return them. My behavior toward her, toward my wife, was despicable.

"She agreed to return those she could, but some, well, most of them, had already been fitted, so the stores would not take them back. And now the bills have arrived. And I have no money to pay for them.

"I am not asking you to give me the money for them, *Vater*. What I am asking you for is a loan, an advance on my salary, so that I can pay these creditors. Both of us have learned a lesson, Celeste and I. And I take full responsibility for this. This is not of Celeste's doing. I let her believe that I was a man of means, that I could afford a wife. Not only have I let her down, but I am ashamed of the way that I told her the truth. I told her in anger, *Vati.*"

He stopped, realizing that this could have been one of the longest conversation he had ever had with his father, the most words that he had ever said to him. Then he recognized that he had spoken without stammering. He had spoken from his heart and he had not stammered.

August willed himself to remain silent. Another mistake, he thought, another mistake for me to fix. And more money going out. For clothes, for God's sake, clothes for Celeste. He closed his eyes.

"*Ach*, Willie, what a child you married. You wanted a beauty. This is what comes of it. You are pushing me to my limits, boy." He put his elbows on his desk, folded his hands, looked directly into Willie's eyes.

"Give the bills to me. I will pay them. You will sign a note, at two percent annual interest, and pay this amount back over the next twelve months. I will see that it is deducted it from your salary. I will handle everything. There is no need for your mother or Clara to know anything about this. But be aware. You are living in my home; you are working for me; you are in debt to me. Willie, this is not a position that you want to be in.

"Your trip to Denver must result in more revenues coming in, but that is only the beginning. We must find more advertisers. You must take on responsibility for some of this if you ever want to get out from this burden you have brought on yourself. And me as well."

August turned toward the window. "Go. We will not speak of this again. I will prepare the document for you to sign. This is not a gift. This is a loan, and you will treat it as such. You will pay your just debts." He stood and watched the carts rolls down Pratt Street, at this hour empty of their wares. The lamplighter had lit the gas lights as far east as he could see.

He turned to face Willie, and pointed a finger. "And you better get control of that girl."

"Yes," Willie said, "Thank you, *Vater*, thank you." He turned and left the office. Before he reached his desk, a sick headache descended. He rushed to the toilet midway down the corridor where he vomited.

110

Forty

Celeste rolled over into Willie's arms. He was lying on his back, his face toward the window.

"Today is my birthday, Willie. I'm seventeen. Your wife is seventeen!"

"I know, my sweet. And I want to make this the best year for you, your very best year."

"Then start by taking me dancing. I want to dance with you, like we did in Denver. You are a wonderful dancer, Willie. You look so shy, but you can dance! And you know all the latest steps. Now that we're married, you can't get behind. Where will we go?"

Willie sat up on his elbow, took her head in his hands, smoothed her hair. "Now you know that tonight is the dinner here. *Mutti* has arranged it. That means that she thinks that you are part of the family. We always have a special dinner on our birthdays. And Saturday, we will go dancing. I'll take you to The Chantilly, to a tea dance there. Then we'll go downtown to the Southern for dinner and more dancing. We will dance until the last dance. Is that special enough for you?"

Without waiting for her response, he continued, "Stay put. I have something for you." He went to the dresser and opened the top drawer. He handed Celeste a small box tied with a cornflower-blue satin ribbon.

She sat up, eager for her first gift of the day.

"Happy birthday," Willie said.

He did not have to encourage Celeste to open it. She untied the bow and tore off the heavy white paper. The gold of the bell-shaped pendant sparkled.

"Turn it over. There's an inscription on the back," Willie said.

111

"For my Belle of Broadway," Celeste read. "Oh, I love it. I'll never take it off."

Willie helped her with the clasp. "This will be the first day of your happiest year ever," he said into her hair. And he wished it to be true.

"But for now I have to get ready for work. Are you coming to breakfast?"

"Of course I am. Who do you think I am, Clara?" she replied. They laughed. In the weeks since Celeste had lived in the house, she had come to know the schedules, the rhythms, and some of the personalities of its inhabitants.

Later that day she visited Annie. She only stayed a few minutes. They had less and less to say to one another, and both slowly recognized how little they had talked when Celeste lived there. Most days Eva was at school, and when she was present during Celeste's visits, the sisters had as little to talk about as they had before Celeste's marriage. When Celeste saw George, she was too full of her own stories and life to notice that he was even more quiet than usual.

"I'll see you tonight, Mama. I can't wait for you to see the Strauff's house, to get to meet them, and Clara, of course. And then tomorrow I'll come over and we can talk and gossip. Seven o'clock. You'll get to meet the Strauffs, finally!"

Annie smiled and kissed her daughter as she bounced out the door. Neither she nor George were looking forward to that evening, although they had decided to make the best of it. Willie's family had been as upset about the marriage as they had been, perhaps more so. But the Strauffs had invited the young couple into their home; they made a home for them while Celeste and Willie got on their feet. Annie and George tried to be loving in-laws who didn't interfere. They hoped for the same from Willie's parents.

When Celeste left her mother's house, she walked the nine blocks to visit with Elizabeth, who had promised to leave school early that day so that the two could have a birthday lunch. Celeste hoped that their conversation would be easier than it had been during her last two visits. She feared that she and her best friend were growing distant, both of them struggling to find common interests. Now that they weren't giggling about teachers and fellow students, they had little to talk about. Even Celeste was tiring of recounting tales of her Western honeymoon. Is this what being married is, she wondered, losing all your old friends?

The Strauff's house was quiet during the day, not unlike her experience in her own home, Meg working, Annie walking from room to room or engrossed in her needlepoint, Eva either at school or reading. The family gathered in the front room in the evenings, to read, much the same as the Strauffs, through there Clara played the piano, incessantly, or so it seemed to Celeste.

She was grateful for her third floor room and often retreated there. But she was lonesome during the day, looking out at North Avenue, at Green Mount Cemetery across the street, studying the trees and their outlines, watching the carriages and the few electric cars coming and going, noting the fashions of the people who walked. It was a quiet life, and one that, if she had let herself admit it, felt a bit sad.

But today was her birthday, she thought, and after today everything will be different. Once you're seventeen, and a married woman, everything will be different, will be all right.

Wearing her new brown kid gloves with pearl buttons, her birthday gift from Elizabeth, and clad in her Denver coat of brown with black trim, Celeste made the long walk back to the Strauffs. She didn't mind; it took longer than when she lived with Annie and George, but she was no longer in a hurry. When she arrived, she would stay in her room until Willie arrived home from work. And then, her birthday dinner. She wondered what gifts awaited her.

Hanne had laid the table, crystal sparkling, silver polished, Dresden plates in place, beeswax candles in each of the candelabra at both ends of the table. Scents of Hanne's mulled pork, the sizzling meat, the wine, the citrus, mingled with cinnamon and nutmeg wafted up from the basement; pickled herring was already set on the table. Hanne wanted this to be a special night for Celeste. She was well acquainted with loneliness and recognized the symptoms in Celeste. She had often spied the young bride standing at her bedroom window as she went to her room in the back of the same floor. She sometimes heard their lovemaking sounds at night, and she was glad that Willie had found some happiness.

That evening the two families met. Both exclaimed how terrible it was that it had taken so much time for the gathering to take place, though both were relieved that theirs would not be a close relationship. Paulina had laid place cards at the table; the group took their seats.

August was at his finest playing the host; Paulina's Bavarian charm came to the fore. August looked over at her and, saw in the candlelight, his young bride. He felt proud that he had been able to offer her this life.

George learned about the newspaper business from August; August learned about the streetcar systems in Baltimore from George, something that heretofore he had taken for granted. August found George to be a serious man. George found August to be boastful, but reasoned that perhaps he had something to boast about. He learned that August had come to this country with nothing and made something of himself. Not unlike George's father, though he would have never discussed it, particularly at a dinner, and especially with strangers. This is what my daughter has married into, he thought.

"I know the Wells and McComas Monument well. Not too far from here. At East Monument and Aisquith Streets, I believe." August said. "Daniel Wells. Is that hero of The Battle of North Point, that luminary of The War of 1812, part of your heritage?" August wanted to be sure that Celeste's father knew that he, this recently arrived German, was aware of the history of the United States.

George quietly explained that he was not of that branch of the Wells family, that both his mother and father were born in Manchester, England and had immigrated to Baltimore in the 1830s. He said this quietly, matter-of-factly, careful not to emphasize the differences in their backgrounds. August, disappointed to learn that Celeste was not of the pedigree he had hoped, was quiet.

Paulina asked about Annie's parents. "They came from Kentzgau. Do you know it?" Annie asked.

Paulina brightened. "You're German, like us. I am from Bavaria also. I've heard of your parents' town. Northern Bavaria, am I right? I left Germany as a young girl; I didn't travel at all, only to Munich once." Paulina lowered her eyes. "And now that I live in the United

States, I see more of Europe than I ever thought or knew about as a child."

The two women liked one another, an easy feeling settling over that part of the dining room. They did not talk about their children, their feelings about this marriage. Paulina asked if she remembered German now.

Annie shook her head. "After I went to school, my parents insisted that we only speak English. They tried to do the same."

"Yes. That is what August insists upon here as well. I think that it is a good way to become American, *yah*?" And both women smiled at Paulina's unwitting mot.

Celeste, sitting next to Willie, held his hand. She leaned toward him. "It seems to be going well, don't you think?" Willie nodded, relieved, but wishing that the evening were behind them.

He looked over at Clara, intent in conversation with Eva. "Clara and Eva seem to be hitting it off. Two blue-stockings," he whispered. Celeste laughed and pressed her forehead to his. No one noticed.

Hanne came in to clear the plates. "We'll have dessert in the front room, Hanne. Thank you for a delicious dinner," Paulina said.

August looked up from his conversation, "Yes, Hanne. Good job. *Wunderbar*." August corrected himself, "Wonderful."

Dishes cleared, Paulina rose. "Let us go to the front room. Celeste, I know that you have gifts awaiting you." Six of the diners left the table. Eva and Clara, engrossed in conversation, remained. After their guests were settled, Paulina called to Clara, "Please, girls, come in and join us. Let us celebrate this birthday. Then, perhaps when we finish, Clara, you will play for us."

The families gathered. Celeste took her seat in the center of the room, the perfect place, she thought, to receive her gifts. From her parents, she received a set of ivory-handled flatware. "For when you get your own home," Annie said, smiling at Celeste and her new son-in-law.

Paulina presented her with tablecloth and napkins, heavy cream-colored linen, embroidered with white silk in a rectangular art nouveau pattern. The napkins were monogrammed with an ornate "S." Celeste fingered the heavy cloth. "This came from our last trip to Berlin.

Little did we know that there would be such a use for it," Paulina said. August frowned at her; Clara's mouth formed a moue. Celeste didn't seem to notice, though she did. As did George, Annie and Eva.

"It is lovely, *Mutti*. We will think of you each time we use it," Willie said, ending the silence that was beginning to be noticed.

"Now I have something for you, Celeste," Clara said, walking to the piano, her limp barely perceptible. She handed Celeste a square package covered in wrapping paper.

"Thank you, Clara," Celeste said, nervous that a public humiliation would accompany her opening of this present.

"It's a book," Clara said, pressing her lips tight.

Celeste unwrapped *Mrs. Beeton's Every Day Cookery and Housekeeping Book*. August saw the gift and inhaled sharply. Paulina closed her eyes. Eva tilted her head to watch. Willie reached over to pat Celeste's hand. Celeste riffled the pages and said, "Well, I certainly will be using this. You have chosen the perfect gift, Clara. Thank you again."

The gathering breathed easier. Crisis avoided.

Clara said, "Yes, there are many recipes in there. It may help you learn how to cook. You know Willie has a delicate stomach."

"Clara, please," August said.

Ignoring her father's interdict, Clara continued, "And it is the new edition, very up to date."

Willie raised an eyebrow at his sister. Paulina, catching August's eye, stood, signaling the end of that part of the evening. "Clara, would you play something for us?" she asked.

The evening ended with a Franz Liszt nocturne.

The three Wells walked back to their home. "Well, that was better than I expected," Eva said. Her parents were quiet, but she sensed their agreement. As they entered the house, Annie said, "Paulina seems a nice enough woman, but I worry about Celeste in that house. They seem so distant."

"Celeste has always found a way to get life to revolve around her, Mama. This may be a bit of a challenge for her, but, watch, she'll maneuver it so that she is the center of attention," Eva said. Before her parents could respond, she continued, "But I do like Clara. It is odd that she and I have never met before. Of course, she went to The

Institute and then to The Music Academy. We plan to get together soon. I think that we could become fast friends."

George turned toward his daughter. "Be careful there, my lovely. All is not well between Clara and Celeste. You don't want to do anything that will hurt your sister." Annie watched the interaction between her daughter and her husband.

Eva stood silent and then spoke. "Must you always put her first? Is this what I get for being the daughter you wanted me to be? That even my friendships must be gauged by what is best for Celeste?"

"Come out of the vestibule, you two," Annie said. "Let's have a cup of tea before we go upstairs."

As the trio went downstairs to the kitchen, George put his hand on Eva's shoulder. She leaned her head against it; all was well for the night.

On the other side of North Avenue, Hanne cleared the dishes from the front room, Willie and Celeste said their goodnights, Clara gathered her music. "You played especially beautifully tonight, *liebchen*," August said. "I could tell the Wells were impressed."

"I don't play to impress, *Vater*," Clara responded, an arch to her voice.

"I like her family," Paulina said. "Don't you?"

Clara softened. "Well, they do seem quite refined. I was surprised. And, yes, Eva is quite nice. She and I have a lot in common; I think that we will see each other again, outside the family, that is."

"Well, good for you. And I do hope that your gift for Celeste was given with the proper spirit, Clara," Paulina said.

Clara looked at her father. "Did you see the gold charm she wore? A gift from Willie, I suppose? I wonder how he is paying for it." August did not respond.

As she headed for the stairs, she said, "Good night. Yes, it was a good night. I'll see you in the morning."

August and Paulina, alone on the first floor, sat by the dying fire. "Yes, she comes from a good home. Though they are not the Wells that I had hoped, not related to Daniel Wells. But a good enough sort, I think," August said. He smiled and leaned close to Paulina. "They certainly are a staid group. Do you think Celeste is the cuckoo in the nest?"

Paulina sat back. "August, what a thing to say." And August placed one arm around her shoulder and rested his hand on her ample breast. "Come, *mien liebchen*, we've had a full day."

On the third floor, Celeste and Willie held each other close; on the second floor, August pulled Paulina atop him. Across the street, Annie held a sleeping George in her arms.

Clara and Eva fell asleep, each thinking about her new-found friend.

*Forty-one*_____

Celeste, enfolded in her coverlet, was basking in the sunlight of a spring Sunday morning. She followed the gentle movement of the tops of the trees in the park across the street, the filigree of the cemetery's pale green birch, the outlines of its branches still visible. Just coming into bloom, she thought, like me.

Willie slept lightly. She watched. He breathes through his nose even in sleep, she thought. She studied his long, thin fingers, his nails trimmed just so.

She felt puffy. She touched her face, leaned down to trying to feel her ankle bones. She knew what was happening. So did Willie. They never spoke of it, their secret. But they both knew that it could not stay private. They must soon make an announcement, view it as a wondrous gift, so that others would see it as just that.

Willie stirred and Celeste placed his hand on her stomach. With all their lovemaking, all their time together, they had mentioned this only twice, once in the living room of Celeste's house, her parents' house, and then Willie's suggestion of it that terrible afternoon in Denver. They both knew; they both thought it best to say nothing.

Willie turned, always reaching for her as he came into morning consciousness. She had grown accustomed to this and she liked it. It made up for some of the discomfort of living in this house where she knew she did not belong.

"Good morning, my sweet," Willie said.

Celeste turned and saw the dark shadows beneath Willie's eyes. He was delicate, that was all, she thought. He will be fine once he was up and shaved. He looks so handsome in his clothes, always fresh, always ironed, though she felt his bones more pronounced these mornings. He rolled toward her.

"No, Willie. Not today. Here. Feel." She placed his hand on her stomach. "I think that we'll need to tell them soon."

"No, not yet. Let it be just us, just you and me. I'll take you dancing."

"Willie, we need to tell them."

This, the first conversation that the couple had about this secret, this baby.

"Not this morning, Celeste. This morning, it is just us."

Yes, this morning, another morning, just us, she thought.

*Forty-two*_____

Celeste stood at her bedroom window looking out at the cemetery. This morning, the lindens had come into bud. Others remained tucked in their blanket of winter. A few more warm days like this one and they all would begin to come into bloom. She would see spring.

This was the day she would talk to her mother. She would tell Annie first, then she and Willie would visit the Wells together that evening for dinner. Celeste would make her big announcement then.

Willie was to tell his parents the next day, at Saturday morning breakfast. Clara would be sleeping in; Celeste would stay upstairs and come down after Willie's news.

This Friday morning, her breakfast finished, the house was quiet. Clara, still asleep, remained in her room, her door closed. August and Willie had left for work. She heard Hanne downstairs, working. Hanne was always working. Paulina, in the dining room, was pasting articles from the German papers onto cardstock.

Celeste put her head around the corner to say goodbye. "I'm going to visit Mama for a few hours. Is there anything I can bring you? Anything you need on my way back?" Though Celeste knew the answer would be "Nothing, Celeste, but thank you anyway," she always offered. At least it was something to say.

She picked up her shawl, a new one that Willie had brought home a few evenings previous, wrapped in delicious pink tissue paper and tied with a wide white satin ribbon. She would surprise her mother with this visit.

Across the street, Annie was putting on her own shawl to leave the house for her morning errands. As she entered the vestibule, she saw Celeste. Standing at the open door, she said, "I was just heading out.

121

Do you want to go with me, or should we spend some time visiting here. I can ask Meg to bring us some tea, and maybe a sweet. What would you like?"

Annie embraced her daughter. So little to talk about, so little to say, she thought.

"Mama, let's stay here. I'm starving. Definitely a sweet. Maybe two?"

They entered the front room and sat on either end of the sofa. Celeste clasped her hands in her lap, trying to wait until Meg finished serving before delivering her news. Annie watched her daughter.

"It is a beautiful day," Annie started. "And I am glad to see you."

"Yes." Celeste waited. Finally Meg arrived and set the tray down.

"Oh, Meg. How are you? I miss you so much. It just isn't the same where I live," Celeste said.

"I miss you too, Miss Celeste. It is much quieter here, but also a little sad," Meg responded.

Annie bristled. "What Meg means is that we all miss you, Celeste." To Meg she said, "Thank you. You've done a beautiful job with the pastries, Meg."

Celeste faced her mother. "Mama, I think I am in a family way." She waited to be embraced.

Annie leaned forward to pour the tea. "Yes. I thought that was what you were going to tell me. Are you pleased? Is Willie? Have you said anything to the Strauffs?"

"Mama, I thought that you'd be thrilled. Aren't you happy for me?"

Annie paused. "Of course I'm pleased. It's just that you are so young. I'm concerned for you. Is this what you wanted? We never really talked about how to prevent these kinds of things."

"Mama, Willie and I are very happy. It will be wonderful. We will get our own house in a little while. Willie is doing very well at his job. It will be just fine when we are on our own. Hanne is teaching me to cook. She has been very kind to me. She really is the best one there."

Celeste added hurriedly, "I mean that she is nice to me too."

Annie was silent. Finally she said, "Do you know for sure? Have you seen a doctor?"

"I'm almost positive. That's why I thought I'd talk to you. Willie said that would be best. Then he'll tell his parents. We have been married for more than three months, after all. It wouldn't be a bad thing, would it? You don't think it would be a bad thing, do you, Mama?"

Annie looked at her younger daughter, outwardly so self-assured, so proud, so silly and sure that everyone loved her. She saw the eager little girl she once had loved so fiercely, before Celeste had realized how beautiful she was, and what a weapon in her quiver that could be.

"Of course it isn't a bad thing. But your life will change, Celeste. You must put this baby first. It will be very different for you. You must learn to be a mother, and a wife. And you are so young."

"You were young when you had babies, Mama. You forget that. And look how easily you did it."

Annie reached out and stroked Celeste's hair. "Yes, you're right. And I will be here with you. You will not be on your own. So, we will arrange a time for you and Willie to come and make your announcement to Papa and Eva?"

"Let's do it tonight. I want to be sure that Papa knows before we tell the Strauffs."

Meg listened from the front hallway. She shook her head and turned to go downstairs to the kitchen. A baby, she thought. Well, now she's in for it.

Forty-three _____

Saturday dawned clear and crisp; the sunlight flooded the front second- and third-floor bedrooms.

August and Paulina had risen early. Willie stood at his bedroom window, pajamas looking starched and pressed despite his fitful, sleepless night. He pushed his hair from his forehead and turned to Celeste.

"This morning it will be. I'll tell them. There's no need for us to be nervous. We've been married for three months now. No one can object."

Celeste turned away at Willie's reference, however oblique, to their situation. Willie noticed and went to her. Sitting on the edge of the bed, he brought her fingers to his lips. "Not to worry. They will be happy. They will love you and the baby. Now we are really a family."

Celeste put her arms around him. "I don't know if I'm ready to be a mother, Willie. I don't feel like a grown-up at all. Sometimes I feel like I'm just playacting, that I'll wake up and worry that I'm late for school, that I haven't done my homework.

"I just want to be with you. Just us. In our own house. I want to watch you read, listen to music that I like, that I choose. I want to go dancing. I don't want to be a mother. I don't want to be old. I just want to be with you. Just us. I just want you to take care of me."

"Oh, my sweet girl, everything will be fine. I'll always be here to take care of you, always." Willie pulled her toward him, held her.

"And you won't be old. We'll make sure that you have plenty of help. Even when we move to our own place. We'll still dance, my Belle of Broadway."

Willie stared ahead as he patted Celeste's back. "Let me get dressed now. We agreed that I'd tell *Mutti* and *Vati* this morning. Clara won't be down for hours. I'll come back as soon as breakfast is over. You go back to sleep. Everything will be fine. I promise you." He walked to the door. I guess this makes me a man, he thought.

Celeste slid under the comforter and watched as Willie left to shave. She was asleep when he returned to the bedroom to dress.

As he descended the stairs to the dining room, Willie rehearsed his presentation. In his mind, he heard himself, firm-voiced, not a trace of stammer.

Hanne stood in the doorway and delivered a happy greeting. A good omen, Willie thought.

Paulina looked up, her notebook and pen beside her, ready for her daily exercise. "*Gross gott*, Willie," she said.

August frowned. "English, Lina," he said. "Good morning, son. And it is a beautiful morning, is it not?" August lowered the paper as he said this and looked at his son. He had noticed Willie's loss of weight, and the glint of perspiration that seemed to cover Willie's face, regardless of the temperature, worried him.

Willie sat, removing his napkin from the heavy silver ring while Hanne poured his coffee. He cleared his throat as he reached for the cream pitcher. "Well, it is a lovely day. And I have something to tell you that will make it even lovelier." He cleared his throat again and breathed deeply, willed himself not to stammer.

"Celeste is *enceinte*." He waited. The room was silent. "You will be grandparents in the fall. What do you say to that!" Willie willed his tone to be jubilant, while he felt the perspiration gather on his upper lip.

August folded the paper and placed it in the corner of the table. He turned to Willie. "Well, it appears that congratulations are in order. Is that not so, Mama?"

Paulina looked over at her son. So thin now, such a young man, a boy, she thought, not ready to be a father. "Well, yes, Willie. This is a blessing come to this house, *yah*? We will make it so."

"I wanted to tell you both when we were by ourselves. Celeste is feeling a bit discomfited about telling people. She is very shy about it."

August stood. "We will make this a celebration for you, for you both. We will start with a special dinner this evening. Paulina, please let Hanne know. This will be a dinner for just family, but it will be special." To Willie, he said, "We will talk about this later. There are arrangements to be made." August walked to the back of the house. Paulina heard the back door close and soon smelled the sweet smell of pipe tobacco coming from the garden.

That evening Celeste dressed especially carefully, tying her hair back with the white satin ribbon saved from one of Willie's surprise gifts. Her dress, now tighter than was comfortable, was a deep blue that she knew drew attention to her eyes. Waiting for dinner to be served, she sat in the front room beside Paulina, her eyes focused on the embroidery hoop she had recently acquired, a gift from Annie. Celeste hated every minute stitch she made while she tried to fit into the quiet demeanor of this house, not unlike the character of the home she left. She didn't fit in there either, she realized.

Clara's entrance was marked by the front door banging open. "The concert was incredible," she called out. "Marlo played beautifully and Belinda's voice, well, you could tell how hard and how long she practiced. It was worth the fifteen-block walk to The Lyric."

Paulina heard her daughter's footsteps, her limp worse this evening. So difficult for her to walk long distances, Paulina thought. Yet she perseveres, not letting her infirmity inhibit her activities. Grit, August called it, Paulina remembered. Another word for her notebook.

Clara paused as she glimpsed the dining room. "Why is the table set with the Dresden?" she asked. "Is there something special tonight? When did this come up?" she added, irritated not to be included in the planning.

"Tonight we have a special family dinner," Paulina said. "Willie has something to announce."

Clara's eyes went immediately to Celeste. "Don't tell me--" she said.

Before she could finish her sentence, August strode into the room. "Enough, Clara. You will have to wait. Now why don't you go to your room and change?"

Hanne was in the dining room putting the finishing touches to the table and overheard the exchange. She shook her head.

An hour later the family of five was seated at the table. Hanne had delivered the platter, filled with thick slices of prime rib ranging from rare to well-done. Paulina served; she knew how each liked their meat prepared.

Once the plates were passed, August nodded to his son. Willie walked to the sideboard and opened the champagne that rested in the silver bucket, relieved that the cork came off with a firm, resounding pop. He rounded the table, filling each fluted glass.

When he returned to his place, he said, "Tonight we have something to celebrate." He paused. "Celeste is in a family way."

August was the first to raise his glass. "*Prost.*" The others followed suit, Clara slower than her parents. Celeste, eyes down, raised her glass to her lips.

August looked over at his daughter and willed her to find some joy in this announcement. "So, Clara, *Mutti* and I are to be *Oma* and *Opa*. And you will be *Tante Clara*. What do you think of that?"

"Well, now we know why they married in such a haste."

Paulina gasped; August put down his glass. Celeste raised her napkin to her lips.

August stood. "Clara, you will leave the table. Such vitriol. What has got into you? You will apologize to Celeste this instant."

Clara looked back at her father. "Which do you want me to do, *Vater*, apologize or leave the table? You are the ruler here, but you give conflicting fiats. Only Willie seems to be the golden boy in this fiasco."

"Clara," August said, "please get yourself under control. Perhaps that would be best done in your room, by yourself. And you will give some thought to the disgrace that you have brought to this house, to this dinner that was to mark a happy occasion. I expect an apology; Celeste deserves an apology, a sincere one. You will not appear again until that has been completed. You will go to your room."

"I will go to my room, but you forget that I am an adult. You have no right, no authority to confine me anywhere."

"Clara, enough. Please go to your room. I will come after dinner and we will talk. This cannot go on."

Clara emptied her glass and rose. "Please tell Hanne to bring a tray to my room, *Mutti.*" Head held high, she left the dining room, willing herself not to limp.

The four who remained were silent. Paulina choked back tears. What is happening to my family? What is happening to my home? Why is Clara so angry, so vicious about Celeste?

August spoke, his voice quiet. Hanne listened from the hallway. "Celeste, Willie, we will not let this incident stay with us. Let us enjoy this evening. I don't know what is wrong with Clara, but she will come around. She is a good girl, headstrong, but a good girl. She will make it up to you, Celeste. I promise you that."

Forty-four

The heat of the summer day clung to the house. Celeste wandered from room to room, looking to fill the hours. She riffled through Clara's sheet music, replete with notes and symbols as unintelligible to her as Arabic. She walked over to the gramophone. Willie had bought a few ragtime records. They played them in the evening sometimes, when Clara was out and the elder Strauffs had retired to their second floor room. Once they asked Hanne to join them as they danced around the front room and laughed as Celeste's expanding middle got in the way of some of the more intricate steps.

Celeste's eye fell on book after book, but none interested her. She kept her romance novels upstairs. Willie had bought an old bookcase to hold them. It was wedged between the wall and the dresser that she had claimed as her own.

Hanne came into the room, feather duster in hand. "Miss Celeste, would you like to learn to cook some German dishes?"

Hanne worried that she might be overstepping herself, but the young woman looked so lost, so alone. Maybe cooking would help. Some people said that gardening was a pick-me-up, Hanne thought. Others said that creating a dish for the family had that same effect. She had never understood that. It was all a job to her, better than her life back in the old country, but only just. But she thought that she understood some of Celeste's loneliness, the isolation of someone who didn't fit it, who wasn't really part of the family.

Celeste stopped what she was doing. A dinner, she thought, fixing a German dinner. That might be just the thing to make Willie happy, to make him realize that we could have a home, a house of our own, and that I can certainly manage a household.

"Hanne, I'd be delighted. Do you have an apron that would go over this?" Celeste rubbed her swelling abdomen.

"Oh, *yah*. Of course, Miss Celeste. Ve vill haf a gut time, no?"

The two descended the stairs.

*Forty-five*_____

The coolness of the basement met them as they entered the room. Celeste rarely ventured down to the kitchen. She was content to eat Hanne's delicious, and some days not-so-delicious, meals, without knowing, or caring, how they were made. On her days off, Hanne left dinners prepared, and Paulina, or more often Clara, heated them up. Clara and Hanne sometimes worked together to develop new recipes for the family, Clara helping Hanne with her English.

"Now we want to do something that we can cook on the stove. No oven. We don't want to heat the kitchen more than we have to in this weather," Hanne said. She moved to the shelf where a dozen cookbooks stood, most of them in German.

Clara helped her with the ones in English. "It's the only way you'll get ahead in this country," Clara would say. "To speak English, yes, but to read English, that is your portal to success in this country. Do not be afraid to make mistakes, Hanne. That is the way that all of us learn." Clara, Hanne thought, always working on things, on people.

"Let us try two recipes," she said to Celeste, as she handed the younger woman an apron of blue and white mattress ticking. "Here, tie this around you. For now, you watch. Then you work."

Hanne moved to the cupboards. "No sauerkraut these hot days. I do not want to smell it down here for days. So, some lentils, some bacon, some sausage, bockwurst. Do you know the different sausages, Miss Celeste? I will teach you."

As she chopped onions, carrots, celery stalks, a leek and a parsnip, Hanne recounted the differences in sausages, all of which seemed identical to Celeste. "Okay, now you know sausages. Now you watch." Hanne sautéed the vegetables and added a few bay leaves. "Always add bay leaves. You don't want your family to have gas, *yah?*" Celeste blushed.

"Next the lentils. Cook one hour. So now we chop up the bockwurst. And when lentils done, put in for twenty minutes. Maybe add more water, or meat stock if you have it. And you're done.

"You see, you have made soup. I will taste it before I serve tonight. You can say to all that it is you who make it, *yah?* You who cooked."

Celeste sat on the kitchen stool and watched Hanne move deliberately around the kitchen. Yes, she thought, it is just as if I have made this soup. This is not hard; cooking is not hard at all. I can do this when we get our house.

"Now the meat." Hanne's words brought Celeste back to the kitchen. "Rouladen, good German dish. No recipe for this either. Just feel your way," Hanne said, as she sliced the beef into thin slices and pulled out the mallet. "Here, you beat. That way you can say you cook this also."

And so, Celeste, clad in her blue striped apron, beat the already-thin slices. She was getting tired of this cooking class, but she felt she had to be polite, kind, to Hanne.

"Okay, now spread this mustard, then put in onion, pickle and bacon on top." Hanne had prepared these while Celeste was pounding.

"Now I roll up together and put in ice box. Then I fry later on. But after fry, simmer for an hour. You remember that now?"

Celeste nodded, praying that the cooking lesson was coming to a close.

"*Frau Celeste*, you are now German cook. Ready for anything."

"Oh, Hanne, you are so good to me, so kind." Tears came to Celeste's eyes. She hadn't realized how much she longed for someone in this house to be thoughtful, to act as if they cared because they really did care, not because they were being polite.

"So now I call you *Frau Celeste*, just when *Herr Strauff* is not in."

Celeste reached to Hanne and kissed her hand. "Thank you, dear Hanne."

Forty-six————————————

That evening the family gathered after sunset to take advantage of the cooler evening air. Celeste heard Hanne climb the stairs to go to the dumbwaiter that held their dinner. Soup bowls had been set at each place.

As Hanne brought in the tureen, she announced, "Lentil and bockwurst soup tonight. A bit heavy, but not too much for this evening."

Paulina looked up, puzzled that Hanne would speak while she served. She'd observed that Hanne had opened up, become livelier recently. Paulina was happy for her, thought that perhaps she had a gentleman friend.

As Hanne placed the tureen in front of Paulina, she said, "Miss Celeste make the soup."

All turned toward Celeste, who had taken special care with her dress and hair this evening. "Yes, though it was really Hanne who walked me through every step. I hope that you like it."

Paulina smiled. "I am sure we will. It wasn't too much for you, the heat of the kitchen?"

"No, I want to learn to cook, the things that Willie likes."

August lifted a spoon to his lips. "*Zehr gut!*" and even he laughed at his use of the forbidden German in his house.

Celeste giggled. Maybe the family liked her. Maybe cooking was a way to get them to like her, even love her. Especially now that the baby was coming. She laughed some more, not able to stop herself, giddy from a word of praise from this family.

Clara was silent, though her bowl was empty when Hanne came in to clear the first course.

"Rouladen," Hanne announced. "Also made by Miss Celeste, though I was the one to do the finishing touches. Not good for her to be in hot kitchen in her condition."

"Oh, yes. Hanne was wonderful," Celeste said. "It was such a hot day and I am feeling so fat. I'll bet I weigh more than Willie now."

"You've always weighed more than Willie." Clara's first words of the meal.

"Clara, please," said Paulina, who closed her eyes and prayed for a quiet, restful meal.

"What? Why are you always saying that to me, *Mutti*? Why can I not open my mouth in this house without your saying 'Clara, please.' I meant nothing by it; it was simply an observation."

Celeste waited for August to chastise Clara. She waited for Willie to say something, to come to her defense.

August put down his knife and fork. He looked directly at his daughter. "Clara, you are too intelligent to expect us to believe that. Now please apologize and let us finish our meal in peace. Celeste, a very good job with tonight's dinner. Thank you."

Celeste waited for Willie to speak. He was quiet. Finally, she sat straight in her chair and looked at Clara. "Clara, I would like us to get along. If I have done something to offend you, something to make you dislike me, please tell me and I will make it right. If that is not the case, I think that you need to treat me with respect. I respect you. I admire you. Please stop being so mean to me." Celeste's voice broke on this last sentence. She considered leaving the table, but knew that she must see this through.

Clara held Celeste's eyes and said nothing. She then put her napkin down and stood. "Hanne, I would like my dinner brought to my room." Her limp pronounced, she left the room and went to the second floor.

The quartet remained silent, the only noise the clatter of silverware on china.

August broke the silence. Addressing Celeste, he said, "I want to apologize for Clara. I truly do not know what the problem is, but, Celeste, it is not your fault. I will talk with her later this evening. You did the right thing. You must stand up for yourself. She will respect that."

To Willie, he said, "Has your sister said anything to you? Do you know what is wrong with her?"

"*Vati*, Clara and I have barely spoken since Christmas. We are polite, but we don't talk."

"Yes," August replied. "But you must talk to her. You must defend your wife, son. It is not only my place to do that. You must put yourself in a position where Clara respects you. Your wife needs you to do that."

Willie looked down. I have failed again, he thought. And the headache came.

Forty-seven———————

Dear Elizabeth,

You are so lucky to be at Cape May this month. It is hot, hot, hot here these August days in Baltimore. We (did you notice I wrote we?) keep the curtains drawn all day to keep the heat out and the cool in. This means that the first floor is always dark. I spend time in our room, which is very sunny, and also very hot, but most mornings I am in the backyard, on the porch. I usually have my breakfast there and then go for a walk before the sun gets too high in the sky. Sometimes I cross over to Green Mount Cemetery and sit on one of the benches there. It seems like all that grey stone and the trees make that area much cooler than just on the other side of the wall. I should ask Willie about that. He knows everything!

I must tell you that I am lonesome with you gone. I do visit Mama a few times a week, but it is not the same as having a girlfriend to laugh and gossip with. Clara is still being absolutely horrible to me. Sometimes it is all I can do not to slap her. And she and Eva are friends. Can you believe that? You would think that Eva would have more loyalty to her sister, but she doesn't. When she comes over she and Clara talk about books. I hear them in her room. Either that or Clara is playing the piano. Oh, Elizabeth, there is music, music, music here all the time. And boring classical music. Once in a while when everyone is out, or in their rooms, Willie will put some ragtime records on. It is like a minute of heaven. I have even come to like silence – yes, anything but Beethoven, Brahms, Debussy. You see, I even know all these composers' names. It must come through osmosis to my brain.

Do you know what osmosis means? Willie told me. It means something filtering through even though you don't want it or even know it. I am expanding my vocabulary!

Mrs. Strauff works with her notebook every morning. I finally figured out that it is difficult English words that she is trying to learn. Mr. Strauff speaks very well, although with an accent. He lived in England when he was a boy, so the language is not so hard for him.

And, guess what. I cooked. Yes. I made soup and a beef thing. Well, Hanne cooked it, but I was there watching, so that is almost the same thing. And then Clara had a hissy fit at the table. And I stood up for myself. I was so scared, but I just had to say something. After all, I am the married woman in the house, not Clara.

I am waiting for the baby and that is very boring. But I can feel it move sometimes. Can you believe that I will be a mother? This fall when you are heading off to Bryn Mahr, I will be out with a baby carriage. Who do you think is the lucky one? Maybe both of us.

So write and tell me when you are coming home. The exact day. I do so want to see you before you leave for Philadelphia. I will come visit you there for sure. You can show me the sights.

Love to my very best friend,

Celeste

Forty-eight _____

Celeste addressed and sealed her letter to Elizabeth. She sat on her bed and stared ahead. How to spend the rest of the day? She would dress and walk to the mail box. She thought that might make her feel a bit more like herself.

She moved to the bureau and pulled out one of her everyday corsets. She could no longer manage to hook the clasps, but the drawstrings were long enough so that she could still use it. She pulled the garment around her and began lacing up the front, then she lay on the bed on her back and pulled the laces tighter.

It is so hot, she thought, but since she was leaving the house, the corset was a must. Even with the corset, her skirt no longer buttoned, though she had moved the button to the end of the waistband. She pulled the skirt above her stomach. It sat just below her breasts, but she could close it. That made the beige linen skirt was now too short to be fashionable, but she decided that her ankles would just have to show. She picked up a beige straw hat, wrapped a long red satin ribbon around the brim, and pinned white silk rose at the front. Maybe people will look at my hat rather than at my skirt, she thought. Finally she donned a white linen jacket, cut to hang loosely from her shoulders to her knees.

As she approached the front door, she called out that she was leaving. The late morning sun beat hot on the pavement as she walked the two blocks north to the mailbox on 21st Street.

Letter deposited, she decided against visiting Annie. It was too far to walk in the heat, and in these months since her marriage she and Annie had less and less to say to one another. Celeste sensed that, as she was becoming a mother, she had lost her own. Her steps slowed as she returned to the house that was now her home.

Once inside, the climb to the third floor bedroom loomed interminable, but she choose that over joining Clara in the front room, listening to her practice four-octave major and minor scales and arpeggios. At least upstairs she could close the door and listen to the quiet.

In her room, Celeste threw off the jacket, unbuttoned her blouse and pulled the constricting skirt over her head. She lay atop the bed, chemise and petticoat damp with perspiration. Earlier that morning she had lowered the window shades to keep out the heat. The room was dim. She closed her eyes.

She awoke when she felt a kiss on her forehead. Willie was home. "Oh my. What time is it?"

"You just rest. It has been so hot today. I think that we're setting a record temperature," Willie said. "Dinner will be late this evening; *Mutti* said that we'll wait until after seven. You'll feel better by then. It will be cooler downstairs."

Celeste watched as Willie changed out of his white linen suit. How, she wondered, could he get through the day and come home unwrinkled? When she opened her eyes again, Willie was placing a cold wet cloth on her forehead. "This might help, my sweet one."

She smiled. Willie loves me, she thought. Yes, he does. And she closed her eyes again.

When he came into the room to tell her that it was almost seven, she sat up. Her hand had been resting on her stomach while she had slept. "Willie, come here and feel this. It is the strangest thing. Watch. My stomach moves; it gets hard and then it softens. Feel."

Willie frowned. Celeste normally did not like any reference made to her condition. He sat on the side of the bed and held her in one arm. He placed his other on her abdomen. She was right. It did move; it rose and became firm, then softened.

"Are you in any pain?" he asked. "Do you think that the baby might be coming?"

"Oh no. There isn't any pain at all. It is just interesting to watch, isn't it? And it takes my mind off the heat." Celeste kissed Willie on the side of his face. She smoothed back that lock of hair. "But maybe you could ask Hanne to bring my dinner up on a tray. I'm just so tired. I'm sure it's the heat. No baby would want to be born in this weather."

Willie stood. "I'll tell Hanne. You rest. I'll come up after dinner. We can stay up here and read."

Paulina was concerned when Willie requested a tray for Celeste. "In this heat? She wants to stay in her room? Is she not feeling well?"

"She said that she was just tired, too tired to dress and come downstairs," Willie answered.

"Let me go up and have a look at her. I don't like that she's baking up in that room. She has a time to go, but she has to take care of herself."

Paulina went to the stairwell. Her trips to the third floor had been few; she liked to give the couple their privacy. The door to the bedroom was open. Paulina tapped lightly as she entered.

Celeste was lying atop the spread, Willie's headache cloth over her eyes.

"*Liebchen,* are you not feeling well?" Paulina asked softly. Poor child, she thought, Clara giving her such a wicked time.

Celeste opened her eyes. She heard the soft tone of Paulina's voice. Unbidden tears came, and Paulina sat down on the bed. She noticed Celeste's abdomen with alarm.

"Celeste, how long has this been happening?" she asked.

"I first noticed when Willie came in this evening," she said. "I don't think it means anything, do you?"

"We call Dr. Bergdorf. I want him to come to take a look at you. You just lie here. Perhaps you can get into a nightgown and straighten the room a bit before he comes. I'll tell Willie. You stay here."

An hour later the doctor ascended the stairs. He had seen Celeste a few times over the past months. "Now what have we here?" he said as he entered the room. Celeste was sitting in bed, clad in a long-sleeved white cotton gown. She had added a blue ribbon to tie back her hair.

After he examined her, he said, "You may have an interesting night ahead of you, my dear. I think this baby has decided that it is time to come into the world."

Celeste's eyes opened wide. "Oh, no. Not now. Not until the fall."

The doctor answered, "It is not we who decide that. Now you just rest as long as you can. Those are contractions you're having. And you say that you are not feeling any pain, any discomfort," he asked. Celeste shook her head.

"Well, it will be quite a while then," the doctor said. "You rest. I'll make sure that your mother knows. She will want to be with you, I presume."

Celeste nodded. Why I didn't go to see her this afternoon, she asked herself. And what is going to happen to me? Celeste closed her eyes. "Could I see Willie, please?"

Dr. Bergdorf nodded. "I'll tell him when I go downstairs. Meanwhile, you rest. You'll need it for the night ahead." He closed the door as he left, then opened it to take advantage of any air that might find its way to the hallway.

Once downstairs, he said to the assembled group, "It looks like there's a baby on the way. It would be wise to let Celeste's mother know so she can be with her. I'll stop by tomorrow morning. Nothing will happen before then." He reached into his bag. To Paulina he said, "If the pains get bad, here is some chloroform. Just put some on a cloth and let her inhale it. Make sure that you don't put too much on. You can always add more. You don't want her to become unconscious. That will just prolong the process.

"And if there are any problems, contact me and I will come. She's young, healthy and strong. I don't think that there is a thing to worry about. Willie, she'd like to see you. I would go up while I could. Once her labor starts in earnest all you can do is wait here. I'll stop by on my way to the hospital tomorrow morning."

The doctor bid his goodbyes as August came in the front door.

"Is there trouble?" he asked, seeing his family gathered in the vestibule. "Is it Celeste?"

Paulina told him of the afternoon's activities. She turned to Clara. "Would you go to Mrs. Wells and ask her to come? Hanne is involved in making dinner. I can't ask her to leave that." Clara glanced at her father, then agreed. Willie left to be with Celeste.

August faced his wife. "Well," he said, "an August baby, *yah?*" He put his arm around Paulina's ample shoulders as they walked to the front room.

The sky darkened before nine that night. Celeste lay in her bed, relishing the attention paid to her, and wondering when the pains would start. Hanne had brought up some soup and crackers and a plate of cookies for Celeste and the women who had gathered. Paulina had the bottle of chloroform. How nice, she thought, and wished that it had been available when she was giving birth to her two babies.

By midnight, Celeste was no longer wondering about the pangs of labor. Her abdomen heaved rock-hard as the contractions started in earnest. "Best not to cry out, dear. Try to swallow your cries. It will make things go faster," Annie said. Paulina pulled out the clean white cloth, ready to administer the dosage when Annie gave the signal. Annie turned to Paulina. "Not yet. I think it best to wait until she is in real pain. We can tell because she will be wet with perspiration. That hasn't happened yet. I think that this will be a long night." Annie was glad that Eva was home with George.

In the early hours of the following day, Paulina first poured a few drops of chloroform onto the cloth. "Breathe in, breathe deeply. Dr. Bergdorf said that this would help." Celeste coughed as she inhaled the acrid fumes, but she was soon asking for more.

Annie asked Celeste if she could look between her legs. "Just to get an idea of where we are." Celeste nodded, and Annie was surprised to see the top of the baby's head.

"Do you feel like pushing?" she asked, but Celeste was drifting off.

"I think it might be best not to give her any more of that for a while," Annie said to Paulina. "I think the baby's coming."

Suddenly, Celeste raised her shoulders and screamed, the first cry that she uttered that evening. With an animal grunt, she pushed and fell back on the bed. Annie looked and saw no change. Again, Celeste raised herself from the bed and pushed again. Annie saw a river of bright red appear on the white cloths that had been placed beneath Celeste's hips. Then she saw the back of a baby's head. "I think he's stuck," Annie said, willing herself not to cry.

Paulina shoved Annie aside, immediately wishing that she had been gentler. Let me see if I can help," she said, and grasped the sides of the tiny, slippery head with her fingers. "Can you push, *liebchen*?"

"Push down on her stomach," she commanded Annie. Annie did as she was told.

"Can you push hard, just one more time?" Paulina asked. Celeste did not hear her, but reared up on her elbows and bellowed. "Get this thing out of me." With that, a baby boy emerged into Paulina's hands.

"*Mein gott*, he is a tiny thing." Paulina saw that the limp infant wasn't breathing and gave his buttocks a slap. A soft mewl emerged. Relieved, Paulina took the blanket that Annie held for her and wrapped it tightly around him.

Annie looked at her daughter. "You have a son, Celeste. A tiny son."

Celeste lay back on the pillow. "Do you think you could help me change my gown? I want to look nice when I see Willie." She looked over and saw Paulina washing a little scrawl of red.

An hour later, Celeste lay in clean linen and fresh gown, hair brushed and held back by another blue ribbon, the baby in her arms.

"Here he is, Willie. Here is your son."

Willie fought back tears as he embraced his wife.

Forty-nine —————————————————————

Hanne answered the doorbell. Dr. Bergdorf had arrived, carrying his black leather medical bag. "You are too late. The baby is born already. But he is little."

Paulina, hearing the bell, had come into the hallway. "It is the infant. He is so tiny. Please, could you go to --"

Before she could finish, Dr. Bergdorf headed to the steps. Paulina followed close behind. "He was born around 2:30 this morning. Mrs. Wells just left an hour ago to get some rest. She was here. The baby looked like he was stuck, but we managed to get him out." Breathless from the climb, Paulina stopped on the second-floor landing.

"You stay here, Mrs. Strauff. I'll look in on the mother and baby," Dr. Bergdorf said, and continued up the stairs.

Celeste was sleeping, the baby in a basket beside her on the bed. The doctor tapped lightly on the door. She didn't stir. He heard the baby mewl. "Celeste, it's Dr. Bergdorf. Can you open your eyes?"

Celeste turned her head toward him.

"Well, you've had quite a morning, I hear. A lovely baby boy. And how are you this morning?"

She struggled to open her eyes. "It was terrible, but I am better now. Mrs. Strauff gave me some of this medicine. That helped." She reached for the white cloth, damp with chloroform beside her. "Now it helps me sleep." The room was redolent with the drug's sweet odor.

"Let's get rid of that cloth now and see if we can air the room out. It is not good for the baby." The doctor threw the cloth into the hallway and raised the shades to let in the morning sun and the few wisps of breeze that stirred.

Bergdorf walked to the white wicker basket and picked up the infant, still tightly swaddled in a blue cotton blanket. *"Ach*, Paulina must have been ready for a boy."

He examined the baby and returned him to the basket, resting the blanket loosely atop him. "Let him breathe in some fresh air. We'll hope he perks up. I will come back this evening. When he cries, put him to your breast. No milk will come yet, but you'll need to get him used to it, his feeding trough."

The doctor left the room. Celeste turned her head toward the baby, though she couldn't see him over the sides of the basket.

Paulina, August and Willie waited as they heard the doctor come down the stairs. Hanne hovered behind them. Clara remained in her bedroom.

The doctor greeted them with a smile. "Don't look so worried. The young mother is doing fine. The infant, well, let him get some air. I raised the shades. Let some cooler morning air get in. and no more chloroform. The room reeked of it when I entered. That won't do the baby any good. He is small, but he has all his fingers and toes. It's his lungs I'm concerned about, but we can address that later. Meanwhile, Celeste is to feed him whenever he cries. Let's try to fatten that boy up. I'll stop in tonight on my way home.

"Congratulations, Willie. What is the boy to be called?"

Fifty ————————————————————

A few mornings later, August and Willie sat in the carriage as it made its way to the paper's offices. The driver took the Aisquith Street route. He told the pair that the horse liked the change. As they passed the Institute of Notre Dame, August thought of Clara's days at the school. She had mastered every subject the German nuns taught – rhetoric, orthography, etymology, composition, history, religion. Religion, how she had taken that to heart. But the music, he remembered. The nuns recognized her talent and prepared her for acceptance at The Music Academy. He closed his eyes. Ah, Clara, he thought, such a smart, educated young woman. Such a mind, such drive. He worried about her future, hoped that she could find a way past her anger at Willie and Celeste. It was giving her a pinched look.

He looked over at Willie, now the father of a three-day-old son, a second generation of Strauffs born in this country. He noticed his son's pallor, grey this warm morning. August had grown so accustomed to his son's nervous gestures that he didn't notice Willie's repeated clearing of his throat.

"*Vater,*" Willie started, "We've decided on the baby's name. I wanted to tell you first, before we announce it to the family."

August turned to his son. Yes, he thought, a boy, born in August. "Tell me. Your mother and I have been waiting." August could not contain his smile. "Tell me."

Willie breathed deeply, and felt both saddened and satisfied by the look on his father's face. "He will be called Stanley Wells." Willie announced, and was taken back at the pleasure he experienced seeing the shock and hurt in his father's eyes. His father was vulnerable; he had not expected that. And immediately, guilt came to sit with this unannounced and unexpected satisfaction.

He knew that he owed his father, that he was indebted to him for much more than the money he was struggling to repay. He considered all of this, and yet, that glimmer of pleasure, that spark of satisfaction remained. I have the power to hurt this important man, he thought, and felt a strength, an energy that he had not before experienced. This time I will stand with Celeste, he told himself. It is, after all, her child.

August cleared his throat and looked out the window of the carriage. "Well, I do understand the Wells. Where does the Stanley come from? Is that a family name?"

Willie coughed, willed himself not to stammer. "No, *Vater*. It is just a name that Celeste, that we, like. It is a strong, English name, and she, we, thought that it was good that he carry the heritage of both his p-p-parents."

August looked at his son, cleared his throat once again. "Well, yes. I see. Thank you for telling me. But before you make any announcement, let me tell your mother. I think that she had other hopes for the baby's name. I don't want her to be surprised by this decision." He turned his eyes toward the street and commented on the twelve-story office building going up at the corner of Charles and Fayette Streets. Construction cranes were visible from the carriage windows. There would be no more discussion of the name, or the child.

When he arrived at the paper, August strode into the building. Willie followed. The older man went directly to his office, nodding silently to Franz who was heading to the pressroom on the first floor. Franz opened his mouth to greet them, and then closed it, noting his employer's determined pace.

Once in his office, August closed the door and stood at the window, staring at, but not seeing, Pratt Street and its early morning rumblings. So, he thought, there will be no August Strauff II. He studied his fingernails, rubbed them against his mustache, surprised at the intensity of this ache.

Seeing his reflection in the glass, he inhaled deeply. I hadn't realized how sure I was, he thought. Before this morning, I hadn't grasped who much I had anticipated, counted on this namesake, how

I had imagined that I could, that I would, make this child into my son. A son, a grandson, to take over what I have built, to carry on the business, to carry on my name.

And now his name is to be Stanley.

August pressed his forehead against the cool of the window. Well, he thought, Willie has stood up for himself, for his wife, just as I have counseled him to do. I never suspected that the strength would be shown against me. I was sure that this would be their gift to me, a child named August. I thought, hoped that it would be a sign of their gratitude for my support through this whole fiasco.

He walked to his desk, reached into the humidor and extracted a cigar, a Cuban *El Luxardo*, one meant to celebrate special occasions. He pulled the gold guillotine cutter from his waistcoat and snipped the cigar's end, warmed it over the flame of his lighter. Finally, he lit it and drew the smoke into his mouth. He sat, opened *The New York Tribune*.

Irony, he thought. A good English word.

Fifty-one _____

August left early that day. He directed Willie to close up. "You can get the streetcar home. I'll see you there." He didn't wait for his son's reply.

Paulina, sitting in the first floor sunroom, started when the front door opened. Raising the gold chain that held her watch, she saw that it was a few minutes after three p.m. Willie, she thought, sick, and she hurried to the front of the house. But it was her husband she saw. "August, what are you doing home? What is wrong?"

He took her elbow and led her to the sunroom. "I wanted to have a chance to talk to you while we have the house to ourselves. Clara is out, correct? Where is Celeste?"

Paulina told him that Celeste was in her room with the baby. August sat on the sofa and motioned for her to sit with him.

"Oh, August, tell me. What is it? What's happened? Is it Willie?" she asked.

He patted her knee. "No, no, not an emergency. I just wanted to talk to you, by ourselves." He stopped, looked out at the flowers planted in the back yard.

Paulina put her hand to her chest. "What, August, what is it?"

"They have decided on a name for the baby." He held his hand up, signaling that she should remain silent. "He is to be called Stanley. Stanley Wells Strauff."

"But no, August. That cannot be. Not after all you have done for them, all you have been for them. Willie would not let that happen. He would not have done that. Not to name the child for you, it is not possible." Her face became red with fury

She stood. "I will talk to that girl. I will talk to her before Willie gets home. She will not do this to you, to us, not after we've allowed

149

her into our home. I will not let this happen. I will not let them do this to you, this -- what is the word, August? What is the English word for this? Humility, I think, humilation."

"The word, Lina, is disenchantment, a dream unrealized. But that is for me, for us, to deal with." He reached for her, drew her back to the sofa.

"I knew that this would be your response. That is why I didn't want Willie to announce it at dinner, before I had a chance to talk to you. He told me this morning, on the way to work. This is Celeste's work; I am sure of that. But, that is the way it is." He held his hands out, shrugged his shoulders. "She is, after all, his wife.

"And some of it is my fault, our fault, for indulging in our bedroom conversations, you and I talking, whispering about August Strauff II. This is not our child. But yes, I am disappointed. I thought that Willie would see, would sense, how important it was to me. But we still have Clara. She understands family. She is the smart one, you know."

Paulina was silent, suffering the blow from this choice of Celeste's, for she too knew who had made the decision. She wondered who would tell Clara, and dreaded the result of that announcement, her family already fractured. She worried about the baby, so tiny, his cries so quiet. Will he survive? Will he be sickly, like Willie? What kind of mother will Celeste be? And *Stanley*? What kind of a name is that?

Fifty-two_____

August went into the backyard, sat beneath the catalpa tree, a rare afternoon visit to this sanctuary. Paulina headed to the third floor. She had made her morning visit earlier, to see the baby. She tried to keep her climbs to once a day; the steep stairways took so much of her energy.

The doors stood open to take advantage of any cross ventilation. She tapped on the door as she entered the bedroom. Celeste stood at the window, her back to Paulina. She had heard her mother-in-law's footsteps. The baby lay on the bed. Paulina went to him. She worried that he was such a quiet baby. So was Willie, she remembered.

Celeste turned, smiled at Paulina. Willie was to tell his father the baby's name that day, she knew, and she had seen her father-in-law arrive home in the carriage an hour earlier. She sensed what was coming. But, she reasoned, the baby is my baby. I have a right to name him what I wish.

"Mrs. Strauff, nice to see you again today," she said, and walked toward the bed. Paulina picked up the infant.

"How has he been today?" Paulina asked. "He doesn't seem to be getting any fatter."

"The doctor said that it would take some time, not to worry, that often infants lose weight right after they are born. I am feeding him, all the time. It seems like that is all I do. It is exhausting. I'm so grateful to Hanne for her help. I don't know what I would do without her, Mrs. Strauff. Thank you for allowing it."

Paulina bristled and placed the baby in the basket by the window. "Celeste, I do need to talk to you about that. Hanne is very good to us. She has been with us for a long time. When you came to be part of

151

the family, it meant that Hanne had one more person to care for. She did this with no complaint. But now that the baby is here, I cannot ask her to take that on in addition to all her other work. It would not be fair to her." Paulina went to the wardrobe, closed the half-open door.

"So, for the remaining of your confinement, of course, she will bring you your meals, and take care of the baby's laundry. But after that, I must insist that you be responsible for the baby, his washing, and all that goes with it. I'm sure you understand and would not wish to put an undue burden on her. I assume that your mother will instruct you on what to do. If that is a problem, you can meet with Hanne and she will show you. But you are not to impose upon her once your two week recovery is completed." Paulina paused, waiting for Celeste's response.

Well, Mr. Strauff must have told her, Celeste thought, and this is what has come of that. She placed her hands behind her back.

"Of course, Mrs. Strauff, I do understand. And I am prepared to care for my child, you can be sure." She said these words with more determination than she felt, for not only did she not want to take on this burden, she had no idea what to do. Annie was acting increasingly distant, even with the baby. I am paying the price for asserting myself in this family, she thought. I'll talk to Willie when he gets home. Maybe he can do something to make it better.

Fifty-three _____

Celeste took her place at the dinner table. The baby remained on the third floor, his basket placed in the middle of the double bed.

Earlier that day Hanne had overheard the conversation between Paulina and Clara. Now, at dinner, she placed herself in the hallway, close enough to the dining room that she could hear, far away enough that she would not be seen. *Ach*, she thought, my presence will be the least of what they will be concerned about.

A few minutes after the meal had been served, Clara put her fork down and addressed Celeste. "You know that it is our custom to baptize babies quickly, within the first week of their birth. The child is now almost three weeks old. Would you like us to make the arrangements for this to take place?"

They never call Stanley by his name, only the baby, the infant, child, Celeste thought. She waited for Willie to speak. He was silent. Another time it falls to me.

"Well, Clara, this is something that Willie and I have not yet had a chance to discuss. We will certainly do so and then let you know of our plans."

Hanne smiled. Celeste was turning into quite a challenge for Clara. My, my, my, she thought, and then realized that the words in her mind were English ones.

Celeste waited for August to comment, but he remained silent. She remembered that he, not Willie, had been the one to stand up for her, for them, and she realized that he was no longer an ally. That was over. Her insistence on Stanley's name had cost her her only advocate. She had worked hard not to be swallowed up by Clara's force, her anger. Though it was poised against her, Celeste couldn't help but admire it. She couldn't help but wish that Willie had inherited some of it. It seemed as if Clara had drunk the well of strength dry.

Paulina broke the silence. She could not stand the tension in her house, especially in the dining room, at dinner. "We have Clara's and Willie's christening gown. I don't know if your mother has yours. Perhaps you would prefer to use that, but we would be honored if the baby could wear it. It would mean so much to us."

Clara glared at her mother. Always simpering, Clara thought, trying to smooth over important issues. August concentrated on his meal. He was finished fighting for this couple who had betrayed him.

Celeste smiled at Paulina, and the older woman took it to be genuine. It was.

"Thank you, Mrs. Strauff. I think that would be a lovely idea. Don't you think so too, Willie?"

Willie reached for her hand and drew it to his lips. "That would be lovely, Celeste, *Mutti*. We want Stanley to strengthen up a bit before we take him out. So it will be a while."

Clara stood and hurled her napkin to the floor. "Absolutely not. That is exactly the point, Willie. The child must be baptized and baptized soon. If he should die unbaptized, then his soul would not go to heaven. You don't want your son to be consigned to Limbo for eternity, do you? Surely you are not that selfish?"

"Clara, enough," August said. "Everyone has their own beliefs. That is yours. It is not that of everyone in this room. Please respect that."

Clara turned to face August. "Oh, yes, *Vater*. You don't go to church and you think that I should say that that is fine. Well, I don't believe that. I pray for you every day, that you will return to God's arms, that you will be saved. I pray that you will come back to the church so that you don't suffer eternal damnation. And now you allow Willie to act the same as you. I am only saying this because I care, about you, about this family. *Mutti* agrees, but she is too timid to speak up. We want the child baptized and soon. This must happen."

"Clara, when you marry and have children, then you can decide what will happen. But Stanley is our son and we will do what we think best." All eyes went to Willie. Celeste felt her heart pound. Willie was speaking up. He was defending her. Finally he was speaking up. It was only later that she realized that Willie had reacted to Clara's attack on his father, not on her.

Clara stood. "Please ask Hanne to bring my dessert to my room. And I'd like a pot of tea as well." Hanne scurried to the back of the house, out of sight and beyond hearing the rest of the dinner conversation.

Fifty-four

Dear Elizabeth,

Oh how disappointed I am not to see you before you leave for college. I'm sure that by now you know about the baby. He is a tiny thing, and surprised us by coming in August, on one of the hottest days imaginable. He cries and cries, and sometimes he just wears himself out and falls asleep. I would not like to tell you what it was like giving birth. I don't think that I'll do it again. My mother talked to me about ways to, well, about ways that it won't happen again, at least for a long while. I guess we can talk more about that once you marry.

I am still in my room on this hot, hot third floor. I stayed here all the time for two weeks after the baby was born. Now I can go downstairs, and then in another week of two I'll be able to go out. Which I will. I am already planning where I will take Stanley in his perambulator. Mama went out and purchased lots of baby clothes in addition to the ones that she had made. And Mrs. Strauff, and even Clara, have made outfits for him too. He has more outfits than I do!

And did you notice what the baby's name is? Yes, I named him. Stanley Wells Strauff. Don't you think that sounds regal? Certainly a name for a very important person. And that is who he will be. I know that the Strauffs wanted him named for Mr. Strauff, and I really did consider it, Elizabeth. I really did. He, and really only he, has been nice to me and defended me against Clara. And Willie, of course.

But, this is my baby, and I wanted him to have a name that I liked. And also an English name. Strauff is enough German for anybody, wouldn't you say?

And now, here is the next part. I'm telling you this as a secret, so don't tell a soul, at least for a little while. You know that Mrs. Strauff and Clara are Catholic. So is Mr. Strauff, but I don't think it is so important to him. He doesn't go to church on Sunday. Neither does Willie. And now that I live here, neither do I. They don't like it, but neither Mrs. Strauff nor Clara has said anything to me about it. So, Stanley must be christened. But not Catholic. He is my child too and it is not something that I want.

So Willie contacted the priest who married us, and he said that he would be delighted to christen our little boy. We haven't told anyone about it yet. We have plenty of time. But I want them to know that I can stand up for myself. Willie says so too. Maybe you could be his godmother. That would be another wonderful connection for us, don't you think so too?

I am so sorry that I won't get to see you before you leave for Philadelphia. And by the time you come home for Christmas, Stanley will be almost grown up, or at least stronger than he is now. He is beautiful, but bald. His eyes are blue, not as light as mine. I think that he will look like me.

Elizabeth, I want to hear all about your life. You have been traveling all summer and I miss you a lot. I love your letters but they are not the same as spending time with you. I hope that you won't forget me once you become an important college girl.

I guess I have to tell you that I am lonely for you. It is such a quiet life here, and I spend most of my time in my room. I don't know what it will be like being a mother. Sometimes I think that everyone was right, that Willie and I were too young to be married. Please don't tell anyone that I said that.

But I know that Willie loves me and we are happy and he is so smart. And he promised to take me dancing as soon as

I can go out. So how could I not be happy? A lovely baby, a handsome husband, and you for a friend.

Please write soon. Please.

Celeste

Fifty-five_____

Stanley now slept in the third-floor's middle room. It had formerly served as the box room; it had no window, but received some air from the hallway. Celeste, Willie said, needed her rest. August brought the crib that his children had used from the basement. Paulina had insisted on bringing it to this house when they moved here almost twenty years ago. He liked seeing his grandson lying where Clara, then Willie and Clara, had spent their first years, vying for space in that small rectangle.

The baby, August called him, still not able to say the name Stanley. Silly for a grown man to be so wounded. Stanley, not so hard to say. Today, he thought, I will call the boy by his given name. Enough weakness.

Stanley was looking healthier, but not yet robust. His cries remained soft and weak. A blessing, August thought, for those others of us who live in this house. He watched Paulina with the boy, who now spent his days in the sun porch, ensconced in the white wicker bassinet. Paulina held him, rocked him, grateful that she no longer had to climb to the third floor to be with her grandson. Celeste seemed more than happy with this arrangement.

August watched Celeste take the baby for his daily measure of fresh air. One of Celeste's favorite events, he thought, taking Stanley, (there I said the baby's name, at least in my mind, a first step) for a walk on North Avenue. She didn't seem to mind struggling with the perambulator in the vestibule, bumping it down the three steps to the street, with Stanley (there, he thought, that came much easier) bumping right along with it. She was normally quiet at dinnertime, except to comment on how exhausting caring for a baby was.

He thought that the household was regaining its equilibrium. Even Clara had softened, clucking at the baby as she whisked by him on her way out the door. August had seen her move the bassinet into the front room while she practiced piano. The boy would grow up to either love or hate music.

Fifty-six

The September night brought a wave of wind and cooler air. All slept more soundly than they had in weeks. Clara, sitting in her bed reading *The Wings of the Dove*, quietly put the book down. The house was settled for the night. She went to the stair landing and listened. The third floor was quiet. Even the baby was sleeping.

Stopping in the bathroom, she poured a glass of water and picked up a clean washcloth. She proceeded up the stairs, holding tightly to the banister to balance herself. She moved slowly, wincing silently each time her left leg bore her weight. For the last five steps, she led with her right one, bringing the weaker leg up behind her. She heard Hanne's quiet breathing. No sounds came from the bedroom she had been forced to give to Willie. She walked directly into the middle room and looked down at the baby. The light from the gas sconce in the hallway showed him sleeping, his fist resting on his closed right eye.

She placed the cloth beneath his head, careful not to wake him. Placing two fingers in the water glass, she made sure that the liquid was not too cold. Clara lifted the infant's head. He stirred but did not wake. In an emergency, it doesn't have to be holy water, Clara said to herself.

"I baptize you in the name of the Father, the Son, and the Holy Spirit." She dipped her fingers in the glass and sprinkled a few drops of water on the baby's forehead. His face formed a moue; he stretched, and continued sleeping.

Clara realized that she had been holding her breath and exhaled, relieved. Removing the washcloth, she patted the stomach of the newest Catholic in the house. He was baptized; she could rest easy. He would go to heaven.

Descending the stairs while carrying the water glass was more difficult than she had anticipated. Clara put the glass down and moved down four steps. She picked it up and placed it on the step, going down four more steps. Finally she reached the second floor. Returning to her bed, she put Henry James aside. She sat up for a while, feeling holy.

Fifty-seven ────────────────

Willie and Celeste watched as Stanley Wells Strauff was baptized on Saturday, December 13th at Trinity Episcopal Church in Towson, by The Reverend Richard Powers. Elizabeth Owens Gittings was godmother. There was no godfather. Stanley wore his father's christening gown.

George and Annie were also present, as was August. After the ceremony, the group gathered at the Wells' house for a light supper. August did not attend.

Fifty-eight ———————————————

Celeste was in the basement, standing at the wash tub, pulling the rinsed diapers into the tub. In the hour allocated for them to soak, she filled the large metal pot with water and placed it on the burners on the laundry stove. Then she transferred the wet diapers to the pot so that they could simmer in boiling water for an hour. When the water cooled, she would ring them out again, place them in the laundry basket and carry that upstairs to the back yard to hang in the drying yard.

She looked at her hands, saw her fingers red and raw from her task, and longed for the warmer days of spring, So much work, she thought, for such a little baby. And now he was eating, nursing, all the time. I do nothing but nurse, diaper, and wash, she thought. But Stanley is a beautiful baby, fat and round. No one would believe that he had been such a string bean for so many months.

But this nursing has to stop. His teeth are coming in; he'll have to learn to drink from a cup. Her mind was made up; she had read about it. It was the modern way. She pushed the last clothes pin to the last diaper of the batch. No more nursing. If he gets hungry enough, he'll learn. Celeste picked up the laundry basket and returned to the house. Standing at the door to the basement, she threw the basket down the steps.

Stanley now sat up on his daily carriage rides, and sometimes waved or smiled to the women who peaked in to look at him. He liked the attention. So did Celeste, especially when passers-by commented on the beauty of child and mother. This was not the life that she envisioned, especially after Paulina had told her the rules with Hanne, but Hanne still helped when she saw that Celeste looked overwhelmed. Celeste made sure that she often looked overwhelmed.

Hanne is a love, she thought. Stanley smiled and reached out for her whenever he saw her. In the mornings when he woke it was Hanne he called for. That he called for Hanne and not his mother didn't bother Celeste, not in the least.

Paulina also bustled over Stanley. She had set up the high chair, once Willie's, in the dining room, ignoring crumbs and pabulum that were sometimes strewn about the room. Even Clara propped him in the chair beside the piano while she practiced. Stanley listened intently, and seemed entranced when she showed him the black notes on her music books. On more than one occasion, Celeste found him on Clara's lap at the piano, Clara moving his stubby fingers on the keys to play a German nursery rhyme. On these occasions, when Clara saw Celeste, she moved Stanley back to the armchair, pillows around him to prop him up.

Celeste knew that she was fortunate that she could leave Stanley with the family, that she could go out, to lunch, shopping, visiting. Paulina was happy to have him to herself. Celeste noticed that the Strauffs still referred to him as "the baby," but she was not about to risk losing the freedom they gave her by insisting that they call him by his name.

She visited Annie, often at first after Stanley's birth; but now her visits were reduced to once a week. When she did visit, the two women were awkward with one another. Their conversations focused on Stanley and the pastries that Meg served. Celeste heard about Eva's studies. That fall, Eva had left the Women's College and was in Massachusetts studying architecture at Wellesley College. Celeste thought how interested Willie would be in that, and was glad that Eva was far away. Now that it was just Annie and George and Meg, Celeste thought, Mama should be even more interested in me and my life, but that doesn't seem to be happening.

"Maybe the three of us could come for dinner on Sunday, Mama," Celeste said during one visit. "I hardly ever get to see Papa, and Stanley needs to get to know his grandfather. I think he is beginning to look like Papa's father, like that oil painting of Grandfather we have in the living room, when he was a boy in England."

Annie was quiet, her hands in her lap. "Celeste, you father isn't feeling so well these days. It takes all his energy to work. He needs his weekends to rest. But I know that he would like to see you, perhaps not for the time it would take for a dinner. Why don't you come by this Saturday afternoon for an hour or so, with Willie too? We miss seeing him."

Celeste had a brief thought that Annie was more anxious to see Willie than she was to spend time with her, but she brushed it from her mind. "Yes, Mama. Saturday afternoon." And she gathered Stanley, his zwieback, his rabbit, and lifted him into the carriage by the front steps.

"I love you, Mama," Celeste said. Annie stood at the door and watched as her daughter, outfitted in a white shirtwaist, navy skirt, and navy jacket with red piping, adjusted the red ribbon that tied her long hair back. Celeste pulled a few curls forward around her face.

Fifty-nine

Celeste heard the baby, soft cries at first. She pulled the blanket over her head as the sounds escalated to wails. She would get up in a minute, she said to herself. Just another minute.

An hour later, her eyes opened to sun streaming thought the windows. She stretched and reached over to touch Willie. Then she remembered. The baby. Could he have fallen back to sleep? Ah, precious gift from her blond son. She rose quietly, trying not to disturb Willie, who slept so fitfully these days. Pulling on her silk robe, a reminder of Denver, she walked softly to Stanley's room. She would wake him, be the first to see his morning smile.

She heard herself gasp when she looked into the crib. Empty. Then she thought, wonderful Hanne. Giving us a few hours of precious sleep. Celeste peered into Hanne's room at the back of the house. She saw the bed made, spread placed as perfectly as the maid did for all the Strauffs.

She walked softly to the basement kitchen, the smells of coffee and yeast meeting her in the first floor hallway. Stanley must be sleeping in the straw basket they kept in the kitchen.

"Good morning and thank you so much, Hanne. Oh, what a luxury to seep in the morning," Celeste said.

This child, Hanne thought. Would she ever think that I might like the luxury of a lie-in? But she said nothing.

"Hanne, where is the baby?"

"I don't know, Miss Celeste. He was quiet when I came downstairs. He's not in his crib?"

Celeste didn't answer, but ran to his third floor room. The crib was empty. Her heart pounding, she willed herself to stay calm. All was quiet in the house. She could not bear to admit to them that she had allowed Stanley to be kidnapped. Who knew he was there? Her mind raced. She could not burden Willie with this, he sleeping quietly for the first time in weeks.

Clara. She had to turn to Clara, ask Clara what to do. Clara always knew what to do. Celeste bit her lips, willed herself to be calm.

She descended the steps once again. Outside Clara's door, she stood tall, tightened the sash of her robe. She tapped on the door lightly, using just her fingertips.

"Clara, are you awake?" she whispered. Celeste could barely hear her own voice.

There was no response. Celeste put her hand on the door knob and turned it gently. Opening the door a few inches, Celeste whispered, "Clara?" The room was darkened, the shades drawn.

In the shadows she saw Clara asleep, lying on her back. She noticed a glint of yellow. Stanley's blond head. She stopped. Clara held Stanley in one arm. He was sucking on the fingers of her other hand, content, his eyes closed.

Standing in the doorway, Celeste thought, Clara loves Stanley. She left the door ajar and returned to her room to dress.

Willie's eyes opened when she went to the wardrobe. "Good morning, my lovely one," he said, and raised himself on his elbow.

Celeste leaned down to kiss him. Then she sat straight and placed his fingers on his lips. "Oh, Willie. Clara loves the baby. She loves Stanley."

Sixty

The trees were in full bloom. On this Saturday morning Celeste and Willie stood at their bedroom window gazing at Green Mount Cemetery. They called it their own Central Park.

"Which is your favorite?" Willie asked. A few weeks ago, he had brought home a book that showed the trees of North America. They laughed as they tried to identify those they could see across the street.

"My favorite is the beech. I like that it holds its leaves through the winter, even if they are brown" Celeste said.

"Me too," said Willie, and put his arm around her waist. Celeste, he thought, is finally adjusting to the baby, to the house.

She leaned against him, inhaling the scent of bay rum. She remembered a fall that seemed long ago. Suddenly she pulled away and said, "Oh, Willie, take me with you. Please. It will be such fun, just like our honeymoon. Just you and me again. Like it used to be." She reached up and touched Willie's forehead, smoothed his hair. "It will be wonderful. I'll bet that your mother and Hanne would be glad to take care of the baby. It would only be for two weeks. We could have such fun. Oh, Willie, don't you think that we deserve some fun? It's been so hard for me, taking care of Stanley all by myself. A whole two weeks, just us, in a hotel again. Another honeymoon, alone?" She kissed his neck.

Willie removed her hands from his waist, took a step back from her. "Celeste, this is a business trip. You know that. Denver, well, that was special. But it can't be that you come with me on every trip. Think of the cost. If we ever want to get our own house, we have to start putting money aside. I can't ask *Vater* to pay for your expenses.

That would not be right. And besides, when I'm away, *Mutti* goes to the newspaper office. She wouldn't be here to take care of Stanley."

Celeste interrupted him. "Then Hanne. Hanne could do it. I know she could. And she would love it. She would, Willie. She loves Stanley. It would be good for her."

Willie laid a gentle hand on her lips. "Celeste, no. Not this time. Maybe the next trip, but not now. Stanley needs his mother. He needs you to be here. I would love for you to go; I know how much you deserve this." He smoothed her hair and turned to the window. This child, he thought. When will she grow up? When will she see that they are adults?

Celeste moved in front of the bookcase; she ran her finger along the spines of some of the volumes. Then she walked to the mirror to check her hair. She turned back to Willie.

"You don't know what it is like for me here, Willie. All day with the baby, working, working, working. No one to talk to except when I take him for a walk. Just waiting for you to come home and be with me. And Clara, so mean to me."

Willie squared his shoulders. "Celeste, I know it is hard for you. But I am working to earn enough money for us to be on our own. And when that happens, you will have to care for Stanley on your own, without *Mutti* or Hanne. And you are doing a wonderful job. Stanley loves you; I can see it in his eyes. When I look at him, I see you, my sweet one."

Celeste allowed her eyes to fill. "Willie, you just don't understand," she said, and stiffened when he took her into his arms. Willie held her and stared straight ahead.

Sixty-one

The next day Willie oversaw Hanne put as she placed his clothes in his luggage: two suits, with waistcoats; twelve shirts, four pairs white pajamas, fourteen sets of underclothes, with the same number of monogrammed handkerchiefs. Willie chose the ties, stickpins and cufflinks. It would be warm in Texas. He was glad that he wouldn't have to deal with heavy outer garments for this journey.

Celeste stood at the window, watching. Willie knew she was upset, but felt sure that his decision was the right one. This trip was not a vacation. It would not do to bring a wife, especially now that Stanley was here. Stanley needed her, Willie thought, and felt a frisson of worry as he questioned how important Stanley was to his young wife. Thank God for Hanne and *Mutti*, he thought.

He returned to the tasks at hand, placing his jewelry in the case of Florentine leather, lined in navy blue velvet. He held the gold cufflinks, a gift from August for his 21st birthday, and remembered the prior week's conversation that led to this trip.

August had called him into his large corner office. "Willie, I have just been in touch with Michael Brauerschmidt, the publisher of the *wolchenblatt* in Texas, in Fredericksburg, Texas. My sense is that they are having a rough go of it, although he did not say that. Of course, we are also having a rough go of it, so perhaps I heard some of the same evasions that I myself have made." August leaned back in his chair, measuring his words.

"During our conversation, I suggested that our papers enter into the same sort of agreement that you negotiated when you were in Denver. Brauerschmidt appeared receptive to it, or at least to meeting and talking about it. Now I think this would be another opportunity for you. This time you are much more knowledgeable. I think that it will be primarily a one-sided arrangement in our favor, but I want you to help him see the benefit to his as well. We will provide information from Germany, and also information about Germans on the East Coast. We don't have any interest about those Texas Germans; their activities are of no interest to our readers. So he will not have to provide anything to us.

"You see, *John*, you will be operating from a strong position. And I know that you can do this without making Brauerschmidt feel inferior. That is a very important tactic," August paused. "Is that the right word? *Yah*, a very important tactic in this agreement." August pulled at his mustache, put his hands flat on the desk.

"What do you think about it? Are you ready to go west? Are you up to it?" August watched his son's face.

Willie smiled broadly, and August realized how seldom he saw his son smile.

"*Vater*, thank you for having this faith in me. Yes, I will do it. And yes, I think that I can bring us an even more lucrative arrangement now that we have experience with sending information by wire. And, yes also, I think that I can work with Mr. Brauerschmidt to make him feel that he has struck a bargain for himself, use that tactic." Willie could not help but laugh as he delivered these last words. August did not smile.

Willie continued. "Do you have any preference for the most effective way to start? With sending the information by wire, or mailing copies?"

The two businessmen spent the rest of the afternoon working out financial details. Willie left the office with a light step. This is what it feels like to be a businessman, he thought. If I can make this deal, there will be money for me and Celeste to live on our own.

Franz tipped his hat as Willie left for the day. Even he noticed the spring in Willie's step.

*Sixty-two*_____

Dear Elizabeth,

It was wonderful to hear about your life – your classes and all your trips to New York City. I still haven't gotten there, but that is definitely on my list of places to go. I am pretty well stuck in Baltimore with the baby, not even stuck in Baltimore, but stuck in those blocks I can wheel the baby carriage. But Stanley is the most beautiful baby. He is now quite fat and heavy, and I carry him down the steps and up the steps and down the steps. It is exhausting.

He is blond, like me, and his hair is growing in loose ringlets. His eyes are brown, like Willie's. The Strauffs love him a lot and make over him all the time, though they prefer that I be there to take care of him. I am just about worn out with all the work that is involved, and don't think that Clara would lift a hand to help me. Oh, no, she is either out all day (I still can't figure out where she goes or what she is doing – it has to do, of course, with music) or she is practicing at the piano. Music, music, music, all the time. Well, at least Stanley seems to love it. She props him up in the big chair in the front room and he is mesmerized by the sound, and, I must say, by Clara. A few times I've come in and she has had him on her lap, putting his little fingers on the keys, picking out a song. He giggles, and, really, it is the only time I've seen her face with a soft expression. Of course, as soon as she sees me, back he goes to the chair, and she goes back to looking like she's been sucking on a lemon.

I've lived in this house for over a year now, and I don't think that she and I have ever had a real talk; it is all very *polite make-talk, like you would if a friend of your mother's had come to visit from far away. All polite, nothing real. I hate it.*

Oh, Elizabeth, I feel so alone and lost here all day. Willie works, and that seems to be going fine. He is going to Texas for two weeks. I will stay here with the baby. I am hoping that we will soon have enough money to have our own place. I just hate it hear.

I visit Mama a few times a week, well, really only once a week, and that just makes me feel worse. I know that she loves Stanley, but she doesn't pick him up and hug him and kiss him like Mrs. Strauff does. And we just don't have a thing to say to one another anymore. It is almost as bad when I go there as when I am in this house. Here at least I have my own room on the third floor. I spend a lot of time here, looking out the window. I am so glad that we have the park across the street that I can look at. Of course, you know that it is a cemetery, but to me it is a park, like New York's Central Park. That is what I imagine when I look out.

And Papa is quiet too. I guess they miss Eva. I thought when she went to Boston that they would be even happier with me and Stanley, and Willie, of course, but it is not the same. Oh, Elizabeth, nothing is the same anymore. I miss you so much. And I worry that when I do get to see you, we won't have anything to talk about either.

I am so lonely. I am so sad. I just never thought that my life would be like this.

Your friend,
Celeste

Celeste looked at the light blue stationery, saw her downward-slanting handwriting. She took the pages in her hand and started to read them. By the third paragraph her tears had made the letters too blurry to decipher. She pulled her handkerchief from her skirt pocket and wiped her eyes. Then she tore the pages into tiny pieces and tossed them into the wastepaper basket.

Sixty-three————————————

The driver unloaded Willie's luggage and carried it into the station. Willie stepped down from the carriage and turned back to his wife and son. Celeste, looking decidedly glum, held Stanley on her lap, the child with a biscuit clenched in his fist.

"Don't worry, my sweet one. It will be fine; I'll be back in two weeks. I know that this trip will be a success. Then we can talk about getting our own place, the three of us. We'll be a real family. You've been so patient with me. Can you wait, just a few more weeks?"

Willie reached to touch Celeste's cheek. She pressed her lips together. Stanley bounced in her lap, pulled at her hair. She moved the child's hand from her face.

"Oh, Willie, it will be horrible with you gone. Please write to me every day, and wire when you get to Chicago, and Little Rock, and Texas. You are so lucky to be able to travel. Think of me when you're gone. Don't forget me. Don't."

Willie took her hand, kissed it, and placed it atop Stanley's head. "It's St. Louis, Little Rock and San Antonio." He smiled as he answered. "And forget you, never. Now don't worry, and take care of my little boy. Make sure that he doesn't forget his father." He leaned in to kiss his the top of Stanley's head, evading the wet crumbs that stuck to the baby's face.

Stanley smiled and waved his biscuit. "Hanne, Hanne." The boy laughed as he called out his favorite word. Celeste took his left arm in her hand and helped him wave goodbye. They watched as Willie entered Camden Station.

August had booked a drawing room for his son's journey. He knew that the trip would prove arduous, and he wanted Willie to be fresh when he met with Bauerschmidt. Willie was looking forward to the days of solitude and had packed his valises heavy with books.

He entered his compartment to await the train's departure. He sat, thinking his life with Celeste and Stanley. Despite the tension in the house, when the three of them were in their third-story haven, life was most often filled with delight. He was happy, though he knew that life there was not easy for Celeste. But Stanley cried less now; the women in the house clucked over and spoiled him. He had turned into a hale, happy baby. Even August loved him; Willie once had heard his father singing a German folk song to the boy. August called him Stanley; Paulina and Clara, not yet. Willie closed his eyes and wished a peaceful time for Celeste.

The first days of the journey followed those of his and Celeste's, taken the year before. Willie sat, remembering the delicious days and nights of their young love, thinking of how his life, their lives, had changed. They had been but children then.

Early the next morning, his breakfast completed before the train pulled into Cincinnati, Willie gathered his sketchpad. As soon as the train stopped he entered the station to make rough sketches of its interior. My work is not very good, he thought, but this will help me remember. He wished that he knew how to take photographs, and resolved to learn when he returned home. He could take photos for the paper. August would like that.

When the train pulled out of the Baymiller Station, he returned to his compartment, grateful for hours of quiet, anxious to catch up on his reading. He would wait until he reached the Texas border to think about the meeting that faced him. He pulled out the maps that he had brought. Such an immense state, he thought. There will be plenty of time to prepare before he reached Fredericksburg.

Arriving in St. Louis, Willie relived that evening months ago, when he had led Celeste through the station, pointing out the splendor of the building, the archways, the mosaics, the Tiffany window. He checked into the station's hotel, just as he and Celeste had done, though he did not return to Tony Foust's, the restaurant where they had enjoyed such a delightful meal. Willie remembered lobster, champagne, Nesselrode pudding, even the carriage ride that frigid night. But this evening he used his time for more sketches, capturing images of the most magnificent station in the country.

*Sixty-four*_____

The next day, after breakfast at the hotel, Willie took a trolley car to Forest Park. He looked out at the mansions on Chatou Street as he headed to the western part of the city. He studied the city map he had picked up at the hotel, orienting himself for his journey. He'd get off the bus at the southeast entrance of the park. He marked that on his map in preparation for his return journey.

Preparations were well underway for the following year's World's Fair; The Palace of Fine Arts was already completed. Willie took out his sketchbook, and drew, as best he could, the structures that he saw. He tried to guess their use. He approached one of the workmen to ask, but the mason simply shook his head.

After a time he put away his pencils. He marveled at the activity taking place in this bustling, yet serene, setting. A sudden dizzy spell came over him, and he realized that he had not eaten since his early breakfast. He pulled out his pocket watch and was alarmed to see the time. He had lost his sense of direction, and had to ask several people for help to find the streetcar stop. He quickened his pace, and arrived as the trolley pulled to the curb. Heart pounding, he arrived back at the Union Station where he gathered his luggage and boarded the train with only minutes to spare. Once in his seat, he closed his eyes. To miss the train. What would August have thought?

To quiet his mind, and to stop his hands from shaking, he picked up the pamphlet on the table in his compartment. The St. Louis, Iron Mountain, and Southern. A romantic name for a railroad, he thought. He made a note to himself to find out just where Iron Mountain was.

Once his heartbeat slowed, he brought a wet cloth from the lavatory. He placed it on his forehead and lay back, hoping to pre-empt the incipient headache. He slept briefly, and when he awoke, he was grateful that he felt better. A headache on this train ride would have been torture. He removed two books from his valise, and placed them on the table. He would read after dinner.

Later that evening he walked to the dining car, found it resplendent with candlelight and white linen napery. Now two full days into his trip, he continued to revel in the solitude, the silence, his time to think. The waiter sat him at the empty chair at a table for four; the two men and one woman seated there were deep in conversation. They nodded politely at Willie and continued talking as if he weren't there. Willie was relived.

He finished dinner quickly, and, nodding to his tablemates, headed for the club car. An after-dinner drink, he thought, and then Emerson awaits.

Willie was met by the redolence of cigars past embedded in the upholstery of the chairs and lounges. I'll not stay long, he thought, as he found a seat, his chest already tight from the smoke. He gave the waiter his order: whiskey, neat. The noise of the car, men's raucous laughter, felt jarring after his days of silence. He looked around, wondered what August would have thought of these men. Would he have sneered at their rude manners? Or would he have eased into conversation with them, thinking that a deal might come of it, that they might be useful to him?

His drink delivered, Willie nodded and raised his glass to the foursome beside him. Cards were splayed across the polished Philippine mahogany table in front of them.

"Care to join us for a hand?" one of them asked.

"Sorry, not a card player, I'm afraid," Willie responded.

"At least allow us to buy you a drink, or, another drink, sir," and the man motioned to the waiter. "Bring the gentleman a bourbon, if you would."

Willie raised his glass to them and finished his whiskey. He did not leave his seat. When the next round of drinks appeared, the waiter place one before him.

"Well, this will be a new taste for me. I've heard of bourbon, but have not had the pleasure." I'm even talking like these mid-Westerners,

Willie said to himself. Good practice for Texas. He inhaled the sweet smell of the liquor, swirled it in the glass before he lifted it to his lips. He savored the liquid, then swallowed. Smooth, honeyed, easy going down, he thought.

"Gentlemen, I thank you, and will certainly add this drink to my collection." Willie caught the waiter's eye to order another. The men watched him, and took note that it was his third drink since he came into the car. Raising an eyebrow to one of his companions, the man with a drooping brown mustache asked Willie to join them, "for a friendly game."

Willie noted the mustache, in less-than-pristine condition. Snuff, no doubt. He finished the drink in his hand, then smiled and responded, "Gentlemen, I have had just enough liquor to give me the courage to say no to your tempting offer. Thank you, and goodnight."

He stood, caught himself before he stumbled, and concentrated on walking in a straight line as his left the car. He congratulated himself. Willie, you are quite the man.

"Eastern pansy," said the man to his cronies. They laughed. One responded, "But he outfoxed you, didn't he?" Willie heard the exchange. He straightened his shoulders and smiled even more broadly.

Sixty-five

Celeste stretched and looked out of the window. Across the street the trees were coming into full leaf. I'll visit Mama today, she thought. I'll ask her. She won't say no, she couldn't, not when I tell her what it is like for me here.

She dressed and headed downstairs for breakfast. At this early hour, Clara will still be asleep, she thought. Perhaps Stanley and I can leave the house before she awakes.

Paulina sat at the dining room table, finishing her breakfast. With Willie was away, she went to the paper almost every day. Celeste hated being in the house alone, almost as much as she hated being there when the Strauffs were at home. She felt that only Hanne's presence saved her. Stanley was ensconced in his high chair. Someone, either Hanne or, more likely, Paulina, had given him his breakfast. He had his cup now, and was banging it on his tray, laughing at the noise it made.

When Hanne heard Celeste's tread, she went to the dining room and scooped the baby up in her arms. She met Celeste at the landing. "Miss Celeste, would you mind keeping Stanley for a few minutes? I must talk to Mrs. Strauff in private." Without waiting for a response, Hanne handed Stanley to his mother. Celeste held him out away from her, turning him from her so that she could sweep away the crumbs. She took him to the sun porch. Something is happening, she thought, and tried to work out a way that she could keep the baby on the porch and still hear what was being said in the middle room.

Hanne returned to the dining room and pulled the pocket doors closed. Celeste planted Stanley in his play pen and went to the door.

The voices were quiet. She strained, but could only hear Paulina's voice.

"Oh, no, this cannot be, Hanne. Surely you will reconsider. Go for a time, but come back to us. Your home is here; this is your home. We will pay your return fare."

Celeste closed her eyes. Hanne leaving? Her heart pounded. What would this mean? What would it mean for her, for Stanley? She strained to hear Hanne's response, but all she could hear was crying.

The women were speaking German now. Celeste returned to the sun porch. She heard Hanne leave the dining room. The maid went directly to the stairs, to her room. Celeste walked slowly to where Paulina sat at her place at the table. Her hands were folded beside her notebook.

"Mrs. Strauff, what is the matter? What did Hanne say?" Celeste asked.

"Oh, my dear child. Hanne wants to go back to the old country." Paulina placed her elbows on the table, rubbed her temples. "After all these years with us, she wants to be with her mother. I am trying to make sense of her decision. Everything that this country offers, everything that we offer. And she wants to return to Germany. *Ach*."

Celeste heard Stanley in the background. He was pulling on the handles of the play pen, hitting them with a rattle. "Oh, Mrs. Strauff, she really wouldn't leave us, would she? She wouldn't leave Stanley. She loves him."

Paulina laid her hand on that of her daughter-in-law. "We must let August work this out. Hanne says she wants to go home, that Germany is her home, not here. She has been like family to us. I thought that we were family to her. But we must think of what is best for her. We owe her that gift. I will talk to August. He will know what to do. I must gather my things now to leave. We will talk at dinner."

Not waiting for Paulina to leave, Celeste rushed upstairs and into Hanne's third-floor room. "Oh, Hanne, you cannot leave me. You cannot." Celeste words rushed out. She grabbed Hanne's hand and pulled it to her lips. "You can't leave us, Hanne. What will become of me here without you?"

Sixty-six

Willie spent most of the day in his compartment, reading, thinking, watching the scenery of Arkansas, nursing what he remembered from earlier years as a hangover. Four cups of coffee and two headache powders cleared his head. He thought about his life in the East, knew that was where he belonged. He thought of two friends from school who left Baltimore to make their fortunes in California. Not the newness of the West for him. He belonged to the East; he fit in there, where things were settled, where people knew what was expected of them.

He closed his eyes and pictured his wife, his beautiful Celesté. And now Stanley. Alone these days, alone with his thoughts, he admitted to himself that this love, this marriage, could have been a mistake, that following one's heart might not always be best course of action. But acting as a gentleman, well, that must always be. One must do the right thing. One must take responsibility for one's actions. No choice there.

Willie picked up one of the books he had brought with him. Best to read, he thought. It is not a good thing to wish things different, to wonder. Yet this day his mind would not focus on Emerson.

Newspapers, he thought, this is not what I'm interested in. I should have gone away to school. *Vati* would have supported me; he wanted me to go to college. He wanted a son who went to college. Architecture, that was what I could have done with my life. And now, Celeste, Stanley, it is too late for me. I had to do the right thing.

He stood, looked out at the green vista. When I return to Baltimore, I will make some changes. Surely what I've learned in my years with the paper, surely the people I know in the city, there must be something that I can do, something of my own.

183

He stared out the window. Such a long ride, so many days, so much time to think. And days to go. He pressed his forehead against the glass. Not good thoughts to think, not thoughts for a husband, a father, a business man. He adjusted the cuffs of his shirt, pulled himself erect, and walked to the dining car. On his way, the conductor announced that they were crossing the border into Texas. Soon they would arrive in Longview, with a change of trains to the International Great Northern line. Willie was too tired to take out his sketchpad.

Several hours late, the train pulled into San Antonio. Willie wired Celeste. *"Arrived San Antonio. Thinking of you every minute. Love to you and Stanley. Willie."*

Four days of travel and Willie's trip was still not completed. Taking advantage of a three-hour layover, he ventured onto Flores Street. Though the sun was setting, the heat and humidity rushed at him after the coolness of the Sunset Depot, its construction still not quite completed. He stared at the pink adobe, glowing like a coral star in the salmons and scarlets of the darkening sky. He had only read about this material. He studied the architecture, mission style, he thought. He imagined what its stained glass window would look like in the daylight, with the sun streaming through. It doesn't compare to that window in the St. Louis station, he thought, but it has a certain beauty in this stark western part of the country. He recognized the Texas star in the middle. Not very literary. He thought he saw an art nouveau touch, and wondered if were just coincidence.

At the station, Willie made arrangements for the rest of his trek. Late that night, he would board the San Antonio and Aransas Pass, the fourth rail line of his journey, that would take him to Comfort. He smiled at the name of the town where he would spend the night. The ticket master in San Antonio wired ahead for him, reserving a room at the Hotel Faust. Willie smiled at this also, and wondered if these Texans read, or even knew about, Goethe. Well, at least I am in German country, he thought, something that I know a bit about.

When Willie arrived in Comfort after a two-hour train ride, he was surprised and gratified to see a village that looked more than adequate to provide food and lodging. The sky was dark, but gas lights illuminated the empty streets. A carriage waited for him outside the station. The stationmaster in San Antonio had given him directions to the hotel, and Willie passed his luggage to the carriage driver while he walked the four long blocks, like Baltimore blocks he thought, to the hotel. He was glad to get some exercise and relieved to be off the train. A late dinner would be waiting for him and he looked forward to a comfortable, if abbreviated, sleep. For the San Antonio stationmaster had imparted some news he hadn't anticipated.

Sixty-seven_____

Willie was awakened by a gentle knock on his door. He looked over at his pocket watch. Six a.m. He had arranged for breakfast at seven; the coach would come to the hotel at 7:30. He smiled to himself as he shaved. A stage coach. What a story to tell when I return. What a story for Stanley, who would surely only know of such things from books. I will write to him, Willie thought, put all these adventures down for my boy to keep, a record that his father actually experienced such adventures.

After breakfast he went onto the porch. A flash of red and yellow caught his eye. A stagecoach, like a prop from a burlesque act, he thought. Pulled by two horses fresh for the day's journey, the shiny coach with its yellow trim and gold scrolls, stopped in front of the hotel. A black canvas tarp formed the roof and sides of the carriage. Light weight, Willie thought. That will help us make good time. The driver jumped down and went inside to get Willie's luggage.

"Looks like you'll be my only passenger this morning. Well, you and the mail sack." The driver looked Willie over. An Easterner, for sure, he thought, and wondered what his business was. He looked like one of those lawyers from the East.

"The team is fresh, so'ins I think we can make it without stopping. That is, if you can. Just pull the bell if you need me to stop."

Willie climbed into the cab, and rubbed his hand over the red upholstered seats. The coach could accommodate six passengers, and he was relieved that he would be the only one that morning.

The driver stepped up to latch the coach door. "You picked a good week to be here. Last week the rains made muck and mud of the journey; I think this morning we can get you where you want to go before ten this morning.

Willie prepared himself for a rough ride, remembering what he had read about Conestoga wagons taking pioneer families west. He hoped that the coffee he had drunk that morning, boiled he suspected, would keep his headaches in check.

He was pleasantly surprised at the roll and lull of the vehicle, though once on its way, some of the rolls became more pronounced. He found himself swayed into a reverie as the coach made its way through the green hills. Not the flat brown he had expected from his readings about the Lone Star State.

At precisely the three hour mark, the carriage slowed as it approached the town of Fredericksburg. Willie looked out. At first glance it did not look as prosperous as Comfort. The streets were wide, as wide as Baltimore's North Avenue, though they were dirt, unpaved. The wooden sidewalks were well-swept, and the pedestrians were better dressed than he had anticipated. He remembered that Fredericksburg was the county seat.

"Are you going to the courthouse, sir? I can take you there, or I can stop at the hotel," the driver said.

"I'm not sure where I'm staying this evening. It would be best to take me to my appointment. *Der Wolchenblatt*. Do you know where the offices are located?"

"That I do, but if you are staying here tonight, I would venture that you will put up at the Nimitz Hotel. That's the coach stop. I can leave you at the paper and take your luggage directly to the hotel if you would like that, sir." The driver's experience was that most Easterners were big tippers. He pegged Willie as one.

"That is quite kind of you," Willie responded, and pulled out a paper note for the driver.

"Well, thank you, sir. Mighty generous."

Willie looked around before he entered the newspaper's office. The town's buildings were a mixture of brick and wood, two stories high, and saddled horses, buggies, and wagons were hitched along both sides of the street. Horse droppings lay drying in the heat, and it gave both a sweet and acrid bouquet to the town. His teenaged reading of Karl May's, of Ned Buntline's stories of the West came to him. The land of Buffalo Bill Cody, Calamity Jane, Wild Bill Hickok, cowboys, another world, this Texas, this Wild West. Here I am, experiencing what I have only read about in *McClure's* and *Collier's* and *Harper's* magazines. Such stories to tell Stanley, he thought.

As he turned to enter the building, a man of his father's age, though significantly larger, came to greet him. Taking Willie's hand, he shook it with vigor, as if testing the younger man's mettle. Willie stood straight and matched the man's grip. "Mr. Bauerschmidt, I am glad to meet you."

"Young man, you have had quite a journey and you are looking none the worse for wear. The driver has taken your luggage to the hotel, I see. Good decision. Let us go into the office. I want to hear how your father is. We met a few years ago when I was in the East. He has done a masterful job with his paper. I am hopeful that we can work together for our benefit."

Bauerschmidt led Willie to his office and the two men concluded their business in less time than Willie expected. Bauerschmidt had definite ideas about the arrangement. They were not what Willie had anticipated, but he knew that August could adapt, with Fritz's help, and deliver what the Texan wanted. For the first six months, paper issues would be mailed. Bauerschmidt wanted that time to gauge if it would be worth his while to take on the typesetting. Willie saw that, behind the boisterous *gemutlichkeit*, his business partner was a shrewd businessman.

The exchange completed, the men repaired to The White Elephant Saloon on the city's main street. Willie resolved to sketch the building, with its four columns and wooden doors, as a record for Stanley. He was in the Wild West, even if it had a decidedly German feel. Such a long, arduous journey, such a short meeting. Well, Willie thought, this is how business gets done out here. He had a glimmer of recognition that August just might have assigned him task not only to give him a boost about business, but also to save the older man the rigors of such a journey.

Once the two men entered the saloon, Willie was surprised to hear German spoken. The menu was in German, offering German food. He compared this with his life in Baltimore, where, while there were certainly German restaurants and German societies, for the most part, those who arrived in this new country did all they could to become Americans first, Germans second. That didn't seem to be so here, though the town was settled by Prussians more than eighty years before. Willie saw that these citizens might be more interested in what was going on in the old country than he had presumed. Maybe this wouldn't be such a bad idea for August.

The lunch lasted well into the afternoon. Willie watched as Bauerschmidt drank draft after draft of lager. Willie did not match his stride. Finally, the older man rose. "Please take dinner with us this evening. I will send a carriage to the hotel. Six-thirty suits, *yah?*" Willie nodded, shook the man's hand, and walked the three blocks to his lodging.

As he approached, he noticed the hotel's odd architecture. More adobe, but this time framed in white wood. The building was three stories tall, with an odd fourth floor room that jutted out over the street. He would ask about that when he checked in. He wanted to have a much bath before dinner. He would wait to wire his father until he was back at the Comfort railway station.

Dinner at the Bauerschmidts was not unlike those on North Avenue. The same food, the same china, linen, a German maid in the background. Mrs. Bauerschmidt clucked over him. Willie felt at home, yet was anxious to return to his hotel, to repack his luggage, to start his long journey back. Too much time alone, perhaps, he thought. He missed the blue eyes of his wife, his son's laughter when he came in the door each evening. He even missed Clara's sarcasm. Perhaps he really was meant to be a family man. That is what he would be when he returned. He would find a home for his family. He would be a business partner with his father. Yes, he would make changes, and those changes would be for good.

Back at the Nimitz, he lay out his clothes for the next day, indulged in a second bath of the day, and wrote to Celeste. He enclosed a separate letter to Stanley.

189

My darling boy,

I have been on an incredible adventure to the West. I grew up calling it the Wild West, and I think that the stories I read of wild Indians and cowboys will soon be just memories. It took many days for me to arrive in Texas. I rode trains and trains and trains through many states. Now almost each state has at least one railroad company. I think that this will soon change as well.

Here in Fredericksburg, Texas, there are no streetcars, no trains, and I have yet to see an automobile. It is a small town, with only one main street, and it is a dirt street. It is wide, but it is still dirt. The weather has been very hot and dry here, but when it rains, the street turns to mud and no one can use it. People are stranded as we sometimes are when a big snowstorm comes to visit us. Everyone has a horse here, some have more than one, and men ride them as easily as we would take a trolley car. There are open wagons that families bring into town to get their supplies for the week. Most people are farmers and live in the country, each house very far apart from the other. I'm sure that they would look at us, in our town houses, and wonder how we can live on top of one another.

It will take a long time, many days for me to return home. I will have to go back through all those states I passed through on my way here. And every morning and every night I think of you and miss you. I can hear your laugh, I can hear you calling in the morning for Hanne, I can see you reaching up to tug on your mother's blonde curls.

My dear son, you have brought such sunshine into so many lives, especially mine. I am proud to be your father. You have made your mother and me a family. I will work hard to give you everything that you deserve.

You are my dear sweet little boy.
Forever, your father,
Willie

The next morning he returned to the offices of *Der Wolchenblatt*. Bauerschmidt had drawn up the agreement. Willie read it slowly, carefully, aware of the older man's eyes upon him. He would not let himself be hurried; he would not allow himself to sign something that he didn't understand.

The agreement reflected their conversation. Willie affixed his signature with a flair he had not before employed. He folded his copy and put it in his breast coat pocket.

"It has been a pleasure working with you, Mr. Brauerschmidt." The men shook hands and Willie returned to the hotel to take the coach, the stagecoach, that would mark the first leg of his journey home.

*Sixty-eight*_____

That afternoon Annie waited by the window. George rounded the corner of Aisquith Street and turned onto North Avenue. She noted his labored pace, his eyes focused on the pavement as if willing each step, so different from the way he used to be. He had always been serious, focused, but never like this. He had told her nothing, but she knew. She frowned and gnawed at the cuticle on her thumb. He thought he was protecting her, but he was protecting her from nothing. His reserve only served to isolate the two in their worries. For Annie, knowing, yet not knowing, was worse. And now this.

She opened the door as he entered the vestibule. "Beautiful spring day today, wasn't it?" she said, trying to set a lighter tone for the evening. He had been so quiet these past weeks, more reticent, more self-contained than usual.

George smiled when he saw his wife waiting for him, remembering an earlier day, a younger Annie, and a younger George. Life, he thought, I must make the best life for us for as long as I can. I must think of Annie.

Annie felt a lump rise in her throat. Such a fine man, such a good husband, father, she thought. I must tell him that, make sure he knows that I think that. She took his hand. "I've asked Meg to bring us some tea and sandwiches. Let us go into the front room."

George leaned against the door. "What is it? What is wrong? Has something happened to Eva?"

Annie noticed his pallor. Ashen. How long has this been? she wondered. How long since I've really looked him? How long since I would see him as I would a stranger? Something was wrong. It was

192

no longer possible to hide it, ignore it. But, for this evening, another problem was more pressing.

"Let me take your coat, George. Annie will hang it up. You sit." Annie moved her knitting from the footstool, folded his jacket over the chair.

George sat; she lifted his feet to the ottoman. "I'm not an invalid, Annie. What are you doing?" His voice was gruff. He heard its harshness, and immediately regretted it. He leaned forward to touch Annie's hair. Annie looked up. How long had it been since he had done that?

Meg entered the room carrying a tray. She had seen the touch as well. Something brewing besides the tea, she thought. She greeted George, then laid the cups and sandwiches out. She stationed herself in the hallway, out of sight, though not out of earshot.

"No, not Eva. She's fine. In fact, her weekly letter is waiting for you in the dining room. She goes with her class to Salem, Massachusetts next week, and she says that her drawing is getting better. She is happy, George. We are blessed in that.

"No, it is not --"

George interrupted her. "Then it is Celeste; it has to be Celeste. What has happened? What has she done?"

"George, she hasn't done anything. Why do you talk that way? You know how she is; she is a child. She can't help that. We must bear the blame for that, I must. I am her mother, after all."

"Annie, don't do this. Just tell me, what is wrong?" He winced; his breath caught on his last word. Annie saw him hold his stomach with his right arm.

"What is it?" Annie came to his chair.

"Nothing." He held his breath, picked up his tea cup. "What has the girl done?"

"George, have you turned on Celeste? I always thought that she was your favorite, that she was special to you. Now she worries that you don't love her anymore, that you disapprove of her." Annie paused to gather her thoughts.

"And that doesn't make what I have to say any easier. Just talk to me; tell me what is wrong."

He placed the cup and saucer on the table beside them. "Oh, Annie, my dear Annie, I am sorry. I am allowing my stomach to be the boss, and hurting my family because of it. I think it may be an ulcer. I promise to see Dr. Bergdorf about it. Soon. And meantime, lots of milk and cream for me, coat my stomach. I'll watch what I eat; you help me with it." Annie stood beside his chair and pulled her husband's head to her breast. She moved George's feet to the side of the footstool and sat before him. She took his hands in hers.

"George. Celeste wants to come home. With the baby, with Stanley. You know that she's never been happy there, and now that Willie has been away she says it has been horrible for her. She stays in her room all day, except when she takes Stanley for his walks.

"It is Clara who seems to give her the most trouble. You know, that has never been good. She's complained before, but today when they came, she was hysterical, crying so hard that I could hardly understand her. She begged us to let her come back. She is a different girl, George. I wouldn't bring this up if I weren't worried about her.

"And now she's learned that Hanne is going back to Germany. She told me that Hanne was her only friend there, that she feels that she is in a prison, and if Hanne goes she will be totally alone.

"I'm afraid that she will leave, one way or another. If we don't take her, where will she go?" Annie placed her hands in her lap.

George looked at his wife. "And what do you think is the best? That she leave her husband? What do you think that will do? Willie is a good boy. He has his hands full with his father, with Clara, with Celeste. What good will come of Celeste leaving him? To come here? What will that do? No, Annie, her place is with her husband, you know that. She belongs with Willie. Once he gets home they will have to work it out. She and her child belong with her husband."

He shifted in his seat, stretched his back. "I don't doubt that the situation is grim for her in that house. But that is the choice she has made. Willie is the one she needs to be talking to, not you. You must give her good counsel. A wife's place is with her husband, especially now that Stanley is part of their lives. You have shown her how to be a good wife. She needs to think about that."

"She said that she wanted to talk to you, that she wanted to ask you, that you would never turn her away," Annie said. "I think that she is counting on your letting her come home. I don't know what she will do if you say no."

George looked at his wife, his countenance stern. "You surprise me about this. Our job is to help Celeste see and do the right thing, not to indulge her childish wants. That is how we show that we love her. She may not see it now, but she will once she gets on the other side of this problem. We will talk to her together, help her see her way through this. Willie is a good boy; he will do the right thing."

Annie exhaled. "Of course. You are right. And you can talk to her, you can make her see. Willie can't get home too soon. *Ach*, Willie."

Sixty-nine———————————

On his San Antonio layover, Willie telegraphed his father. *Agreement completed. Willie.*

Seventy———————————

Clara entered the front room and drew the pocket doors closed. Celeste fought the feeling of being trapped. I will be strong; this is my house too. I deserve to be here as much as *la grande Clara*. I will not quake; my voice will not quiver, she said to herself. I will be strong. Though for all her resolve, she wished she had Stanley to hold onto, and was sorry that he was upstairs for his afternoon nap. What was Clara doing home this early anyway, she wondered. Should she not be lunching, playing the piano somewhere with her high-brow friends, arranging some entertainment to benefit the poor and needy?

Clara stared at Celeste. For the Celeste, the silence was worse than Clara's biting tongue. She forced herself to meet and hold Clara's gaze.

"What is it, Clara? Why have you shut the doors?"

Clara walked toward her. "You know perfectly well what the matter is. Hanne. Leaving. This is your doing. You have put such a burden on her, caring for Stanley when he is your responsibility, adding so much to her workload that she is leaving us. How could you do this to us? Your selfishness has brought even more hardship to us. I hope you are satisfied." She turned with such force that Celeste heard the swish of her taffeta underskirt.

"But don't think that our next housekeeper will do you bidding like Hanne did. Stanley is your responsibility. You will take care of him. This is a disgrace. Hanne has been with us since Willie and I were children. And now you have ruined that. She had a good life here. Now she is going back to Germany, a place that she hardly knows. This is her home. You are responsible for making her leave." Clara's face was scarlet with the effort of controlling her anger.

Celeste's heart pounded. She went to Clara, towering over her short, stout frame. I must be strong, Celeste thought, I must not let her talk to me that way.

"How dare you come in here like some kind of jailer. I am not responsible for Hanne's leaving. She loves Stanley. She would not leave because of Stanley. If she is leaving, have you thought that maybe she has no real life here? Taking care of you, of us, that is her life. Maybe she wants more. Maybe she wants a real family, not one where she is the servant, bringing you tea, or coffee, or your dessert, or your breakfast." Celeste's voice rose. "Don't you dare talk about my taking advantage of Hanne. You do it all the time and don't even see it. You need to look at yourself, Clara, before you stomp around accusing someone else, someone who has treated her with respect."

Clara leaned on the piano, then pulled herself erect. "How dare you talk to me like that? I have taught Hanne to read English, to improve her vocabulary. I want the best for her."

"How can she have the best if all her time is spent in this house, taking care of you, of us?" Celeste countered. "Where is her life? I don't blame her; I don't blame her a bit. And it is I who will miss her. You will only miss a servant, and you can replace that, I'm sure, with your fancy connections."

Celeste pulled the doors open and walked up the steps to her room. I did it, she said to herself. I stood up to her, again. I won, she thought, though she felt bad that she used the word "stomp" with Clara, an unveiled jibe at her limp. Too bad. She should have thought of that before she came in. I won.

Seventy-one

Hanne stood in her third-floor bedroom, the one she had known for the past twenty years. Home, I am going home. This America, this family, has been good to me, provided me with a place to live, good food, some money. But not a real life, she thought. So lonely.

She didn't mind the work, and she found Celeste a ray of sun, though the turmoil that she spun the family into, well, that was something to watch, like a book. She thought of Stanley. She would miss him. She hoped that he, and wonderful, sad Willie, would soon be off on their own, Willie to find his own life. Clara, who knows what would become of her, but she would be the boss, that much Hanne knew.

She held the ticket in her hand, purchased weeks ago. Third-class, just the same as when I came here. Not much progress, she thought. And who knows what I'll find when I return. *Mutti* wrote that she cried when she read that I had decided to return. I wonder if my little town will be the same. *Mutti* said that jobs are waiting for me. I hope she is right. All these American dollars I've saved. They will be a blessing.

Ha, she thought, a new life when I'm almost forty. Maybe I'll even work for the vote, like Clara. The sounds of Clara ascending the stairs interrupted her reflection. A final goodbye, Hanne thought, and remembered the years with Clara, a willful little handful when she first met her, hair in tight braids flying behind her as she raced around the house, telling everyone what to do. Hanne smiled. Some things never change. Such a disciplined child, hours spent at the piano, at her books. August's pride. Then that terrible summer. Tuberculosis, that dreaded word. But tuberculosis in the bone. No one had ever heard of that. And the treatment at Hopkins. Radiation to kill the germ, to make Clara well. And that it did, but left her crippled. Not a cripple, as Clara, the little girl Clara, once screamed to her mother.

"I am not a cripple, *Mutti*. I have trouble walking, but I am not a cripple. Don't ever say that about me again." Clara shouting, Paulina weeping, Willie watching, silent. Things were never the same in that house. Oh poor Clara, Hanne thought. Who will look after her?

"Hanne," Clara's voice at the head of the stairs. "I have brought you some books to take with you. They are in English. You must not forget your English. You must try to speak it every day, and read a chapter of a book, any book, in English, every day. It will set you apart. It will tell the world that you are intelligent. You can find work based on your knowledge of English, Hanne. You can. You do not have to stay in a little town. You can make something of yourself, Hanne, even in Germany. You can. I know it."

Clara spoke sharply, not looking at Hanne. Her eyes were red-rimmed. She placed the books on Hanne's bed and walked over to her, making no attempt made to camouflage her limp. She put her arms around the older woman.

"I want to thank you for making my childhood happy, Hanne. I will miss you more than I can say. I wish the best for you. You deserve it. And I love you." These last words were whispered into the side of Hanne's head. Hanne did not hear them.

Clara turned and, without looking back, descended the steps. Reaching her room, she closed the door. No one would hear her cry.

August left the office at noon. He had the carriage ready; the driver brought Hanne's trunk downstairs. She left her room for the last time. Celeste remained in her room across the hall, her door closed. She wouldn't join the family for this goodbye, but Hanne remembered Celeste's words to her.

"Hanne, you have meant the world to me. I don't know what Stanley and I will do without you. I will say my goodbye now."

Celeste and Clara, two girls, Hanne thought, and saw no solution to their antagonism. Poor Willie, she thought. He will have to make a choice. *Ach*, choices not so easy for him.

Paulina stood at the bottom of the stairs, weeping, holding Stanley in her arms. "Hanne, it is not too late to reconsider. You will always be part of our family. I don't know how we will manage without you. You have seen our family grow. We will never forget you." She embraced her servant, her helpmate, the baby wedged between them, and walked with her to the front door.

"I have left a note for *Herr* Willie. I will miss him. And Stanley," Hanne said. She spread her arms. Stanley mimicked her, spreading his arms and screeching, "Hanne, Hanne."

Paulina stepped back; Hanne moved to the front door. August stood waiting.

"Let us go, dear Hanne," he said. The two entered the carriage for the ride to Hanover Street and the dock. Both were quiet as it wound through the traffic of downtown Baltimore. Hanne looked out the window, trying to fix in her mind the scenes she had known for so long, the row houses, the Jones Falls, the Fish Market, the a'rabs and their wagons full of produce, the harbor, full with ships and rotting produce. This had been her life. Now back to a small town. She took her ticket from her purse, turned it over, read the German script, and wondered if she had made the right decision.

The carriage pulled up to the dock. Hanne saw *The Carpathian* towering above them. August turned to her. "Hanne, give me your ticket." She looked at her employer, nervous at his request.

"I want to give you a final gift. I do not want you to travel back to Germany with a third class ticket. I cannot give you first-class, but I can make sure you have a good room to yourself, second-class."

Hanne's eyes filled." I don't know how to thank --"

August interrupted her. "No thanks necessary, Hanne," and he left the carriage.

A few minutes later he returned with a new ticket. Handing it to her, he said, "And here is an extra gift for you. It is American money. Save it, Hanne. It is a strong currency. I don't think that you'll have, as they say here, 'a rainy day,' but this can be a little nest egg for you." He folded her fingers around the notes and led the way to the gangplank, the driver following with her trunk.

The two Germans stood together. August stroked his mustache and looked away. *"Auf Wiedersein, Hanne."* He reached out and shook her hand. He turned immediately to return to the carriage. Hanne stepped onto the ramp that would take her home. Neither looked back.

Seventy-two _____

Stanley stood in his playpen, teethed on its railings; Celeste had curled up on the sofa there, a magazine in her hand. Clara came in and sat across from her sister-in-law.

"Until *Mutti* finds a replacement for Hanne, we must make arrangements for running the house. She is at the paper with *Vati* every day that Willie is away. They are going to bring in a girl for day work, but it will be up to you and me to make sure that the household runs as it should." She paused, waiting for Celeste to look up. When she didn't, Clara cleared her throat and continued.

"To that end, I will take over the meals. I will cook. I would like you to help me serve and clean up after. Since I am cooking, I think it appropriate that you take over the household chores. We will send the laundry out, so you will not have that to do. It should not be an undue burden on you, since you live in this house and enjoy all its benefits."

Celeste had not expected Clara's proposal. She decided to approach it obliquely. "But Clara, I have Stanley to take care of. How can I possibly take care of the house as well?"

Clara was prepared. "What I have proposed should not be a burden. You need to be part of this household; you need to help. If you find it a difficulty to clean and take care of Stanley, I can look after him while you are working.

"This is what I have decided to be the best way to deal with this situation. It is temporary, after all. We both can work together, do you not think so?" Clara fixed her eyes on Celeste.

"Yes, Clara." Celeste gathered Stanley and took him to her room. She flounced on the bed. Housework, she fumed. She walked to the window. Well, Clara would be cooking; that was a lot. And she said that she would care for Stanley. And it will only be until they find another Hanne. Maybe it will be good practice for me for when Willie finds us a home of our own, until we hire a live-in.

The next morning, after Paulina had left for the newspaper, Clara presented Celeste with the cleaning schedule. "I thought it best if it were spelled out. No room for disagreement that way."

Celeste moved Stanley from her lap to let him crawl. "Floors will need to be scrubbed and swept daily if you allow him to do that," Clara pointed out. Celeste ignored her and picked up the sheet of paper. Clara had mapped out, by day, all that was expected of her. Sundays had been left free.

Celeste folded the sheet and put it in her pocket. "Thank you, Clara. I will see what I can do." Scrub and sweep, she thought. We'll see about that.

But scrub and sweep she did, as she counted the days until Willie returned home.

Across the street, George stood on his front steps as he left for work. He looked to the west, to the house where Celeste and Stanley lived, and saw his blond daughter, kitted out in a blue mattress-ticking apron, scrubbing the white marble steps of the Strauff's home. He stared. Finally, he turned back to the house.

"Annie," he called, "come here. I need to talk to you." When she came into the vestibule, he looked at his wife. "She can come home."

*Seventy-three*_____

The next morning Celeste wheeled Stanley in his carriage to visit Annie. She made a return trip with the carriage empty. Soon it was filled with diapers, baby clothes, her jewelry and as many outfits as she could carry from the third floor. She wanted to take advantage of the time when Paulina and Clara were away. A third trip and she decided that she had all that she could take for now. Before she left the house, she returned to her room, their room. She pulled out her box of blue stationary to pen a note, to Willie. This she left on the table in the vestibule, beside that of Hanne's. She closed the door, locked it and headed east. She did not look back.

Seventy-four ─────────────────

Clara saw the note as soon as she entered the quiet house. She dropped her satchel filled with music scores and headed to the stairs. She climbed to the third floor, this time not worrying about her awkwardness in ascending the steps. The front room stood as usual; the bed made, not nearly as neatly as Hanne's work. Clara entered the room and opened the wardrobe. Willie's clothes hung precisely arranged, each hanger an inch from the next. The section where Celeste's clothes hung, always a jumble (this Clara knew because this was not her first foray to this room when no one was home), was empty. She went into Stanley's room. Diapers, normally stacked on the changing table, had disappeared.

Clara returned to the first floor and went straight to the hall table. She picked up the light blue envelop, staring at Celeste's florid scrawl, "Willie." She did not hesitate as she tore it open.

> *Dearest Willie,*
>
> *I cannot stay in this house any longer. It is a prison to me and you know why. I want to be with you, but I will not return to that house. It is up to you now. You say that you want us to be a family. Then you cannot continue to be the boy in yours. Please Willie. I love you but I cannot stay here.*
>
> *Celeste*

Clara crumpled the note in her left hand. Then, rethinking her action, she smoothed it out and returned it to its envelop. *Mutti* and *Vati* would soon arrive. She would have a plan worked out by then.

When August came in, Clara showed him the note.

"This letter is to Willie, is it not?" her father asked.

Clara fumed. "This is not about privacy. This is about someone kidnapping your grandchild. Can you not see that?" Always taking Celeste's side, she thought.

"Celeste is the child's mother. This is something between her and Willie. We must decide whether to notify him of this or wait until he returns. Stay out of this, Clara. Do you not think that you have done enough?"

Clara fumed. "Oh, you are not blaming me for this? This is impossible. Why is it that I am always seen as the villain? I am your daughter, *Vater*. Can you not be loyal to me? Can you not see that I am offering you good advice?"

"Clara, *liebchen*, leave this to Willie. He will be able to reason with her. Your involvement will make things worse, believe me. You may think you are doing the best thing, but leave this to your brother."

"But Stanley. We cannot let her take Stanley from us." Clara's voice wavered; she turned her back to her father.

"Making things worse with Celeste will not bring Stanley to us. Leave this, *liebchen*. Leave this." He reached to take his daughter into his arms, remembering how long it had been since he had last held her. Clara pulled away.

Mutti, she thought, *Mutti* will listen to reason.

Seventy-five —————————————

Celeste slept in her room, her old bed, Stanley pressed in beside her. The house was quiet.

Annie sat at her dressing table and rubbed lotion into her elbows. George came into the room and closed the door. Annie saw his reflection in her mirror. He is not well, she thought. And now this.

He turned back the spread and fluffed up the pillows. Annie went to sit on the bed beside him.

"What do you think will happen, George? How long should we allow her to stay? What will become of them?"

George took her hand. "Ah, Annie, I don't know what to say. You know Willie would have made a better match with Eva. She would have made a man of him, supported him, and I think that he would have made her happy, the two of them sitting and talking books."

He put her hand down, held the top of his head. "Why did I think of that? Not good, I know. But Celeste, she is such a child, even with all this unhappiness around her. She needed –" George stopped himself. "Well, no matter. Willie will be home soon and he will take care of it. Once she sees him, she'll go back. And all this will be a tempest in a teapot. So let us not worry. Let Celeste enjoy her days here. I have no doubt that life was made very difficult for her while Willie was away. And then with the servant leaving. Well, all will be well when Willie comes back. Not to worry."

Seventy-six

Clara sat at the dinner table. She had made the meal and brought it up on the dumbwaiter. August sat. "Let us have a meal in peace. Let us not discuss this afternoon's activity. At least let us have an hour of peace," August said. The meal was eaten in silence.

Finally, Clara spoke. "I cannot be quiet any longer about this. We must tell Willie. He must do something. We cannot let her take Stanley. If she doesn't come back, if she doesn't let us have Stanley, then we should do something. We cannot let her get away with this."

August moved his plate to the side, folded his hands and placed them on the table. "Clara, I will not say it again. This is none of your business. Do you understand that? Keep out of this.

"I have decided to wait until Willie arrives home before notifying him of Celeste's leaving. He is already on the way; he can't get here any faster. There is nothing that he can do from such a distance. I will meet his train and tell him. And then he will decide what to do. If he asks for my advice I will talk to him. Clara, you are not to get involved in this. You do understand me." August looked hard at his daughter.

Why, he thought, are we at loggerheads so much, my beloved one. His eyes softened. Hers did not.

Seventy-seven _____

August was waiting at Camden Station when Willie's train pulled in. He stood at the doorway as the passengers filed through. He saw his son leave the car and walk slowly toward the station. Willie's walk is labored, August thought, not the spry step of a young man who has just concluded a successful business trip. Tired, that is it, he is just tired. Well, no matter, after two weeks of travel, anyone would be weary and exhausted. And what I have to tell him will only drain him more.

Willie saw his father as he neared the station, surprised that he was there. Perhaps another congratulation. That certainly would be in order, he thought.

"*Vati*, a surprise. Nice to see you," Willie said as he shook the older man's hand. "Should we go directly to the office, or head home? I would like very much to see Celeste and Stanley. It has been a grueling two weeks. I have missed them, and you and *Mutti*, of course."

August took Willie's arm and led him to the Gentlemen's Waiting Room. "Willie, we will go home directly, but there are some things we need to discuss." The two men sat on one of the long wooden benches. The room was empty except for them and another small group who sat by the window.

"*Sohn*, much has happened since you left for Texas. It is hard for me to believe that it has only been two weeks. First of all, Hanne has left us. She decided to return to Germany. You can imagine how difficult this has been for all of us." Willie started to respond, but August stopped him.

"However, that is not the most distressing event," August continued. Willie opened his mouth to speak, but August raised his hand to continue. "Willie, you know that Celeste has had a difficult time getting used to living in our home. She has not had an easy time of it, that I will admit. And it seems that, with you away, that time became even more difficult for her."

"*Vati,* what is it? W-what are you saying? Has s-something h-happened to Celeste? To the b-baby? Tell me." Willie struggled to get his voice under control.

August cleared his throat. "*Nein, nein,* not to worry about that. They are fine. It is just that Celeste has taken Stanley and returned to her mother's house. She has left our house, Willie. She did leave a note for you. I think when you read it you will understand more.

"This is a terrible thing for our family, and you must do what you can to make it right. Pay no attention to Clara. You must work this out, Willie. You must be a strong husband and get your wife under control."

"When did she leave? How long has she been gone? Why did no one wire me about this?"

"It happened just a few days ago. You were already on your way home. It was I who decided not to get in touch with you. I wanted you to come home strong to deal with this, not even more exhausted with worry." August paused. He had no more words for his son.

"Let me go to Celeste," Willie said. "I will come to the house after I see her. I must see her and Stanley." August nodded and the two men left the station and entered the carriage. The driver stopped first at the Wells's home. "I will see you, *Vater.* Thank you for telling me," Willie said, and left the carriage without looking back.

211

Seventy-eight _____

Willie rang the bell. Celeste was not surprised to see him at the door; she knew that he would come. But his appearance disappointed her. Bedraggled, thin, weak, he was not the strong man she had fantasized coming to her rescue, sweeping her into his arms, kissing her, telling her that he would do anything for her, telling her that their house was ready, calling a carriage and taking her to her fine house on Mt. Vernon Place.

He tried to take her into his arms. She flinched and backed away.

"We must talk, Celeste. Tell me what has happened. Tell me what is wrong."

She walked to the front room; he followed.

"My note said it all. I cannot live in that house. It is too awful for me. We are married. We need a house of our own."

Willie reasoned with her, telling her of his meeting in Texas, promising that he would have more money soon, pledging that they would get a place of their own if only she would give him time. He saw that she was not convinced. "Is your mother here? Can we talk with her? Please, Celeste, please come home."

"Don't expect Mama to take your side, Willie. Don't expect Mama to do your work for you."

Annie heard them and came to sit with the pair. She looked at Willie, sad, pale, unhappy, and promised that she would talk with Celeste. She struggled to explain just how miserable Celeste was living with his parents, with Clara.

Finally, Celeste stood. "You talk about me as if I were not in the room, as if I were a child. Willie, it is you who are the child." She looked at her husband, her eyes hard, without compassion. "I want you to leave this house. Don't come back here, Willie. Don't come back until you have a place for us to live. I mean it. I will not see you until you have done that. That is my condition of seeing you again." She walked toward the stairway. "And don't think you'll see Stanley either."

Annie sat with Willie; they didn't speak. Finally she said, "Can you do what she asks, son?" Willie nodded. "Go home then. Get some rest. Find a house for your family." Annie kissed him on the cheek and he returned to the house across the street. She saw him stumble when he reached the sidewalk. He righted himself and started his journey.

*Seventy-nine*_____

Willie managed to walk to the corner at North Avenue and Holbrook Street. He coughed, then leaned against the lamppost and vomited into the gutter. A passerby looked away, repulsed, but stopped when he saw Willie take a white handkerchief from his pocket and wipe his mouth. He approached, asked if Willie needed help. Willie refused, politely. He folded his handkerchief and noted the stains. Holding back his sobs, he continued his journey home.

Paulina stood in the vestibule; she went to him as he mounted the front steps. "Oh, Willie, I am so glad to see you," she said, wrapping him in her arms. "Come, come inside. We will talk. We will get you a cup of tea, something to eat. We will make this right, somehow."

Willie stood straight, braced himself to speak. "Thank you, *Mutti.* Where is Celeste's note?" Paulina started to go to the hall table. Two letters waited there, one from Hanne, the other from Celeste. Willie picked up the blue envelope. "Who has opened this?" he asked, his face flushed with anger.

Paulina chose not to answer. "Come, come onto the sun porch. Let me fix you something to eat. Let me call you father. He can talk to you. He can help; he can make this right."

"*Mutti*, stop, please. No one can make this right except for me. Who opened my letter?" Paulina looked away.

"It was Clara, wasn't it? She could not even respect my privacy in such a personal manner. It was she who opened this, wasn't it? Tell me, *Mutti.* It was she, no?"

Paulina nodded, and reached for her son. "But she is not home now, Willie. Let us concentrate on what is most important. You can talk to Clara later. Yes, it was wrong of her to do that, but you know that she has only your best welfare in her mind. She wants to help you. You know that. Sometimes she does not go about it in the best manner."

Willie banged his fist against the wall. Paulina flinched.

"Have I no privacy? Have I no standing in this house. It is no wonder that Celeste has left. I must have my family. I must get my family back. I cannot do that living in this house. Surely, *Mutti*, you see that."

August had come onto the porch as Willie spoke. He led his wife to the sofa. "Let Willie speak, Lina. We must listen to his thoughts."

Willie addressed his father. "Celeste will not come back to this house. That is her mandate to me. She will not consider coming back until I have a home for her. That I must do. I promised her that, months ago. So I must find a place to live, a place for us."

August turned toward Paulina. "Can you give us some time alone?" he asked, his tone gentle. "There are business items we must discuss--"

Willie interrupted. "This is not a time to discuss business, *Vater*. I must make plans."

August waited until Paulina was out of earshot. "Willie, you must know what the facts are as you make plans. I wanted to wait to talk to you about this, wanted you to recover from the rigors of your journey. But now we must face facts; you must face facts. Please do not share this with your mother or Clara." He walked toward the garden, waited before he continued.

"The paper cannot pay you the salary that you need to afford a home of your own. There are the cold facts as they say here. I don't know what else to say. I can certainly pay your living expenses while you are under my roof, yours, Celeste's, Stanley's, but there is not enough revenue coming in, even with your Texas arrangement, to pay you a wage to keep a wife and child. This should not be a surprise to you, Willie. You see the subscription numbers; you see the returns. You are not a child. You must have discerned how little takings the paper has."

Willie's head pounded. He pressed his temples to lessen the throbbing. "I cannot think about this now, *Vater*." He looked at August.

"I do understand what you have said. My mind is reeling. I cannot think. I must be by myself now. I hope that you understand."

August reached for his son, put his hand on Willie's shoulder. "Go rest. I will have *Mutti* bring some tea, some sandwiches, a sweet, to your room. Eat; have a bath; get some rest. We can talk about this tomorrow. It will work out, Willie. She will come home to be your wife. Just rest now."

Paulina stood in the hallway and watched her son climb the stairs.

Eighty_____

Two evenings had passed; Willie remained in his room. Paulina brought his meals to him. August had directed Clara to stay away from the third floor, to let Willie work this out on his own. Willie had agreed to accompany August to work the following morning. He would be back to normal; they would talk then.

Franz greeted Willie when he arrived at the office the next day. The boy looks grey, he thought. The Texas meeting a failure, he assumed.

At noon, Willie went to his father's office. "*Vati*, the throbbing in my head is so bad, I must leave. I am sorry that I am not stronger for you. I think that once I lie down it will be better. Could we talk this evening? Would that suit you?"

August had an engagement that evening, but told Willie to go home and rest. They would talk later. He arranged for a carriage.

Willie prayed that the house would be quiet; that *Mutti* would not be there to cluck over him, that Clara would be out. Before he turned the key in the lock, the sounds of Beethoven came to his ears. She's home, he thought, and made a silent plea that her passion for music would prevail over her passion for imparting advice.

She heard the door open and lifted her fingers from the keys. She recognized Willie's step. Sick, she thought, sick again. She walked to the hallway.

"Willie, are you not well?" she asked, resolving to be kind, helpful to this brother whom she loved. "Let me bring you some tea. Why don't you sit in the sun room? I can use the dumbwaiter."

Willie nodded and Clara went to the kitchen. He sat, willing his head to stop aching. Maybe a cup of tea would help. And he had to stop avoiding Clara, that he knew.

She soon returned and set out the light meal. "Willie, I know that you think I interfere. I know that you are offended because I opened Celeste's letter to you. I want to apologize for that. I have no excuse. It was an unpardonable act, I acknowledge that and I hope that you will forgive me."

Willie looked up, not quite trusting this unfamiliar aspect of Clara. His head throbbed. He reached for the tea that Clara had poured. He didn't mind the silence. Clara did.

"I have been thinking about the best way to handle this situation, Willie. You cannot let Celeste get away with this, with telling you what to do. You are her husband; she must obey you. You are the one to tell her what life will be like, where you will live. She cannot tell you. That will not do. She will never respect you if you do not act the man.

"Now I know that you cannot drag her back. But you must get the child. She is not capable to raising a child, Willie. You know that; she is a child herself. You must get Stanley and bring him here. Tell her that she cannot see him until she sees reason. Tell her that her leaving you shows everyone that she cannot be trusted, that she cannot raise a child. Let her stew about that for a while." Clara became more sure of her plan as she spoke.

"She will come back; she will beg you to take her back. Where she lives will be the least of her worries."

Willie slammed down his cup. Tea splattered; the cup split into even halves. He looked at Clara. "Leave me alone. Can you not leave me alone? Do you think you are making things better for me? Do you care about my happiness at all? Is it all about you getting your way? Can you not just leave me in peace?"

*Eighty-one*_____

Willie had finished dressing and was sitting on the edge of the bed. He willed himself to venture downstairs, to start his day in the normal way, to go to work, to get though the day. He walked to the mirror to comb his hair a final time. He saw Clara's reflection. She came into the room.

"Willie, please, we are family. Let us not be like this with each other." Willie stood firm; he did not to face her. Clara went to him. "It is just that you cannot allow her to treat you this way; you cannot allow her to treat the family this way. Stanley is your child, your son. You must not let her take him away, play you for a fool. You must bring Stanley here. I have been thinking about this. I have talked to *Mutti*." She reached for his arm.

"Go and get Stanley; go and bring him here. We can keep him until she comes to her senses. If you do this, you will show her that you are the husband, that she must do what you say. You want to be a family, you want this? Then you must act."

Willie turned to face her; his fists were clenched at his side. "Clara, can you leave me? Can you leave me in peace in my own room? Why do you hector me like this? What is it you want?" A wave of nausea came, a flash of heat throughout his body. Perspiration soaked his undergarments.

"Willie, I am saying this because it is important, to you, to the family. I know about these things. You do not. You must act like a man. You must get your son."

"Clara, stop it, stop it. I cannot stand this, can you not see? I cannot stand this." Willie pushed past his sister and ran down the steps. Clara heard the front door slam. She looked out of the third floor window to see her brother running east on North Avenue, to Celeste.

219

PART II

Baltimore Sun
June 19, 1903

SUES TO REGAIN HER BABY
Mrs. Celeste W. Strauff Says, Child Was
Taken From Her.

Mrs. Celeste A. Strauff obtained a writ
of habeas corpus yesterday for the purpose
of regaining possession of her 10 months
old infant Stanley Wells Strauff who, she
alleges, was forcibly taken from her by her
husband and the infant's father, William
Strauff. The writ was obtained yesterday
morning through William Colter attorney,
and was directed against Mr Strauff and
his parents, Mr and Mrs August Strauff.
The Court ordered the writ to be served at
once, and the deputy sheriff soon returned
with Mr Strauff s parents, who said their
son had left their house with the child
Further proceedings in the case were then
postponed until this morning before Judge
Harlan

Mrs Strauff said that while she was
standing in the doorway of her parents'
home, 1123 East North avenue, last Tuesday
her husband came up and grabbed the child
out of her arms she then said her husband
told her he intended to take the child out
of the state and that she would never see
the baby again it is supposed Mr Strauff

221

took the child to the home of his parents,
1108 East North avenue.

Mr and Mrs Strauff, it is said, ran
away about two yers ago and were married
at Towson her maiden name was Wells they
separated recently and since then Mrs
Strauff has been living with her parents
Her husband also lived with his parents,
across the street

At the time of her marriage Mrs Strauff
was attending the Eastern High School.

Baltimore Sun
June 20, 1903

SAYS HUSBAND TOOK BABY
Mrs. Celeste A. Strauff Asks The Police To
Help Find It
SAD SEQUEL TO AN ELOPEMENT
Wife Testifies Husband Seised Infant From
Her And Ran To His Mother's Home—Both
Disappear

Mrs Celeste A. Strauff yesterday asked
Police Marshal Rarnan to aid her in
locating her husband. William Strauff, who
is charge by her with having taken from
her by force their 10-months-old infant,
Stanley Wells Strauff. Mrs Strauff sought
the aid of the police after her attempt
to learn the whereabouts of the infant
and regain his custody by habeas corpus
proceedings had proved unsuccessful.

The writ of habeas corpus was directed
at Mrs. Strauff's husband and his parents,
Mr. and Mrs August Strauff. In obedience
to the summons Mr. and Mrs. August Strauff
appeared in Judge Harlan's court yesterday
morning. Their son was not with them,
and neither was their infant grandson.
They repeated the statement they made in
court Thursday, that they did not know the
whereabouts of their son and grandson,

and as their statement was not disproved the writ was dismissed as to them.

Mrs. Celeste Strauff is a decided blonde, with a mass of light colored hair, blue eyes and a fair complexion. She said when giving her testimony that she and her husband ran away to Towson to be married and separated about five weeks ago. Before the separation she and her husband were living with his parents at 1108 East North avenue Since the separation she and her child have been living with her parents, Mr and Mrs. George W Wells, 1123 East North avenue, just across the street from her husband's parents

Mrs. Strauff said her husband rang the doorbell of her parents home about 12:30 P M last Tuesday, and when she answered the ring with the child in her arms he grabbed the little fellow from her and made off across the street Mrs. Strauff declared that she followed her husband as soon as she could, but she was not permitted to enter the home of his parents No one answered her persistent ringing of the bell and rapping on the door Her husband, she said, threatened to cut her throat if she attempted to get the child Mrs Strauff saw her husband Wednesday evening At that time he said he would return the child to her the next evening He did not keep his promise, and she does not know where he is

Mrs George W Wells, mother of Mrs Strauff, corroborated her daughter as in the taking of the child by his father

Mrs. William Kline, 11 East North avenue, testified that she saw Mr Strauff go into the home of his wife and come out with the child He took the child across the street and into his parents' house The child's mother ran across the street after her husband and banged at the door and rang the bell of the Strauff house, but she was not admitted

Mrs. John Guy, 1121 East North avenue, next door to the home of Mr and Mrs Wells, testified that she heard Mrs Strauff screaming after the child had been taken, and that was the first she knew of any trouble

William Colton, attorney for Mrs Strauff, called upon both Mr. and Mrs Strauff to testify in the case. They both denied knowing where their son is They said their son has consumption and his mother said he purposed some time ago going with her to Asheville, N.C. and that he had a railroad ticket for that place. The last time they saw their son, they said, was about 7 A M Wednesday at their home. Mr. Colton made a close inquiry as to Mrs Strauff's relatives, in hopes of learning whether the infant had been taken to one of them. William C Smith appeared as attorney for Mr. and Mrs August Strauff

Baltimore American
June 20, 1903

HUSBAND AND CHILD HAVE DISAPPEARED
William Strauff's Parents Testify That They Do Not Know His Whereabouts

In the case of Mrs. Celeste A. Strauff against William Strauff, her husband, and his parents, Mr. and Mrs. August Strauff, to recover possession of her 10-month-old child, Judge Harlan yesterday dismissed the petition for a writ of habeas corpus as against Mr. and Mrs. August Strauff.

As before reported, Mrs. Celeste A. Strauff and her husband are now separated, and a few days ago, as alleged, her husband took forcible possession of the child and carried him away. Mrs. John Guy, 1121 East

North avenue; Mrs. William Klein, Mrs. Annie Wells, 1123 East North avenue, the mother of young Mrs. Strauff, and the latter herself all testified as to William Strauff taking away the child. Mr. and Mrs. August Strauff both testified that they were not aware of the whereabouts of their son or of the child, and there was nothing for Judge Harlan to do as to them except to dismiss the petition.

One

August sensed an uneasy quiet as he entered the house. No music, no sounds or smells of dinner cooking. Something untoward had happened that day, that he knew.

"Lina, Clara, are you home?" he called. Silence. He looked to his right, to the table in the vestibule. No note.

He walked up the stairs, looked into Clara's room, glanced into his and Paulina's. All was quiet, normal. He climbed to the third floor. The door to Willie's room was closed. August knocked. He had expected Willie to come to the office. Willie's headaches had returned, but August believed that the boy was doing his best to conquer them. If something had happened to Willie, Paulina would have contacted me, he thought; she would have left some kind of note.

He opened the door to find Willie, ashen-faced, lying on the bed, fully dressed, even to his shoes.

"Willie, what is wrong? What happened? Where is your mother?"

Willie sat up, put his head in his hands. August bristled, "This is no time to wallow, Willie. Tell me what happened. What is wrong? Pull yourself together, son. Now." August was unapologetic for his harsh words; the boy could not stew in this misery that had befallen him. August stopped himself from slapping his son. He took a breath and waited for Willie to respond.

"The baby --" Willie started.

August interrupted him. "Has something happened to Stanley? Tell me. What is the trouble here? What is going on, Willie?" August felt his patience break. He turned away from his son, swallowed, then turned back.

"*Vater*, I have ruined things. Stanley --"

227

"Just tell me what the hell happened, boy. Out with it."

"I took him. Clara --" Willie stopped. He would not blame this on Clara; he would stand up to what he had done. "I took him, *Vater*. I saw Celeste and grabbed him and brought him here. She came running after; we wouldn't let her in. It was terrible. I think that the police were here. I didn't answer the door."

"Where are they? Where is the boy?" August said.

"*Mutti* and Clara have him. They left by back door, the alley. They're going to Washington; Stanley will stay with Julius. They went to Camden Station; I don't know how they planned to get there. They said for me to stay here and not answer the door."

Willie walked toward his father. "I have made a t-t-terrible m-m-mistake, *Vater*. I know I need to face the c-consequences, but I don't know w-what to do. I would have taken the b-baby b-back, but now he is gone. The p-police, scandal, for you, for Celeste. I have ruined everything."

August stood in place, working to keep his composure, trying to work out a best way to manage the situation. He faced his son. His anger prevailed.

"What a cockamamie thing to do. What in God's name were you thinking? Did Clara put you up to this? Was she involved in this? Tell me. I want the truth."

Willie saw his father's face, red with anger. "I must take responsibility for this, *Vater*. I did this. I acted alone."

August paced the length of the room. "I must talk to your mother. She left no note. That is not like her at all. When did they go? How was she when they left?"

"Clara seemed in charge, *Vater*. She had the idea. She said that she would handle things. She said that they would try to be back this evening." Willie stepped toward his father. "I know that I have disappointed you, again. But Clara is right. Stanley is a Strauff. He needs to be with us. She is right there, isn't she?"

August turned to walk out of the room. "I must think. I must think. And yes, do not answer the door. We need time to think."

August returned to the first floor. He first went to the dining room and poured a glass of whiskey, larger than his usual two-fingers.

228

He took off his suit coat and hung it on the back of one of the dining room chairs, the one that Celeste had used, and walked to the back of the house. He stood, looking out at the yard. He noticed that the spring flowers had wilted, not yet replaced by summer's annuals, Paulina too busy running the house, helping out at the paper, missing Hanne. What a time she has had, August thought. She deserves better.

He sat down in the sun porch. Stanley's toys remained, no longer scattered, but placed in his toy box, awaiting his return. He remembered Clara's and Willie's toys in this same room. His eyes rested on the tea service, hurriedly left on the table near the door, dregs remaining in the cups. Dresden, he recognized, brought back by Paulina from one of their trips back to Germany.

What has happened to my family? Willie, Celeste, Stanley, Clara, such turmoil. And now this. I am the man, the *Pater Familias*, August thought, liking that Latin phrase. Now my family is in disarray. He closed his eyes and smiled at his understatement. He pictured them: Willie, distraught, sick on top of it; Paulina, rushing to her cousin, surely telling him their personal business, business which should stay under this roof; Clara, so hateful, so frustrated and angry that her good intentions are misunderstood, so sure that she knows best. He thought of Celeste, such a willful child, nowhere near ready for marriage or motherhood. It was her thoughtless actions that had brought this tumult upon them. What was she thinking in that house across the street? How were the Wellses managing? Had the police visited their home as well? What scandal she had caused, had Willie caused?

It is up to me to restore tranquility, equilibrium to this household, some peace, he thought. He missed Hanne's presence; how much easier it would be if she were still here. So many changes.

He put his hands on his knees and pushed himself up. Standing straight, he decided. I will talk to Willie, bring him to his senses. When Paulina and Clara return I will talk to them as well. I will make sure that this situation is resolved.

Returning to Willie's room, he addressed his son, who stood staring out the window, looking at the trees of the cemetery. "Come, let

229

us take dinner. Dunlop's. It will be good for us to walk there. Good air for you, clear your head a bit. We will talk about this. We will devise a way to make it right. Come, dress. I will meet you in the hallway in ten minutes. Come, Willie, it will do you good."

Two————————————————————————

Willie, smelling lightly of Bay Rum, joined his father in the vestibule. August suggested that they leave by the back door. Two blocks to the west, they turned onto North Avenue; after fourteen more blocks they reached Howard Street. August noticed that Willie had difficulty keeping to his pace, and hoped that a hearty dinner would remedy this. The pair entered Dunlop's Restaurant fifty minutes later. Willie's face was drenched with perspiration.

When they were seated, August addressed his son. "Willie, I am concerned about your health. Let us deal with that first off. You must work hard to regain your strength, your vigor. You cannot begin to address the issues you face until that happens. Fresh air, exercise, good food. I believe you have not recovered from your trip west. Then to come home and face your, ah, domestic situation, well that has affected you both physically and mentally. You do not have the strength at this time to cope. Hanne's leaving, the unrest of our own household, has obviously added to your predicament." August placed the starched linen napkin in his lap.

"So, I believe it is this that is the cause of your precipitous, perhaps calamitous, action where Stanley is concerned. Therefore, before we can address the resolution of that issue, I must insist that you concentrate on your health. Hearty meals, yes, that is a start. And we will start with this evening."

August ordered for the pair: fortified beer, Jaegerschnitzel, red cabbage, dumplings. That, he thought, should toughen up the boy. When the food arrived, August hungrily tucked into his plate. Willie picked up his stein and drank. He knew it would ill-advised not to finish this meal that seemed so important to his father.

Willie put down his knife and fork and looked at August. "I want to apologize again, *Vati.*"

August stopped him. "Let us not belabor that, my boy. You had a major lapse in judgment, no doubt due to the stress of the situation. Now you must eat. We will talk about what to do after the meal. I think there is a way that we can work this out. My question to you, and I want you to think about this before you answer, is what is that you want? What kind of life do you want for you, for Celeste, for your boy? You must answer me honestly. I will do what I can to advise you, but you must be the one to take this situation as your own. You must be the one to handle it. You must act like a grown man, not a boy."

Willie looked at his father, saw a man successful, sure of himself, the husband of a wife who respected him, who honored him, who loved him, a man who would never tolerate his wife taking his child and returning to her mother. Willie felt himself to be a photographic negative of August. His father had the strength that he lacked. Willie swallowed his sense of shame, of failure, together with the veal.

Three

Willie was silent during the long walk home. They turned north at Aisquith Street and entered the house from the alleyway. Lights shone from the back of the house. Paulina and Clara sat in the sun porch. Paulina looked up as August entered; she stood and embraced her son.

Clara went to her father. "We did what we needed to do, *Vater*. We took care of the situation. The child is as much Willie's as it is Celeste's. He is a Strauff; he should be raised as one. When Willie brought him home, we thought it best that he be taken somewhere safe, at least until the situation is resolved." She had rehearsed this speech in her mind on the train ride home. Stanley was safe at her cousin's home.

August looked at her. "The situation cannot continue, Clara. I don't know what you were thinking when you took the child away, but we must deal with what has been done. The day has been a long one for all of us."

August looked over at his wife; she appeared to be as distraught as his son. "Let us get some rest. Willie, you will have to see Celeste tomorrow, try to calm the situation down. You can think about what you will say to her. She must return as your wife. That is how it must be.

"Clara, please bring a pot of tea upstairs to your mother and me. Willie, help her with the tray." August reached for his wife's hand. "Come, Lina. Let us go to our room." Willie and Clara were silent as they descended to the kitchen. When the tea was ready, he brought it to his parents' room.

"I am sorry, *Mutti, Vater*. All I can say is that I am sorry."

"Enough apologies. Use your energy to plan tomorrow," August said. "Good night. I hope that your sleep is sound."

As Willie turned to leave, Paulina walked to the door and kissed him goodnight.

August expected Paulina to begin dressing for bed. Instead she stood, motioned for August to sit in the chair in the bay window. "Let us talk about this, August. I have been thinking, thinking of a way that we could make this right." August was surprised at his wife's strength. He looked up at her, nodded for her to continue.

"What Willie did was rash, but it is not against the law. He did not kidnap, could not kidnap, his own child. He took the child to be better cared for. Celeste has shown that she is not a fit mother, running away like that. Anyone can see that George Wells is a sick man. He will not be able to offer the child a stable home. And not even properly baptized. Anyone, well, any Catholic, would see that that just will not do.

"Now, I think that we should leave the child with Julius for a while, see that he is properly baptized, and see that he has a proper name, your name August. That is how it should have been. Once that is taken care of, we can see about Celeste. She is too young, too immature to be a proper wife, much less a proper mother. We must convince Willie of that. We could offer her an enticement so that she could start a new life for herself. As pretty as she is, that would not be hard for her. Yes, we can offer her something and then raise the baby as our own. We can somehow have that marriage annulled, give Willie a new start."

Paulina paused, grateful for her mornings of studying new English words, pleased with her ability to reason with August, proud to meet him as an equal. Clara had helped her rehearse on the train back from Washington.

August looked at his wife. What had brought about these changes, he wondered. She talked of raising this child, when she had yet to call him by his given name, cooing about him, calling him *liebchen*, darling boy, but never Stanley?

Before he could respond, Paulina continued. "Willie has done nothing wrong. He has taken his own child. He will take care of his own child. You must support him in this. It is the only way not to bring scandal to this house. We will support our son, August." Paulina delivered this pronouncement with more force than August had seen in his wife.

"We will keep the baby away from Celeste until the matter is resolved. I think that she will listen to reason. Perhaps her mother will help her see that this is the best way for everyone, especially the child. He will have a fine life with us. We will be able to give him what she cannot. She chose to leave Willie. She must pay the price for that rash action."

How different their thinking was, August thought. Here she is standing over me, lecturing, such a different Paulina, like Clara. "What you say, Lina, I will think about it." August paused. "We both will think about it, sleep on it, as they say here. Maybe you are right."

The next morning, August sent word to Franz that he would not be in that day. It was August who opened the door to the sheriff; it was August who accepted the blue envelop; it was August who read that he, Paulina, and Willie were to appear before the magistrate. He thanked the sheriff and said that he and his wife would comply. Closing the door, August walked into the sun porch. He stood at the window, working to stop his mind from racing. The paper, the household, Stanley, Willie, Clara. Such a maelstrom. How to work things out, how to restore peace to this house, to his life.

On the following day, Willie remained in his room. August and Paulina, with their attorney, appeared in court, testified that they had no knowledge of the whereabouts of their son or grandson. The writ was dismissed. When they arrived home, August directed Willie to leave the city. That afternoon, Willie boarded the train for New York. He would stay with relatives in Courtland. Clara helped him pack his bags.

Across the street, Celeste stood sentinel at her bedroom window, watching the house across the street, waiting for any sign of Willie. Annie sat at the dining room table, thinking. George was worse. He was to see the doctor the following week.

Four

On the sixth day of July in the year of Our Lord 1903, at The Church of the Mother of God, St. Mary's, Washington, D.C., wearing his father's christening gown, Stanley Wells Strauff was christened William August Julius Strauff. Godparents were August Strauff and Julius Griebel. His paternal grandmother and aunt were also in attendance.

What poppycock, August thought, as he stood for the ceremony, all this ado. But he went along with it; it was important to Paulina. She believed that the child now was saved. From what, August wondered. It had been Paulina's idea to give Stanley the name she thought he should have had in the first place. "It is only right," she said. August silently agreed.

Clara remained silent about the midnight baptism those months ago. And the name, yes, she agreed, it was only right.

Five

Willie, in New York, spent his days alone, thinking of Celeste, of Stanley, struggling to find a way to make things right, grappling with what a proper man would do. His evenings were spent with his uncle, loyal to August, but clear in his disapproval of Willie's actions and the part that his parents played in them. The family had not condemned Willie. On the contrary, they tried to understand. Willie had confided in his Uncle Gerhard, talked from his heart, and the old German seemed to know what he was trying to say.

"Go back," he said. "What is this saying about you that you ran away? Not a good thing, my boy. Not good at all. Find your son. Take him to his mother. It was an atrocity to take him as you did, you know that. Do not listen to anyone but yourself. Your conscience will tell you what is right. And I will tell you what is right. Get the boy; get your wife; find a job away from your father, away from his business. Find your own life. You have too many talents that you do not recognize, that are hidden from you because you don't believe that you can stand up for yourself. Go back, beg your wife's forgiveness, then tell her what she must do. Be the man, Willie. Leave the house of your father; return only as a visitor. You will see. You will have your good life."

Willie believed him and followed his counsel.

Willie rang the bell and waited for Meg to let him in. He heard the maid call to Annie, who now was behind her. Meg stepped away as the door opened, and Annie looked at her son-in-law, then drew a breath. "Oh, Willie, what have you done?" she said as she ushered him into the front room.

"Mrs. Wells, I am trying to make this right. I am Celeste's husband. She needs to return to her home with me," Willie said. His eyes were downcast; his arms lay at his sides.

"You know this is the worst thing you could have done. Where is Stanley? What have you done with him? Do you realize the scandal that you have brought upon us? Do you know how ill Celeste's father is? Do you think of anyone other than yourself?" Annie's voice shook with anger.

"You must make it right, Willie. Bring Stanley back here. Then you and Celeste can work things out. What did you think would be gained by your taking the boy? What?" Annie struggled to keep her voice modulated. She did not want to disturb George. She did not want to bring Celeste downstairs to continue her hysterical outbursts. She wanted her home back, her peace of mind; she wanted George to be well again.

Willie stood straight, willed himself not to stammer. "Mrs. Wells, Stanley is my son. I have a right to him. Celeste wants a strong husband. I will be that. I must show her who rules the house. She cannot desert me, leave me a note to find when I return from my trip. She humiliated me. I cannot have that. I have to show her. She must listen to reason; she must return to her rightful home."

Annie looked at Willie, saw him struggling to be someone he wasn't. She put out her hand to him. "Talk to Celeste; bring Stanley back. You will be able to work things out then. But never this way."

The pair heard Celeste descend the stairs. She had brushed her hair and changed into a fresh outfit, white, with flecks of yellow. It was one of Willie's favorites. She stood in the doorway. "How dare you come into my home? You bring my child back. You had no right to take him from me. He is my child, Willie. How could you do such a thing?"

"Let him speak, Celeste." Annie moved to the door. "I will leave you two alone. Nothing will be accomplished by this bitterness. Stanley is safe, is he not, Willie? You will assure us of that?"

Willie nodded to Annie, but his eyes were on Celeste. Annie pulled the room's pocket doors closed as she left.

Willie took Celeste's hand; she didn't pull away. He led her to the settee. "Celeste, what I did, I did for us, to try to get you to listen to reason. I want us to be together. I love you. We belong together. I want us to be a family. Stanley is fine, but I will not let you see him until you come to your senses. I am doing this for you, for us. Please believe me. I will get the money for us to have our own home, but it will take time. I need you by my side; I need you to be my wife."

Celeste noticed the dark circles under Willie's eyes. She knew that he was suffering. But I am suffering too, she thought. He has no right to expect me to live in that horrible house. He wants us to be a family. He must provide a home for us, a home of our own.

She stood, smoothed the skirt of her dress, adjusted the white stand-up collar. "Get us our own house, Willie. If you want me to come back, get us a house." She turned and left the room. The doors remained open. Willie let himself out.

Six _____

Annie's days circled to a new normal. Her thoughts moved between Celeste and George. Once in a while she thought of her grandson, hoped that he was adjusting to wherever he was. So many changes for that baby, she thought. No mother, no Hanne, for Annie knew that Hanne had been the one to care for Stanley while he lived across the street. With strangers now. She wished him well, wished that she was a praying woman. Too late for that now, she thought, not the time to learn when you are in the middle of a jumble. She smiled to herself. A jumble, she thought. If only.

George continued to rise each morning, dress silently, now unable to swallow his morning coffee before he left for work. His clothes hung on him, his collar so loose that his necktie could not hide it. Annie wondered if Celeste saw this change in her father. No need to add to her worries, she thought, no need to add to the responsibilities that Eva had taken on with her studies. Theirs had always been a quiet house, except for Celeste's banter. Annie missed that. Even Celeste was quiet. Now the house was a hushed one, the inhabitants quiet with their own thoughts, worries.

Celeste stood at the window of her bedroom most days. Her tears had dried. She too tried to find a rhythm to her days.

And then they found the baby.

**Baltimore Sun
July 11, 1903**

MRS. STRAUFF GETS BOY BACK
*Friend Got On The Trail And Followed It
To Highlandtown*

Probably the happiest woman in Baltimore
is Mrs. Celeste A. Strauff, 1123 East North
Avenue, the cause of her joy being the
recovery of her 11 months-old boy, Stanley
Wells Strauff, who has been sought for by
police, detectives and friends since June
16, when, she says, the child was taken
by force from her arms by her husband,
William Strauff.

Mr. William Hall, 1219 East North
avenue, and Mr. Carroll Mann, 1183 East
North avenue, both intimate of friends of
Mrs. Strauff and of her parents, Mr. and
Mrs. George W. Wells, have devoted a great
deal of time since the child was stolen
in endeavoring to find a clue to its
whereabouts in order that the baby might
be restored to his mother. Last Wednesday
afternoon Mr Hall entered Camden Station
to get a drink of water, when, he says,
he noticed Mr and Mrs August Strauff,
the parents of Mrs. Strauff's husband,
standing in the ladies' waiting room.
According to Mr. Hall their actions were
such as to awaken his suspicion, and he
placed himself in position where he could
watch their movements.

"Soon afterward," says Mr. Hall, "a
lady about 25 years old got off a car
and went into the waiting room. Almost
immediately an elderly woman came out,
carrying a baby in her arms. Mrs. Strauff
and the young woman left the station,
walking up Howard Street to Lombard,
where they boarded a Highlandtown car.
The young woman was carrying the baby and
Mrs. Strauff a basket, in which were the

241

child's clothes, I suppose. I followed and got on the car, taking a seat well back. Mrs. Strauff was sitting a couple of seats ahead of me, while the woman and the baby were in front.

"At Eastern avenue and First street they got off the car and Mrs. Strauff took the baby while the other carried the basket. Up to the end of the 1200 block of First street they walked, with me about a block behind, when they suddenly turned the corner, and though I ran to the corner they had disappeared.

"I came back to Baltimore and told of what I had discovered, and the following night Mr. Mann and I visited the neighborhood, but failed to locate the house where the child had been taken, and, although we succeeded in getting the residents very much exercised over our movements, we again failed to learn anything.

"Thursday night we again went to Highlandtown, and this time we mentioned the matter to a couple of officers we met there and they advised that we see Constable Pfeffer, who resides in the block, and who perhaps could give us the information we desired. We waited about the Constable's home, 1218 First street, until about midnight, when we saw him. As soon as we stated our business the officer said that his wife had heard a baby crying for the last day or two at the home of a Mr. Kraft, 1222 First Street.

"Yesterday morning about 6 o'clock Mr Mann and Mrs.Wells, together with Constable Pfeffer, called at the house, and while Mr. Pfeffer was explaining the matter to Mr. Kraft Mrs Wells went back to the kitchen, where Stanley was found in Mrs. Kraft's arms. The latter at first refused to give up the baby, but after her position in the case had been made plain to her she gave in, and we soon had the long lost child in our possession."

It was said at the home of Mr. and Mrs August Strauff, 1109 East North avenue, that both were out, but Miss Clara Strauff, who came to the door, told the reported for THE SUN that the child ha been recovered by its mother and that they were satisfied that this had been done. She also, said that her brother had taken the baby out of the city as soon as he had secured the boy from his mother, and that he had returned to Baltimore only a few days ago.

On June 19 habeas corpus proceedings were begun by Mrs. Celeste A. Strauff against her husband and his parents. The case came up before Justice Harlan. Mr. and Mrs Strauff there denied that they were aware either of the whereabouts of their son or their grandson, and the writ was dismissed. After the habeas corpus proceedings had proved unsuccessful the Police Department was appealed to.

Mr. and Mrs. Strauff eloped to Towson and were married about two years ago. They lived together at 1109 East North avenue until about two months ago, when the young wife left and returned to her mother's home, almost directly opposite. The causes that led to the separation are not known.

Baltimore Sun
July 13, 1903

GLAD TO GET BABY BACK
For The Present, Mrs. Strauff Says, She Thinks Of Nothing Else.

Mrs Celeste A. Strauff, who, as told in THE SUN Saturday, has recovered her 11-months-old baby, which, she claims, was snatched from her arms on June 16 by her husband, William Strauff, from whom she separated about two months ago, refused to say last night what action she intends to take in the matter. She declared that she was so glad to get the child back that she had not thought much about anything else.

She declined to state whether she would institute divorce proceedings against her husband, who, it is said, left Baltimore yesterday morning for New York, accompanied by his parents, Mr. and Mrs. August Strauff. The latter have been living at 1108 East North avenue.

Seven

Celeste held Stanley in her lap. He was screaming, struggling to be let down. "He's forgotten me, Mama. He doesn't remember me; he doesn't know who I am," Celeste said. She cried, making sure that her mother saw her tears.

Annie left George's side and went to comfort her. She reminded Celeste of the ordeal that Stanley had been through. "So much time with strangers, strangers coming, taking him hither and yon. He needs time to get used to you again. Don't force him. Let him come to you. He'll do that. He'll remember your smell, your feel. Be gentle with him. He has been through it, poor little fellow."

The women looked at the boy, his face splotched with red, wet with tears and teething. Celeste let him slide to the floor. His sobs became soft hiccups. He stopped writhing and lay quiet, looking up at the faces staring down at him. Meg came into the room, offered to help, asked if the women would like tea. She stooped to look at Stanley.

"There's my little one," she crooned, "there's my little boy." Stanley reached his hand to try to touch her. Meg looked at Annie for permission to pick him up. Annie nodded. Stanley rested his head against Meg's shoulder; his eyes closed, his fist in his mouth.

Celeste's lip trembled as she watched. She said nothing. Meg came to her, Stanley now asleep in her arms, and placed him in Celeste's lap. "He will see his mama when he opens his eyes. He'll remember, Miss Celeste. He will. It will be fine." Annie heard Meg's words and nodded, wishing that it would be so. She breathed a prayer of thanks for Meg. Maybe, she thought, I am a praying woman.

George went to his daughter, smoothed her hair, patted her head. "All is well, now? Stanley is back. And Willie will be here. He will make it right, you will see."

"I don't know how you can forgive him, how you can overlook what he has done to me. Don't you want us here? What is it, Papa? Don't you love me anymore?"

George took her hand. "I believe his letters, sweetheart. I believe what he says. He is a weak man, yes, and he has let his family rule him, have too much influence over him. I know that he has let you down; he has let us all down. But he is a good boy. And now we have Stanley.

"He said that he tried to get him and bring him back and I believe that. When they learned that he had started out for Washington to get him, that is when Clara brought the baby back to Baltimore. Something is wrong with those people, but we cannot blame Willie for the faults of his family. He said that he would do everything he could to make it right for you, for Stanley, and I believe him. It is not good for you to live here, away from your husband. Perhaps this dreadful situation, this frightful scandal that has come about, perhaps this will teach both of you a lesson that you can use. Perhaps this will make you grow up." George, breathless from the exertion of his speech, went to the sofa.

"We will help you get settled again. We will do that for you, but only as you start out. Then you two must make your own lives, as a family. Willie loves you, I am sure of that. You must show him respect and loyalty. You must be a good wife to him."

Annie listened to her husband speak, more than he had spoken in many months. George pulled Celeste closer, kissed her cheek. He turned to take Annie's hand. "I think that I'll go up and lie down for a while. Annie, you come with me." To Celeste he said, "Willie will arrive soon. You will need your privacy."

Yes, Annie thought, Willie would arrive soon. Celeste had received the telegram. So much apology; so much confession, so much regret. The child needed to be with him, Annie thought, and then realized that she was thinking about Celeste. Three children in that small family, two of them adults.

Annie was standing at the window when Willie arrived later that evening. She watched as the carriage came to the house, watched as he unloaded his suitcases. She saw him draw himself erect, smooth his hair as he came up the stairs to ring the bell. He was even thinner than the last time she had seen him. His color was grey. He was not well. But she could not take on the worries for another invalid.

She opened the door. Willie took her hands in his and kissed them. "Oh, Mrs. Wells. There is nothing that I can say to you. I do not deserve your forgiveness. But it is that I am begging. Can you forgive me?" Annie drew him into the house. Meg brought in his two valises.

"Celeste has been waiting for you. She is with Stanley in the front room." Annie led him in. She closed the pocket doors as she left. If I were a praying woman, she thought, I would surely pray now.

Eight

As the sun came up Willie looked over at Celeste, savored her lying beside him, her arm slung over her head. He heard wet, slurping sounds, and he turned to his left to see Stanley, sitting in his crib, sucking his fist mightily, rubbing his blanket on the top of his head.

Willie rose to pick up his son, taking care not to disturb Celeste. Last night had been the first time Willie had seen Stanley since that horrible day in May. I must get beyond that, he thought. I cannot let that failure take over my life. I am better than that. I have learned from that.

Nine

Celeste had her house. It wasn't Mt. Vernon Place, it wasn't actually a house, but it was a start, and it was theirs. Annie visited and worried; George shook his head. The Strauffs had yet to be invited, and knew enough to stay away without an invitation. August had arranged for their bed, his gift to the couple when they married, and the rest of the furniture from that third floor room, to be delivered to the apartment. Clara regained her third floor bedroom in the North Avenue house.

The bed and dresser filled the back room; Stanley's crib was squeezed in behind the door, so that the couple had to turn sideways to enter. The mammoth mahogany wardrobe was set on the long wall of the living room, where it was bordered by two arm chairs, rescued from the Wells's basement, upholstered in forest green brocade. A yellow pine drop-leaf table stood between the windows and served as dining table, writing desk, and temporary lodging for folded diapers and laundry. The middle room functioned as the kitchen, and came with a coal stove and ice box. The living room rug, another relic from the Wells's basement, already bore the tracks of ice and coal deliveries, and Celeste was learning that a daily cleaning and scrubbing was a necessary fact of life. The bathroom contained a sink and bathtub. The toilet facilities were outside, shared with the family renting the first floor. Chamber pots, discretely placed under their bed, were used during the night.

The couple had moved into their first home, a converted second-floor apartment at 1716 Harford Road, on the last day of July. With George's help, Willie was now employed by the United Railways and Electric Company, not as the up-and-coming manager that all had assumed, but as a conductor assigned to one of the longest routes, the

Druid Hill Avenue line, car #17. George had advanced the couple the not inconsiderable sum of $100. He had said nothing as he handed over the plain envelop to his son-in-law. Willie had accepted gratefully, humbly. George shook his hand and turned away. Willie, without opening the envelop, went to him.

"Sir, p-please accept my, our, sincere thanks for this. I will repay you. Know that I intend to p-provide a g-good life, a g-g-good home, for Celeste and Stanley, on my own. You have given me a s-second chance. I will p-prove myself to you."

George looked at Willie, saw his sincerity. The triumph of hope, the gift to the young, George thought. Give the boy a chance. "Yes," he replied. "I have no doubt you will." The older man reached out and shook Willie's hand, again.

Ten

A few mornings after the move, Celeste and Annie sat at the Wells's dining room table. Meg had cleared the dishes except for coffee cups and a second piece of kugel that sat in front of Celeste. Annie cleared her throat, and placed her hands, fingers entwined, on the table. Downstairs, Stanley sat in his high chair in the kitchen, watching Meg wash the breakfast things.

"Celeste, I'd like to talk to you, to give you some advice, sound advice. I want you to listen to me. I know of what I speak. I want you to pay attention."

Celeste looked up, surprised by both her mother's grave expression and tone of voice.

Annie continued, "You have a chance, you and Willie, to make a new start. You have your own home now. It is not what you are used to, but you must start out somewhere. You wanted your own home; now you have it. Be grateful." Annie again cleared her throat, a nervous gesture.

"You must learn to be a wife, Celeste, and that is more than looking beautiful. You must think of your husband, put him first in your life, put his welfare before what you think you want. Willie is a good boy, a fine man, struggling to do the right thing. Now he can be the man of the house. You be sure that you treat him as such. He is a bright boy; he can make something of himself. But he is a dreamer, his head in the clouds, all that thinking, all that reading. He is not strong, not schooled, learned, in the ways of the world. I think that you are wiser in this. You can help him. You can look out for him, help him be more suspicious of what life presents. It is up to you to bring him to earth, to take care of him.

251

"I want more than anything in this world for you to be taken care of as well. Eva, she will manage, that I know. She is quiet, but she knows her world, how to find her way in it. You, you always appear so sure of yourself, but I know, I know, how much you want. You have a good boy there. Don't throw away your chance at a good life."

Celeste sat quietly, watching her mother. Mama just doesn't understand, she thought. Willie wants to take care of me. He doesn't want another mother. He does want someone beautiful and gay. He said so; he's told me how happy I make him, how he likes it when people look at me, at us, admiring. Mama just doesn't know him.

Annie saw Celeste's eyes upon her, intent. Finally, Annie thought, she is listening to me.

"Meg and I will help you until you get used to keeping house. But you must prepare to be on your own, to be a wife and mother. It will not be easy. You have led a much pampered life until now. Yes, you have had some unhappy times. You have had the situation with Willie and Stanley, but that is behind you now. You be a proper wife to Willie, a good housewife, a good mother. Let him concentrate on his job, doing well there. He will be able to provide a respectable life for you. But you must put him above everything. Your father and I have had a fine life, no? Remember that. Think of this house. You can have that too one day."

Celeste smiled, picked up her mother's hand, drew it to her lips. "I love you and Papa." To herself she added, I'll have more than this kind of house, more than your dull life.

*Eleven*_____

George had done what he could. The company needed conductors, motormen, not clerks, and certainly not managers. Willie was unremittingly grateful – for the job, for the forgiveness that he received from this family. In the weeks before the move to Harford Road, living in the Wells's house, he had experienced a peace that he hadn't realized had been missing in his life. Maybe it was acceptance, he pondered; maybe it was love; maybe, it was respect. After all the trouble, the disgrace, he had brought to this family and to his own.

The Strauffs, on the north side of North Avenue, had been slower to forgive, their obstacles more complex than the Wells's.

"How could he leave like that?" Clara demanded of her father. "Just capitulate to that spoiled brat of a girl, to give in to her like that. To leave this house, his family, his job. How can you not feel betrayed, *Vater*? How can you continue to find excuses for Willie, his mistakes, his weakness? What kind of a son do you have? Don't you ever think of that? Does that not come to your mind?" Clara's face was blotched, with anger, with frustration.

"Do you not see, do you not acknowledge the disgrace he has brought to our name? That scandal follows all of us. And now he leaves, moves across the street, like nothing has happened? How can you bear that? And say, do, nothing," Clara gasped for breath.

August regarded her, his expression stoic. He paused, knowing that his words must be measured, willing himself to stay calm.

"Clara, this is not your affair. You have done enough to worsen the situation. You must see that. It is too late, not the time to review. But we go on with our lives. The dishonor, yes, it was. But people will talk only until the next scandal, new gossip. We must hold our heads high through his time."

"I took the baby to save Willie, *Vater*, to, once again, fix his mistakes. You cannot blame me for this," Clara responded.

"Let us talk of something else. Let us agree that it will not be a topic of our conversation. Let us concentrate on helping your mother get over losing Willie. Let us think of her."

Clara looked at her father. Always Willie, always something else, never me, she thought. She turned and left the sun porch. A minute later August heard scales; he recognized a four-octave minor, A-flat, played loud, with no touch of grace.

Twelve _____

Celeste stood in the doorway, watching him adjust his tie, his cufflinks, the ones from August, real gold, and his hat. He could be an Army officer, she thought. Yes, definitely an officer.

Willie stood before the mirror, taking care that the stiff collar of his shirt was straight, the hang of his navy jacket even, the four brass buttons aligned. He checked that his hat was positioned, and looked at the gold numbering in its center. The first digit, "3," represented his route number; the trolley that went from the entrance to Druid Hill Park, down Druid Hill Avenue to Paca Street, past Camden Station, all the way to Ridgely's Delight. The second number, "2," told the world, if they wanted to know, that he was the trolley's conductor. The last numbers, 89, indicated his seniority. His first day working on his own, official conductor of the Druid Hill Avenue line.

He boarded the trolley at North Avenue and rode it to Druid Hill Avenue. He was assigned to the second shift, starting at 2:30 p.m. and would stay with the trolley until it returned to the car barn at 1 a.m. Willie didn't mind the long hours; it gave him an extra thirty minutes of work time, a total of $1.05 a day. He was committed to repaying George's loan as quickly as he could manage. He would not make the same mistakes he had made with August, always borrowing, never being in a position to settle his account. He had already made two payments, one dollar a week, paid first, before even the rent, the honorable thing to do, what a proper man would do.

He patted the eight pockets on his jacket, four on each side, each one designed to hold a different sized coin, the bottom two, longer than the rest, ready for the transfer slips. He was responsible for collecting

255

fares, making change, and, at the end of his shift, balancing the fare worksheet for the night manager.

His hours walking the length of the trolley, collecting fares, answering questions about routes, transfers, timetables, provided him with an unexpected sense of accomplishment. This was a real job. He hadn't gotten it on his own, he allowed, but still, he wasn't working for his father. He was his own man. He wondered what Clara would think, what she would say, when she found out. Well, this was not her business. He had started a new life, a life where he would be the pilot or, he smiled to himself, the conductor.

Summer afternoons were sweltering; heat rose from the asphalt-paved streets, the iron rails. Only when the trolley moved was there a breath of breeze. But the evenings, after the sun had moved far into the western sky, when the crush of workers ended and couples out for an evening boarded, brought with it a calm coolness. Willie then had time to think, to wonder about the stories, the lives, of his passengers. I could write a book, he thought.

The fresh air, being in the open, being free of his family, all that love and attention from the Wells, and some from Celeste, being the head of his own family, having his own house, however cramped, had a salutary effect on Willie. The hollows of his face filled out, the dark circles under his eyes lightened. He had to loosen his belt two notches. That lock of hair still fell into his eyes, but his gesture smoothing it back became less anxious. He couldn't remember the last time he stammered. He had a job, not one for a thinker, or a reader, perhaps, but a job, and it was his.

Celeste packed his dinner each day, a sandwich, an apple, and three cookies, baked and delivered by Meg. Each afternoon the family of three left the house together. Celeste held Stanley as they said goodbye, Celeste and Stanley, dressed for their afternoon walk to Annie's, Willie, handkerchief in hand, prepared to wipe off traces of drool and teething biscuit as his son kissed him goodbye. As he started his walk to catch his trolley, Willie turned around for one last glance, always delighted to see his wife and son watching as he turned the corner onto Lafayette Street.

At the end of his shift, he walked the sixteen blocks from the Charles Street car barn to his home, tired in those early morning hours, but also grateful for the quiet of the streets, the calm of the city. At North Avenue, he began the second leg of his journey. Each night he passed Green Mount Cemetery, its tall, imposing granite wall cool to the touch. Each night he paused and looked at 1108 E. North Avenue, tucked in tightly for the night. He thought of his mother, of August, and was sad that, for now, their estrangement had to be. His eyes went to the third story, to that bay window that belonged to the room that once been his and Celeste's, now, most assuredly, he thought, once again belonging to Clara.

On his day off Willie studied the routes of the different streetcar lines, their terminals, where they intersected. He tried to work out why particular streets were chosen, why there were different intervals between stops. He noted his suggestions to make things run more smoothly and waited for someone to ask about them.

Thirteen —————————————————————————

While Willie worked, Celeste developed her own rhythm. She was a wife now, a proper wife. She kept house, practicing for when they moved to their real house.

With Willie's second shift assignment, their days started later in the morning. Even Stanley sensed this, and played quietly in his crib until his father came to rescue him. He would carry him into the living room where the window shades were kept down to preserve the cool of the previous evening. The windows of the room faced east, so the apartment was spared the scorching afternoon sun. The drawn shades gave the room a gloomy feel, but Willie and Celeste agreed that the cooler air was worth it.

Willie sat Stanley in his high chair and filled his bottle. Allowing the baby his morning bottle had been a concession, proposed by Meg, to make up for the upheavals in Stanley's life. "Surely one bottle a day won't hurt him," she said, surprised at the intensity of her suggestion, delivered before she had had a chance to remember her station.

The milk was cold, a small shard of ice still in the top of the box. The iceman had told Celeste that he didn't make deliveries to a second floor, but he'd make an exception for her. Willie emptied the melted water that had accumulated in the pan below, then turned to the stove to heat water for coffee for him, tea for Celeste. Still in his robe and slippers, Willie would bring up the morning paper that had been delivered to the front door one flight down. Stanley contently drank his breakfast milk, knowing that soon his mother would appear from the bedroom.

Willie had Celeste's tea waiting for her on the table by the window. Stanley banged the glass bottle on his tray. "Good morning, my sweet boys" was her daily greeting, and she took the baby back to the bedroom to change his nappy. Returning to the living room, plunking Stanley back in his high chair, she sat to savor her tea, the first order of her day. After that she would walk to the kitchen stirring hot water into pabulum for Stanley while Willie made toast, buttered just as they both liked it. Meg's homemade preserves followed.

After breakfast, Celeste dressed Stanley for the day and settled him in his playpen. The baby held onto the railings and walked his way around the perimeter, screeching to Willie, throwing his books at his father's feet. "Ree, ree," he squealed.

Willie called out to Celeste, "I think Stanley's talking. His first word, 'read.' Isn't that a delight!" and he leaned down to scoop his son into his arms, settling him into his lap and opening *The Tale of the Squirrel Nutkin*, one of the set of Beatrix Potter books Willie had brought as a peace offering when he moved from his parents' home to the Wells's house.

Celeste emerged from the bedroom carrying a wicker basket and a bucket filled with Stanley's soiled diapers. "You read to him, keep him occupied. I'll take care of these."

Willie looked over at his wife. "Do you want me to carry those down for you?" he asked.

"No, just keep him occupied. I'll be back up soon."

She's doing such a fine job here, Willie thought, and his attentions returned to his son.

Celeste made her way down the steep, narrow staircase. She maneuvered around Stanley's pram which took up a large part of the vestibule. They were fortunate that the Pokilovs, their downstairs neighbors, didn't complain. The stairs to the basement were at the rear of the house and the basement contained two washtubs. She didn't complain; she knew that there were some houses that still did not have running water. There was a small stove in the corner where she heated the water for the soiled napkins to soak. She would come down later in the day to rinse them and hang them outside to dry. Mrs. Polikov had offered to watch Stanley when she was in the back yard, but so far Celeste had refused. With Willie home in the mornings, she could manage. And besides, she didn't think that the Polikovs were her type of people.

By the time Celeste returned to the second floor, Willie had made the bed and washed the breakfast things. They had the rest of the morning to themselves. Some days they went for a walk, the three returning to the house in time for Willie to dress for work and Celeste to prepare for her visit to Annie and George. Some days they did the marketing together; some days Willie stayed with Stanley while Celeste ran out to shop. It was quicker and easier that way.

The evenings were hardest for Celeste, not used to being alone, on her own. Most days she returned from her parents' home in the late afternoon, carrying a basket containing dinner and lunches for the next day. She was surprised that Annie did not invite her to stay there for dinner more often. Back in the apartment, she dusted, cleaned the floors, played with Stanley before she put him to bed. His bedtime, the time with him that she liked best, when she could stand over the crib and stroke his head, pushing back the blond hairs that stuck to his scalp from the heat of the day. He wanted to walk; he wanted to be out of his playpen; he wanted to be read to. But that was Willie's job. In the evenings she let him crawl on the floor. Now he was pulling himself up on any piece of furniture he could find. He stood at the windows, looking out, gnawing on the woodwork. In the quiet of the night Celeste read magazines, *The Ladies' Home Journal, Life, The Delineator*, looking for ways to be a good wife. She skipped the mothering advice.

Meg came two afternoons a week, mainly to iron. It would not do for Willie not to have crisply-ironed shirts. She demonstrated her techniques to Celeste, but so far Celeste had mastered only Willie's underwear. She showed Celeste how to cook, but knew that the young woman had neither the aptitude nor interest for this. Meg didn't mind; she loved seeing Stanley, and Celeste was, in her way, doing her best.

Annie had lightened Meg's workload at home. Meals were simpler now; many nights George did not eat at all, simply asked for a glass of milk and a plate of crackers which he ate in the front room. Annie picked at her food. At least Celeste and Willie appreciated her cooking, Meg thought more than once.

Fourteen————————————

Celeste stood in the kitchen, packing Willie's dinner. "Let's give Stanley a birthday party. We can ask your parents to come. They can see him again, and they can see our house, how well we're getting along without them, how we don't need them."

Willie looked up from his chair. Stanley sat on his lap; Willie had been reading *The Jungle Book*; pointing to picture of the animals. He paused before he answered. "Do you think that is a good idea, Celeste? Are you ready to have them here?" Willie's heart softened at the thought of seeing his mother, his father again. He had decided that he would not contact them, not until Celeste was ready. It was a proof of his loyalty to her. He wanted them, and Celeste, to understand that.

"I want them to see that we are getting along just fine; that you have a good job; that I am capable of being a good wife. And mother," Celeste added.

"It would be simple; just a birthday cake and some drinks. Maybe champagne. I think that we need to do this." She looked over at Willie, put down the waxed paper she was folding for his sandwich, and waited for his reply.

"Our place is so small, Celeste. Where would they sit? We have only two arm chairs and the two at the table. And the heat." Willie saw from Celeste's face that it would be best if he not continue his objections.

"There are four chairs and four adults; five if Clara comes, if we invite her. And if we do, she will just have to stand."

Willie smiled at Celeste's remark. "What about if we asked them here over the Labor Day weekend? It should be a bit cooler then; it will give us more time to prepare. I want to help you with this. I can visit

261

them, or write to them, or you could be the one to issue the invitation. That might be the best idea, you, as the hostess, invite them. And it is up to you if you'd like to include Clara, but I think that it would be the gracious thing to do. Not that you have any cause to be gracious. They, I, have wronged you, Celeste. You have been, you are, wonderful to put that all behind you and forgive." He put the book down, placed Stanley on the floor and went to her.

Willie put his arms around her. "You have shown your character, my dear wife. I cannot tell you what it means to me. You have shown me how much a better person you are than your poor weak husband. But I will make it up to you, I swear it."

Celeste put her head on his shoulder. I will not complain, she thought. I will make the best of this. This is our home; I will make it our home.

"I'll write them today. I have to think about Clara though. I'm not sure." Celeste took time to make sure that the edges of the paper were folded so that the sandwich would not be exposed, so that Willie could have as fresh as dinner as she could manage. She would have a happy life, she decided. Nothing would stop her.

The first Monday in September arrived. Paulina had sent a note that she, August, and Clara would be delighted to come and celebrate both Stanley's birthday and the couple's new home. They were to arrive at 4 p.m. Celeste hoped that the sun would be at the back of the apartment and that the front room would be cooler than it had been for the past several days. The day before, Meg had visited, and had helped Celeste baked a two-layer cake. "It's a grand job, you've done, Miss Celeste," she said. "Let me work on the icing while you clean up. That way it will have a chance to harden a bit before tomorrow. With this heat, you don't want it running down the sides onto the plate." Which is exactly what it did.

At three o'clock Celeste looked at her offerings. Two bottles of champagne were resting on the ice at the top of the ice box. Stanley's cake was beside the sink. The top layer was tilting. Holding back tears, Celeste used a knife to maneuver it back into place. She was less than successful.

Willie came into the room. "It is wonderful, and what a beautiful cake. It is for Stanley, don't forget, and he will love it. That is all that matters." He took Celeste's hand.

"It's frightful, isn't it? Now your family will know that they were right. I am not fit to be a wife, or a mother. Do you think there is time to go out and buy something? I don't even know that a bakery is open today. It is a mess." Celeste drew the white dotted-swiss apron to her eyes. The apron covered the dress she had chosen for the day, blue gingham with short sleeves for the heat of the day. Her hair was tied back, but hung without its usual bounce. Circles shown under her eyes.

"It is lovely, and if they don't love it, then more's the pity. They just can't see beauty," Willie said. "But I surely can," and he lifted her hair and piled it atop her head. He took her hand in his other hand and drew it to his lips. "My sweet beauty," he said.

A rap came at the door precisely at four o'clock. Willie went downstairs to meet his family. Paulina, leading the trio, followed her son up the stairs. She carried two parcels, wrapped in green and yellow sprigged paper. August followed, holding a large cardboard box, tied in twine. Clara was the last to ascend the steep steps, slowly. She too carried two packages, wrapped with the same paper. She left her cane at the bottom of the stairway.

"Welcome to our home," Willie said, and escorted them from the landing into the front room. Stanley, dressed in white, stood in his playpen. He looked sternly as the adults came toward him.

Celeste stood in the doorway to the kitchen. This is my home, she thought. I will not be nervous. "Hello, Mr. and Mrs. Strauff, Clara. Welcome to our home."

August spoke for his family. "Thank you for inviting us. We are happy to be with you and share this celebration." He walked over to Stanley.

"Our birthday boy has grown," he said, and laid the box he carried at his feet. Paulina went to the baby and opened her arms. Stanley stood and opened his arms as well. She picked him up, straining at the unexpected weight. Stanley allowed himself to be kissed, but no smile appeared on his serious face. Clara stood at the entranceway. "He is a beautiful boy, Willie. No doubt of that."

The three entered the front room; Willie showed Paulina and August to the armchairs; he had turned their dining chairs to face the center of the room. "Clara, you sit here, would you?" The couple stood. No one spoke.

Uncomfortable with the silence, August began. "We brought some gifts for the boy, for the birthday. I hope that you, that he, will like them." He handed Willie the brown box. Willie unwrapped a wooden fire engine, complete with ladders that could be put together and extended as high as the window sill. "*Vati*, this is lovely. I know that he will enjoy it," Willie said.

"Yes," August answered. "It is from Germany, of course. You can see the insignia on the truck. Stanley is American, but it is good to remember Germany."

Paulina handed Willie the packages she brought. Celeste remained at the kitchen entry. "One is for Celeste," Paulina said. Celeste came forward and carefully opened the paper. It was the table linen that Paulina had given her for her birthday the year before. Celeste had not taken it with her when she left the house those months ago.

"Thank you, Mrs. Strauff," she said, and left to put it in the bedroom. Paulina's other gift was a light brown colored Steiff bear. "Also from Germany," Paulina said, nodding her head. Stanley took the proffered bear and smiled. "Bee," he said.

"Now from me," Clara said, and handed one package to Celeste and one directly to Stanley. The toddler tore the paper gleefully, *Mother Goose as told by Father Gander*. "Beautiful illustrations there, Willie. I think he will enjoy them." Clara looked over at Celeste, who had yet to unwrap the package. Celeste knew it was a book. "No need to unwrap that now," Clara said. "It is *Mrs. Beeton's Every Day Cookery and Housekeeping Book*. You forgot to take it with you. It should be a great help to you now, I think."

Celeste did not respond, but turned around to bring out the cake, complete with one candle. The rest of the afternoon was spent watching Stanley walk around the apartment. Champagne was drunk; cake was eaten. All present commented on how delicious the cake was, how difficult it was to make a cake in such heat, how wonderful it was that Celeste took the trouble to make it rather than buy from a bakery. Everyone in the room, except Stanley, was trying. Everyone in the room, except Stanley, and perhaps Celeste, was grateful to be together, grateful that this first awkward meeting was taking place.

As the Strauffs prepared to go, August took Celeste's hand. "You are doing a good job here." He looked at Willie, "You too, my boy."

Paulina walked to Celeste and said, "May I kiss you?" Celeste nodded, but did not bend down as the shorter woman stretched to reach her cheek.

Clara stood, silent. Finally she said, looking at the young couple, "I know I have made things more difficult for you. I am sorry." The last three words were barely audible, but Willie heard them. He stepped forward to embrace his sister, but she had turned and was making her way down the stairs.

August and Paulina followed. Once on the sidewalk, Paulina turned and faced the other two. "Now we will be a family again, *yah*." August took her arm; she leaned against him. Clara, three paces behind, followed the couple as they made their way home.

Fifteen

"Take me to the park. Oh, Willie, let's go. We can even take Stanley. Please, please, please. Look, I've made Hanne's lentil soup for us tonight. Remember how she taught me to cook?"

Celeste danced around her husband. He could smell her freshly ironed blouse. Meg must have been there that afternoon, Willie thought. Celeste's eyes sparkled. "I've been thinking about it all day. Gwynn Oak, the Ferris wheel, the carousel. I haven't been there in years. We can take the streetcar. Maybe the conductor will let us on without paying."

Willie looked at his wife, saw a freshness, an energy that he hadn't seen since the early days of their marriage. "I've asked to work an extra day on Saturday, but, yes, Sunday, we will go to Gwynn Oak. It will be Stanley's first visit; we can go as a proper family."

Celeste came to Willie, kissed him hard on the mouth. They forgot about dinner, though not about the french letter. Stanley stood in his play pen happily gnawing on the railing. He looked down and saw a piece of biscuit. He sat, contented, and chewed.

Later that evening Celeste fixed scrambled eggs; Willie made toast over the burner. "Feast for a king," he said. Celeste smiled. Stanley had fallen asleep in his playpen, biscuit in one hand, a stuffed rabbit under his left arm.

That Sunday, before noon, the couple dressed, Willie in his white linen suit, a new straw boater with a maroon hat band, shirt crisply ironed by Meg. Not as good as Hanne's work, he thought, but a lifesaver over Celeste's attempts.

Celeste wore her red boots, making sure that they showed beneath the black serge skirt that just touched her ankles. Her long-sleeved white blouse was softened by a floppy bow of black satin at the neck. She added a white straw hat banded with the same black fabric. To help hold up her hair, she placed a black silk rose at the nape of her neck. It showed under the hat's brim whenever she bent down to tend to Stanley, which she did each time she felt the admiring eyes of passers-by. They looked the perfect family, she knew, perfect for the cover of *Ladies Day* magazine, maybe even *McClure's*. She held Stanley as they rode the carousel, she side-saddle, holding the toddler on her lap with her right hand, her white-gloved left hand clasping the bar. Willie, his hand on Stanley's stroller, watched his family as they rode. Celeste met his eyes at each rotation. She smiled. Yes, she thought, this is what he wants, a beautiful wife.

Stanley wore a sailor suit of white and robin's egg blue, a gift from Meg. His blond hair was growing in, though the top of his scalp still showed. His eyes were hazel, like his father's. Pity, Celeste thought, and touched her lips.

Sixteen

That October weekend Willie had two consecutive days off from work. He looked forward to getting in some time to read. Annie had invited them to lunch on Saturday. He hadn't seen the Wells in several weeks, although he made sure that his weekly payment was sent.

They started out shortly after noon, the Wells's house only a few short blocks away. The couple left Stanley's stroller at home, allowing the toddler, who was now walking steadily, to make the journey on foot, holding on to his parents' hands for balance. If he got tired, Willie would carry him. Stanley, dressed this day in a sailor suit of white and navy blue, pranced out ahead of his parents. Willie ran to catch up with him before they reached the corner. With a firm hand, he guided the toddler the rest of the way. Celeste followed behind, watching her two men, twirling the parasol that had charmed Willie only a few short years ago. A lifetime ago, she thought.

Meg was waiting at the door to greet them, and the family went to the front room where Annie and George were seated. They fussed over the baby; George greeted Willie warmly. Willie handed George an envelope with the week's repayment of the loan. Annie leaned down to take Stanley into her arms.

A few minutes later Meg announced that the meal was ready and the group moved to the dining room. George sat at the head of the table, looking out at his family. Celeste, settled, happy, he thought. He reached for his wineglass. "Let us toast this family," he said.

Celeste looked at her father and laughed. "Papa, I don't think I've ever heard you say that before." He must be feeling better, she thought. The group raised their glasses and drank. Even Stanley was given a sip of wine.

Meg, standing in the doorway, surveyed the scene. Maybe Mr. Wells is feeling better, she thought. Annie looked over at her husband; she caught his eye, and smiled.

Before the meal was over, Stanley had slumped in his high chair, asleep. Willie picked him up gently and placed him on the sofa in the front room while they gathered their belongings for the walk home.

"Thank you, Mr. Wells. We had a wonderful time," Willie said as he shook his father-in-law's hand.

George put his hand on Willie's shoulder. "Take care of my girl," he said, "and Stanley."

"Always," was Willie's reply. Meg had wrapped the leftovers of the meal for Celeste to take home. Celeste carried the basket, Willie carried Stanley as they made their way back to their apartment.

That evening, the couple sat in their front room, reviewing the day. Stanley, dressed in his pajamas, played on the floor at their feet. Early the next morning, before light, they heard pounding on the door. Willie ran down the stairs to answer. It was Meg.

Baltimore American
October 11, 1903

SENT BULLET CRASHING THROUGH HIS BRAIN
George W. Wells Dies at St. Joseph's Hospital from Self-Inflicted Wound
George W. Wells, 1123 East North avenue, sent a bullet crashing through his brain last evening about 8 o'clock and dies about an hour later at St. Joseph's Hospital. The deed was committed in the middle room, second floor, of his home. Mrs. Wells, his wife, was the only person in the house when the shooting occurred. The cause for the act is assigned to Mr. Wells' ill-health. He had been suffering from stomach trouble for the past two years.
Mr. Wells was a watchman employed at the Charles street barn of the United Railways Company he went home yesterday morning from his night's work and complained of feeling ill. He immediately went to his

room, where he went to sleep. He arose, apparently, about 5:30 o'clock and dressed himself. Mrs. Wells, who was busy in the dining room, noticed nothing unusual and proceeded with her work. About 15 minutes later she heard a muffled report of a revolver. She became frightened and ran to her husband's room, where she found him lying on the floor, face downward. He was still alive, and pressed his right hand to his head. The revolver was lying on the floor, smoking, with one chamber empty. A ragged hole appeared just above the right temple and his left hand was burned, noting that the muzzle of the revolver had been held with the left hand against the side of the head.

Mrs. Wells was nearly prostrated when she entered the room, and a messenger was dispatched for Dr. Harry C. Hyde, 1100 East North Avenue. When Dr. Hyde arrived he made a hasty examination, and ordered the wounded man to be sent to the hospital. He was removed to St. Joseph's Hospital in the Northeastern district ambulance. The hospital staff were summoned, and after an examination discovered that the bullet had passed through the brain from right to left, and there was no chance for his recovery. He expired about 35 minutes after being admitted to the hospital.

Mr. Wells was a native of Baltimore and had been in the employ of the United Railways Company for many years. He is survived by a widow and two daughters – Miss Irene Wells and Mrs. Celeste Stauff. He was a member of the Shield of Honor and was well know in Northeast Baltimore, Coroner Hirsch, of the Northeastern district was notified and is making an investigation. The funeral arrangements have not been completed.

Baltimore Sun
October 11, 1903

FIRES SHOT INTO HIS TEMPLE
Mr. George W. Wells Had Suffered Long With
Stomach Trouble.

Unable to endure the pangs of stomach trouble, from which he had suffered for the past two years, Mr. George W. Wells, 60 years old, sent a bullet from a 32 caliber revolver into his right temple about 5:30 o'clock yesterday afternoon in the middle room on the second floor of his home, 1123 East North avenue. He was taken to St. Joseph's Hospital, where he died several hours later. Coroner Hirsh has been notified and is making an investigation.

Mr. Wells was alone at the time the shot was fired, but his wife, Mrs. Annie E. Wells, engaged in domestic work on the first floor, heard the report. She rushed upstairs and found her husband lying on the floor with blood streaming from a wound in his right temple. R. Harry C. Hyde, 1100 East North avenue, was summoned and ordered that Mr. Wells be removed to the hospital.

Mr. Wells had complained of stomach trouble for a long time and during the past two years he had lived almost entirely on milk and crackers. He had been attended by a number of physicians, all of whom pronounced his case incurable. It is believed by the members of his family that his mind had become impaired by his affliction, as he had acted peculiarly during the past few months.

Mr. Wells partook of a light lunch before the tragedy and was unusually pleasant during the afternoon. He chatted with the members of his family, and on going upstairs he told his wife that he would take a much-needed rest.

Mr. Wells was born in Baltimore and for a number of years was in the employ of the United Railways Company. Several months ago he was compelled to retire on account of ill health. He was a member of Victory Lodge, No. 25, Shield of Honor. Besides a widow he is survived by two daughters – Mrs. William Strauff and Miss Irene Wells.

Seventeen

Annie sat in the front room, reliving the past day and night, trying to believe it, trying to understand. At the hospital she had told the police, the doctor, all she knew. More police had come to the house before she had even arrived home that night. The hospital must have notified them, she thought. Meg had let them in, shown them the room.

The noise. She replayed it in her mind; running upstairs, finding him, screaming for Meg, begging her to get the doctor. It was he, she remembered, who had called for the ambulance. The trip to the hospital. She had ridden up front with the ambulance driver, directly in back of the horse, George's body strapped to the stretcher in the carriage behind them.

She was sure that George had been still alive when they arrived, rushing up the steps, going into the room. Perhaps he was; she had waited hours at the hospital before the doctor came to her.

"He's gone," he told her, then asked if she wanted them to contact someone, someone who could come for her. Annie shook her head. She didn't need anyone to come.

She had taken the news without showing emotion. The doctor shook her hand and turned back inside the double doors. Annie sat alone, then gathered her things. She walked the seven blocks home from St. Joseph's Hospital. As she came to Harford Avenue, she looked to the north, to Celeste and Willie's apartment. No, she thought. Later. Now I need to gather my thoughts. A wry smile crossed her face; she wondered if they would ever be gathered.

Meg had stood at the window, watching, waiting for news. She opened the front door before Annie's foot touched the steps, and led her to the front room. The two women sat together, silent through the night.

As the sky lightened, Annie turned to Meg. "We must tell Celeste, Eva." Meg nodded and left the room. A few minutes later she returned, carrying a cup of tea and a thin slice of cake for Annie. Her shawl was over her arm. "I will go. You stay here. I will be back in a few minutes. Mr. Willie can wire Eva."

Celeste pushed open the door and ran into the front room. "Oh, Mama, how is he? How is Papa? What happened?" Meg had told them that there had been an accident, that she didn't know the details. She said nothing about the second-floor room, its door locked for now.

Willie stood behind her, silent. He saw Annie's face. He knew George was dead.

Annie took her daughter's hands, stiffened her arms so that Celeste stood away from her. "He is gone."

Standing in the doorway, Meg stifled a cry, putting her fist to her mouth. Celeste was silent, staring at her mother. Willie stood close.

"Mama, what happened? What happened?" The last two words came as a bleat.

"Later," Annie said. "Later." She walked to the divan and sat. Meg motioned to Willie. He led Celeste to sit beside her mother and went to join Meg.

When the two were in the vestibule, Meg pulled the pocket doors to the front room closed. "He shot himself, Mr. Willie. In the middle room, upstairs. The police were here, said I could clean it up. I've closed those doors. I couldn't go in. I don't know what she would want me to do."

Willie put his arm on Meg's shoulder. "Leave it for now. We just need time to think."

On Monday afternoon, the hearse stopped at their front door. Meg stood at the doorway, Annie at the window, waiting. Eva sat beside her mother. The women had said little since Eva's arrival late the evening before. The police had come again, earlier that day. Annie showed them the room; showed them the note he had left. They transcribed it, for their records.

The undertaker delivered George's body to the house, placed it on the bier in the front room. Annie thanked him. He stood in the vestibule. "Are you up to making funeral arrangements?" he asked. He knew there would be no insurance moneys coming.

"Burial in the family plot in Green Mount Cemetery. Directly from the house. There will be no church service." Annie's voice was flat, direct. The undertaker nodded. He had seen responses, reactions to death. He knew that emotional outpourings were no indicator of love, or caring, or hatred. He nodded and tipped his hat as he left.

That afternoon, Annie sat with the body. Eva joined her, and spelled her mother during the night. Meg answered the door, to friends, to neighbors who came to offer condolences, and to gawk. More than one brought a newspaper clipping. "I thought you should have this, thought you should know," they said. Annie was stoic; Eva more so.

The priest visited. The Reverend Charles May knew the rubrics of the Episcopal Church. No church service, nor burial service for those who "laid violent hands upon themselves." Yet it was he who had suggested the service at the gravesite to Annie. His ministry focused on the living, he told her, said that some type of service, short, simple, might offer solace.

Annie agreed to the service, though she knew that her solace would not come from the words of a priest. Perhaps someone would benefit, she thought. She was beyond caring for herself.

Celeste spent her mornings at the house on North Avenue, returning home to Stanley in time for Willie to leave for work. She waited to be embraced, by her mother, by her sister, even by Meg. None came. The women sat, each with their own thoughts. Celeste, thinking that this was the proper procedure for mourning, was silent as well.

Wednesday morning was brisk and clear, the sky an azure blue, a few feathery clouds giving a crisp balance. The hearse pulled up to the house shortly after nine-thirty. The undertaker and his helper, wearing the customary black top hats, moved George's body into the carriage, its glass windows uncurtained. The spray of white lilies atop the casket slid to the ground as they lifted the coffin. The assistant bent to pick it up, replaced it, not quite centered.

The driver turned the horse and carriage in the direction of the cemetery. The undertaker and his assistant walked in the street, behind the carriage. The family used the sidewalk, Annie between Eva and Robert, George's brother, then Willie and Celeste. The women wore black, their hats shrouded in black tulle, their faces covered. Willie wore his United Railways uniform, a black arm band attached. Meg walked six paces behind them. Celeste had borrowed a black jacket from Elizabeth's sister. It didn't fit. No one noticed.

The group walked the five blocks on North Avenue and turned left at Greenmount Avenue for the final distance to the cemetery's gray stone entranceway. Annie knew the way to George's family plot. So did Celeste. Willie remembered their visit there, and tried to brush it from his mind. Birth and death, the cycle of life, played out in a cemetery, he thought.

They walked up the hill to the plot, the golden gingko leaves rustling in the wind, the leaves of the chestnut tree swaying gently. Annie heard the sound of her breathing. She counted each one. As she reached the crown of the hill she saw the crowd that had gathered. She identified neighbors, she recognized August and Paulina; she saw a phalanx of employees of the United Railways, the conductors and motormen in uniforms of navy blue, the clerks who had worked in the office with George in their black suits, most shiny with age. All had black armbands. Annie recognized only one member of George's lodge.

Willie saw his co-workers and nodded to them, pleased that they had come, that they were showing his family respect and caring. The group had taken a collection, including the ones who couldn't be there, the ones who were on duty that day, to give to Annie at the end of the service.

The Reverend May met the family at the graveside. In the distance the group heard the bells of the trolleys as they plied their way on Greenmount Avenue past the cemetery. Each car slowed, stopped for a moment at the entrance, and rang the bell twice, in remembrance of their co-worker.

"I am the resurrection and the life, saith the Lord; he that believeth in me, though he were dead, yet shall he live; and whosoever liveth and believeth in me, shall never die," The Reverend intoned. He stopped, looked at those gathered. He had no sermon. "Let us remember George in life and know that he is now in a better place, free of suffering. Let us turn our thoughts to his family and do what we know George would want us to do."

Clad in his black single-breasted cassock, the black stole, edged in white lace, around his neck, he proceeded with an abbreviated version of The Order for The Burial of the Dead.

"Forasmuch as it hath pleased Almighty God, in his wise providence, to take out of the world the soul of our deceased brother, we therefore commit his body to the ground; earth to earth, ashes to ashes, dust to dust; looking for the general resurrection in the last day, and the life of the world to come, through our Lord Jesus Christ."

Annie came forward with a handful of dirt, threw it on the coffin. Her thoughts were her own, to be shared with no one. Eva stood straight, her face impassive. Celeste sobbed; Willie held her. The Reverend May hoped that the Bishop would not learn of his service. There was no wake.

Clara stood at the window in the Strauff's front room, holding Stanley in her arms. The two watched as the group made their way from the cemetery. Willie looked over and saw them, touched Celeste's arm. She looked up, smiled and waved at the baby in Clara's arms.

Clara carried the toddler to the armchair by the doorway. He knew that was his place to sit and listen as she played. She leaned down to riffle though her music scores. Massenet, she thought, and chose *Meditation from Thais*. Stanley sat quietly, listening, watching Clara's fingers as they floated on the keys. Once she had played the first bars, she closed her eyes and played from memory. To lose a father, she thought, no matter what Celeste had brought upon herself, upon them, a tragedy.

Eighteen

The afternoon of the funeral Annie and her daughters gathered in the dining room. Meg had set it for tea. Willie had returned to work; Clara kept Stanley. Celeste struggled with conversation; the other two didn't try.

After some minutes, Eva spoke. "I've made arrangements to return to Boston tomorrow if that is all right with you, Mama." Annie nodded.

"Do you have enough money for a while?" the older woman asked. "Your tuition is paid through the winter, your board. Do you have enough spending money until you come home again?"

Eva nodded. She swallowed, folded her hand together in her lap. "Mama, this is a terrible time to bring this up, I know. If it could be different I would make it so. I had written Papa about it, but received no response from him." She kept her eyes lowered.

"I plan to remain in Boston. My life is there now, and I have found friends, friendships that I was never able to find here. I will not be returning here to live. I want to spend my time there. I do hope that you understand." Eva reached for her mother.

Annie allowed Eva's hand to remain atop hers. She looked at her daughter, smiled as much of a smile as she could manage. "Yes. You go where you will find happiness. It will not be in this house, I'm afraid."

"But I must tell you." Annie paused, gathered her resolve. "I must tell you." She hesitated, inhaled deeply, removed Eva's hand from hers. "There is no money to keep you at Wellesley, Eva. There is no money."

Celeste, who had been quiet, inhaled sharply. "What is it you mean, Mama? Are you talking about Eva's school?"

Annie stared straight ahead, not at her daughters. "What I am saying is that there is no money, for school, for anything."

Celeste jumped up from the table. "Surely, that cannot be right. Papa would not do such a thing to us. He would never leave us, leave us with nothing. Mama, you must be wrong. Why do you think such a thing?"

Annie clasped her hands together. "Celeste, he was suffering so much that he didn't know what he was doing, couldn't know. And yes, I am wrong in saying that there is no money. We did have a bit put aside. But there will be no insurance money, after all the years that every week he paid in, every week. But there is none." She shrugged.

"Why not?" Celeste demanded, and then immediately regretted her tone.

Eva looked at her sharply. "Don't be stupid, Celeste. Just keep still."

"But I don't understand. What is it you're not telling me? Why? That is all I want to know," Celeste said.

Annie looked at her daughter. "Sit down," she said gently. "Eva, Celeste is a child. Do not be so hard on her." Annie looked over at her younger daughter. "Because Papa took his own life. There was no church service; there should not even have been a graveside service except for The Reverend May's choice. And there can be no insurance payment.

"We will not speak of this again. I will work out a way, Eva, but for you to continue your schooling is impossible for me to manage."

"Oh, Mama. Not to worry about that. I can find work. I am ready to find work. I have made friends there. They will help me, I know. I must worry about you, not have you worry about me." Eva answered.

Celeste continued. "But those newspaper articles, Mama. What did they mean? They said that Papa was a night watchman. They said that he didn't work there. What did they mean? Why did they write all those things?"

Annie looked up sharply. "Where did you see those papers, Celeste? Who showed them to you?

"My neighbor, Mrs. Polikov, saved them for me. She said that I might want to know what they said, so that I would not be surprised. Willie didn't want me to read them, but I did. Were they lies, Mama? That is what Willie said they were, that papers had to print something

279

to make people buy them, that it was all sensation. That's what he said, sensation. Is he right? Were they all lies?"

Eva stood up. "Oh, Celeste. What difference does it make?"

"It makes a difference because I have to face my friends, Eva. I am not like you. I cannot run away, leave my family behind, start a life somewhere else. That is why it makes a difference."

Annie reached for her daughters. "Let us sit. Let us be together in this time.

"Celeste, some of the things were true; some were made up. Your father had been sick for a long time. He was not a night watchman; he still went to work every day. He was a good, kind man who was in indescribable pain. And he couldn't stand it anymore. He loved you, he loved us very much. He was a good husband; he was a good father. That is all you need to know.

"You do not need defend him or yourself. Those who know you, who care about you, will know that. The others will forget it when the next scandal appears. All you need to remember is to hold your head high. You remember that from before, no?"

Celeste knelt and put her head on her mother's shoulder. Even Eva came to her side.

After Eva left, Celeste visited Annie every day. She sat with her mother, waiting for words of comfort. None came. Annie said that she was not up to seeing Stanley yet, that he brought too much commotion into the house, that she needed quiet. She spent her time sitting at the dining room table swallowing cups of tea, tasting nothing.

One day, with Meg out of earshot, Annie said to Celeste, "I must talk to Meg soon. We will have to think out our plan, what we will do, she and I." Celeste realized that those were more words than her mother had spoken to her since George's death.

Earlier that week, Willie had visited Annie, alone, without Celeste. She embraced him when she opened the door. "Mrs. Wells, I am so sorry."

"I know. I know," she replied. They walked to the front room where Annie sat on the sofa. Willie sat beside her. He pulled an envelope from his pocket.

"I promised to repay Mr. Wells for his loan. I want you to have this. It is the balance of what I owe. And I can never thank him, or you, enough, for your forgiveness, for your caring. And I will be here, always, to do whatever I can to help you. You have accepted me as part of your family. I will never forget that."

Annie reached over and drew his head to her lips. "Dear boy," she said, although he could not hear her.

Baltimore American
October 18, 1903

WELLS PREMEDITATED TAKING HIS LIFE
Letter to Wife Among Papers – Shot Himself
on October 10 at His Home
    Among the papers and letters of the late George W. Wells, who committed suicide on October 10 by shooting himself in the head at his home, 1123 East North avenue, was found a letter addressed to his wife and children. Mrs. Wells found the letter last Friday, and its contents clearly indicate that the suicide was premeditated. The letter was written in ink, and was not dated, except the month. It reads as follows.

October
    Dear Wife and Children – Feeling so very weak and not being able to sleep, as you know, I have suffered for the last two and a half years. I have made up my mind that there is no early chance for my recovery, so I hope you will forgive me for this rash act. May God bless you and have mercy upon my soul. Knowing you to be a good wife, I pray to God to help you and the children. Bury or burn my remains, as

you choose. One of my last wishes is for
Robert and Cousin Joe Walker to attend my
funeral. Let me say good-by to you once
more.

Yours affectionately,
GEORGE W. WELLS

Mr. Wells refers to his brother as
Robert. Another letter was found telling
his wife several matters of interest to
the family.

Nineteen

August brought in the newspaper early that Sunday morning and took his place at the dining room table. Inger, the new Hanne as he thought of her, had not yet served breakfast. Paulina and Clara were at Mass. A few hours of silence for me, August thought.

Hearing her employer, Inger came up from the kitchen bearing coffee, extra strong, the way he preferred it. She placed the silver pot on the table, the creamer iced and filled. The sugar bowl remained on the table from the night before. "Thank you, Inger. Now just give me some time before the women return." She bowed her head and returned to the kitchen.

As he turned the page of the local section August's eye went to the headline. More, he thought. More scandal. Can they not leave that poor woman to herself? He put down his cup to concentrate on the article. He did not know Celeste's father well, but it did not seem to him the letter of a suicide. Anything to sell papers, he thought. Sometimes, he admitted, he did the same thing, although never so egregiously. Willie, Celeste and the baby were to visit that afternoon. What a horror for them, for George's wife, for all of them.

An hour later, with Clara and Paulina seated at the table, August told them of the latest *Sun Paper* article. "We must ignore it; say nothing. Another scandal will be upon the city soon, and all this will be forgotten. Let us do what we can to help Celeste through this."

Clara did not object. Her view of Celeste had softened over the past week. She knew that August had loaned, or given, money to Willie so that he could repay his debt to George. She knew that Annie would receive no insurance money. She knew that Eva, back in Boston, would not return to Baltimore. She knew that she had lost a friend, a kindred spirit.

In the early afternoon, Willie and Celeste stopped at Annie's house on their way to visit the Strauffs. Willie picked up the paper on the front step as he, Celeste and Stanley walked up Annie's front steps. Stanley ran to the front room, Celeste and her mother close behind. Meg was downstairs fixing lunch. Willie sat in the chair by the window and opened the second section. He saw the headline, read the article, and placed the paper on the floor.

He addressed Annie. "Mrs. Wells, there is another article in the paper about Mr. Wells's death, about the note he left. I am sorry that you have to know this, that you have to go through this, so sorry that it seems that this nightmare won't end."

Celeste jumped up and picked the newspaper from the floor. "Where? Let me see it. Let me read it." Willie reached for her. "Celeste, don't do this. This will not make it easier for you, for any of us."

"I have to know what it says, Willie. Don't you see that? Everyone knows everything except me. I am always kept out of things. I am not a child. I want to read that. I want to see what everyone else is reading." She turned away and stood in the doorway, the newspaper held in front of her. She read, then turned back into the room.

"Oh, Mama, how could he do this to us? Why didn't he care enough for us not to do this, not to put us through this?"

Annie remained silent. Celeste cried. Stanley looked up. "Mama crying," he said.

Willie picked him up, held him, smoothed his curls. "She will be fine, Stanley. Mama is just a little bit sad."

And he wondered who had written that note.

Twenty_____

The grey days of February had arrived. A boarder had come to live in Annie's house; she was looking for a second, perhaps a third. Meg had found a new job, a new family to care for. She had promised to keep in touch, to look in on Stanley, but she had visited only once. Clara had heard from Hanne. She had found work in a shop and was trying to keep her English. She said that it was hard to find books. No one in her town spoke English, but they all said that they wanted to learn. Clara posted a box of books to her the day after her letter arrived. Clara was now going to the Music Academy three days a week. They had asked her to take on some students who needed advanced training, discipline.

Willie and Celeste celebrated the Christmas holidays at the Strauffs. Paulina had asked Annie to join them; Annie replied that she preferred her own company. Annie had lost some of her graciousness. Eva had written; she would not return home for the Christmas holiday, the expense and the crush of studying; she hoped everyone was well. She wrote Clara as well; Clara knew her friend had left her.

The North Avenue house was bedecked for the holidays. The rooms on the first floor gleamed with painted nut crackers; a candle pyramid stood on each mantle. A tall fir tree, trimmed with ornaments, all from Germany, stood in the bay window of the front room. On Christmas Eve, August took Stanley into the sunroom. The baby sat beside his grandfather as he split walnuts in two, carved out the meat, and place a nickel, a dime, a quarter into the shell before gluing the pieces back together. "See, Stanley, a nut of money here." The child laughed, reached for the walnut and shook it. "Ha," August said, "now you know that money talks." He lifted the child onto his lap and kissed him on his wet, red cheek.

"*Opa*, say *Opa*," August said. Stanley laughed, reached out to touch his grandfather's salt-and-pepper mustache, but did not speak. Willie watched from the doorway, called to Celeste to come. He put his arms around her, whispered into her hair, "Two years, my sweet one. Two years today."

Celeste rested against him. They watched, their son with his grandfather.

In all except the most bitter weather, Celeste took Stanley out for his walk each afternoon. She tried to concentrate on the baby, not her father, not her questions. Sometimes the pair went all the way to the park at Johnson Square where the toddler could run and Celeste didn't have to be at his side every moment. Celeste hoped to make friends with other mothers there, but the children were mainly tended by nannies and maids. She resolved to try another park, maybe Madison Square, though it meant a longer journey.

Annie cleaned, cooked and went about her day. She had given that middle room to the first boarder. No use making it a shrine, she thought. Celeste's afternoon visits had dwindled. Both women were relieved.

August went to the paper each day, Paulina on Mondays, Wednesdays and Fridays.

Willie's walks home from the car barn each evening became less agreeable, less pleasant, as the temperatures dropped. Frigid winds whipped down the streets' dark corridors; ice that formed after the daytime thaws made walking treacherous. His cough returned, though no one mentioned it.

Rising in the morning became harder for him; he often let Stanley stay in his crib until Celeste retrieved him. Without Meg's help, meals became less palatable, although Willie knew that Celeste was trying. She went out each morning to shop; he stayed with Stanley. A washerwoman came each week to pick up the sheets and towels, but Celeste did all the other laundry. Without Meg, Willie ironed his own shirts; Celeste still had not developed the knack, though she did a fine job, he thought, on his undergarments. The couple agreed to keep this to themselves.

Celeste and Stanley still came to the front door most afternoons to watch Willie as he left for work. But on this frigid Sunday afternoon, Celeste said that she and Stanley would stay upstairs, perhaps lie down for a nap. As Willie opened the front door to leave he smelled a sharp, acrid scent. He looked to the south; the sky was dark. He turned up his coat collar, coughed as he turned toward North Avenue. He passed a man on the street; they shared a few words. Willie turned abruptly and returned to the house. He ran up the stairs.

"Celeste, get up. The city is on fire."

Twenty-one _____

Celeste jumped up, startled at Willie's return, more startled at his words. "What's wrong? What are you talking about?" she asked.

"The city is burning. A fire downtown, and it's spreading. They can't control it. They've called in help from Philadelphia, Wilmington. You need to leave. It isn't safe here until we know more. It's spreading north. Pack a bag for yourself and Stanley and I'll walk you to your mother's. It's not safe for you to be here by yourself." Willie's words were strong, commanding. Celeste went to the closet, took out the suitcase she had used on their honeymoon.

"You'll just need a few things. I'm confident that it won't last long. It will be put out soon, I'm sure. But in the meantime, I don't want you to be alone." As Willie spoke, he gathered Stanley's clothes and placed them in a pile in the middle of the bed. Celeste hurried to the wardrobe and returned with her arms full. She threw her clothes on top of the baby's.

"I don't think you'll need that much, Celeste. Just pack a few things. Hurry. I need to see you safe and then I need to get to work, to see what they need from me there."

Celeste ran to the window, saw the darkened sky. "What about you? How can I be sure that you are safe?"

Willie finished packing the bag and snapped it shut. "I'll come to your mother's when I get off work. By that time I'll know more and things should be settled down. I don't want to worry you; I just want to be sure that you're not alone, that you have someone to look after you and Stanley."

Celeste stuffed the baby into his winter coat, leggings and hat. If he wanted to make sure that someone would look after me, she thought, surely he could have made a better choice than my mother. But Willie looked to be in such distress that she did not press him. A fire. Certainly the Fire Department can handle it.

Celeste pulled on her boots, her coat, her hat, two scarves, and carried the kicking, squirming toddler down the steps. Willie picked up her suitcase and locked the apartment door.

Celeste stopped at the vestibule. "Should we warn the Polikovs?" she asked.

"I'll get the stroller down the steps. You knock on their door; if they answer, let them know that there is a major fire downtown, and that it's spreading. Don't wait for them if they don't answer the door right away. We must leave now."

Celeste did as Willie said. There was no answer at the first floor apartment.

The couple walked the five blocks to Annie's house, pushing the stroller against the heavy winds. Stanley cried the whole way, tears and drool freezing on his face.

The three arrived at Annie's a few minutes later, and after a brief explanation, and kisses for Celeste, Annie and Stanley, Willie was on his way. He waited at his normal stop for the trolley to pick him up for the first leg of his journey to the Druid Hill Park station. The sky to the south remained dark, the smell of smoke even stronger than when he had left the apartment a few minutes ago. He saw the cinders in the air.

When the streetcar arrived, he spoke to the motorman and the conductor. They had no more information than he.

The trolley stopped just before it reached the intersection of North and Linden Avenues. The motorman pressed the pedal, but there was no movement. He pressed it again. Nothing. He looked up, checked the electric connector. All was as it should be. As Willie and the conductor made their way to the front of the car the motorman looked across the street. The eastbound trolley had stopped midway between Madison Avenue and Eutaw Place. The conductor said to the motorman, "You stay with the car. Strauff and I will go and see what's going on."

When the pair came back, he said, "Our guess is that the power plant was hit. His car has no power; neither does ours. Looks like they'll be no trolley service until this fire is put out, and who knows when things will be back to normal?"

They looked around them, slowly realizing that there were no lights shining, that there was no electricity anywhere around them. They helped the passengers leave the car; patrons were leaving two nearby restaurants, looking to take the streetcar home. The men told them that they could not help them. Some knew what was happening; others grumbled about service.

The motorman and conductor from the east bound train joined the men. The group decided to head to the car barn on Charles Street; perhaps the managers there could give them direction. "Looks like we're walking right into the fire," one said. The other laughed. "What choice do we have? Fire or be fired." The motormen locked the brakes and ignitions on the cars; one wondered aloud who would venture to steal a streetcar. As they turned right onto Park Avenue, several carriages passed them, carrying Bolton Hill women heading north with their jewelry, and their children.

Willie pondered as he walked: no electricity, no trolley cars, no job.

The sky grew more menacing as the men walked south, although they were two miles north of the business district, where they had heard the fire started. The wind whipped cinders around their faces; dense smoke made their eyes water.

"This fire has to be closer than the harbor," one man said. The rest remained silent, tense.

The doors to the car barn were open when they arrived there thirty-five minutes later. Only two trolleys were in place. Other employees had gathered, waiting for word on what had happened, on what to do next. Each gave an opinion.

"The fire took out the power plant. They're dynamiting all over, trying to stop it, but it's got away from them. It is coming this way. You can see that, the wind is blowing north. The whole city is going up. Everything."

"No use worrying about that. God will tell the fire when to stop."

"Well, I hope God loves streetcars, that's all I have to say."

When they saw the shift manager come down the steps from his office, all conversation stopped. The men looked to him. He stood erect, attempting to look in control; he prayed that his voice would not break.

"As you know by now, there is a major fire that is not under control as of this time. The Fire Department has called for help from surrounding cities and towns. They are on their way, by train and by highway.

"There have been several major explosions in the business district, and the power plant that we use to move our equipment has been destroyed. Most of you were working when the electric supply stopped, when your car stopped. There is nothing more that we can do at this time until the fire is put out, or at least is under control. We are praying that there is no loss of life.

"As for you, since there is no more to be done here, at least for the time being, we suggest that you return to your home and families and do the best you can to protect them. We anticipate that we will know more by tomorrow morning. If it is possible, we ask that you return here at nine. We will have more information then, and we should be able to give you some direction about what to do next." He cleared his throat, wishing that he had taken some water before he began.

"This is a terrible fate that the city is suffering. We ask your prayers. We will be closing the barn in ten minutes. If you have any valuables in your lockers, I suggest that you gather them and take them with you when you leave. Thank you." He turned and walked back to his office. The men were silent, and then, in groups of two or three, they turned and left the building.

Willie took his normal route home. The wind was still strong, but he sensed that it had turned to the east. He made a stop on the way to Annie's. He wanted to talk to August, to see what he thought.

Clara had been standing at the window watching the sky. She opened the door when she saw her brother. Paulina greeted him, coming from the sun porch where she had been saying her rosary. The beads were still entwined in the hands.

"Oh, Willie," Paulina said, "isn't it terrible. *Vati* has left, gone downtown, trying to get to the paper. I am, we are, so worried about him. And we will not leave here until he comes back. Our neighbors on both sides have packed up and left. There are not too many of us in this block who remain.

She went to her son, touched his scarf. "What about you? You smell of smoke. Where have you been?"

Twenty-two————————————

Dear Elizabeth,

I'll bet you have read about the excitement here in Baltimore, and, yes, I was part of it, and Willie. He was the one who told me about it. He left for work and came right home to rescue us. He was covered with cinders just from being out those few minutes. So, we packed up and went to Mama's, the baby and I. Then Willie, such a hero, really, went to work.

Well, all the electricity went out. We didn't know what was going on. Then Willie came home that night. We stayed at Mama's, really stayed with Mama to make sure that she was all right, and then we went home the next day. The fire didn't get anywhere near our house, but the air was still full of smoke. In fact, you can smell it even now.

Elizabeth, the wind that day was horrific. That is why the fire spread so quickly. It started near the harbor, and spread all the way to the Jones Falls. That is where it stopped, but it was over a day later before it was out. Such destruction. Margaret and I went downtown to see it. I didn't tell Willie or Mama. My downstairs neighbor kept Stanley for me. She is very nice.

The destruction was awful, and there were soldiers from the National Guard there, standing at attention. I guess to keep the looters away, but there were more people like us, just there to sightsee. I didn't see any looters. And they discovered when the fire departments from other cities arrived to help that their hoses didn't fit the hydrants. Isn't that something? Well, Willie said that there would be steps taken to fix that problem.

293

And Mr. Strauff's business escaped. How about that? He said he thought it was because the building was only two stories, and that the flames jumped right over it. And he is probably right, because it was the tall buildings that really were the worst.

So, that is my exciting news. You see, even an old married woman and mother gets to have some excitement! And I miss you. Please write. I want to hear about your life.

Your friend,
Celeste

Three days after the fire August and Paulina sat at the breakfast table. August put the paper down. Paulina sensed that he had something to say.

"Look at these pictures of the destruction, Lina. That fire burned for thirty hours before it was contained, eighty city blocks gone, just about the entire business district. Something so fortunate for us that the building was spared, not even singed, no damage, like nothing had happened. A miracle for us. They had to use thirty-seven engines, all at the Falls, to stop it. And they couldn't have done that had the winds continued. Like hell it must have been. The fires of hell."

He picked up the paper to show Paulina. "*Ach*, look at this, Lina." Paulina nodded and looked at the pictures from the fire. She knew that her husband wanted to talk.

"Well, something to be said for having a small building, I guess. But all the dailies, their buildings, gone." August paused.

He knew that his small press would be of no help to the daily papers, *The Sun*, *The American*, but he could offer his services to some of the weekly publications whose buildings had been destroyed.

He wrote an editorial for his paper, for the first time in English, the German version beside it. He felt quite patriotic, and grateful for a quirk of fate. The business, he knew, could not have survived if the building had been destroyed.

Willie also was grateful that he was not one of the thirty-five thousand men were left without permanent employment, though he, like countless others, had been affected by the fire.

Electric power gradually returned. The transit company worked with the city to determine the order in which the trolley routes would be restored. In the meantime, those trolleys that did run operated on an abbreviated schedule. There was no evening service. The shift manager said that he was sorry, but that Willie would not be needed until full service was restored.

The couple did without his income, stopped sending out the laundry, ate only one meal a day. Celeste gave Willie the money she had saved to buy a gramophone, five cents a week from the grocery money. They were not the only ones suffering, they knew, but it felt to them like they were.

August offered a gift to the couple. Willie gratefully accepted, and told his father that he would take it only as a loan, to be paid back as soon as he was called back to work. He would not go back to where he started, taking money from his father. Bu his cough, and his color, worsened.

Twenty-three _____

By mid-March Willie and Celeste, along with the city, were getting back on their feet. The company called Willie back to work, his Druid Hill Park run abbreviated until the track was restored. The line was not a priority for the city or the company.

The trolleys were not running late into the night, so Willie's shift, and his pay, were reduced by half. They told him that they hoped to be back to full service by the end of April. When they asked him to cover another route, this time on the day-shift, he accepted. It meant that his mornings started at 4 a.m., but it was work, and a full paycheck. And he would have his evenings with Celeste now, a more normal life, the life of a proper family.

Celeste had grown to like the routine of life with Willie and Stanley. Willie read. Sometimes he read to her; it seemed he was always reading to Stanley. Twice a week, the three ventured downtown to Mulberry Street to visit the Enoch Pratt Library. On their walks, Willie pointed out different architectural styles to Celeste. At the entrance to the library, he said, "Look at the belvedere, Celeste. Now think, compare it to the one at Camden Station. Which do you like better? Can you see the differences?"

Celeste told him that she preferred the one at the station, because that brought back memories of their honeymoon, their trip to Denver. In reality, she couldn't remember what the station looked like, much less the belvedere. But, she thought, Willie is feeling better, all this knowledge he's giving me.

It was a long walk, almost two miles, to the main library, but Willie preferred it to the branch on Miller Street at Broadway, a few blocks closer to home. He loved his city, its architecture, and saw something new each time he made the journey. Sometimes though, loaded with books, they took the trolley back home, Stanley wedged in his stroller between stacks of books.

With Willie's change of schedule, Celeste's days took on a distinctly different rhythm. She realized how much freedom Willie's mornings at home had provided. While he stayed with Stanley, she was free to do her errands and chores without the tugging of a toddler. Now she took pains to be friendly to Mrs. Polikov, and most mornings left the baby with her.

Annie appeared to be too busy with household chores, with cooking, with taking care of the boarders to help out. Afternoons found her too tired to see Celeste and Stanley, or busy starting supper for the now three boarders who now lived in the house, or so she said.

Many of Celeste's mornings were given over to laundry, first boiling the clothes in the tub, then scrubbing them on the drain board before she pulled them into the sink for a rinse. The landlord had installed a wringer (Mrs. Polikov called it a mangle), so she no longer had to twist them out by hand. Lifting the wet clothes into the wicker basket, she would then, depending on the weather, hang them in the dark basement, or struggle up the basement steps to the back yard clothesline. She pretended that she was in a play, a New York play, on Broadway. Or maybe the heroine in a book, waiting to be rescued, waiting for her house of Mt. Vernon Place.

Almost every day she'd go to the alley when she heard the a'rab's call and the brightly jangling bells attached to the horse and wagon.

> *"Holler, holler, holler,*
> *'til my throat gets sore.*
> *If it weren't for the pretty girls,*
> *I wouldn't have to*
> *holler no more."*

She grew to anticipate and love his distinctive call. I must be turning into Willie, getting pleasure from such incidentals, such trifles. Incidentals. Willie's word, she thought.

When she'd hear the horse's bells and distinctive song, she'd run to the window and call for him to wait. He was always willing to stop his flat, open wooden carriage to wait for the beautiful blonde to come out with her change purse. Celeste would take a nickel, some days a dime, and give it to him.

"Don't let me spend more than this," she'd tell him, and he'd nod, and fill her dark green woven basket with lettuce, tomatoes, greens, whatever he had picked up that morning at the Pratt Street market. Some afternoons he would come around again, with fish, shrimp, crabs that he had picked up from the Fish Market as it closed. Once, when Willie was home to carry it in, they bought a watermelon. Never again, she thought, too big, too messy, impossible to keep.

Toward the end of summer, Willie approached his father about repaying his latest loan, as well as the moneys August had advanced to repay the money that George had loaned them almost a year ago. The couple had saved five dollars, the bonus from the company to those who had been out of work. August told him to "put it aside for Stanley's education," then wondered if it would have been better to set this account up himself.

The next afternoon Willie journeyed to the Savings Bank of Baltimore. As he passed the corner of Charles and Lexington Streets, his eye was drawn to a gramophone in Eisenbrandt's window, and he entered the store. The $10 price tag was out of his range. As he turned to leave, Mr. Eisenbrandt approached him.

"If you're looking to save a bit of money, we just got a new one in. Well, a used one," he added, "from an estate. I'd be willing to give it to you for $5.00"

Willie left the store with a spring in his step. He had paid two dollars down, with the balance to be paid, fifty cents a week. They would deliver it tomorrow. A gramophone for Celeste. She deserves it, he thought. After all, she did begin saving for one on her own. And he still had most of the money for Stanley's education account.

He came to a camera shop in the next block. He looked at the window display A Brownie Kodak, a new invention, easy to use, with film in a roll. One dollar. A good price, he thought, to have a record of Stanley as he grew. Something that would last forever. He bought it.

He placed the remainder of the money for Stanley's account, and was saddened to see how little it was.

Celeste danced when the gramophone was delivered. "Oh, Willie. It will be like before, when we lived at your house. Only now we can dance every night now that you're home. We will have music in our home, music again!"

Willie read his books on photography and practiced every day. Stanley in his high chair; Stanley eating; Stanley holding a book. Pictures of Celeste, Stanley, filled the house; the gramophone sat on the dining table, ready for the records that Willie had retrieved from North Avenue. Clara didn't mind that he took the popular ones; she had her Caruso, Kreisler.

"Does *Vati* know you have a gramophone? How did you pay for it?" Clara's words to Willie.

Some things never change, he thought. But so delighted was he to have a happy Celeste again, he touched his sister on the nose and said, "Let me worry about that."

Clara bristled and turned. Willie was becoming a man, she thought, and smiled.

Throughout the summer, Willie photographed Celeste and Stanley, on their outings to the Pratt Library, in the back yard, Celeste standing with the a'rab, his cart and horse.

On the day of Stanley's second birthday, Celeste said, "All these pictures of us. Let me take one of you, of you and Stanley."

Willie showed her how to use the camera, and took his place beside his son. Such a characteristic pose, Celeste thought, as she looked through the lens to see Willie, kneeling on one knee, that lock of hair falling forward, his arm around Stanley, the boy's wavy curls tumbling around his face and ears. Celeste stood behind the camera, just as Willie had instructed her. "Now I have you two, just like this, forever!" she exclaimed. She realized that she was full of love. She realized that she was happy. Even the cake she baked tasted good that day.

The cool weather of fall arrived. Annie received a letter from Eva. She was engaged to a professor at The School of The Museum of Fine Arts. He specialized in Decorative Design, an up-and-coming division of the school. She would like to come home to marry, either in Annie's front room, if she consented, or at City Hall. She was sorry that Annie would not have a daughter who had a formal wedding, but she didn't think it was all that important to Annie anymore, not to mention the expense. It would be soon after the anniversary of George's death. She hoped her mother would understand. They would come for the weekend and then return to Boston. Would she please let Celeste know and ask The Reverend May if he would perform the ceremony?

On the morning of November 13th Celeste dressed for the wedding, glad that it was chilly enough for an outfit from her Denver trousseau, even if it fit more snuggly than it did two years ago. Willie got up to dress, but soon had to lie down again. Celeste went to him, felt his head, hot with fever. "It must be a cold that you caught from one of the passengers," she said, sorry that her handsome husband would not be at her side, a contrast to Eva's plain, some might say ugly, fiancé. She struggled to fit Stanley in his finest linen suit, his too a bit snug, and set out for Annie's house. She'd bring a piece of wedding cake home to Willie.

Twenty-four _____

The Monday after the wedding Willie came home from work early. He went directly to bed. Celeste brought him some broth. He slept. He didn't wake when she brought Stanley to him to say goodnight. Later that evening she slipped in the bed beside him.

The next morning he rose at 4 a.m. to dress and leave for work. He returned home early that day as well. When Celeste arrived home from the market, Willie had changed into his pajamas and was in bed. His jacket lay on the dining room table; the rest of his clothes lay on the floor beside the bed. She ran downstairs to ask Mrs. Polikov to keep Stanley a few hours longer. She sat beside Willie, lay cold cloths on his forehead, brought him more broth.

On Wednesday Celeste sent word to the company that Willie was ill and would be unable to work for the next few days. At the end of the week she had a visit from John Ellsworth, a manager of the United Railways. Celeste let him in, asked if he would like to visit with Willie. He greeted Willie and soon returned to the living room where Celeste sat with Stanley. She offered him a cup of tea. He declined, and, clearing his throat, began what later Celeste realized was a rehearsed speech. He stared down at his hat, turned the brim in this hand several times.

"Mr. Strauff has been a model employee in the time his has been with us. We were sorry to learn of his illness." Celeste looked up at him. She wondered if he knew that she was George's daughter. He must, she thought. Why else would he take the time to visit?

The man cleared his throat once more, coughed, then continued. "I have his pay envelop with me. For the days that he has worked, and through the end of this week. Since he has been ill so often, and since it appears that his recovery will take some time, I'm afraid that this is all that we can give him."

Celeste noticed the perspiration on Ellsworth's upper lip. She felt her heart drop. She reached to pick up Stanley and held her breath.

Ellsworth stood, handing Celeste the small manila envelope. "Please give him our best wishes for a speedy recovery. We hope that he will be able to return to work soon. Tell him that we will find a position for him once he is strong enough, well enough, to return to work."

Celeste took the envelop from him and stood, unthinkingly dropping Stanley to the floor. He landed with a thud she did not hear. "Yes, thank you. I will tell him," she said. Ellsworth shook her hand and left the apartment, exhaling a long breath as he reached the street.

A week later, Celeste looked up as Dr. Bergdorf entered the living room. She had been staring out the window, her hand resting atop the gramophone. She was counting the carriages and wagons going past on the street below. Once in a while she saw an automobile. Stanley played on the floor, placing the bear in the seat of the wooden fire engine, pieces of its wooden ladders strewn across the floor.

The doctor walked toward her, stepping around the child's toys. He paused before he spoke. "Willie's resting now, his fever, the coughing, have worn him out. But I'm afraid that I have some bad news for you."

He took the other chair at the table, facing Celeste. "My dear, it is consumption, I'm afraid. You know that he has always had a weakness in the chest. He made a fine recuperation for a time last year, but his condition was simply in remission. He needs treatment now. He won't be able to return to his work."

Celeste sat, not moving. She had imagined this scene in the days leading up to Willie's allowing her to contact the doctor, but had pushed it out of her mind. Willie sick, no job, no money.

Dr. Bergdorf saw anguish in her face, reached for her hand. "Would you like me to talk to the Strauffs about this? I know that they will do what they can to help. May I do that for you?"

Celeste held her back erect, felt her heart pound in her chest. Back to the Strauffs; back to the Strauffs. She tried to think, tried to come up with an alternate picture. Dr. Bergdorf waited.

She straightened herself even more. "I can think of no other course right now," she answered. "They know that he has been ill. Perhaps they have been expecting this. Yes, if you could talk to them for me, that might be the best thing." The doctor leaned toward her to catch her words.

"I will do that. I will stop by and see them this afternoon. Meanwhile, it would be best if you kept the child separated from his father. I can help you move his crib into this room if you'd like. And be sure to take care of yourself. Take a daily walk, breath in fresh air; keep the windows open, and each morning and evening inhale deeply and force the air out of your lungs completely. Do this ten times for each session. That way you will keep yourself strong. You need to do this, for Willie, and for Stanley. And it would be best to cease any marital relations until Willie totally regains his strength."

Celeste listened, then leaned down to touch Stanley's hand. She drew him toward her; her arms closed around his waist. Stanley looked up at the doctor and raised his bear. "Bee," he said, his hazel eyes serious as he studied this strange man in his house who was making his mother unhappy.

Twenty-five ——————————

Clara walked into the front room where August sat reading the evening paper.

"I have been studying this, *Vati*. There have been many developments since I was diagnosed. And Willie has tuberculosis in the lung. That is easier to treat. He is young. That is a good thing. He has opportunity to be cared for by the best. All this is good. He will recover; he will get well. Now, here is what must happen."

August put down his paper. Yes, he thought, Clara has been studying.

"There is a sanatorium in North Carolina" she continued. "It is run by a German doctor, vonRuck. It is the Germans who have made remarkable progress in treating this. It is all about fresh air and exercise, and this North Carolina climate is supposed to be the best for fresh air, all those forests, I think. Pine trees. That is where Willie must go. He can recover there at first and then come back here and fully regain his strength. I have studied this, *Vati*. This is the best thing for him."

Clara sat on the piano bench, facing her father, her notes in front of her. Earlier that week she had visited the medical library at The Johns Hopkins Hospital, told them that she was a doctor from New York. They gave her full access to their documents and studies.

August looked over at his daughter. Always knowing the best thing to do, he thought. Always taking charge. What man would want this, day in and day out?

He faced his daughter. "*Yah*, I have heard of this clinic. Dr. Bergdorf mentioned it. And, yes, we can send him. But, you know, he is a grown man. We cannot decide this for him. This is his decision."

August paused. "I don't think that he will want to leave Stanley and Celeste."

Clara bristled. "He has no choice in this, *Vati*. This is his life. He must see that. He must see that sacrifices are to be made, that everyone in this family must make sacrifices to ensure that he recovers. He cannot go on just being a weak boy, just worried about how he *feels*, making things right for Celeste. It is time that he acts like a man, *Vati*, way past the time he should act like a man."

Clara, August thought, always right, always sure, tiring to be around, but so smart. He reached for her hand. She came to his chair and stood before him.

"Clara, you have done a commendable job with this. I appreciate all your work, but have you not learned that you cannot force someone to do your bidding, even if it is the best thing? You cannot present Willie with an ultimatum to leave his family. He must come to a decision on his own. It must be his, and Celeste's, decision. Don't you see how that will only help him recover more quickly?

"Let Dr. Bergdorf present this mode of treatment to him, to them. Let him be the one to explain its efficacy. I have told the doctor that we will pay for any treatment that Willie needs. That is as far as our involvement should extend. This has to be up to Willie. Do you just think that following your advice, your orders, makes him a man?" August delivered this last sentence with more force than he intended.

Clara's eyes filled and she quickly turned away. I know what is right, she thought. Why can't everyone see that? And why can't they appreciate me? Why can't they thank me?

August walked to the front window and looked out at the street, at the grey stone wall of Green Mount Cemetery, the tree limbs, stark in the winter sky. He reviewed the names of those whom he could contact for yet another loan.

Twenty-six

Asheville, North Carolina

Dearest Celeste,

I arrived here yesterday evening. The train journey was long, and I did manage to sleep a few hours. The rest of the time I looked out the window at this beautiful scenery. Mountains, not as high, not as majestic, as the ones we saw on our trip to Denver, but beautiful in their own way. A misty blue emanating from them; they are softer, just row upon row of undulating heights. Quite relaxing in their own way. I guess they fit with the reason I am here.

The campus is quite lovely. My room is in the main building; there is a wing on either side. The buildings are of a light grey stone, I've not seen anything quite like it before, and the architecture is Romanesque. Do you remember what that is, my sweet? Red tile roofs do a good job in tying the buildings together. They sit proximately on a hill and there is 360 degree mountain view. It is much like a resort, not like a "sanatorium" at all. Some of the patients go into Asheville in the afternoons. I am looking forward to exploring the city. I have not had the opportunity to visit the South, except for my trip to Texas, and that really isn't the South, is it?

I count the hours since we were together, and cannot bear to think of the days that we will be apart. I am determined to complete this regimen and be home to you and Stanley before Christmas. We must spend Christmas together, as a family. The Railway Company has promised that I will have a job when I am strong enough to return to work. That is very *comforting to me. I know that soon I will be able to be a real husband to you, that we will have our own house and that the three of us can be a real family once again.*

I close my eyes and see you, my dearest one. Think of me, please. Write to me. Be strong. It will not be long until I am home and with you once again. Then we will have our own house. Stand up to Clara if she acts up. I am smiling just thinking about it, and I smile even more thinking of you.

With all my love,
Your Willie.

Asheville, North Carolina

Dearest Celeste,

It is hard to keep track of the days here. I have a calendar and I mark off each day so that I can remember what day of the week it is, how long I have been here. Every day is the same.

Four weeks into my regimen, I am feeling stronger most days. I feel that I do nothing except read and eat. They try experimental treatments sometimes; they always tell me when it is an experiment. For the past ten days they have been trying a compound of iodine and creosote which they rub on the inside of my thighs and in my armpits. I don't know if it helps or not, but everyone certainly knows when I am approaching! We try to keep some humor here. I think that I am one of the more hale patients. They try to keep the ones who are on the way out (not the way home) secluded. Those of us who can go to meals at the dining room have developed what we call a "gallows humor." I hope that it doesn't upset you. None of us believe that such a fate will befall us, not as long as we keep it at bay by ridiculing it.

Let me tell you about my days. They are all the same. At 7:30 a man comes in and wakes me up. He then rubs me all over with a coarse towel. This is to get my circulation going. We have breakfast at 8 am. And it is always fresh milk (they have their own cows here), bread, butter and coffee. Then we

307

go out to an open pavilion where we sit, wrapped up, and have yet a second breakfast. This is where I do most of my reading, though I must admit to a nap more days than not. Sometime during the day I am treated to a "forest douche." That is where they pour ice cold water over me. Someone stands on a ladder and pours the water out of a tremendous vat. Then I am dried off and scrubbed. This is torture for me, and I don't think that it does a bit of good.

We have dinner at 1 p.m. and then go back to the pavilion where we stay until we are called for dinner. That is served at 7 pm. After dinner we play cards, or games, or chat, or read. In the afternoon and evening they serve us all the brandy, sherry, wine or beer that we desire. I do like the brandy. Maybe that is why I find it difficult to concentrate on my reading!

I am thinking that I could do all this resting and breathing and cold water treatments right at home where I can be with you. My fever is gone completely; I will talk to the staff tomorrow to see if I am well enough to venture into Asheville for a look around. But mainly, I want to come home to you.

Please write as often as you can. I wait for your letters. I am glad that things at home are going as smoothly as they are and that Stanley is thriving. I hope that he will remember me when I return. Please don't let him forget me.

Give my love to Vati and Mutti; I will write them a short note tomorrow. And give a wink to Clara from me, however you want to manage that! Also give my regards to your mother. I hope that she is managing.

I long to see you,
Your Willie

Celeste realized that her days with the Strauffs afforded her a chance of freedom and rest that had not been part of her life for those months with Willie on their own. Keeping Stanley out of Inger's way, doing his laundry, was a small price to pay for three splendid meals each day and a respite from cleaning and shopping. Even Clara treated her with more civility, and Celeste often joined the family for their evenings of music. Stanley was clearly beloved by this family. Seeing this made her mother's distant manner sting a bit less. Annie had retreated into her own thoughts; there seemed to be no room for anyone else there.

In the evenings, when she put Stanley in his crib, she sat and read Willie's letters to him, and counted the days until his return.

Twenty-seven ————————————————

Clara delivered her pronouncement to the family. "Fresh air is what he needs. We can put in a sleeping porch connected to his, to their room. He can sleep out there. We can do whatever they did in North Carolina. There are enough of us here to take care of him, to bring him back to health. If he won't stay there, then we must do what is necessary. Celeste can help. I think that she will follow my direction."

Willie returned, taking the train from North Carolina to Baltimore. August called in the carpenters. The porch, attached to Willie's room and above the sunroom, and a door replacing one of the windows, was completed in less than a week. The carpenters needed the work.

August had seen to it that Willie and Celeste's bed was moved from their apartment, as was Willie's wardrobe. Some of the furniture was stored in the Strauff's basement; the rest was left. Annie said that she had no room, couldn't help them out. Mr. Eisenbrandt himself came to take back the gramophone. He was sorry, he said, and refunded their initial two dollar payment.

Inger bristled when the Strauffs told her that the three would be moving in. "I do not care for children. That was not the job you advertised. And just what kind of sickness does your son have? I will not be in a house where there is influenza."

Paulina took her aside, explained their situation. Inger agreed to cook for the expanded family; Celeste would care for Willie and Stanley, take care of all their needs.

*Twenty-eight*_____

The sun was hidden behind the clouds most of the day. A February day, thought Celeste, but still, my February day. She took care in dressing, placing a new blue ribbon at the back of her neck, holding up her hair. Maybe Willie would notice. The ribbon matched the tie she put under her lace collar. She hadn't worn the blouse since their last trip out, dinner at Haslingers's. She couldn't remember when that was. She even donned her red boots.

The Strauffs went about their day. August left early for the paper; Paulina followed a few hours later. Clara gathered her music, stuffed it in the soft leather valise that August and Paulina had presented to her that Christmas, and left for the Music Academy. She would walk the fourteen blocks that morning; take the trolley home. She would not give in to her limp.

Celeste gave Stanley his breakfast, sitting him at the table in the kitchen, not bringing the meal to the dining room. Inger was busy upstairs; the mother and son had the room to themselves.

"It is a very special day today, Stanley. A very special day for your mother," she sang, willing herself to be cheerful, to be happy. Heading to the sun porch, she placed Stanley in his playpen and went to the second floor, to visit with Willie. He had come inside from the porch where he slept each night and was sitting in the armchair in their bedroom. Inger had delivered his breakfast earlier.

"There is my girl," he said as she entered the room. "And how is my boy, today?" He shook his head. "I long to hold him, Celeste. How will he ever remember me, behind this door?"

Celeste sat on the arm of the chair. "Don't you worry about that a bit. Every day you're getting stronger. I can see it. Yes, I can see it,

311

can't you? It won't be long before the doctor will say that you can come downstairs, that you can see Stanley. And he could never forget you. I tell him about his Papa every day, every day, Willie."

She leaned over and kissed the top of his head, smoothed his brow, touched the back of his head where she had cut his hair just the week before. She waited, waited for him to say something, to remember. But he had closed his eyes, savoring the touch of her hand. And he had fallen asleep in the chair.

After lunch, she dressed Stanley in his coat, leggings, scarf and hat; she put on her coat and hat in the vestibule. "Let us go for a walk, Stanley, to a special place today," she said, and held his hand as he maneuvered down the front steps. Once in the stroller, she pushed it to the corner, then across the street.

She did not speak as they entered the cemetery. Stanley was quiet as well. He studied the limbs of the bare trees. At the top of the hill they turned left, and a few steps later, reached the Wells family plot. Celeste pushed the stroller up onto the grass so that it stood directly in line with the head and footstones.

"George Walker Wells. This is your grandfather, Stanley. This is my father." She reached down and felt the raised lettering.

"Today is my birthday, Papa. I am twenty."

Twenty-nine

Clara noticed the budding maple tree in the back yard when she brought the pen and inkwell to Willie's room. She placed them on his desk, the one he had used throughout his school career, his initials roughly carved by his boyhood penknife.

She helped him into his robe, thinking of the mornings years ago when he had bounded down the stairs to breakfast, rising too late to change his clothes, hoping that his father had already left for work, that he would not be sent back to dress. So many years ago, she thought.

Willie smiled up at her as she helped him to the chair. They communicated without words these days.

"I'll leave you to it. Just ring the bell if you need anything," she said. He nodded; she closed the door as she left the room.

Letters, he thought. These will be what they will have to remember. He tied the sash of his robe tighter, picked up the pen, and dipped it into the inkwell. He sat, holding his pen above the paper. Then, lowering the nib into the ink, he began.

> *My dearest boy,*
>
> *I close my eyes and see your fair hair, smell the sweet sweat of your tousled curls, inhale the sweet perfume of your kisses. These days it is best that we not see each other; it is important that you stay healthy. Your papa is sick and we do not want you to catch this illness.*
>
> *I close my eyes and imagine you, taller, older, preparing for your first day at school. I know that you will already be reading, know that you will be the best reader in the class, the smartest*

boy. Your teachers will recognize your worth and be proud that they have a part to play in your education.

I close my eyes and see you as a young man heading to college, your bags packed, ready to face the world. You will be tall and blond, like your mother. You will look the proper English gentleman. You will be sure of yourself; you will believe in your abilities; you will be strong; you will be a success.

Willie rested the pen on the holder, stopping to regain his strength, to think. This boy, this Stanley, he will be all that I could not be.

I close my eyes and see you with a family, an outstanding father, a loving, dedicated husband, an able provider. I see you surrounded by your children, with your dear mother looking on. My heart aches that I will not be there to see you as you grow, as you become a man.

In our all too brief time together, you have brought more happiness into my life than I could have dreamed of. Dear, dear boy, you have shown me that I could love without bounds. You have made my life worthwhile.

Take care of your mother. She loves you and she needs a strong man to help her navigate this world, and know, my dear sweet Stanley, that I love you with all my heart.

Your loving,
Papa

Willie picked up the blotting paper holder and pressed it over his words. I will not be here for him, he thought. I will not be part of their lives. They will have nothing to remember me by; Stanley will have no memory of our time together except for a few pictures. I will mean nothing to him, and he will grow up without his father. I have nothing to leave, not money, not a fine job. And Celeste, what will happen to Celeste? Willie struggled to stand, to walk to the door to the sleeping porch. He looked out on the alley.

What has it all meant, this life of mine? He put his hand out to steady himself, and returned to the desk to write his final letter.

Dearest, dearest Celeste,

 Please don't forget me, please.

 I wanted to be strong in this letter to you, wanted you to remember me as a strong husband, a provider, someone whom you could count on, someone who was always there for you, someone who always took care of you. I have failed you in so many ways, have not been the husband that you deserve. And now I'm leaving you. My heart is broken, not because I will die, but because I have failed, have failed you.

 I cannot change what has happened, cannot go back and be the husband that you deserve. But this I do know, and write without hesitation.

Willie stopped, wiped the perspiration from his face, rested his head in his left hand. He continued:

 I have loved you with my whole being ever since I knew you. Please remember that when you think of me. I wish that I were a writer so that I could put down words to tell you how much you have meant to me, how delirious you have made me when I just looked at you. And to touch you, to have you as my wife, has been my joy. I have failed you repeatedly, I know. I have not offered you the life that you deserve. And my hope, my dream for you is that the future will include everything that I could not provide for you.

He put the pen down, waited for his hand to stop trembling.

 Please take care of Stanley; please don't let him forget his father. I have written a letter for him. I hope that you will keep it and give it to him when he is old enough to understand. Oh, Celeste, my darling Celeste, please don't forget me.

    With all the love that I ever known,

       Your Willie

He put the letters into envelopes and placed them in the middle drawer. Time enough, he thought. He heard Clara on the landing outside his door. He called to her. She helped him into bed.

Thirty —————————————————————————

"It won't be long now," August murmured, his voice low. Paulina sat on their bed; it took so much effort to dress these days. The house, and everyone in it, was tired. August sat beside his wife, took her hand. "We must be ready to say our goodbyes." Paulina nodded.

While Celeste was in the basement kitchen with Stanley, Paulina went across the hall to Willie's room. Celeste had straightened his bed, her cot beside it. He wore clean pajamas. He opened his eyes when he heard the door.

"Ah, *Mutti*, you're here," he said. Paulina went to him, sat on the bed, took his hand.

"*Yah*, I am here."

Willie struggled to open his eyes. "Thank you, for everything, for all this, for letting us come here." He gasped for air; his coughs were weak.

Paulina took his hand in hers, brought it to her lips. "*Ach*, Willie, my dear Willie. You were always my favorite, my delicate, sweet favorite." Willie, asleep, did not hear her. She adjusted his covers, and went to the dining room for breakfast. She did not eat.

When August heard her steps, and went to Willie. August bent over his sleeping son. He whispered: "I could have been a better father to you. I could have been gentler, more forgiving. I was trying to make a man of you. I thought that was what a father should do. I never let you see how much you meant to me.

"You are my dear boy, Willie." August walked to the back window and looked out on the alley. My boy, he thought, and rested his head against the glass, and silent sobs came.

That night, Celeste, dressed for bed, leaned to kiss her husband's forehead. Willie looked up at her, managed a smile. His eyes, she thought, something is different. It's like he doesn't see me. She listened to his breathing as she fell asleep.

Thirty-one————————————————

Celeste woke to the room in semi-darkness, the suggestion of the alley's street light reflecting in the mirror. Gradually she realized that the background sound that had lulled her to sleep was no longer there. Willie's breathing.

She lay still on her cot a few minutes longer. I am only twenty years old, she thought. This is not my life. It is not my life.

Finally, she went to him. Willie lay on his back, the sheets and blanket smooth around him, his left hand on his chest. Celeste put her hand on his; there was no movement.

She sat on the edge of his bed, stroked his hair. She sat with him until she heard Stanley's call from the third floor. He knew to wait in his crib. Celeste went up the stairs, gathered him up and took him to the kitchen. Inger had started breakfast.

"Can you keep him, for just a little while, Inger?" Celeste's voice was soft; it didn't quaver.

Inger put her hands around his waist, hefted him into his high chair. "Take as long as you need."

Celeste stopped in the bathroom, gathered the basin, a washcloth, some towels. Then she went back to their room, to bathe her husband a last time.

Baltimore Sun
April 24, 1905

STRAUFF

On the morning of April 21, 1905, at his residence. 1108 East North avenue, William G., aged 25 years, beloved husband of Celeste Strauff (nee Wells) and son of Augusta and Lina Strauff. May he rest in peace.

Friends of the family are respectfully invited to attend the funeral from his late residents, as above, this Monday, April 24 at 8:30 A.M. Requiem High Mass at St. Ann's Church at 9 A.M. Interment private.

Baltimore Sun
April 25, 1905

WILLIAM G. STRAUFF

The funeral of Mr. William G. Strauff, who died Friday morning, took place from his late home, 1108 East Nor avenue.

A high requiem mass was celebrated by Rev. Timothy B. Kenny at St. Ann's Catholic Church. The pallbearers were Dr. William L. Burks, Messrs. Henry Starklauf, William Beacham, William Engels and H.W. Gore. The interment was in Baltimore Cemetery, under the direction of Undertaker William M. Gawthrop.

PART III

One

The undertaker brought Willie's body back to the house, placed his coffin in the front room. August and Paulina sat on the sofa, Clara on the piano bench.

Celeste led Stanley by the hand. "We're going to see Papa, Stanley. To say goodbye to him. He's in heaven now, but his body is here for just a little while, just enough time for us to say goodbye," she whispered as they entered the room.

Stanley pulled his hand away. "Papa, Papa," he squealed and ran to the casket. He patted Willie's cheek. "Wake up, Papa. Wake up." He turned to Paulina, "Papa sleep, *Oma*. You tell him wake up. Tell him." And Stanley pounded his father's chest.

Celeste went to the boy, swept him into her arms, put her mouth to his ear. "Stanley, Papa is in heaven. This is how people look when they are in heaven. Only his body is here. His spirit is in heaven. So you need to say goodbye to him. From now on, you'll just remember him. You can close your eyes to see him looking down at you."

Celeste stood beside the body, Willie in the suit he wore when they married. Inger had ironed his shirt; the undertaker had attached the linene collar perfectly, just as he would have liked it. His hair was in place. Celeste pictured him holding that front lock of hair between his fingers, pushing it back into place; she thought of the times that she had reached over and done it for him. She would wait until she was alone and do it a final time.

*Two*_____

Celeste spent the next three days in the second-floor bedroom, lying on their bed, sheets fresh and ironed, her cot folded and put away. At night she brought Stanley in bed with her. Stanley spent his days with Inger. She didn't complain. For her it was an issue matter of expediency rather than affection. This won't last long, she thought. Celeste will leave; she does not belong here.

Clara arranged the service, then informed the family of the details. The day of the funeral Stanley stayed with Annie, who had told Celeste she'd had enough of funerals.

At week's end, Celeste visited her mother. Annie knew why she had come. Their conversation was awkward, stilted, and by the end of the hour, Annie had consented, reluctantly, to allow Celeste and the baby to come there. The two would share the back third-floor room, overlooking the alleyway. Annie would ask two of the boarders if they would consent to share a room; otherwise she would have to let one of them go. That would mean less money, but, she reasoned, Celeste could help with the cooking and cleaning.

She looked over at her daughter. I should love you more. I should put my arms around you and hold you and let you cry until you have no tears left. I should be a better mother to you, she thought. But I feel nothing, not even for the boy.

Celeste and Stanley moved back across the street later that week. How many times have I done this, Celeste asked herself as she packed up her belongings.

The next morning Annie knocked on Celeste's bedroom door at sunrise. "Let the baby sleep. He'll come down when he's ready. Meanwhile there are some items that we need to discuss." Celeste pulled on a robe and went to the dining room with her mother. Once seated, Annie pulled a schedule of Celeste's duties from her apron pocket.

She's like Clara, Celeste thought. I'm trapped here.

Her attempts at cooking proved disastrous. Annie took over that chore. Her efforts at ironing the bed and table linens fared better, but caring for the men's shirts fell to Annie. Celeste found herself consigned to cleaning, heavy laundry and doing some of the shopping, provided that she took Stanley with her.

Each morning in the basement, standing at the metal washtub, she imagined being rescued, delivered to a new life, unaware, or unwilling, to recognize that she was wishing for a fairytale ending. She no longer dreamt of her house on Mt. Vernon Place.

Elizabeth wrote to her when Willie died; Celeste couldn't bring herself to answer. Eva hadn't traveled to Baltimore for the funeral. She was expecting her first child and needed her rest. Annie never mentioned her, although Celeste saw Eva's weekly letters, addressed to Annie alone, when they arrived in the post.

Celeste had no money of her own. She felt that she couldn't ask Annie for money; it was enough that Annie gave them room and board. But she pilfered money from Annie's purse, and felt like a child when she did. If she got caught, she planned to blame Stanley.

Her days were work, and Stanley; she spent her evenings alone. Annie retired to her room after the dinner dishes were washed and the table set for the next morning's breakfast. I cannot go on this way, Celeste thought, not in this house, so quiet, not even music to break the silence. She remembered her days with the Strauffs. They no longer seemed quite so dreadful.

In her room, with Stanley asleep, she thought about Willie. On her walks, especially when she saw the ragged sparking of a streetcar wire, she thought about Willie. It seemed to her that people had forgotten her widowed status; they no longer gave her sad smiles or patted her hand. I am overlooked, she thought.

She and Stanley left the house each day. Once a week they journeyed to the nearest branch library, off Broadway. She read to Stanley each day; for herself, she dipped into Charlotte Braeme regularly, and attempted to decipher the works of Theodore Dreiser, Winston Churchill. She thought Willie would have liked them. She finished *House of Mirth*, although it was a difficult read for her. Her favorite was *Rebecca of Sunnybrook Farm*, though people said that it was for children. Willie would be proud, she thought. All this reading.

The heroines in her books were plucky; they weren't satisfied with a life of cooking, cleaning. Some of them had jobs. They typed; some worked in stores. And so, Celeste said to herself, can I.

I will not stay here; I will not be a maid to boarders. I will find a job. That will give me a new life. I'll get a job, bring in money, support myself. I'll have new clothes, nice clothes. My friends will envy me. I'll be a new woman, just like in a book.

On an evening in early fall, Celeste loaded the dinner dishes onto the dumbwaiter and lowered it to the kitchen. Annie joined her in the washing up. Celeste looked over at her mother. Next week would be the second anniversary of George's death.

"Maybe we could go to Papa's grave, Mama."

Annie looked over at her daughter. Still beautiful, she thought. The death of her father, her husband, and still beautiful. She raised an eyebrow, thought to herself, it's better to be shallow. Nothing hurts you. Better to expect love as your due. Then she saw the sadness in Celeste's eyes.

She put her arm on her shoulder. "Yes, we will go together, remember him together."

Three———————————————————

November brought news of Eva's baby, a girl, Olivia Rose. Annie could not leave the work of the house to be with her; Eva did not expect it. But Annie smiled when she told Celeste the news. And Celeste deemed that smile a good sign. She would talk to Annie.

That afternoon Celeste sat in the front room with her mother, one of the few times when the women could sit without work at hand. Stanley napped upstairs. "Mama, I've been thinking. I think it would be a good thing for me, for us, if I got a job. It would bring in money; I could help pay expenses. It could work out for both of us."

Annie was silent. She knew what she should say, how she should answer, knew that she should be happy, proud, anxious for her daughter to start a new life. She heard herself answer, "What about Stanley? What about the boy? Who will mind him? Certainly I cannot take that on." She patted the lace antimacassar that sat on the arm of the sofa, looked down to adjust it, patted it again. She felt her face flush. Celeste saw it as well.

The words came in a rush, harsh. "Have you thought about Stanley, or me, or are you only thinking of what you want, what's best for you? Have you learned nothing? It is time that you grew up, that you realized that there are more people in this world than you, that everyone may not acquiesce to your whims, your fancies."

Her mother's reaction shocked Celeste; her eyes filled. "Mama, tell me why you are acting this way. Tell me what I have done to make you so angry, to make you hate me." Celeste's voice was high, reedy. She reached for her mother's hand. Annie stood and walked to the window.

"I just want to have more than this. Don't you want that for me? I can't spend my life here with you, cleaning, cooking for other people.

Don't you want me to have a better life? Why you are so angry with me. What have I done? Why don't you love me anymore, Mama?"

Annie felt Celeste's presence at her back, heard her words. She had recognized the cruelty in her response to Celeste and was shocked at the force behind them. Celeste had asked her why. Annie wished that she knew.

She turned to face her daughter. "My girl, I don't know what has come over me. The words just come out, I can't help myself. I know I have hurt you. I should be a comfort to you. Losing Willie, losing Willie was like losing a son."

Annie paused. "I thought I would never get over losing Grace." She closed her eyes, held the lace curtain in her right hand. "She skipped home from school that day, I saw her as she came up the block. At dinner she said her throat hurt. I felt her head and put her to bed. I went in later, to check on her, she had a fever. Two days later she was dead.

"Before you were born. Diphtheria. Now there is some kind of vaccine. If she had been born later she would still be alive. Your father and I decided never to talk about her to you. Eva was just two years old. She doesn't remember her. No one is left to remember her except me. No one." Annie thought that there would be tears. There weren't.

Her words were cracked, garbled. "And George, Papa, gone. And Willie, dear, sweet Willie. Everyone gone." Annie's mouth was dry; Celeste didn't hear the last.

They stood apart, each unable to go to the other. Celeste's held her head in her hands. "Mama, I have lost a husband and a father. You are not the only one. Can you not see that? Can't you, think about me?"

Annie turned to face her. She heard herself scream, "That is what I've been trying to tell you. I don't feel anything." Tears came, ran down her cheeks. "My girl, what I want for you, what I want for you, is to find a good man, a man who will take care of you. I am doing all I can do."

Celeste sank into the sofa. She looked at Annie. "Why can't we be a family, Mama?" she sobbed. "Why can't we just be a family?"

Stanley, awakened from his nap, had maneuvered his way down the two flights of stairs. He clutched his bear and watched from the doorway.

"Mama cry," he whispered.

Four _____

Clara came to the house bearing an armload of new clothes for Stanley. "He is growing, Celeste. You're doing a good job with him." She invited Celeste and Annie for Thanksgiving dinner the following week. Annie declined. No one was surprised. Celeste resolved that she would not spend the holiday in the house with Annie, the boarders away, perhaps with their families. They didn't say. They were as quiet as Annie, each guarded with his own live, his own secrets.

Celeste thought that Clara was making an effort to be kind to her. She was correct. Clara was trying, as August had suggested, to see the situation from Celeste's viewpoint. He helped her realize that it was important not to make an enemy of Celeste. They wanted to keep Stanley in their lives, to make sure that Willie's memory was kept alive for his son.

When the last Thursday of November arrived, Stanley, outfitted in a new linen suit and brown wool coat and leggings, left the house with his mother. Celeste wore another of her Denver outfits, powder blue, the waistband held together with two large safety pins. Paulina met them at the door and welcomed them with smiles and kisses that appeared sincere. Celeste recognized how she longed for smiles, and warmth. They seemed genuine here. A surprise, she thought, a nice one.

Smells of turkey and sauerkraut drifted from the basement kitchen, and Celeste was delighted to have a meal that was served to her, a meal where she didn't have to wash the dishes and scrub the pots and pans. Stanley ran to August who stood behind his wife. "*Opa*," the boy cried out. "*Opa*, S-S-S-tanley!" and August leaned down to accept the boy's kisses.

"I'm teaching him his 'esses," Celeste said.

August smiled and whipped a bubble of drool from his cheek.

"He is looking fine, Celeste," Paulina said. "Clara said that he was triving. Is that the word?" She bent to pick up her grandson.

Celeste draped her coat over Stanley's on the familiar rack in the front hallway, Willie's black winter coat and scarf had hung there the last time she was in the house. Just a few months ago; a lifetime, she thought.

At dinner, Stanley sat Willie's place, atop a pile of pillows and books. Everyone noticed. No one spoke of it. Too soon, they thought.

The meal finished, Paulina and August led the toddler to the front room. Clara and Celeste remained at the table while Inger cleared. Celeste made a special effort to thank the housekeeper, now aware of the work involved, below stairs. The thought came to Celeste that she filled Inger's position in her own house, though without wages.

She dismissed her thoughts with a shake of her head, and enjoyed the soft movement of her loosely pinned hair. It remained beautiful, she knew, still full and blond. She looked at Clara, noticed the maroon tint to her hair. Henna, Celeste thought. I could teach her how to use it.

The two were quiet, listening to Stanley's giggles. "He seems happy, Celeste. Are you reading to him? Three years old; it is time that he learned to read. Does he know his letters yet? I can help with that. Perhaps you could bring him here on Saturdays for lessons.

"And piano. He likes piano, likes to watch me play. I could start teaching him. A little older, if he likes violin, he could use Willie's. It is still here, in the attic."

Celeste thought, oh, Clara, always working on something. Now Stanley is your project. Then she stopped. She thought. Clara. And Stanley.

Celeste smiled. "Oh, yes, would you? That would be wonderful, and a way to keep Stanley close to you, to Willie. So not to forget, not to forget for a second."

Clara's small, dark eyes softened. "Yes, Celeste. Thank you."

Celeste looked at her. Clara was actually smiling, she thought. Good for her; good for us.

You know, Clara, this has not been an easy time for us, has it?" She clasped her hands in her lap. Clara nodded.

"I so admire you and the work that you do. Teaching music. It must be wonderful, helping people. Do you like going to work? Do you have enough time for your own music?"

Clara looked at Celeste and wondered. Was this a sincere compliment, or did she want something? She nodded. "I take only those students with promise, who need the discipline of an exacting teacher. And yes, both they and I are gratified when they make progress. I don't play for myself as much as I once did, but I do have a recital coming up the week before Christmas. You are welcome to come; it is open to the public."

"Yes, Clara, I would love to come," Celeste replied. She paused and took another breath.

"You know, I too have been thinking about a job. Nothing like what you are doing, of course, but I was thinking that I could do something, something more than keeping house for Mama and the boarders. Clara, it is an awful life for me." Celeste had not meant to say these last phrases aloud.

"Yes, I imagine it is," Clara said.

Celeste had resolved to be strong, like Clara; she was surprised at Clara's sympathetic response. She considered reaching for Clara's hand, then thought better of it.

"What kind of job were you thinking about?" Clara continued.

Celeste talked of her idea of working in a shop. "I was really thinking about Hutzler's. I think that I could do a good job there. I know a bit about clothes, what is fashionable. I think that would be a good job for me, don't you?"

Clara was silent, then replied, "Probably a very good job for you, Celeste. And would your mother care for Stanley?"

Celeste looked at Clara. They both knew the answer to her question. The truth, thought Celeste. I must tell her the truth.

"I did ask her. But she said no." Celeste sat erect, her eyes on the carpet.

"I hardly know my mother anymore. It is so awful in that house. You cannot imagine. And I hate to have Stanley live in such a gloomy home. I try to keep my spirits up, for him, you know. I take him out, to the park, to the library, but still we have to return to that house."

She looked up at Clara. "But you don't need to hear my troubles."

Clara wondered if Celeste were acting. Something struck her as not quite genuine. Yet she realized that she had been given an opportunity. If I help Celeste, she thought, I could see that Stanley was raised properly.

"Perhaps I can be of some help to you. Let me talk to *Vater*. Stanley could stay with us. You could see about a job without worrying about Stanley. We could give him a real home here, stability. Possibly we could give you some money to help you get started." She noticed a brightness in Celeste's eyes. Yes, she thought. I am getting through to her.

"You are so young. Your life should not be over. I think that we could help." Clara tilted her head, leaned on her hand.

Celeste stood. "Oh, Clara, would you? That would be so wonderful. Stanley needs a happy home, happier than where he is now. And I could find a job, and start again. Of course, never forgetting Willie. I could never forget him. But it has been so hard these last months."

Clara struggled to her feet. The cold, damp weather was causing her more pain in her knees than usual. "Yes, of course. I'll talk to *Vati* this evening."

Celeste reached down to hand Clara her cane. Their hands touched briefly as Clara grasped the carved wooden handle.

"This has been a good Thanksgiving," Clara said. "I was dreading it, missing Willie, seeing that empty chair. This time has been so hard for *Mutti*, though we never speak of it. But this, having Stanley, this could lift her spirits a bit. Yes, I will talk to him, to them, this evening."

Five

Celeste carried a basket laden with leftover turkey, sauerkraut, mashed potatoes and two slices each of pumpkin and mince pie from the house. Stanley carried his bear.

"Thank you so much for a lovely evening, Mrs. Strauff. Mama will enjoy having this wonderful food. I know that she would have enjoyed today. I'm sorry." Celeste paused. "Well, she doesn't like to go out too much. I hope you understand."

Paulina nodded, and leaned down to kiss Stanley goodbye. "My *liebchen, herzig barchen*, sweet, sweet *liebchen*." Stanley jumped up to receive his kiss, and waved his bear. "*Barchen, Oma. Barchen!* German language, *yah?*" and he laughed.

August stood beside his wife as they watched the mother and son cross the street. He put his arm around her. "Lina, our first Thanksgiving without Willie. It will never be the same."

Paulina turned to him, touched his face, surprised to hear her husband express such sorrow. "No, never," she whispered.

They made their way to the front room where Clara sat at the piano, her hands in her lap. She turned to face her parents. Lina sat in the chair by the window; August stood, looking out at Green Mount Cemetery, his thoughts his own this evening.

Clara sensed the sadness in the room. "*Mutti, Vati,* Celeste and I had an interesting conversation after dinner." She stopped, waited for their attention. August opened his mouth to respond, then thought better of it.

"Celeste wants to get a job. She is having a terrible time of it over there, nothing more than a maid to her mother, those boarders." Clara rubbed her hands down her black taffeta skirt. She saw that she had the full attention of her parents.

"What kind of a life is that for Stanley? He doesn't even have a room of his own. She says that she takes him out, for walks and the like, but I would be surprised if that were true. He needs to be where he is taught, where he experiences music and the things that a young boy of his background should have. I think that you will agree that that is not happening. Celeste is not capable to raising a child, not in the way that Stanley deserves."

August sat. He anticipated Clara's next words. Paulina straightened, sat forward.

"I think that Celeste would agree to let us keep Stanley. She talked about getting a job, at Hutzler's. She's already talked to her mother about it, and Annie said that she would not keep the child. I think that we could work it out so that he could come and live with us."

Paulina put her hands to her mouth. "*Ach,* Clara. Would she do that? Would she let him live here, with us?" Another thought intruded. "Does she want to live here as well?"

"No, *Mutti.* She wants to be out on her own. I think that if we could offer her a bit of help, financially, she would be eager to have Stanley come here." Clara struggled to keep from giggling with happiness. "I do think we could have him, *Mutti.* I do."

Paulina sank back in her chair, closed her eyes. It would be like having Willie back.

August looked over at his wife, recognized what it would mean to her. He addressed his daughter. "Clara, you must tread carefully here. You are working; *Mutti* comes to the paper three days a week. How would we care for Stanley? You must think of that, consider that."

Clara had thought of that difficulty while her parents had said their goodbyes in the hallway. "You could talk to Inger. She seems to like Stanley now; she treats him better than she did during those first days when Willie and Celeste came to live here. You could you offer her a bit more money. And *Mutti* and I would care for him whenever we're home. I don't think that it would be too much for us, do you, *Mutti*?" She knew that August would say yes, for Paulina.

"Oh, *Vati*, consider it. It would mean the world to *Mutti*, wouldn't it?"

August looked over at his wife and saw her cheeks wet with tears. He turned. "Clara, talk to Celeste. Ask her if she would come and see us, talk to us about this. See if she's serious about it, or if it was just another of her fancies. But yes, let us talk with her."

Money, he thought. More money.

Six

The following Tuesday morning, Celeste took the carrots from the ice box and started peeling. She was waiting for Annie to return from the butcher's.

Celeste began as soon as Annie came in the back door. "Mama, I've decided to look for a job. I've thought a lot about it, and I think that it is the best decision for me and Stanley. Clara said that they would keep Stanley. That way you can rent my room again."

Annie turned from the stove where she had laid the chuck roast. "And where are you proposing to live, Celeste? Surely you would not move back there. You are not thinking about living on your own? Do you have any idea how much it costs to rent an apartment, a room?"

Celeste faced her mother. "As a matter of fact, I do, Mama. Willie and I had our own apartment; I know how much our boarders pay. It is wrong of you to talk like I am a child. I am not. I am a widow with a son, trying to make my way in the world."

"Celeste, this is not one of your novels. Don't talk like it is. Life is not easy; you should know that by now. You must make your own way. You cannot expect anyone to come and rescue you."

Celeste looked at Annie. Someone might not want to rescue you, she thought, with your sour face all the time. But once I get out in the world, I know that someone will appear who will take care of me, who will make sure that I get my house on Mt. Vernon Place.

She held her tongue; she knew that her mother would never understand. Yet she still hoped for her mother's blessing.

"Oh, Mama, I know that it won't be easy for me. I just want a chance at a real life. Clara works; she has a job. So I think that I could do that too. Don't you want me to be happy, Mama? Don't you think that I deserve at least some happiness?"

Seven————————————————————

Celeste had presented herself at the manager's office at Hutzler's. He liked the way she held herself, liked her shy demeanor, liked the way she looked. His customers would certainly trust her judgment when she offered her opinion about what would suit them best. Sad situation, he thought. A young widow, no children. She was hired immediately.

The week before, August had met with Celeste, wished her luck in her new venture, gave her a check for $500, "to help get you set up." When Celeste saw the amount, she leaned down to kiss him on the cheek. It was more than she expected. "Thank you, Mr. Strauff. Thank you for everything." She would see Stanley on her days off.

Before she left, Celeste sought out Clara. "Thank you so much, Clara, for arranging this. I think that it is for the best, for everyone, don't you?" Celeste smiled and moved toward her sister-in-law.

Clara turned so that Celeste would not touch her. "There is one thing, Celeste. We will call the boy Willie. It is only right. Since Willie died, the child is our link to him. His name will be William August Strauff, and he will be called Willie. I am sure, had you known how sick Willie was, that you would have called him that from the beginning. So. You will call him Willie also from now on, whenever you see him. It would not be good to confuse the child. That is how it will be. I am sure you agree."

Celeste stopped. So, they named him, renamed him, really. Willie. Still, it was a lovely name. And, without realizing it, she ran her finger over the check that was still in her hand. "I understand," she responded. "Yes. I suppose it is a good thing."

She walked down the front steps of the house slowly. Willie, she thought. They changed his name to Willie. She held herself straight, pulled her shoulders back. I need to find a place of my own, she decided. I will be like the heroine in one of my books. I might just write my own book, about my adventures, and they wouldn't have to be made up.

Stanley moved into his father's bedroom on the second floor of the house on the north side of North Avenue. The double bed that Willie and Celeste had shared was replaced by the single bed that Willie had slept in as a boy. The desk remained against the wall. A small dresser was brought down from the third floor box room. Paulina had talked to Inger; the promise of a raise in her wages was received with a smile.

*Eight*_____

"Mama, I think it would be easier if I found a place to live closer to work."

Annie looked at her daughter. She had expected this; her only surprise was that it came so soon. Annie nodded, but did not answer. She looks like her old self, Annie thought. Proud, confident, sure of her beauty. How can she live like she's forgotten, Annie wondered, and was envious. She felt destined to hold all the sorrows of the family; it seemed as if Celeste possessed an armor of silk.

"I think I've found a place, just a room, really, but a place of my own. I'll still visit, Mama, and help you out when you need it. But this room is wonderful. It's like a bed-sit. You know, like in those books set in London. I'll be a working girl on my own now, Mama. Isn't that just the best thing?"

Celeste saw her mother's frown, but she was determined that she would let nothing spoil this exciting adventure. She would let nothing would ruin this.

She had paid a month's rent, in advance, for the second floor room on Robert Street. It was a few minutes closer to downtown. She would take the trolley to work, the Druid Park line, Willie's line. She would keep him close that way, see him in his uniform every morning and evening, being there, just for her. Celeste thought about him every night. He would want her to be happy, she knew. He would applaud her on her new adventure, she knew.

She resolved to be careful with August's generous gift. She would not be extravagant; she would not waste this money. It was for emergencies, though she did buy a delicate lavender spread and two ivory lace pillows for her bed. She wouldn't have to do heavy laundry.

Mrs. Bellingstone, the landlady, took care of the sheets and towels. She laughed that not having to do laundry made her happy.

I will see Stanley on my days off, she told herself. Now I really must start thinking of him as Willie. That is part of the agreement.

Nine————————————————

Clara was the first smiling face that greeted Stanley each morning; Inger fixed his breakfast; Paulina gathered the sheet filled with crumbs that was placed under his highchair and took it to the backyard for a shakeout. He waved his toast slices with abandon; he was happy. He didn't ask for his mother.

Paulina sat him on her lap. "You will now be 'Willie,' *liebchen*. You are Willie." Stanley stared at his grandmother. "Your name is Willie. Say it, sweet bear. Say 'My name is Willie'." And she struggled to be sure to pronounce the W, like an American.

Stanley looked at her and smiled. "My name Willie," he said, and laughed as she took his hands in hers and covered them with kisses.

"*Ya*, your name is W-W-Willie!" she said, and drew his arms above his head.

Clara taught him to read; Paulina gave him German words to remember; August recited Grimm's fairy tales, recounted the stories of *Hansel and Gretel, The Town Musicians of Bremen, The Mouse, the Bird and the Sausage.* He read to him from Willie's books, brought from the trunk in the attic. Inger cooked, and cleaned, and, once in a while, gave the child a smile. The toddler loved all of them, and laughed to his bear.

Ten _____

Dearest Elizabeth,

I am so sorry that I haven't written to you in so long. And I never told you how much your visits this summer meant to me. I was in such a pickle then, and having a friend like you made me feel better. Sometimes I feel that I am so alone, but with you I don't feel that way. We even laughed. I think that was the only time since before Willie got sick, and I haven't laughed too much since, only with Stanley, my beautiful boy.

I can hardly wait to see you again. When will you be coming home? I do have so much to tell you. I am now a working girl! Yes! I have a job! I am a saleslady at Hutzler's! In the lingerie department! Isn't that exciting news!

And then more exciting news. I have my own place now. I am living on my own. Now, that is grown-up, isn't it! I have a bed-sit at 1217 Robert Street. Now don't you think that is just like Sister Carrie? *Have you read it yet? I haven't had a chance to, but it is about a working girl who becomes rich and famous. Or at least something like that. So, when I become rich and famous, you can say that you have known me since the beginning.*

And Stanley, well, he is living with the Strauffs. It was just such an oppressive atmosphere at Mama's, not a good place to raise a child, and when Clara suggested that he stay there while I am working, well, I thought that it would be best for him. They have the money to give him a good life. I will visit, so he won't forget me. Oh, and yes, we call him Willie now, so he will always remember his father. His name

343

is William August Strauff. It is hard for me to think of him not as Stanley, but that is for the best as well.

So, when you come home for summer, please come and see me. I will serve you tea and cakes, though the cakes will be bought, not made. My room does not have a kitchen, but I can use the one downstairs when I need to. My landlady is very nice. She is sympathetic to my being a widow, as she is one herself.

Please write to me. I feel that I have so few friends. But maybe I will meet new people at my job. My job. Doesn't that sound grown up?

Your devoted friend and working girl,
Celeste

Eleven_____

Celeste rose early; she had set her alarm for six a.m. She hadn't slept well, nervous about her first day of work. Hutzler's Palace Store, the top of the line. She would work in the lingerie department. At first she had been disappointed; Hutzler's had the finest fashion department in Baltimore and she had hoped that she would be assigned there. But lingerie, all that silk and satin. It will be wonderful, she thought, just touching those delicate, soft pieces.

She dressed carefully, black serge skirt, black cotton stockings, a black blouse, the kind that they had told her to wear. She attached a white linen collar, rimmed with lace; she fastened the buttons on the matching cuffs. She piled her hair atop her head. No bow, no jewelry, except a watch with a thin black strap, they said. She had no watch. Celeste pinched her cheeks, bit her lips and waited for her hot plate to heat water for a cup of tea. She wanted to have just a bit of warmth in her stomach before she started out. Her landlady had wished her well the evening before; told her that she would have some toast made for her before she left.

I am a working girl, Celeste thought. I am modern. Everyone will see me and be envious.

She walked the two blocks east to Druid Hill Avenue and waited only minutes before the trolley arrived. Willie's trolley, she thought, as she took her seat. He would be proud of me, I know. She got off the trolley at Paca Street and walked the two blocks to Howard. She crossed the wide boulevard to get a better look at the store. It's five stories, grey stone, and it has carvings around the windows, she whispered. See Willie, I notice everything, just like you.

345

On her first day of work, she used the store's main entrance. After that, she would use the employee entrance on Clay Street. Mr. Warburg, the store manager, met her and escorted her to the second floor. He introduced her to her supervisor.

"Miss Yates will be with you for your first few days. Just follow what she does and soon you will know everything there is to know about women's lingerie. Good luck, Mrs. Strauff. Welcome to the Hutzler staff. I wish you well." He shook her hand, and left the department.

"Have you shopped here, Mrs. Strauff?" Miss Yates asked. When Celeste responded that she had often come to shop, though not buy, Mary Yates smiled. "Yes, I do understand that." She showed Celeste how the garments were organized. "By type, then by size, then by color. You see how they are all stored separately."

Celeste examined the glass-fronted drawers in the mahogany display cabinets.

"Take out no more than two pieces at a time; spread them on the counter. Drape one atop the other, leaving half of the bottom piece showing. The customer can touch them, but we prefer that she not handle them. Use your judgment about how to communicate that. Most of our customers know to act properly, so that should not be a problem for you. When you put pieces away, be sure to fold them correctly. You see the tissue paper that is placed between each piece? Use that; if you need more, I will bring you some."

Mary Yates studied her newest employee. She will be one to watch out for, she thought.

"Also, most of our customers have accounts with us, so you will handle very little money. Just take down their names and write the amount on these blue sheets. I'll come by and collect them at mid-day and at day's end.

"Most will prefer to have their purchases delivered. Our drivers know the addresses, so there is no need to get that information unless it is a new customer. In those cases, please call me and I will handle the transaction. So, for the others, be sure that you fold the items correctly, with the tissue paper, then tie the package with these ribbons." She nodded toward the spools of narrow pastel lace-trimmed strands, pink, green, blue, yellow and white. "You can decide what color you would like to use. At the end of the day, before you leave, take the bundles to the wrapping department; they will box them and give them to the driver to deliver. Deliveries are normally made the next day.

"Now, are you following this? Am I going too quickly? Do you have questions?" she asked.

Celeste shook her head. "I think that I am getting a good sense of things. Thank you."

Yates raised an eyebrow, unsure of what to think of this young woman. Beautiful, that she knew.

"For customers who pay with cash, you will place the money, along with the sales slip in this wire basket." She pointed above, and Celeste noticed the warren of pulleys that crisscrossed the ceiling.

"Elaborate, isn't it?" Yates smiled. This time it was genuine. "The basket goes to the office; there someone will take the money, make change if needed, and then return it and a receipt to you. It should not take more than a minute or two. While the customer is waiting, be sure to ask if she would like to sit down." She stroked the tufted stools, upholstered in varying shades of purples.

"Ask if she would like to have some tea. If she says yes, here is where you send the message to the maid." She indicated a small bell behind the counters.

"I'll stay with you today and most of tomorrow, but you seem to be catching on quite quickly. I do hope that you will enjoy working here, Mrs. Strauff."

"Please call me Celeste," she said.

"It is best that we maintain a formal atmosphere, at least while we are on the floor. That is the way things are done here."

Celeste bit her lower lip. "Of course, Mrs. Yates."

"It's Miss."

Twelve

Celeste found that she liked the work, liked the store, even liked her co-workers. She rose early each morning, and came downstairs to the breakfast that Mrs. Bellingstone had fixed for her. Celeste's landlady felt sorry for her, such a young widow, all on her own. The woman prepared Celeste's lunch each day, a sandwich and an apple, packed in a brown paper bag.

"You could use a little mothering," Mrs. Bellingstone said. "It makes me happy to do this for you. I feel useful."

Celeste leaned down to hug her new landlady. "You are so good to me, Mrs. Bellingstone," she said, and she placed her lunch in the patterned carpetbag she carried. She did not want her fellow trolley riders to know that she had to carry her lunch in a sack.

Miss Yates no longer needed to monitor Celeste's work, and when she had been there for several months, Yates called her into her office, to give her a work review, she said. Celeste sat quietly, her hands in her lap.

"You have done an acceptable job in your first months here, Mrs. Strauff. You know the merchandise; you service your customers well; you handle money and invoices expediently. I have observed, however, that you are a bit sloppy when you return the unsold merchandise to the drawers. You were instructed in the proper techniques to fold each piece. Please follow that exactly. You also are quite profligate in your use of tissue paper. Each sheet has a cost, and I notice that you tend to use a fresh sheet in too many cases. From now on, when you remove a piece of lingerie, you are to smooth the tissue and set it aside, then reuse it, after the customer leaves of course, as you return the properly folded piece to the appropriate drawer. That is the only criticism I have of you at this time.

"You are punctual; you do not tarry at your lunch break; your deportment is exemplary; your style of dress and your posture can be an example to the other girls. I am happy to have you as one of my employees. But do be careful with the tissue paper."

Celeste sat, uncertain of what was expected of her. Finally, she answered, "Yes, Miss Yates. Thank you."

Miss Yates stood. "Yes. You are dismissed. You may return to your department."

Celeste nodded and left the office. Well, she thought, that is what happens to a working girl. Wait until I tell--. She stopped. Who can I tell, she asked herself. Then it came to her. I'll tell Mrs. Bellingstone.

Celeste ate her lunch in the employee lunch room, chatting with the other salesladies. They were not shop girls, as one of the older women had pointed out, bristling when one of the younger ones sang a song about a shop girl. The woman stood up and looked sternly at the rest of those present. "We are part of the staff of Hutzler Brothers, the finest department store in Baltimore. That is certainly not a shop!" The younger woman apologized, and then laughed behind her back.

Celeste's work friends knew that she was a widow, and were quiet about their dates, boyfriends, they called them. As they grew more comfortable in her presence, they spoke more openly. Celeste laughed and giggled with them about their exploits. One dared to ask if she would like to accompany her sometime, that her beau knew some young men whom she was sure would like to meet Celeste. Celeste declined. She was not interested in young men with little money and limited prospects. No, she would wait for a man who would give her her house on Mt. Vernon Place.

That man had yet to appear at the lingerie counter of Hutzler Brothers, but Celeste kept her eyes open and her hair coiffed, in the event that he materialized. Perhaps someone will come in at Christmas time, to purchase a robe, a silk robe, for his rich, old, eccentric mother, she imagined.

She also surveyed the managers. They were all married, but, she fantasized, one will have a son. He will invite me to his home, introduce me, and his son will immediately be smitten. She took advantage of every opportunity to venture to the fifth floor, where the executives had their offices. She made sure that each one knew who she was, and always greeted them with a smile when they strolled down the aisles on the second floor, asking her if everything was working smoothly, if there was anything that she needed.

Miss Yates noted this as well. They did not approach her.

In the evenings, Mrs. Bellingstone had Celeste's supper waiting. At first, she was the only boarder, but Mrs. Bellingstone told her that she enjoyed fussing over her so much that she rented out the last bedroom. "It will keep me busy; they'll keep me company, even if they spend their time in their rooms. I like having young people in the house." She thought she might find a good young man for Celeste. But Celeste was not interested in anyone who would rent a room; she was not interested in a boarder. He could not promise her a house on Mt. Vernon Place.

Celeste was polite to, and sometime amused by, the young man who rented the room beside hers. But she did not flirt, did not offer him hope. She was a widow, and he was intimidated by that.

Her evenings were spent reading; she regularly visited the central library on Mulberry Street, just four blocks from The Hutzler Palace. She sketched her dream house, its layout, where she would place each piece of furniture. Willie, she thought. He is with me, watching me do this, and smiling. It will be our house, no matter whom I marry.

During her third year at Hutzler's, the store announced to its two hundred employees that it planned a special 50th anniversary celebration. There would be special merchandise, special sales, and, for its crowning achievement, they had commissioned Harrison Fisher to paint his vision of the typical "Baltimore Girl."

A painting, Celeste thought. I could be the model. I am from Baltimore; who could represent the city, and Hutzler's, better than I? She resolved to make sure that Mr. Warburg suggested her to the artist. Yes, I could be *The Baltimore Girl*, she thought. That would show everybody.

Thirteen———————————————————

The four-year-old sat at the table, a heavy Saturday lunch spread before the family.

"The child is using his left hand. Do you see that? He uses it consistently," August pointed out.

"Well, his mother is left-handed. So was Willie. I suppose it was born in him," Paulina answered, wary of the direction of the conversation.

"Well, stop it," August responded. "We stopped Willie. You can stop this Willie."

"I wonder if that was the right thing to do. You know, I think Willie was a nervous boy because of that. Perhaps we should just let him be. He's had so much upheaval in his life. Let's not add to that, at least right now. We can work on it later," Paulina said, surprised that she expressed herself so strongly, surprised that she felt this way.

"Nonsense. You must do something before he gets any older. It will only be more difficult then." He turned, "Clara, you will help your mother, no?" August threw down his napkins. All these women; he could not let Willie be raised only by women. He would make a man of him.

Paulina did as she was directed, but only when August or Clara was present. Let the poor little fellow use whatever hand he wants, she thought. For now at least. When he gets older I'll talk to him about it, make him understand how important it is.

The young Willie learned to use his right hand when his grandfather was present, though he developed a stammer that exhibited itself whenever he was nervous or tired or scared, which was more often than his grandparents observed.

August noticed the stammer, and didn't like what he saw. "Now the boy has a stammer, just like his father," he said to Paulina. "Take him to the doctor and get it fixed."

Paulina drew herself to her full five foot height. "This can't be fixed, August. We couldn't fix Willie; we can't fix little Willie. Just leave the boy alone. Let him be who he is, not who you want him to be. Have you learned nothing?"

August took a step back. How dare she use that tone of voice, he thought, then decided not to respond. "You are upset," he said. "We will talk about this later." He turned on his heel and walked out of the room.

Paulina inhaled deeply and found that she was smiling.

Willie heard them talking about him. He sat huddled along the wall on the dark staircase leading to the second floor. He had Willie's room; he had Willie's stammer; he was left-handed, like Willie; and he was nervous, scared, and afraid, like Willie.

Fourteen _____

Celeste worked half-days on Saturdays; her Sundays were spent sleeping-in and preparing for the week ahead. She washed her stockings, her underclothes in the small sink in the bathroom, and spread them on her chairs, tables, windowsills to dry. She removed the collars and cuffs from her blouses and scrubbed them on the washboard in the basement, careful of the lace, and struggling to remove random ink stains and city grit from the fabric. Most of her earnings went to Mrs. Bellingstone, but, Celeste realized, her life was better here than living with Annie. She seldom saw her mother; she tried to remember to write her a note every Sunday evening. Most times she was too tired, or forgot, or just didn't have anything to say. These Sunday evenings she also thought about Stanley. Willie, she admonished herself, I must think of him now as Willie.

She had seen him often in the first months. Now her visits were infrequent. The journey was so arduous, she reasoned, the streetcars, the transfers, the time, when she needed to rest up from her busy workweek. The child seemed to be happy living there; he called her Mama, but clung to Paulina when she arrived. He stood in the doorway of the front room and eyed her warily. He seemed more content to play in the sun room, with his bear and his fire engine.

She had a picture of herself made for him, even purchased a silver frame, not so expensive with her employee discount, and presented it to Clara. "Could you put this in his room, so he'll remember me?" she asked. Clara nodded, but on her next visit, when the child led Celeste up the familiar steps to his room to show her his grown-up bed, the picture was nowhere to be seen. Well, she thought, maybe better that way. It is not good for the baby to miss his mother.

Clara held this view as well, and on Celeste's last visit, suggested that Willie be told that his mother had to go away. "That way he won't be asking for you. You don't want to make the boy unhappy, do you? Especially since he will be facing some big changes in the fall.

"We have enrolled him at Mount Washington Country School. He will live there during the week; we will see that he comes home most weekends. We thought it best for him. He is already so advanced that the school accepted him early. He will be their youngest student, but the nuns are equipped to handle that. And he will be with boys of educated parents. Many of them travel, or are stationed in embassies overseas. He will have good examples there. And then, of course, be with us some of the time."

Celeste looked over at her son. He was not yet five years old. Sometimes he stammered when he talked, like Willie, Celeste thought. Willie's son. I wonder what he would think.

Clara handed her an envelope. "Just a little something to help out."

*Fifteen*_____

That Sunday she took the streetcar. She told no one. There were few who knew of his existence.

It had been too long to count since she'd seen him. He's better off. That's what the Strauffs said. You're better off, so said a small voice inside her whenever she thought of Stanley, which wasn't often. But this day she wanted to see him, see what he looked like, see if he was still blond.

She hadn't planned this day, this trip. But she woke up thinking, dreaming of him. She just wanted to see what he looked like.

Riding the streetcar north on Falls Road, she studied the Roland Park summer cottages to her right. She noticed the rolling hills, the grasslands to the west, where customers at Hutzler's' summered; some had moved here year-round now that the streetcar routes had been extended.

She sat on the straw-seated cushion and watched the countryside roll past. A Sunday morning. Washing her stockings would have to wait. This day she planned to see, to catch a glimpse of, her son.

Celeste left the trolley when it reached Kelley Avenue. She felt the eyes of the passengers as she made her way down the iron stairs. The women were studying her blue linen suit, its ecru lace at the sleeves and collar. The skirt had a hem of the same lace. Her boots were kid, buttoned with small imitation pearls. Celeste was used to envying, and admiring, glances. The men also looked, not at her suit, but at the derriere under it. Celeste was used to these looks too. She liked them both.

She hummed as she crossed the bridge that spanned rushing water of the Jones Falls. Her eyes sought out the building on the hill. She caught a glimpse of the rose brick building before the thick leaves of the maple and oak trees that lined the circular drive blocked her view.

She hadn't realized the walk would be so long, so strenuous. Her hair lay heavy atop her head; the burden of her hat, bedecked with feathers, weighed her down. The heat had made the feathers go limp, and she pushed them away as they stuck to her damp brow. The boots grew tight. Her thighs chaffed with each step. She took off her gloves and folded them into her pocketbook. She continued walking, all the while wondering if the day had been a mistake.

She turned right onto Smith Avenue when she reached the end of the bridge. The sign stood large before her, "Mount Washington Female College." A smaller sign hung beneath, "Mount Washington Country School for Boys." She looked up. The Octagon building stood at the top of the steep hill.

The climb was arduous. Her body was wet with perspiration. Her feet hurt, her boots unsuited to the journey. She sat to rest on one of the benches halfway up the drive, taking temporary refuge under a tree. A soft breeze dried her damp brow, though her feet continued to throb.

Flowers, pink and white, lined both sides of the drive, and she wondered what they were called. As she sat, a new thought came to her. He might not be here. It's Sunday. Suppose they came and took him home for the weekend. She brought her purse to her mouth. Why had I not thought of that? Why did I choose this day, a Sunday, for this journey?

She sat, then folded her hands in her lap. I've come this far, I'm here at his school, she said to herself, and stood to continue the walk. The building stood as a beacon at the top of the hill, a four-story octagonal shaped building surrounded on all floors with wooden walkways painted ivory. As she approached, she thought that it looked like a kind of wedding cake, the cupola replacing the bride and groom.

It was here that Willie spent his weeks, studying, learning what the nuns taught, dressed in the grey military uniform with its gold buttons and navy trim. Little boys dressed up as fancy soldiers, Celeste thought, and wondered who did his laundry. The nuns, she supposed.

Another bench placed was place near the building's entrance;
Celeste walked toward it. She had seen boys from the school, wearing
their woolen uniforms, at Hutzler's. They came sometimes with their
mothers, in the late afternoons, after their classes and sports had
ended. Their drivers brought them; their cooks served their meals.

The campus was quiet, deserted, the only movement a tall,
blond woman who limped to the bench to sit. Celeste sat, unmoving,
recovering from the exertion of her climb, waiting for her pulse to
slow, the perspiration to dry; her feet to stop pulsating.

Suppose this trip has been for nothing, she thought. Suppose I
came here for nothing. Suppose I don't see him.

She sensed movement to her right. A nun, her hands inside the wide
sleeves of her black habit, entered the building. Celeste remembered
the chinchilla muff that she had as a girl, how she tucked her hands
inside it just as she had seen the nun do. A second nun appeared,
leading a line of boys, dressed in grey flannel short pants and maroon
sweaters bearing the school's crest. Lined up by height, they marched,
two by two. Celeste watched, little boys, dressed like men, in tandem,
lockstep. They passed in front of the bench. The nun acknowledged
Celeste with a nod, then looked straight ahead.

Celeste wondered if Willie were in the group. Which one was he?
She picked out one to follow with her eyes, the one with the skinny
legs, the one whose socks were falling down around his ankles. No,
that could not be Willie, she thought. He would be a tidy dresser, like
his father. The boys marched toward a play yard behind the building.
There was no running or romping on this beautifully manicured lawn;
all play was confined to ball fields, play yards.

The line came closer to her. Most boys were unaware of the
woman seated on the bench, so intent were they on reaching their
green freedom. But a few noticed her. The little ones were guileless;
the older ones stared with unrestrained curiosity. A beautiful woman,
not their mother or their sister. They appreciated that, wanted to keep
on looking. One boy, in the last, the tallest, pair, elbowed his partner.
They both gawped, lost the practiced rhythm of their cadence, and
jostled one another. They hid their laughs behind their hands, not
quite embarrassed.

One small boy, a blond, marched directly behind the nun. He concentrated on counting his steps. He loved the marches; he loved the nuns, Sister Sulpice, especially. She often sat on his bed when she came by for night checks. He sometimes woke to feel her cool hand on his head, smoothing a lock of hair from his forehead. He knew to lie there quietly, not to let her know he was awake. He sometimes wondered if she were his mother.

He knew that one day his mother would come and take him away with her. They would live in their own house. He would go to work to make money so that they could live. He knew that he needed an occupation. I could be a fireman, he thought. Maybe a fireman. Or a logger. Then we could live in the woods.

But this day he was thinking about monkey bars. He was counting; he was thinking. He didn't notice the woman to his left. And her eyes passed over him as she surveyed the group.

The boys were out of sight; Celeste could hear their whoops from the play yard. She watched the nun, fingering her rosary as she stood at the yard's edge. She asked herself why she came, why she woke up that morning determined to see him. She hadn't been able to pick him out of the group; the boys, all in their play uniforms, looked so much alike. Those well-bred, well-educated, wealthy boys being groomed to take their places in Baltimore society.

What kind of mother doesn't even recognize her own son? Well, she sighed to herself, maybe it is best this way. It was a mistake to come. The journey was too far, too hard. And now I have the return trip ahead of me.

As she stood to leave, the tall nun came to her. "Is there something I can help you with, or are you simply enjoying this beautiful fall day, this beautiful scenery atop our mountain?" She smiled at Celeste. Celeste felt her eyes fill.

"I came here to see my son, just to look at him, not to cause any trouble," she found herself saying. The words caught in her throat.

The nun put her hand on Celeste's. "We would have to have permission for that, of course. Maybe another Sunday."

And she turned her eyes to her boys.

*Sixteen*_____

The walk down the hill was easier, less strenuous. Celeste did not look back. She concentrated on *The Baltimore Girl*. Surely they would choose her. She would be famous.

But she found that she was crying as she came to the end of the drive. Turning left onto Kelley Avenue, more tears came, and her body shook with sobs. She reached into her bag; she had forgotten her handkerchief. She pulled one of her gloves from her pocketbook and used it to wipe her eyes, her nose. It will not do to board the trolley like this, she thought. She continued down the narrow street that led to the bridge, the red brick mill to her left. She hadn't noticed it earlier, she realized, so focused had she been on the building at the top of the hill.

Stopping midway on the bridge, Celeste leaned against its stone side and stared down at the rushing water of the Jones Falls. Putting her hand to her mouth, she swallowed hard, willed herself to stop crying. She hadn't cried since the day that Willie died, not at his funeral, not leaving Annie's, not saying goodbye to Stanley. But today the tears wouldn't stop. She looked toward Falls Road and started to walk, grateful that there was no one to see her.

When she reached the trolley stop, she looked at her watch, her first purchase with her Hutzler employee discount, one with a thin black strap so she could wear it at work. Four o'clock. She closed her eyes and pictured her room at Mrs. Bellingstone's. She ached to be home, sitting in the chair beside the window, safe.

As she stood she realized that she was hungry. She looked at the stores clustered there. All were shuttered. Sunday, she remembered. Her tears were replaced by a headache that would become worse as the afternoon progressed.

When the trolley finally arrived, Celeste stepped up, handed her token to the conductor, and slid into a seat in the second row, grateful that they streetcar was nearly empty, grateful to be able to sit down. The blisters on her feet had started to sting; one on her left heel, another on the top of the toes on her right foot. She closed her eyes and imagined soaking them in Epsom salts, remembering how Mrs. B. had brought the basin to her during her first weeks at Hutzler's. Mrs. B., she thought. What would I do without her?

She left the trolley at North Avenue to transfer to the line that that would take her nearest to her home. It was too far to walk that day. She decided to get a bite to eat before the last leg of her journey; she entered a small restaurant at Linden Avenue. The manager was uncomfortable allowing such a disheveled woman on her own into his establishment. But when he looked more closely at her outfit, he determined that she was a gentlewoman. He seated her in a corner of the restaurant.

Celeste smoothed her hair as she walked to the Ladies' Lounge to splash some water on her face and rearrange her hat. She unbuttoned her jacket and smoothed the wrinkled blouse beneath it. She knew not to touch her boots or her feet. They would have to wait.

Celeste ordered tea when the waiter came, then added, "And some soup, please. What is your soup today?" She sat and ate slowly, the steaming tea, the navy bean soup strengthening her for the journey home

She thanked the waiter and limped to the door. She willed herself not to cry. Just let me get home, she thought. Just let me get to my room. Just let me get through this day.

Mrs. Bellingstone was waiting when Celeste arrived. "It's getting late; I was worried about you. You had a nice day, did you?" Celeste nodded and went directly to the stairs.

Man trouble, her landlady thought.

Once in her room, Celeste walked directly to the bed. She roughly pulled out her hatpin and tossed her hat on the dresser. I never want to see another feather, she thought. She sat and gingerly removed her boots with one hand, unhooking her stockings from their garters with the other. She pulled off the white hose and looked at her feet, blotched red and purple. The white blisters shone. As she flung the boots across the room the tears came again. She tore off her jacket and unbuttoned the top of her blouse, pulling it over her head and tugging the sleeves over her wrists. She stood and stepped out of her skirt, dropping it on the floor beside her. She untied the strings on her corset, struggled out of it and threw it across the room. Just let me stay here, she thought; just let me be safe.

She pulled the lavender spread down, and crawled beneath the covers. Just let me sleep, she thought. Let this day be over. Willie, why aren't you here? Why did you leave me?

Later that evening, when she knew all in the house were asleep, Celeste went into the bathroom, locked the door, and soaked her feet in the tub.

Seventeen

The alarm rang at its usual 7 a.m. Celeste forced herself to sit up. Maybe today, she said to herself as she threw off the blanket, Mr. Warburg will tell me that I have been chosen to be *The Baltimore Girl*.

She splashed her face with cold water, relieved that her eyes were no longer red and swollen after her afternoon of tears. At least, she thought as she pulled on the black cotton stockings, my feet look better, and she looked tenderly at her comfortable, broken-in, lace-up, low-heeled black work shoes. She glanced in the mirror before she left her room. Not at my best today.

Mrs. Bellingstone had a special breakfast waiting. All this trouble over a man, she thought. And here is a perfectly good fellow living right here in this house that Celeste doesn't give a second glance.

Celeste thanked her and, grateful for a full meal, tucked into the crisp bacon and scrambled eggs. She even had a cup of Mrs. Bellingstone's coffee. Maybe it will make me feel better, she thought, and she willed herself to push the events of the past day from her mind. Focus on being *The Baltimore Girl*. Today it will be yours.

Her walk to the trolley stop and the ride to Paca Street cheered her. She liked her work; she had made friends there; she didn't even mind Miss Yates. Celeste knew enough to ask her advice every once in a while; she deferred to her judgment; she treated her with respect. For her part, Miss Yates knew enough to leave Celeste alone, aware that the young widow was a favorite on the fifth floor.

When she stepped onto Clay Street and pulled open the doors to the employee entrance, she felt that she was home. She hung up her coat and placed her purse and carpet bag in the small locker. She heard the younger salesladies talking about their weekend. She smiled and looked interested. She wanted no one to ask about hers. She would focus on today, she decided. Yesterday never happened.

She was folding merchandise, carefully re-using the smoothed tissue paper, when one of the managers approached her. Her friends referred to all of them as "the fifth floor." She noticed that his black frock coat was a bit wrinkled. "Good morning, Mr. Hayley," she said, and employed her sunniest smile. She raised her eyebrows and bit her lower lip. "Any word yet on Mr. Fisher's choice for a model?" she asked. This will be my lucky day, she thought. After yesterday, this will make things right.

The tall man paused, cleared his throat. "Mrs. Strauff, before you take you lunch today, please come to my office" Celeste nodded, sure that today would be her lucky day.

It was not to be so, however. Hayley delivered the news as gently as he could. Harrison Fisher had chosen his model. "Mrs. Strauff, I know this is a disappointment for you, but Mr. Fisher was looking for a girl. You are a woman, a beautiful woman of course, but your particular beauty did not correspond to the standard the artist envisioned."

Hayley stopped. He used words Celeste did not understand, but she knew not to interrupt him. She did understand that today would not be her lucky day.

"However," he continued, "you have been noticed and I would like you to think about an opportunity. We are planning to model our fashions in the Guilford room, while the ladies lunch. The models would walk about, answer questions that the customers might have about the outfits. I'd like you to consider taking this on, in addition to your other duties, of course. You would, naturally, be eligible for additional pay for this time." Hayley picked up his pen on his desk, unscrewed the top, then returned it, placing it in the middle of the green blotter.

"Thank you, Mr. Hayley. I think it would be lovely to be a model. I do follow fashion, you know. I have other clothes besides the ones I wear here. Not just black." Celeste could not stifle her giggle, and then bit down on her lips to stop herself from smiling.

Hayley stood. Celeste knew that was his signal that she was dismissed. "It would be best if you said nothing to Miss Yates, nor to anyone in the store. Not until we work out the details," he said.

Celeste nodded, and worked hard not to skip out of the room. Her smiles at lunch made some of her co-workers think that she had a man in her life.

Eighteen

The store had few customers late that afternoon. Celeste faced the bank of glass-paneled drawers, making sure that each piece of merchandise was folded, sorted by size and shade, tissue papers placed between each piece. Not a piece of silk was out of place.

She sensed rather than saw a figure behind her. *Molinard de Molinard*, Clara's scent. Celeste hoped that there was another Baltimore matron who wore this expensive perfume. She turned. It was Clara. Of course, she thought.

"Clara, what a nice surprise. Are you here to purchase something? What can I show you?" She turned toward the drawers.

Clara stood, her feet solidly place, girded for battle. "I am not here to buy. You know why I am here."

Celeste glanced around her, nervous that Miss Yates, or worse, Mr. Hayley, would witness this encounter. "Please, Clara, not here. Could we meet after my work hours end?"

Clara inhaled, pulled herself more erect. "Yes, you are right. Not here. As soon as you finish work, come directly to the house. I will be expecting you. And you will come. Do you understand? Is that understood?"

Celeste drew her shoulders back as well, stood straight, her posture belying her emotions. "Clara, I can explain," she began.

"Yes, you will explain. I said that I will see you tonight. Six o'clock." Clara turned and walked out of the store with military precision, in spite of her reliance this day on a cane.

Celeste leaned on the glass counter, heedless of the smudged fingerprints she left. She had to come up with a story, a reason. How had Clara found out so quickly? The kind nun. It had to be the nun.

Not so kind, Celeste thought. Or is Clara a fuming about something else? How can I plan my story, my excuse, if I don't know why Clara is so incensed?

She stopped her thoughts, crossed her arms across her chest, saw the situation from a different focus. What does it matter if Clara is angry? I went to see my son. There is nothing wrong with that. I didn't ask to be with him, I just wanted to see him. And that didn't even happen. How dare Clara come to my work? I will not be afraid of Clara, the Strauffs. I am living on my own. They have taken my son. It is they who should be worried. Clara has frightened me for the last time, she resolved. I will not allow her to ruin this day.

Celeste's hands shook as she dusted the counters and locked the drawers at the end of the workday. I will be strong, she repeated to herself. I will not be cowed by Clara. I have done nothing wrong. They cannot keep me from seeing my son.

She gathered her belongings from the employee lounge and gave her gloves an extra tug as she put them on. I will be strong, she said, surprised to hear her words aloud and relieved that there was no one present to hear them.

She walked the four blocks to Charles Street and took the familiar trolley line to North Avenue. Once off the streetcar, she hoped that the crisp evening air would give her energy, reinforce her resolve. She considered stopping in to see Annie afterward. Get all these prickly tasks taken care of at once, she thought.

The walk proved more demanding than she had anticipated, her feet still not recovered from the day before. So many long walks, she thought, but she had salvaged a bit of her earlier determination by the time she arrived at the house.

Clara came to the door in answer to the bell, her face set just as firmly as it had been in the store. Without greeting, she led Celeste to the front room. Celeste saw that the table was set for dinner, though there were no cooking smells coming from the kitchen downstairs.

Paulina sat in her usual chair. She did not rise to greet Celeste, but her smile was warm. August was nowhere to be seen. Clara asked Celeste to sit; she remained standing. Celeste took August's chair, and sat stiff-spined as she turned toward Clara. She would not allow herself to be treated like a child being scolded.

Clara began. "Celeste, we learned that you went to Willie's school yesterday. This is a very grave matter. We agreed that it would be best for him, best for all, if you were not part of his life. It will not do for you to appear and then disappear. You agreed that we would tell him that you had to go away. That way he would stop expecting you, thinking of you. Well, of course it is fine that he think of you, remember you, but it is not a good thing for him to think that you will be in his life." Clara stopped. She wanted Celeste to understand her words, as well as what was not being said.

"*Vater* was quite generous to you, and made sure that you had resources to begin a new life. We were happy to do that. But you must understand that Willie also deserves a new life. He cannot be pulled every which way. His home is here, with us. We are his family now. You agreed to that, and it is expected that you abide by that agreement. It is not proper for you to see him, or for you to try to see him. If we deem that his meeting you is the best thing for him, we will arrange it. *We* will arrange it. Do you understand what I am saying? Am I making myself clear?" Clara stood, her hand resting atop the piano, as if she were delivering a stern lecture to her students.

Celeste stood, towering over Clara. "I will do what I think is best for Willie, Clara. And you are speaking to me in a most unsuitable manner. I will tell you what yesterday's situation entailed. After you hear me, I will expect an apology."

Clara was surprised at both Celeste's tone and her words. Her time on her own has toughened her, she thought. She listened to her account of the day, but gave no apology. Clara recognized that her adversary had developed a new strength.

Paulina reached up to pat Celeste's hand. "All will be well, *liebchen*," she said. Celeste leaned down to kiss her on the cheek.

She turned to Clara. "I'll let myself out."

Nineteen ————————————————————

The next morning, as she dressed for work, Celeste stared in the looking glass. *How is it that I look exactly the same after so much has happened? Visiting Stanley; losing* The Baltimore Girl, *Mr. Hayley choosing me to model, Clara. All those things happening and here I am dressing for work, just like a regular day. Willie, you see, I am strong. Are you proud of me?*

It was mid-morning when she was summoned to Hayley's office. Miss Yates delivered the message and waited for Celeste to give some indication of the reason for the visit. Celeste smiled and said, "Oh thank you so much for covering for me. I'm sure that I won't be long." She was walking toward the elevator to the fifth floor before Miss Yates could respond, forcing herself not to skip.

Hayley came from behind his desk to greet her. "We're moving a bit faster than we anticipated, Mrs. Strauff. It is a stroke of luck for us to find you in our midst, our model. We plan to introduce this program in two weeks if we can manage that. Your assignment will be from eleven until 2:30 each Tuesday and Thursday. Miss Grey, our buyer, will choose the outfits for you; she anticipates that you will wear five or six different outfits each day. You will be fitted for them each Friday. You will work with her starting this Friday. Is that acceptable?"

Celeste bobbed her head. *Modeling six different outfits every day. What luxury,* she thought.

"Now, we are prepared to give you a bonus for this work, in addition to your daily rate. I think that ten percent for each hour worked is a fair agreement, don't you? We will not compensate you extra for those times that you are being fitted. You will earn your normal rate for that time. And you will have to work with Miss Yates to arrange coverage for your time away. You can do that, can't you?" he asked.

Celeste swallowed. "Actually, Mr. Hayley, I think it would be best if you approached her about that. That is, if it is not too much trouble. I think that she would take it better coming from you, since she is my superior. I don't think it would be good for me to tell her about this myself. That is, if it isn't too much trouble." Celeste knew she was babbling, but couldn't control her words.

Hayley smiled, and held his expression a bit long. "Of course, you are right. I'll see to it by the end of the day. Now don't worry your head about it in the least. I'm glad that we could work this out, Mrs. Strauff."

He paused. "May I call you Celeste?"

Twenty————————————————

When Celeste returned from lunch she knew that Miss Yates had been told. The old sour puss, she thought. She looks like she's just sucked on the biggest lemon at Lexington Market. "Mr. Hayley has spoken to me. I am aware that you will be away several days a week during the lunch time hours. That is, of course, our busiest time, so I will have to take over your responsibilities while you are otherwise engaged. Please see that your work is current before you leave each of those days. It would not be fitting for me to have to pick up after you."

Celeste felt as well as heard the frostiness in Mary's voice. "Oh, yes," she responded. "I know that this is an imposition on you, Miss Yates. I will do everything I, anything I can to make this not too much more work for you. If you see that I can do more, please tell me."

"Well, yes, thank you. I realize that this is not your fault, and it is quite an opportunity for you. I'm sure that you will make the most of it." This last sentence was delivered with more than a hint of venom.

On Friday Celeste walked to the third-floor Guilford Room to meet the buyer and to be fitted for the next week's outfits. Miss Grey had selected six ensembles. Celeste had worn her best step-in and corset, and it was not until she was alone with the buyer that she realized how old and worn they were. Miss Grey noticed as well.

As the fitter worked, Miss Grey leaned close to Celeste and said softly, "Please choose two sets of lingerie from your department. You will wear them under these clothes. They will be part of the modeling wardrobe; they will not belong to you. However, it is expected that you launder them after each session. Please tell Mary, Miss Yates, that I have approved this. And, by the way, Mrs. Strauff, you could stand to lose a few pounds."

Celeste flushed. The fitter caught her eye and raised an eyebrow in sympathy. Still, Celeste thought, two new sets of lingerie. I will pick the most expensive pieces.

On the streetcar ride home that evening, she wondered why she didn't feel happier. Then she shook her head to put that thought out of her mind.

Twenty-one _____

It seemed to Celeste that Mr. Hayley was passing by the lingerie counters more often than usual. "Things going well for you, Celeste? The modeling program starts next week. Are your fittings proceeding well?" He smiled and nodded at Mary. "Good morning to you, Miss Yates."

Celeste had told her supervisor about the lingerie sets for the modeling program. "Well, yes. Let us decide together which ones you will have. We will have to take them off the inventory. We will charge them to Management's account. And it would be advisable to take those models that are not selling well. Do you not agree?"

Celeste did not agree, but remained silent. Sour puss Yates, she thought. She doesn't want me to have anything good. But she responded, "Oh, yes, would you help me choose? I know that Miss Grey wants to be sure that I wear only the finest. At least that is what she told me. And you are so good at this; it would be so nice if you could help."

Mary felt cornered, unconvinced that Celeste's smile was sincere. She had proven herself to be a hard worker. But there was something that Mary couldn't quite identify. She saw how the men watched Celeste, smiled at her and then continued smiling as they walked on. Mary had heard nothing about any man or beau in Celeste's life. She was a widow when started working there. Now, two years later, was there still no man in Celeste's life? Or perhaps she was just discrete, an attribute that the other girls here could use, Mary thought.

Several months later, Hayley approached Celeste as she walked back to the Guilford room to change back into her work attire.

The outfit that Miss Grey had chosen to end the day's modeling complimented Celeste's complexion, her hair, her eyes and her height. The navy walking suit had a long jacket that reached her knees. A shorter woman would have been lost in it. The skirt fell in layers and was the shorter length that was just becoming fashionable in Baltimore that year. Her navy shoes, closed with a thin strap, were shown to their advantage, and her ivory hose caught the light in a way that brought the eyes to her ankles. Miss Grey added a silk and chiffon scarf at her neck, peach and ivory. Celeste had wondered earlier if she could manage to purchase it; thought that perhaps she could convince Miss Grey to give her a larger than usual discount.

"Celeste, you look especially lovely today."

She thanked him and blushed. Blushing at will was a skill that she had mastered as a girl. Men liked it, she knew. She also was aware that she did look especially lovely that day. "Oh, thank you, Mr. Hayley. Actually, I was deliberating how I could afford to buy it!" Celeste laughed. Willie, she thought, how about my using the word deliberating.

Hayley paused. "Well, Celeste, let me see if I can do something to make sure that you can. Why don't you come to my office at the end of your shift? I should have an answer for you by then."

Celeste clapped her hands, then stopped, remembering Hutzler's proper decorum. "I don't know how to thank you, Mr. Hayley. Yes, I will be happy to come to your office. Thank you again; thank you so much."

Hayley smiled and walked toward the buyer's office.

She saw the dress box on the desk as she entered Hayley's office late that afternoon. What a show-stopping smile, he thought, as he handed her the package. "Please consider this as Hutzler Brothers' gift to you for your extraordinary service to us."

He watched her response. What a beauty, he thought. He walked in front of his desk. "Celeste, would you care to have dinner with me one evening? And perhaps a show after?"

Twenty-two ⎯⎯⎯⎯⎯⎯⎯⎯⎯⎯⎯⎯⎯⎯⎯

He suggested that they meet at Miller Brothers at a quarter past six the next evening. "That should give you enough time to get there, and after dinner we can take my car downtown to a vaudeville review. Do you know vaudeville?"

Celeste nodded. "Oh, yes, when my husband and I visited Denver we attended a performance. It was quite different and enjoyable. But I have not attended any since then." She lowered her eyes.

"Good," he said. "I will, of course, escort you to your home afterward. It would not be seemly for a young woman such as yourself to be out alone after dark."

Celeste thanked him again, hugged the box to her, and left his office. She turned her head at the doorway, to give him one last smile before she left.

The rest of the staff had left by the time she got to her locker. Mr. Hayley is interested in me, she thought. He is married, but I'll bet they don't get along. I would marry a divorced man, she thought. Yes, certainly I would.

The next morning Celeste placed the fringed shawl into her carpetbag. She had purchased it when Hutzler's had its "India" sale, and knew that the black background overlaid with dark reds and blues would blend with her black blouse and skirt. She added a wide dark red ribbon to wind in her hair, as well as the garnet earrings that Willie had given to her the Christmas before he died. He had bought them in Asheville. She hadn't worn them since the day of his funeral.

As she walked toward Fayette Street that morning she felt that something was amiss, that something was not quite right. She shook her head to dismiss any sense of disquiet. Mr. Hayley asked me to dinner; he had seen that I was rewarded with a beautiful outfit, one that I could never have afforded, not even with my Hutzler discount. He is taking me to a show. I must be special. I will feel proud about that. He must like me, she thought. And it would not bother me to marry a divorced man, not at all.

At dinner that evening, Hayley ordered oysters and was surprised that Celeste knew how to eat them. They drank champagne. Afterward, he guided her to his car, a dark blue Buick Model C. Celeste had seen automobiles, but had never ridden in one before. She made sure that Hayley didn't know that. She thought that he drove with elegance as he maneuvered the car to East Baltimore Street, gripping the wheel when the tires caught in the trolley tracks. She held on to the leather passenger strap to keep her balance, and imagined that she was a young Roland Park matron, not chauffeured, but riding in a car driven by her husband. Yes, I know how to do this, she thought. I know how to act the part.

As he helped her from the car, she looked up at the marquee: Eve Tanguay. Celeste had read about her in the one of the fan magazines that had just started to be published. She always bought the latest ones at the newsstand at North and Linden Avenues on Saturday afternoons after her half-day shift had ended. She thought it exciting reading, though she knew that Willie would not approve.

She adjusted her shawl, touched her hair. The ride in the open car had loosened it; she made sure that it was pinned tightly enough to stay up, but was still soft enough to appear that it might fall at the slightest touch. Men liked that, she knew.

She pointed to the marquee. "Oh, I know about her," she exclaimed. "She will be in the next production of the Ziegfeld Follies. And she is here, in Baltimore. What a treat! You must have known how much I would like to see her. And now, here I am. Oh, thank you, Mr. Hayley. Thank you so much for this evening."

"For tonight, you can call me Daniel. But, of course, always Mr. Hayley at the store," he said, as he put his arm around her waist and guided her into the lobby of the newly opened Gayety Theatre. The lights dimmed as they took their seats; Celeste sat through the opening acts, anxious to see the famous Eve Tanguay. Wait until I tell the girls, she thought, and then remembered that she would have to make up a story about how she visited the Gayety. The dinner and show would remain just between her and Mr. Hayley. Daniel, she thought, I must remember to call him Daniel.

Celeste gasped when the show's headliner tottered onto the stage, just managing to balance her towering headdress. Why she isn't even pretty; she's pudgy! And her hair, it's all snarled, almost matted. What man would like that? she wondered. Then Tanguay opened her mouth to sing. My goodness, all those yaps and cackles. Why in the world is she so famous? She slurs her words so that I can hardly understand them.

Then Celeste stopped thinking and listened. The chanteuse sang *You'll Remember Me a Hundred Years From Now* with such a saucy irony that Celeste found herself laughing, without even thinking of what Hayley might think. Tanguay skipped off the stage and soon returned in another elaborate costume, this one all beads. It must weigh a ton, she thought. And she could never sit down in it. But doesn't she seem to be having a good time.

Celeste kept track. The star had ten costume changes in all. When she came out for her final number, *I Don't Care*, Celeste thought her heart would burst with laughter and happiness. She could not remember having such an amazing time, not even with Willie.

With a start, she realized that she had paid no attention to Hayley since they had been seated. But he had been paying attention to her, and watched with amusement, and a surprising bit of tenderness, as his companion bounced and clapped with each song the performer performed. A sweet girl, he thought, though surely she is a woman.

Celeste felt that she was walking on air as they walked to the car. "Mr. Hayley, Daniel, thank you for a wonderful evening."

They were silent he drove to the house on Robert Street. He opened the car door and walked her to the front door. Mrs. Bellingstone was sitting in the window, waiting for her boarder.

"I had a wonderful time this evening. Thank you for being a part of that." Daniel reached down and kissed her hand. Celeste turned and entered the house. Mrs. Bellingstone stood, watching as Hayley returned to his car.

Oh, Celeste, she thought. Oh my dear Celeste.

Twenty-three

The dinners became expected, only sometimes followed by shows. It depended what was playing. Hayley knew what Celeste liked, and delighted in watching her reactions. He knew she loved music, and at the end of one evening, as he stopped at the house on Robert Street, he turned to her.

"I'd like to give you something special, if I may." Celeste smiled to herself. An engagement ring, she thought. And so soon. She closed her eyes, thinking of how she would respond, what she would say, how she would look. "It's in the trunk," he continued.

Celeste's eyes snapped open. Seconds passed before she answered. "Oh, may I see?" she asked, and Hayley came around the car and opened the door for her.

"I would be delighted for you to see," he answered, and they walked toward the back of the car. "It was too big to wrap. And I do hope that you like it."

Celeste squealed when she saw the gramophone. "Oh, I can't believe it. It's just like the one Willie and I had!" This was the first time that Hayley had heard her refer to her life before Hutzler's. She had avoided direct answers to his questions, and he was content not to pursue it.

"Do you think your landlady will object?" he asked.

"Oh, no. I will ask her to place it in the parlor so that we all can listen to it. Oh, Daniel, this is one of the grandest gifts ever. Thank you so much." And she scampered to the door to open it as Hayley struggled to carry it up the front steps.

Celeste ran to Mrs. Bellingstone who waited in the front room. "Oh, wait until you see this. A gramophone! Isn't it wonderful? Do you think we can put it in here? That way we all can listen to it, maybe even dance. Mrs. B., isn't this just wonderful!"

Thoughts of engagement rings were replaced by fantasies of musical evenings in the parlor. Just like a family, Celeste thought.

She introduced Hayley to her landlady, who offered him a hand and a cold smile. He set the machine on the floor by the door. "We can determine where it goes tomorrow," Mrs. Bellingstone said, and walked toward the back of the house.

Celeste walked Hayley to the door. "This is a wonderful gift," she said, and reached up and kissed him on the mouth. In all their weeks together, this was the first time she had done more than allow her hand to be kissed.

The next week, over dinner, Hayley told Celeste about an upcoming trip to New York, to meet with some of the store's major suppliers. "Would you like to accompany me, Celeste?" he asked.

"Oh, I've never been to New York. Clara --" She stopped. She had started to tell him of Clara's many trips there. But that was another life. That was not part of her life now.

Hayley smiled. "Clara what? What were you about to say?"

Celeste shook her head. "New York? That sounds just wonderful. Would it be possible to see some shows there?"

Hayley laughed. "As many as I can find for you," he said. "I'll be in meetings during the day, but the hotel can arrange for you to tour if you'd like. And, of course, you would have your own room. I want to make sure that you know that. I would never do anything to compromise you. You are my dear Celeste." And he reached over and kissed her hand. Like Willie, she thought. She shook her head. Oh, Willie, not now.

A few days later, Hayley handed her an envelope. "Here is your ticket. It would be best if we took separate trains. I've put in enough cash so that you will be able to take a cab from the station to the hotel. I'll be in touch when I arrive." He paused. "Celeste, I know that you will be discrete about this."

"Of course, Daniel," she responded, and was uncharacteristically quiet the rest of the evening.

And uncharacteristically quiet was Mrs. Bellingstone when Celeste told her that she would be traveling for the next several days.

Celeste boarded the morning train. She carried the train case that she had purchased for her trip to Denver, her honeymoon case, she thought. And in the hours that the train passed through Maryland and Pennsylvania, she thought about that trip west. It felt like a lifetime ago to her.

At the Knickerbocker Hotel she unpacked the few outfits she had brought. She stood at the window, watching for Hayley. The sky darkened; she paced in the small room.

She jumped when she heard the phone ring. He had arrived. Would she meet him in the lobby at 7:30? He had a special dinner planned for them. She dressed slowly, slipping into the lingerie that was designated for the Guilford Room. No one would see it, she thought, and remembered what she had read about Mr. Ziegfeld and his show girls. He wanted them all to wear silk underwear. "No one will see it," he had said, "but they will know it. And they will walk differently." And Celeste resolved to walk like a Ziegfeld Girl.

Hayley pointed out Union Square as their carriage took them to 14th Street. They entered the dark, plush atmosphere of Luchow's. Celeste tried to remember the restaurant that Willie had taken her to in Denver. That was German, she thought, and, like this, dark and opulent. She shook her head. Please Willie, leave me alone, just for this night.

They walked through room after room, one with a glass ceiling higher than she had ever seen, another with frosted skylights of etched glass. She looked up, taking it all in. What would Willie have thought? He would have identified everything; he would have told me all about everything. He would have loved it here.

But Hayley's eyes followed only the waiter. Celeste watched him. All this opulence, all these details were lost on him, she thought. Willie, leave me alone.

She saw ferns and more ferns. Like the Strauff's house, she thought. Something everywhere; no space without a piece of furniture, a piano or a plant. She had a glass of May wine; he had bourbon and water while an oompah band played. "Oh, I love that song," she said. "*Lili Marlene*. That is one of my favorites. So sad. It's on my list to buy for my wonderful gramophone."

The waiter led them to yet another room, another table, where Celeste ordered a saddle of Canadian hare with kronsberries and potato dumplings; Hayley dined on Koenigsburger klops with caper sauce. As at every meal, he marveled at Celeste's appetite. Here was a woman who was not afraid to eat in front of a man, he thought. Such a comparison to his wife, who ate almost nothing at their meals together, but who he knew hid cakes and sweets in her bureau drawers, behind her handkerchiefs, underneath her stockings.

Celeste laughed and sang along when another band marched into the room. When that group was replaced by a Vienna Quartet, she listened intently. All this music, she thought. It is like being with the Strauffs again. But to think about that family is not what I want for tonight. This is my night, with this man, this man who will surely ask me to marry him.

"You look especially lovely tonight, my dear," Hayley said as he helped Celeste into the horse-drawn carriage for their ride back to The Knickerbocker. "I am always amazed and humbled by your beauty."

Celeste smiled and settled back, watching New York. Here I am, in New York City, she thought. Something more for my book.

They entered the elevator together; Hayley walked her to her room. They stopped at her door. "May I come in?" he asked, gently.

Celeste stood, quiet. Then she nodded.

Twenty-four ————————————

She and Hayley had returned from New York earlier that week. The three days and two nights there had been a blur to her. She had toured the city, riding in a horse-drawn bus. The tour leader noticed her, a beautiful young woman, alone, and gave her special attention. He was even more gratified when the carriage returned to The Knickerbocker and she tipped him with a dollar coin. She had thought that he would give her change, but soon realized that she had been mistaken. "Well, thank you, miss. You have a wonderful time in New York," he had said, and tipped his hat. He followed her with his eyes as she entered the hotel.

She had brought her own money with her. Hayley might be paying for her hotel and dinners, but she wanted to be on her own during the day. She wanted to be a modern woman. The dollar tip critically depleted her reserve funds. But, she thought, I have learned a lesson. I do not want to live in New York, where people smile at you and then take advantage.

Mrs. Bellingstone had dinner on the table when she arrived back in Baltimore. She had taken a cab, a motorcar, from the station. Hayley had moved his seat when they reached Philadelphia; she had not seen him since. But she understood. Discretion. That was reasonable. And she was sure that he would ask her to be his wife, very soon now. She wondered why she didn't feel more content, then shook her hair and decided not to think about it. Mr. Hayley, Daniel, loves me, she thought. He does, surely.

The landlady waited for her boarder to talk about her trip. Celeste talked about New York, the train ride. Finally she said, "Mrs. B., I went with Mr. Hayley. I just had to tell you, had to tell someone. I hope that you don't think me a bad girl."

Mrs. Bellingstone looked over at her boarder, her now-beloved boarder. "Oh, my girl. I do not think you are a bad girl. I think you are a foolish girl."

Celeste smiled. "Oh, no, Mrs. B. I am sure that Mr. Hayley, Daniel, loves me. I am sure of it." And she walked over to her landlady and kissed her on the cheek.

Twenty-five_____

Three days after their return Warburg called Hayley into his office. He did not rise from behind his desk when the younger man entered.

"You are to stop it. Now. Do you understand? There will be no scandal brought to this store, not while I am in charge. Do what you have to do. There will be no more discussion."

Warburg uncapped his pen and went back to his papers. He did not acknowledge Hayley's departure from his office.

Twenty-six ——————————————

The next morning Hayley sent word to Miss Yates that Celeste was to report to his office at 11 a.m. She sensed that all was not well and smiled as she delivered this message to Celeste.

Celeste smiled as well. She had not seen Daniel since their return. He'll set a time for us to have dinner, she thought.

Hayley did not rise from his desk when Celeste put her head around the corner of his office door. "You asked to see me, sir?" and she smiled in what she thought was a coquettish way.

"Mrs. Strauff, please come in and sit down." Hayley indicated the chair in front of his mahogany desk. Celeste felt her heart clutch. She entered his office and sat in the chair he had indicated, the one she had sat in so many times before, times of giggles and laughter. It was not to be so on this day, that she knew.

Hayley cleared his throat. "We have found that your services are no longer necessary at Hutzler Brothers. You have served us well for several years now. We are prepared to give you an exemplary reference, and severance pay that should do to tide you over until you find other suitable employment."

Celeste sat, her hands in her lap. She looked down, trying to catch her breath. She looked across the desk. Hayley's eyes were set, his chin raised.

Finally she found words. "But why, Daniel? Why are you doing this?"

"Mrs. Strauff, you will address me as Mr. Hayley. Anything else is quite inappropriate."

"Daniel, Mr. Hayley, what will I do? I need this job. I thought that you loved me? What did I do, Daniel? Just tell me; I'll make it right. I swear I will. I'll make it right. But please don't take my job from me. Please, Daniel."

Hayley rose, offered Celeste his handkerchief. Celeste had shed no tears, but was gasping to catch her breath. He stood beside her. "I have some contacts at Stewart's. I think that I can work it out so that you may have a position there. I will be in touch with you. By post.

"If you want my help, you will not contact me here. Ever." He swallowed and looked at the girl, the woman he had loved, at least a bit.

"I am sorry that it is this way, Celeste. I truly am. But I have no choice. I wish you the best." He handed her an envelope that contained her severance, a week's pay, $2.50. "It is best that you go now. And say nothing to anyone about this."

Celeste gathered herself, wiped her eyes, and placed the handkerchief on Hayley's desk. She turned and left. She said nothing.

The employee lounge was empty when she gathered her belongings. She would not see Miss Yates nor any of her colleagues. She walked toward Paca Street, glad for the cold, biting wind. She carried her hat, let the wind blow her hair.

She walked the two blocks from the streetcar stop. Mrs. Bellingstone, returning from the market, saw her walking toward the house. Something was wrong. She hurried to meet her.

"What is it, love? Are you sick?"

Celeste, who had held herself stoic through the walk to Paca Street, through the long wait for the trolley and the journey home, looked at her landlady. Just let me get to the house, she thought, she willed. She managed a smile for this woman, who she knew loved her.

As they walked up the front steps together Mrs. Bellingstone said, "Just let me get these things into the ice box. You go into the parlor; I'll put on a kettle."

Once settled, Celeste's related the day's events. "I thought he would marry me, Mrs. B. I did. I really did. And now this. He took my job away from me. I've done a good job there. Why would he send me away? Why would he do that?"

Mrs. Bellingstone patted Celeste's hand. "Oh, my girl. You must learn the ways of the world. You are too old not to know more of life." She poured more tea into Celeste's cup.

"You will get over this. But remember your lesson. You must be wary, especially of men. They are usually not what they seem. There are a few good ones; perhaps your husband was one of them. But they are few and far between. If you want to find a husband, you must be wary. And if a man is married, that means that he is not interested in marrying you." She smoothed Celeste's hair. "What a hard lesson for you to learn, my dear girl." Celeste picked up her cup. "Why don't you go upstairs and lie down for a while. I'll call you when it is time for dinner. We can put this behind us. Everything will be all right. You'll see."

Celeste stood and walked toward the steps. "But my job. Why did he take away my job?"

Twenty-seven ——————————

Hayley was good for his word. A few days later a handwritten letter arrived at Robert Street. Celeste was to contact Wilfred Price, the senior manager at Stewart's. She was, of course, to say nothing regarding her departure from Hutzler Brothers. He wished her every success in her new endeavor.

Celeste sat on her bed, running her finger across the envelope, studying Hayley's signature. The next morning, she wrote a letter of her own, requesting a meeting with Mr. Wilfred Price, at his convenience.

The following Monday, she walked toward Stewart's main entrance at Howard and Lexington Streets, almost directly opposite that of her former employer. As she approached, she studied the six-story building. It is certainly more beautiful than the dark stone of Hutzler Brothers, she thought, this white palace. Willie would know exactly what style it was, and she studied the columns, the carved laurel wreaths and fierce lion heads protruding from the cornices. Italianate, perhaps, and made a mental note to stop at the library on her way home.

Price came out to greet her in the anteroom and escorted her into his sixth-floor office. She wore the navy suit that she modeled on that significant day those many months ago. When, thirty minutes later, she left his office, she had a job at Stewart's. For the present she would fill in where she was needed. Price called her a floater. As soon as a permanent position opened, she would be eligible for that.

"I am quite knowledgeable of lingerie, fine lingerie," Celeste stated, more emphatically than she had intended. Price raised his eyebrows and smiled. He said that he would keep that in mind. She was to start the following Monday.

Once back on Howard Street, she used Clay Street as a shortcut and walked toward her trolley stop on Paca Street. She passed the glass-fronted door of Hutzler's employee entrance. I won't walk this way again. I'll use Lexington Street, she thought. I'll walk past Hochschild Kohn and look in their windows. That extra distance will do me good. I will forget Hutzler's; Hutzler's never happened.

Celeste was up and dressed early for her first day of work. Mrs. Bellingstone made her a special breakfast and sat with her while she ate. "A new start for you today, Celeste. I wish you the best."

"Thank you. Your words, always so kind; just what I need. Always."

At the store, her days soon settled into a comfortable routine. She met other salesladies; they welcomed her with more warmth than she expected. A month later she was assigned to the lingerie department. The woman who had worked there was given an opportunity to move to the notions area. She was given a one-time bonus for agreeing.

The managers, "the sixth floor," smiled when they saw her. Price had given no explanation for this new recruit, but they knew that she went by "Mrs." and had noted that she wore no wedding ring. "Divorced, I'll wager," one of them remarked, "fair game." And the rest laughed.

Celeste was always aware of the men, clad in their black frock coats, but kept her eyes lowered as they passed. Mrs. Bellingstone was right. She would not be so foolish again, ever.

Hutzler launched its *Baltimore Girl* campaign. Celeste winced each time she walked by a display window which featured the dark haired beauty, for sometimes she did take that Clay Street shortcut. She flinched each time she picked up the paper and saw the heart-shaped face, dark curls cascading around a bonnet, staring at her. Yes, Celeste agreed, she was beautiful, and, yes, she was a girl. When Celeste looked in the mirror each morning, she saw that she no longer was. She was a woman, unmarried, and most likely to remain so.

As serene weeks turned into contented years, Celeste stopped at the library every Saturday, and never forgot to think of Willie as she picked out a book, sometimes two. She spent her evenings with Mrs. B; often they played records on the gramophone. "No use letting that go to waste," she said. And both women laughed.

Twenty-eight————————————

Celeste continued her days standing behind glass counters, perfectly-folded lingerie, good quality merchandise, but no imported brands, nothing French or Italian. Customers who wanted, who could afford, those, went to Hutzler's. Celeste found that the women who shopped at Stewart's were friendlier, open to her suggestions; sometimes they even laughed together over a particularly difficult corset fitting. Celeste liked her fellow employees, appreciated the piano that sat in the employee lunch room, and laughed and sang along when Albert, from Fine Menswear, played some of the group's favorites. She also liked her twenty-percent discount, and, piece by piece managed to acquire a wardrobe that she was proud of. She rarely ventured out in the evenings, and when she did, mostly with other girls from 1st floor, she walked with a flair. Stewart's did not model fashions in their lunchroom; she was glad.

Once in a while she saw her friends from Eastern High School. Most had gone to college, some had actually graduated. Elizabeth lived in Philadelphia, married, two children now. Her husband was a banker; they lived on the Main Line. She had invited Celeste to visit. Perhaps one day she would. Celeste hadn't been on a train since her New York trip. Best to leave that, she thought. That day, those days never happened.

She sometimes met friends for lunch on Saturdays, after her half-day schedule. She always wore her finest outfit, always in that year's style. They thought her quite sophisticated, and didn't ask about Stanley. She hadn't told them that he was now called Willie. When they were by themselves, they were sometimes sympathetic, sometimes caustic. "If only she would tell us the truth," one said. "I wonder what happened. She never mentions her son, or her mother for that matter. It seems that her landlady fills that role. And a room. She calls it a 'bed-sit,' like she's a heroine in some kind of book. But really she's just a boarder in someone else's house. And all those airs she puts on. I'll bet she'd trade places with any of us in a second."

Celeste focused on her new friends, her work friends, and found many in the same situation as she. The younger ones plotted and planned to capture a husband; the older ones seemed resolved to lives as spinsters. She didn't know where she fit in, but she did know that it would be a long time before she would look at a man and wonder. In the meantime, she talked to Willie every night as she fell asleep.

She decided that it would be best not to see Stanley, and when she thought of him, which was rare, she reminded herself that he was "Willie" now. Clara was right, she told herself. It was best not to confuse the child. Maybe she would see him later, when Clara thought the time was right. And I will call him as Billy. Yes, in my mind, Stanley, from now on, will be Billy. That's more American. I'm sure that's what Willie would have wanted.

Twenty-nine _____

The buyer brought it to her, a soft silk kimono with wide Magyar sleeves, candlelight colored. "It's a one-of-a-kind," she explained. "We found a consigner in Japan and thought we'd give this a try. Not sure if it suits our customers. More like Hutzler's, don't you think, Celeste?"

Celeste reached to touch the fabric. "Oh, Miss Lynn, once people see this, they will know that this is quality. They won't have to go across Howard Street once they feel this softness. This is definitely the best piece that we've ever offered. I know that it will be a success."

The buyer smiled. "Well, we knew that we could count on you to make sure that the customer likes and appreciates it. I'm glad you are pleased, Celeste. I'll leave it to you to decide how to display it."

Celeste went to her supervisor. Best to let her take the credit for this. Not wise to be singled out, not this time, she determined. She suggested to that a mannequin be placed in the department. "It will make people stop and look, Miss Loftus," Celeste said. "I'll bet that at first they'll think it's a person; then they'll see the robe. And they will stop and look. And buy," she laughed.

She was right. They placed only one robe on the floor. As that was sold they brought out another. The purchaser was assured that she was getting a one-of-a-kind.

Celeste caressed each new kimono as she displayed it. She stared down at the price tag. More than she made in a week. Perhaps with her discount, she thought. When a peach colored kimono appeared, she took it behind the counter. Perfect with my complexion, my eyes, she thought. She folded it, smiling as she inserted the tissue paper, and placed it in the bottom of the lowest merchandise drawer. No one asked about it. That afternoon, she placed a yellow version on the mannequin. Celeste waited to be asked about the peach robe, wondered if they had forgotten about it. Each day she had her story ready; each day, while Miss Loftus took her lunch break, Celeste opened the bottom drawer and looked at the kimono, made sure it was still there, safe.

That Saturday, as she was closing out the department, she returned from the employee lounge with her carpetbag. She gently placed the kimono in the bottom of the bag, and covered it with her scarf, gloves, hat, and library books. She walked toward the employee entrance. The staff was preparing to leave, all of them wishing each other a pleasant weekend. Celeste joined in, and walked toward the door. "Celeste," a friend called out, "aren't you going to put on your scarf. It's a blowing wind out there." Celeste turned. "I just want to feel the air for a while. I'll fix it while I wait for the trolley."

That afternoon, after calling a hello to Mrs. Bellingstone, Celeste went directly to her room. She unwrapped the kimono and laid it out on the bed. She would save it until after her bath that evening. I'll be wrapped in silk. Just like someone in a book, she thought.

Thirty_____

For the next week, each morning Celeste drew in a quick breath as she greeted her supervisor, a pleasant woman of the last century, Celeste thought, much like most of Stewart's clientele. Faith Loftus treated Celeste kindly, like a daughter. She, as well as the rest of the staff, assumed that Celeste lived the life of a quiet widow in reduced circumstances. Which was not far from the truth.

As each kimono sold, Celeste breathed a sigh of relief. They had a complement of ten; only one remained to be displayed. Surely, she hoped, they had forgotten about that one. Yet she knew that their inventory system was meticulous. They had trained her to use it, counting each piece of merchandise, completing long sheaths of paper with numbers and descriptions for each piece. They trusted her, and sometimes, though not often and not for long, she felt a bit guilty.

Three weeks later she was told to report to the manager's office. All remaining kimonos had been sold. As she walked to the elevator, Celeste held her breath; she had planned the story she would tell if this happened, and had rehearsed it several times, each time making it a bit more believable. She remembered bringing the peach robe to the floor, but she hadn't seen it since. She thought, with the rush of the holiday season, that perhaps someone from another department had included it with a customer's purchases. Perhaps.

Price met her as she entered the executive suite. "Mrs. Strauff, would you come into my office, please. We have much to discuss."

Celeste's heart plummeted. Caught; now what? I'll lie, she thought.

But Price was not thinking of kimonos.

He returned to his desk; Celeste sat in one of the pair of blue brocade upholstered chairs in front of it. "Mrs. Strauff, we have noticed the quality of your work in the years that you have been with us. Your experience at the other retailer has stood you, and us, well. You obviously have an eye for quality; you know how to help customers choose what they think they would like. I've heard about how you talk with them, about quality lasting, about how quality feels against the skin. You have been the top seller in the department since the time that you arrived with us. We do measure these types of things, you know."

Celeste sat, her eyes lowered, her hands folded in her lap, quietly waiting for the indictment. "And you have quite a supporter in Miss Loftus. You have done a good job in making your supervisor like you, a not unimportant factor in what I am about to say." He paused.

Celeste raised her eyes, forced herself to take a breath, nervous that Price would hear her gasp for air.

He continued. "We have been talking with Miss Loftus about taking a less demanding position. She is getting older and it is obvious to us that it is difficult for her to manage an area that is as physically spread out as our lingerie department. We have talked with her about taking over notions. That is a department that is quite complex as far as its merchandise is concerned, but its counters are more compact. She would not have to cover as much territory and she could discharge most of her duties while seated. The staff there is first-rate and we think that this transition would be a good one for her." Price folded his hands and looked at Celeste.

"I'd like you to know that she has recommended you to take her place. She is a tough taskmaster, so that is quite a feather in your cap."

Celeste's breath caught in her throat, though she managed to cough out a thank-you.

Price held up his hand. He was not finished. Celeste put her hands back in her lap.

"Additionally, we feel that this employee change gives us an opportunity to expand the scope of the department, to add a higher quality stock to our offerings. We would like you to collaborate with Miss Lynn, our buyer, on this project. She is amenable to working with you in this regard.

"Now, this position will entail a different kind of work than what you have been doing; it will no doubt be a challenge for you. We still expect you to work the floor, especially with our selected customers. In addition, you will work with Miss Lynn to bring in a new line of more luxurious garments. And you will supervise the salesladies under you. Furthermore, and this is a key component of the position, you will be responsible for keeping financial and merchandise records. You will work with Mr. Moore, the finance director, and he will train you on the forms and procedures that we use here. I believe that you have a good head on your shoulders and should have no trouble mastering that aspect of the position." He drew a typed sheet from the middle drawer of his desk.

"We are prepared to offer you a ten percent increase in salary. I hope that you will give this offer serious thought. Do not make your decision now. Think about it over the weekend and let us have your answer on Monday. I do not want you to underestimate this opportunity. If you are interested in a career in retail, and I do think it is one to which you are very well suited, this can be just the first step." He stood and extended a hand to Celeste.

She rose and shook it with a firm grip. "Thank you, so very much, Mr. Price. This is such a surprise; I never expected that you would offer this to me. I am very interested. This is such an honor." She stopped. She knew she was babbling and bit her lip to silence herself. She drew herself even more erect; she was taller than Price.

"Yes, I will think about it and let you know on Monday. But I think I know what my answer will be." She smiled and left the office.

Now won't this be something for my book, she thought.

And so Celeste became a supervisor. She was a good one, except for a minor problem with pilferage. Price asked her to watch her employees carefully. She responded that she had every confidence in their honesty. But every month or so, a piece from the Fine Lingerie collection disappeared. Price suspected that they were misplaced, mixed among the regular lot of petticoats and chemises. Pilferage, he thought, is a cost of doing business; perhaps it was shoplifting by a particularly accomplished thief.

The sixth-floor respected and valued Celeste; she had some responsibility, they thought, for upgrading the image of the store. She no longer kept a low profile, no longer kept her eyes lowered when they passed. She called out cheery greetings when she saw them on the floor, when she delivered the day's receipts to Mr. Moore in his sixth floor office. She saw them as a way to help her career in retailing, as she now thought of it, nothing else. Her experience with Halsey never quite left her; she would not make that mistake again.

In her new role at Stewart's, Celeste had more options with her work wardrobe. No longer confined to black blouses and skirts, she spent some of her cherished earnings on the new styles, and she tried not to notice that the lines and fashions of the 1910s did not do justice to her figure. She also wore the finest of undergarments, most of which she had paid for.

Thirty-one————————————————————

That April morning, she dressed with extra care; she wore the garnet earrings he had given her on their last Christmas; she wore the boots she had bought in Denver, and the grey suit with the black piping at the skirt bottom. She had to use a safety pin at the waist, but the jacket covered it. She wanted him to recognize her, remember her as she was when he knew her. She brushed her hair an extra one hundred times, but she knew that it was darker now, not the same as when he was here.

She lingered at the breakfast table. Her landlady noticed. She had asked for permission to take the day off the week before.

"Are you going in to work late this morning?" Mrs. Bellingstone asked. Celeste stirred her tea before she answered, weighing what to say.

"No, Mrs. B. I'm not going in today."

The older woman waited. Celeste took a breath. It would be the first time she had talked about Willie, other than to tell Mrs. Bellingstone that she was a widow. "My husband died five years ago today. I thought that I would visit his grave. What I'm wearing, all these things, he knew, he'd recognize. I wanted to be sure to wear what he knew, so that he wouldn't forget me." She looked down at the almost-empty cup.

Mrs. Bellingstone looked over at her, patted her hand. "I know, my dear. It is not easy, is it, no matter how long ago." She paused.

"You are so young. It is good that you visit the grave, but it is a grave, Celeste. You don't have to worry that he won't remember you."

Celeste nodded and stood. "I thought I'd walk there. It's far, but then I can take the trolley home. Baltimore Cemetery. His grave is on a hillside. You can stand there and see the whole city. You can look straight up North Avenue and when the leaves are off the trees you can almost see Mt. Royal. He has a wonderful spot. He loved architecture, buildings. He read, he thought, all the time. He taught me so much, and he was so handsome, Mrs. B." She stopped.

"Well," Celeste cleared her throat, "I'll just get my shawl from my room."

Mrs. Bellingstone stopped her. "Would you like me to go with you? I couldn't walk that far, but we could go on the streetcar. We could have some lunch on the way back. You shouldn't be alone this day, my dear."

Celeste smiled. "Thank you, but I'd like to talk to him, I hope you understand, I'd like for there to be just the two of us today."

The landlady nodded and started to clear the table. She is under such a cloud, she thought. Such a child. She has not listened to life's lessons, much less learned from them. Not yet.

Thirty-two —————————————————————

Clara went into Willie's room. The boy would be home soon, for his two-week summer visit. The family had visited him once or twice during the school year, taken him out to dinner at the *Deutches Haus*. His manners were impeccable. They saw no use of his left hand. The nuns were training him well, they thought.

She thought it imprudent to visit too often; he needed to think of the school as his home. It would make a man of him. The school, whose boarders included many whose families lived abroad, scheduled classes and activities throughout the entire year except for two weeks in August. Students went to their families or stayed with the families of friends

Willie waited on the front steps, his suitcase beside him. He had packed it himself. I'll have my own room; I'll have some time without a class, or a study period, or a game, or chapel. I'll see *Oma*, he thought.

Inger still took care of the house, a much easier job now that all the adults were occupied during the daytime. She had time to read in the afternoon and still have dinner on the table for them at six-thirty. She was looking forward to Willie's homecoming. He was no trouble, she thought, and a handsome, tall boy, mannerly. The nuns were teaching him right.

Clara smoothed the spread and fluffed the pillows on his bed. She opened and closed the drawers of the dresser. She walked to the small student desk by the doorway, opened the middle drawer. Willie's father's desk, she thought, while she pulled out old papers that had been carelessly shoved in. Her brother's drawings before he went away to school, school papers, marked up in red pencil by the nuns, always with an encouraging remark at the top. She gathered them, tapped them together to neaten the pile. Underneath were two envelopes. She recognized Willie's handwriting. One was addressed to Celeste, the other to Stanley.

Stanley, Clara said to herself. How long has it been since we've called him that? He doesn't even know that that was his name. She slipped the envelopes into her pocket and climbed the stairs to her room. Her knees were bothering her; she had to use the second railing that August had installed earlier that summer. She went to her desk that sat in the bay window and opened the letters.

Oh dear, dear Willie, she thought. Such a sweet man, such letters, written all those years ago, all this time unnoticed in the desk drawer. Willie should have this. He should have something to remember his father by, to know, at least a bit, the man who was his father.

She read the letter again. Willie called his son Stanley. How to explain that? Perhaps by telling the truth, not about the kidnapping, but about why he was now called Willie. She sat and stared out at North Avenue; her eyes moved to the granite walls of the cemetery, the dark green canopy of trees. She sat, quietly, waiting for an inspiration that would help her decide what to do.

Thirty-three————————

That Thursday morning, Celeste lingered over breakfast; she glanced through the *Sun Paper* as she munched a third piece of toast. Mrs. B. sat in the front room, watching the children on their way to school, some running, always one lagging behind.

"Well, how about this," Celeste said, surprised that she had said it aloud.

```
The Sun
November 24, 1910

MARRIAGE ANNOUNCED
    Announcements of the marriage of Miss
Clara Strauff, 28 years old, of 1108 East
North avenue, to Dr. H. Stanley Gorsuch, 34
years old, 501 East Twenty-second street,
were sent to their friends yesterday. Dr.
Gorsuch and Miss Strauff went to Wilmington
Tuesday for the purpose of having a quiet
wedding, and were there married by Rev.
Dr. George I. Wolf. They will live at 501
East Twenty-second street.
```

"Clara married! And she's lied about her age. And," Celeste allowed herself a laugh, "they eloped, just like Willie and I did. "Whoo," she chortled, "and no Catholic priest!"

Mrs. Bellingstone came into the dining room, reading over Celeste's shoulder, anxious to see what made Celeste so boisterous.

Celeste looked up, patted her hands on the table. "Oh, Mrs. B, they made such a fuss because Willie and I were married in an Episcopal church, insisted that a Catholic priest marry us for it to count, and now, Clara has run away and been married by somebody who's not Catholic. Isn't that rich?" Celeste hadn't realized how angry she was about her second marriage service, angry with Clara, with Paulina. And why, she thought, had Willie not stood up for her, for them?

Mrs. Bellingstone's words cut Celeste's thinking short. "Well, you know how Catholics are. They have all the answers, for everyone else. The Irish are the worst, with their drinking and having all those children. Like rabbits, they are."

Celeste looked up at her landlady. In the years that they had been together, that this was the first time she had heard Mrs. B. speak unkindly. Well, Celeste thought, she must have a reason. But then, everyone hated the Irish.

Celeste reread the article. H. Stanley Gorsuch. She wondered if Clara flinched at having another Stanley in the family. And she opened her mouth and laughed so loudly that Mrs. Bellingstone looked at her. Then she laughed again. And when she left the house to catch the morning trolley that cold day, she could not keep herself from skipping.

Thirty-four —————————————————

Spring 1913 brought the earliest Easter most could remember. Celeste had made plans to walk in the Easter Parade with friends from Stewart's. She would visit Annie for lunch and then take the trolley to Mt. Vernon Place where the group would meet. Or maybe she would walk, she thought, depending on what Annie served for lunch.

Her visits with her mother were rare now; they had little to say to one another. Annie told Celeste about Eva and her little girl; she said little about her own life. It was better for her now, the house filled with enough boarders that she could afford help three days a week for the heavy work. She thought that Celeste had found her way; she didn't think about Stanley. He was in boarding school, that much she knew. It has all worked out for the best, she thought, though when her few friends talked about their grandchildren, she sometimes felt an emptiness, which she soon replaced by telling herself sternly, that what never makes you laugh never makes you cry. Best to just get on with life, be content with what you have. She felt lucky that she didn't have to move; George's brother had taken on the mortgage, had said that she could stay in the house as long as she liked. He even paid part of the taxes when he could; most years all she needed to do was to pull together enough money together to keep the house going. He was a good soul and she appreciated it.

Celeste left the trolley at North and Greenmount Avenues. She wanted to walk beside Green Mount Cemetery, wanted to look at Willie's house. She remembered how they had laughed and talked of their house on Mt. Vernon Place. She had forgotten that, until today, until she saw the house. She looked at the bay window on the third floor, wondering if Stanley, no, she told herself, if Billy, stayed there when he was home from school now that Clara had married. Billy, she whispered, and wondered if he spent Easter with them.

She crossed Hope Street, arriving at the third house. She thought of it as Annie's home now, memories of her girlhood days there just that. Her mother met her at the door. They embraced gingerly; Celeste's flamboyant straw hat, much too spring-like for this chilly day, precluded any warm embraces. Both were grateful that they could blame the hat.

Annie led Celeste to the front room where she sat, a visitor. She inhaled the aroma of yeast rolls. "Mama, everything smells delicious. Thank you so much for inviting me. It's been so long since we've seen each other, but I think of you every day, I do." Celeste smiled at Annie.

"As I do of you," Annie responded, then rose immediately. "Let me check on lunch. Two of the boarders are here. You haven't met them. They will be in shortly. James Confly and Robert Wickson. They work downtown, for Alex Brown, some kind of financial work. But they are very clean and quiet. Gentlemen, both."

Celeste felt both disappointed and relieved when she learned that she would not be alone with her mother.

"I walked by Willie's on the way here. Do you know if Stanley is home for the holiday?" Celeste asked. "Do you ever see him when he's here?"

Annie turned. "Do you not know? I thought that they would have told you." Seeing Celeste's face, Annie continued.

"The old Kraut sold the house, sold the business, I heard. Moved, I think outside of Baltimore, somewhere in the county. Since Clara married, it was just the two of them. I don't know why they moved. The neighbors said that the mother was ill. I don't know. Eva does hear from Clara, I think, but she doesn't tell me what her letters say."

"Mama, I had no idea. I cannot believe that Mr. Strauff wouldn't have notified me. I have kept my part of the bargain, you know. Let Stanley, Willie, I think of him now as Billy, grow up without worrying about me. But to move without telling me? I just don't understand it."

"Nothing to understand. They have their lives, Celeste. You are not to be part of that. Neither am I. So, a decision made, a promise kept. Who knows what is right? And it seems to be working out for everyone. You are free. How is that life for you?"

Celeste looked at her mother, unsure of how to respond. Annie's face was set firm. Celeste saw neither softness nor censure.

"I thought my life would be different, Mama. Now I'm just trying to make the best of it. I don't think that I was cut out to be a mother. I wouldn't know what to do, not on my own, not without Willie. If he had lived, well, if he had lived it would have been different. It is not right to condemn me; it is not my fault Willie died and left me."

Annie turned and walked toward the steps to the kitchen. "The men will be here soon. I want to have lunch on the table for them. I'll put the food in the dumbwaiter; no need for you to help."

Thirty-five

Sister Sulpice came into the classroom, whispered to the nun at the front of the class. He heard his name. "William Strauff, please come with me." The class fell silent. He put his pen down, straightened the books on the desk into a neat pile, and stood. She held her hand out. Everyone knew something was wrong.

> **Baltimore Sun**
> **June 25, 1914**
>
> STRAUFF
>   On June 23, 1914 at 2:45 P.M. after a lingering illness, LINA STRAUFF at the age of 59 years, beloved wife of August Strauff.
>   Funeral from her late residence 16 Catalpha avenue, Alsa Terrace Harford road, on Friday morning, a high Requiem Mass for her soul, St. Dominic's Church, Hamilton at 9 o'clock. Interment private at Baltimore Cemetery.

Willie attended the funeral. He wore his school uniform, though the weather was sweltering that day. Clara's husband Stanley drove him back to school after the luncheon following the service. Sister Sulpice was waiting for him at the door.

Thirty-six———————————————

Celeste visited the notions department; she bought a dark green leather notebook with a lock and "Diary" embossed in silver. She bought a red Waterman fountain pen, trimmed in gold. She stopped at Woolworth's on the way home for a bottle of Sanford ink, violet. Just for writing in this book, she decided.

She lay in bed that morning, seeing the clear blue winter sky. This day was going to be hers. She had asked for the day off. She remembered the last time she had asked for a special day off, almost five years ago. That day had been for Willie. But this day, this one would be hers. A special day, she thought. It will be one I will celebrate. I will not think bad thoughts. No, I am a working girl; I am someone people envy. I have made something of my life.

She rose and wrapped the peach kimono tightly around her waist, pulling in her stomach as she did so, and put her kettle on the hot plate. She would start with tea in her room, just like one of those ladies in the books she read. Except they did not have to make their own tea. No matter, she thought. I will sit at my table and look out the window and sip my tea. On this special day.

She picked up the pen and placed the point in the square glass bottle, watched as it drank up the ink, then replaced the round cork firmly. Violet ink, she thought, just perfect for this book. A new pen; a new diary; a new era. Yes, I like that. I am beginning a new era.

February, 1915

Dear Diary,
Today I am thirty years old. I am a working girl; I am the supervisor of Fine Lingerie at Stewart and Company. It

*is a fine department store in Baltimore, Maryland. I live on
Robert Street in a bed-sit. I am an independent woman, just
like those in books, only I am real. I will write about my life
one day. It will be a life worth reading about.*

Celeste capped the pen and stared at the paper. I
should write about my life, she thought. I should write
about what I do every day; I should write about what
I want for myself. I should write about who I am. She
opened the pen turned to a new page.

Today I am 30 and alone.

She swallowed.

*I never thought that I could be this old. I never imagined
that I would be alone. I thought that I would have my house on
Mt. Vernon Place, have a husband who took care of me, have
so many beautiful clothes that I couldn't get around to wearing
them all, that I would have servants, or at least one. But truth
be told, here is my life. I work in a department store. I live in
someone else's home; I have a room of my own, just a room. My
friends are all married and are living the life I thought would
be mine. Honestly, they are not my friends anymore. I think
they feel sorry for me, if they think of me at all, or maybe they
feel smug. I know all these fancy words, from Willie. He taught
me so much, and I still read every day. But I am not married;
I am a widow, and even that people forget.*

*Mama has forgotten me; she seems relieved that we see
each other hardly ever. I miss her, and then when I visit I can
hardly wait to leave, to get home, to my room here, and Mrs.
B. She is more like a mother to me. I think that I make her
happy, make her laugh sometimes. I guess I am lonely. I am
30. I thought that I would be married. I thought that my life
would be different.*

*I still talk to Willie sometimes. I wonder if he's forgotten
me. It's been ten years almost. When I read, when I'm in the
library, I try to find books that he would like. Sometimes*

they're not very interesting. And then Stanley. I am sure that
he has forgotten me. For the best, most likely. Clara said so. I
see her every once in a while. I read the Society Pages. She and
her husband are in them often. She has a good life. I would not
mind that for myself. And Stanley is now Willie, or Billy. He
will be thirteen years old in August. I wonder what he looks
like. He is still at the Country School. I am sure that he is a
proper gentleman.

Eva has a good life I hear. Everyone has a good life,
but me.

Celeste sat back, looking at the words in purple.

This is not a good way to start my birthday! Today I am
thirty years old. I have a wonderful job. It is a career. I meet
lots of lovely women, and sometimes, at Christmas time, even
some men who are shopping for their wives. Once in a while I
think I wait on a man who shops for someone who is not his
wife! Then we smile. Sometimes I think that they think that I
am "easy," but I am not. No men in my life. Not since. I am
hoping that someone will find me.

I have nice clothes and an eye for fashion. Maybe I could be
a dress designer, in New York. I would be a success and make
lots of money and have magazine articles written about me.

And I miss Willie. We were so young. Today I will imagine
what my life would have been like if he hadn't died and left me.
I know that I would be living on Mt. Vernon Place, serving tea
and a special birthday cake from Fiske's, and Stanley would
come home from boarding school for a long weekend. He would
wear his uniform; he would be tall, with beautiful blond hair.
He would be a gentleman!

Celeste thought that the purple ink was perfect. She closed the
journal, and ran her hand over the leather cover. Now I have a diary, she
thought. Willie would like that. She placed her pen diagonally across
the cover. Now that looks just like something a proper lady would do.

Thirty-seven _____

Stanley, who knew himself only as Willie, who thought his name was William August Strauff, celebrated his fourteenth birthday with his grandfather and aunt and uncle at the *Deutsches' Haus*, downstairs, in the *Rathskeller*. August was known there, and now, after years of celebrating birthdays and holidays, so was Willie. He smiled shyly as the waiters congratulated him.

"*Ach*, you are no longer a boy. So tall. Ready to take on the world, no?" the waiter said. Willie hung his head, nodded and felt his cheeks and neck redden.

August laughed. "Look, Herman, he is taller than all of us here. Next time, he can pick up the check!"

Stanley Gorsuch, Clara's physician husband, looked over at the boy, and then at Clara. She had suffered two miscarriages, the second one a tubal pregnancy that resulted in a hysterectomy. No children for them. He was content. She never let him see her cry, although he knew that she did.

The waiter brought the menus to the table. "So, *Herr Willie*, you go to Calvert Hall like your papa? Carry on the name?"

August spoke up. "*Nein*, Fritz. That is not possible. So, the boy goes to boarding school, Mt. St. Joseph's, in Irvington. Do you know it?"

"Oh, *yah*. Lots of good German boys go there. Good school makes strong-minded men."

Willie stared down at the menu. He had visited the school, but was reluctant to leave the comfort and familiarity of the place that he thought of as his home, the nuns as his family. He had graduated in June; his classmates had dispersed. Most would go to boarding schools in New England. He felt fortunate that he would not have

412

to go so far away. His grandfather's new house was in Hamilton, off Harford Road, but since he had sold the paper, since Paulina's death, August was managing a resort in the Walbrook neighborhood. It seemed that all was unsettled, for both of these males. August felt untethered. Willie didn't know the word for how he felt.

The week before, August had received a letter from the school, requesting a number of forms, one of which was Willie's birth certificate.

August contacted Clara, asked her for advice. Clara saw that her father had lost much of his bluster, his confidence ebbing with the loss of his wife, the loss of his newspaper. He was a different man from the father she had known.

"It will not do to send the birth certificate to the school," she answered. "There will be much too much explaining needed, and our decision was no one's business but ours. Tell them that a birth certificate is impossible at this time, but send a copy of the baptismal certificate. That should suffice. They will not question you."

Willie overheard this conversation, and knew enough not to ask about it. A problem with his birth certificate. It had to do with his mother, he thought. That could be the only explanation.

A few days later, when August was out of the house, Willie went to the large mahogany desk that sat in the front window. He opened the middle drawer. Nothing. He examined the contents each drawer, always careful to close it gently, to leave the papers in the exactly as he had found them. The bottom right had drawer was packed tight with files. Most folders were not labeled, and Willie pulled each one out cautiously. He found the file with his baptismal certificate, from a church in Washington, D.C. Why would I have been baptized there? he asked himself. Maybe family friends, some Germans, always Germans.

As he replaced the parchment, he noticed an official-looking document behind it. A birth certificate. But not his. The name was Stanley Wells Strauff. He wondered if he had a brother. He looked further. His father's name. And his mother's, Celeste Alba Wells. I have a brother, he thought. He looked at the birth date. August 13, 1902. I have a twin brother.

Willie sat, the certificate in his hand. Maybe my mother took my brother, he reasoned. Maybe that was the problem. Maybe that was why I couldn't see her. Something had happened when Father died. Maybe she took Stanley and left me with *Oma* and *Opa*. Maybe that's why she didn't want me. She couldn't take care of both of us. Maybe she loved me but had to choose. Maybe now that I'm grown she'll want to see me, want to know me.

Willie's heart pounded. Celeste Wells was her name before she married. He found a piece of paper and copied down the name. Maybe I can find her, he thought, let her know how I am. Maybe I could get to see her.

He carefully placed the document behind the baptismal certificate, returned the documents to the folder. As he went to replace it, he realized that he had neglected to mark its space. He shoved it in the middle of the drawer, packed tightly between manila folders of varying hues.

Later that week, he took the streetcar to the downtown library. He used the Mulberry Street entrance. He approached the main desk. "I'd like to look at your City Directory, please." The librarian, thinking what a well-mannered young man he was, delivered it to him as he sat at the long wooden table.

Opening it to "S," he began his search. No Strauffs except those he knew. His mother's name was not there. He sat. Her name was Wells before she married. He turned to "W". So many Wells, he thought, a full column of them. He decided to start with the top and work his way down. And he found it, Annie Wells, the third in the listing, the North Avenue address. He had forgotten to bring paper or pen, but the librarian noticed him and came to him with a half-sheet of paper and a sharpened pencil. "Will this help?" she asked, and he smiled his thanks. A fine-looking boy, she thought. So refined.

He copied the address and returned the Directory to the desk. "Thank you for all your h-help," he said. "You have been very helpful. Th-th-thank you again." Poor fellow, she thought. A stammer. Lucky he is so good-looking.

He walked to Charles Street to catch the first of three trolleys he would use to return to August's home. Sitting beside the window, he pulled the paper from his pocket. 1023 E. North Avenue, right across the street from his old house. She lived right across the street. Why had she not come to see me, he wondered. She lived right across the street.

It has to be complicated, he thought. All this secrecy, all these questions. But I am fourteen now, a man. I will find out. I will find my mother, my brother. Then everything will be all right. We can be together. We can be a family. And I won't have to go to that school.

Thirty-eight _____

Willie was sorry that he no longer had his school uniform. He felt comfortable wearing it, like himself. But those days were over; he was to enter high school in the fall.

He attached the collar to his white shirt, and stood erect as he buttoned the top two buttons on this linen jacket. He gave his shoes an extra shine, and then left the house to meet his grandmother. He had practiced what he would say. He willed himself not to stammer.

He walked by the house on the north side of North Avenue, the house he considered home, and then crossed the street. At the house third house, he paused, then mounted the stairs and used the door-knocker.

Annie looked out the window before she answered the door. She knew who it was.

As she opened the door, the young man before her stretched out his hand to shake hers. "How do you do, Mrs. W-wells. My name is W-w-william Strauff. I am your g-grandson." Annie stood, motionless. She saw Celeste in this child who stood before her, his dark hair so painstakingly combed, yet it was Willie's lock of hair that fell into his eyes. Willie pushed it back, swallowed, and waited.

Annie opened the door wider. "Come in, child. Come in."

"I would like to thank you for seeing me," he began, before he reached the vestibule. "I would like to see my mother, and my brother. Could you help me do that?" He relaxed. One entire sentence completed, not a stutter.

Annie led the boy into the front room. He sat on the edge of the sofa cushion, his back stiff with effort. She sat beside him, mirroring his posture.

416

Annie reached out and smoothed his hair. "Oh my dear boy, my dear boy. You remind me so of your father, his gentle ways. You are so tall, like your mother." Annie tried to think, to plan what she would say in answer to this boy's request.

"You want to find you mother, certainly. But I don't understand your question about a brother. You have no brother, Stanley, I mean Willie. Why would you ask about that?"

So, he thought, she knows about Stanley; she called me by his name. Willie remembered his rehearsed speech. "I found his birth certificate. Stanley Wells Strauff. He was born the same day I was. Do I not have a twin brother? Is he dead? There is so much secrecy about this, about my mother, I thought this was why. I thought perhaps my mother took care of him and left me with *Opa* and *Opa*. I thought that was why she left." His voice broke with his last word.

"Oh, sweet boy." Annie moved closer to him and took his hand in hers. "I will tell you. So many secrets, so much misunderstanding. So little thought given to what you might think."

And Annie related the tale, of Willie's death, of Celeste's youth and inability to take on the duties of a mother, of August's and Paulina's changing his name to that of his father.

"But all of us did what we thought was best for you. Perhaps what we did was what we thought was best for ourselves. So the birth certificate is yours, Willie. Your name was Stanley, but it was changed when your father died, when you went to live with the Strauffs."

"No, Grandmother Wells, that is not s-so" Willie struggled to remain calm, like an adult. "I saw my baptismal certificate. My name was on that. I was baptized when I was nine months old. My father was alive then." He rose abruptly and stood at the window, looking out on North Avenue.

Annie sat. "Willie, I have told you what I know to be the truth." She paused. "But I have not told you all; I told you what I thought would help you understand. Now I see that you need to learn more." She told him of the kidnapping, of his being taken to Washington. "They must have had you baptized then. You had already been baptized here earlier, but it wasn't in a Catholic Church. So, they must have done that then. I didn't know about the name, Willie. Truly I didn't."

He rubbed his eyes and willed himself to be brave, to be a man, before he turned to face her. "Can you help me find my m-m-mother? Do y-you know where s-she is?"

Annie nodded. "Would you like for me to arrange for you to meet?"

Willie felt his face crumple, his eyes, his nose filling. He put his hands to his sides and made fists. He inhaled deeply. "Y-yes," he said, and his voice cracked. "How will I find out about it?" he asked.

"Can you come back on Sunday? I will see what I can do," Annie answered. "Willie, will you tell your grandfather what you are doing?"

The boy shook his head. "I d-d-, I th-th, n-no," he stammered. "Not at this t-time."

He turned toward Annie. "Thank you, Grandmother Wells. I know this must be quite a s-s-shock to m-m-meet me. You have been very g-g-gracious to allow me into your h-h-" The last word would not come.

"Come on Sunday, dear Willie. Come back on Sunday. Three o'clock. You can come at three?"

Thirty-nine _____

Dear Diary,

Today I met Willie. He is so handsome, so much like my Willie, even a stammer. He looks like him, I think, and like me. He is tall, taller than I am. I am glad that he got that from me; and he has dark hair now, almost black. The last time I saw him it was blond. He even has that piece of hair in the front that flops down. I had to reach over and put it back in place. He seemed a bit startled when I did that.

And, he knows everything. Mama told him when he went to see her. He found his birth certificate and thought that it belonged to his brother. Can you imagine that! So funny. But then I can understand. He always thought his name was William. Well, I like that name too.

Mama had told him that it was just too hard for me to take care of him by myself. I think that he understands. After all, he has had a nice life, really the life of a gentleman. I told him that I went to see him one time when he was at the Country School. He was very quiet all afternoon, and I kept seeing him stare at me. I hope that he thought that I was pretty. It is important for young men to think that their mothers are pretty, I think. It gives them confidence. They can look for a pretty wife later on. They will know what to look for, how she dresses and such. I think I showed him a good image to look for. I wore a white cotton blouse with a lot of lace trim, and a mauve linen full skirt and an ecru walking coat. The skirt stops right above my ankles, very stylish. And white *stockings, and a straw hat, a big one, with purple and pink flowers attached to the brim so that my face shows, and one long white feather. I think that more than one would have been too much. He seemed impressed, though he never said that he thought I was beautiful. Maybe he was too shy. He is shy, like Willie, I think.*

He will go to Mt. St. Joseph College in a few weeks. It is in Irvington, so it is not so far away. Frederick Road, he said. He could take the streetcar to his grandfather's for the holidays. He is not sure what he wants to study, he said.

So, Willie has met me and I think that he was impressed. Maybe we will be able to spend more time together. I asked about Clara and he said that he liked his "Uncle Stanley." I didn't mention anything about their not being married in a Catholic church. Probably he isn't aware of anything, not that he should be. And how about that, another Stanley in the family. I wonder if Clara thought of that, if she ever remembers my Stanley.

He is a very sweet-natured boy, very quiet, but then, we are strangers to him, I realize. Mama seems to like him very much. She was more lively in conversation that I can ever remember, even before Papa died. So, we will see.

He asked if he might call me Mother. I told him to call me Celeste. I think it would make him feel grown up, and it would be best that way if we were to meet and there was someone else around, someone who didn't know about him. Right now I am needing to concentrate on my work and my career. It would not do to advertise that I have a son, much less a son who is almost grown.

I am glad that I have you, dear diary. I can record important days, and I do think that this was an important day.

Forty

Clara answered the phone on the second ring. Without a greeting, August said, "Willie is gone. They just called me from the school. They haven't seen him since last night at bed check."

She leaned back in the chair by the fireplace and stared at the blue Delft tiles as she formulated her response. "What is it you know, *Vater*? Is there anything more to this? When did you last hear from him? Has he been writing to you? He's been there less than two months. Did anything happen? Are you going to the school? Do you want me to go with you?"

August listened to the barrage of questions. "Clara, I saw him yesterday. Somehow he had left the school and had walked, or hitchhiked, or taken the streetcars all the way here. I was in the front room when he came to the door.

"He told me he hated the school, begged me not to send him back. He was full of nonsense, said that he would work, that he would find a job, that he would do anything not to go back. His stammer was so bad that I could hardly understand him. He wept, like a child, Clara. The boy wept." August removed his glasses, rubbed his eyes.

"I told him to buck up, that he must act like a man, that it was a school where he would learn what he needed in order to make his way in the world, that we expected him to go to college, to be a gentleman. This sniveling, this quitting because he 'didn't like it,' was unacceptable. I will not mollycoddle him, Clara. It will do him no good. I know I was right in doing that."

Clara waited for her father to continue. In the past months, it seemed to her that he had lost his bluster. But here it had returned, she thought, so anxious was he for the boy to be a man.

"He finally stopped wallowing. I called for a car to take him back to Irvington, to the school. I rode with him to make sure that he got there. We shook hands as he left the car, Clara. I thought that it was settled. And now he has run away. Is he with you? Have you heard anything?"

Clara shook her head. A fourteen year-old boy on his own in the city, and a sheltered boy at that. She put herself in his place. What would her actions be if she were in his situation? He would try to find someone he knew to take him in. He would not be on his own, she thought.

"*Vati*, let me think and then I will call you back. He has gone somewhere, to someone. He would not just leave with no place to go. Let me think. Let me think."

August agreed to remain at the house in the event that Willie came there. Clara told her maid to be on the lookout for him. Then she called for her driver. Stanley had been at the hospital that morning and had office hours all that afternoon. She would not disturb him.

At four-thirty, her car pulled up in front of Annie's house. The driver waited as Clara rang the bell. The daily was working on the first floor. She called to Annie as she went to the door. "A lady here to see you, Mrs. Wells. She's come in an automobile."

Annie was standing in the vestibule when Clara reached the door. "Clara, come in. Is there something I can help you with?" The child, she thought. It has to do with the boy.

Clara used her cane all the time now; she walked directly into the living room, preceding Annie. "Willie has left school. Have you seen him? Has Celeste had anything to do with this? You must tell me. The child is missing. If we do not locate him soon, we will be forced to go to the police. If Celeste is involved, you do not want us to do that. You must tell me. Does she know where he is? Has she been in contact with him?"

"Oh, no," Anne said. She put her hand to her forehead, the spoke. "He came her a month, no, about six weeks ago. It was still summer. He had found his birth certificate. He thought he had a twin brother named Stanley."

She gathered her strength to confront Clara. "You have done a terrible thing keeping all this from him, Clara, all this secrecy, about his name, about his mother. He asked about her, wanted to see her, wanted to find out why she couldn't keep him."

"He is a poor lost boy, Clara. I did arrange for him to meet Celeste, here. They met for about an hour. So, he knows the truth, or as much of the truth as he can understand. He is a mixed-up boy."

Annie stopped, clasped her hands in her lap. "Oh, I've made a muddle. He did come here early this morning," she admitted. "He told me how he hated school, begged me to let him stay. I sat with him, gave him some tea and cake, told him how important school was, that he had just started, that it would get better. I told him that he could not stay here, that he had to go back. I offered to ride with him, to Irvington, but he said no, that he would take the streetcar. He had his duffel bag with him. I kissed him goodbye and he left.

"Clara, he is such a mixed-up boy, so confused, so unhappy. He is sensitive, I think, like Willie."

Clara glared. "Well, sensitive or not, he is missing. Where is Celeste? I want to see her."

"Celeste is working, you know that. And she lives on Robert Street; she's been there for over ten years now, the same place. She would never to anything to jeopardize her job, or her home. I don't think that he went to her; he wouldn't know how to find her. And she would be at work. Or, if he did see her, she would surely have told him to go back to school. I don't think that she is involved in this, Clara, truly I don't."

Clara stood. "Well, perhaps you have more faith in her than I, Mrs. Wells. But I will visit her tonight if he is not found by then." Clara extended her hand. "Thank you for your time. It is unfortunate that the few times that we have met have been so difficult. I do hear from Eva every once in a while. I consider her a friend, Mrs. Wells. I do." Clara looked down. "And I wish circumstances had been different."

"Well, yes. I presume that we all feel that way."

Annie walked Clara to the steps. The driver sprang out to open the right rear door.

That evening she and Stanley drove to Robert Street. They met with Celeste in the front room of Mrs. Bellingstone's house. Celeste corroborated what Annie had said; she had not seen Billy; she purposely called him Billy, since the summer. And yes, she would let Clara know if he contacted her.

Clara went with August to the school the next day. The prefect was apologetic, but showed no remorse. "Mr. Strauff did not seem to appreciate the rigors and expectations of the school," he said. "Perhaps if he had stayed longer he would have adjusted. But under the circumstances, the Brothers feel it best if he were disenrolled. When you locate him, it would be advisable that he seek another school.

"The young Mr. Strauff appeared to take his belongings with him. He left only his textbooks and notebooks here. Should we find any other personal articles, we will be happy to mail them to you." The short, gaunt Xaverian Brother extended his hand to August, nodded to Clara, and stood at the doorway to see them out.

They did not go to the police. They did not want another scandal associated with their name. Clara employed a private detective who watched Clara's and Annie's houses. Willie did not appear.

Three weeks later, August received a letter, postmarked Norfolk, Virginia.

November 1916

Dear Opa,

By the time you receive this letter I will be at sea. I have joined the Navy. Please don't try to find me; I did what is best for me. They told me that they will teach me a trade. That will be a good thing. I appreciate all that you have done for me. I want to be a good grandson to you, and a good nephew to Tante Clara. Please tell her that you have received this letter. I am sorry if I worried you, but I know what I did was the right thing. I am enjoying being in the Navy; they think that I am older. I like that. I will write you again when we reach port. I think that we are going to Belfast. I will be a seasoned sailor by the time we arrive. I have already learned the semaphore.

That is my first job here. It is very exciting being in the Navy with Europe at war. Everyone is a bit nervous. I hope that the U.S. will join in soon. Then it will be for real and I will have better stories to write to you.

Your loving grandson,
Willie

August called Clara. Clara wrote the Assistant Secretary of the Navy demanding that Willie be returned home. She received an immediate response, the letter signed Franklin D. Roosevelt, who promised to locate Willie and send him home.

However, Willie remained in the Navy until he was discharged in 1919. He regularly wrote to August and Clara; he did not contact Celeste or Annie. His fellow sailors knew him as Bill.

Forty-one

Celeste sometimes thought of Billy, of his adventures. Such an exciting way to start off his life, in the Navy, and at war. She knew that Clara heard from him, but only knew where he had been, not where he was. Clara's attempts to get him back home had failed. Celeste took some satisfaction in that. Clara seemed to have everything, a doctor husband, a big house in Peabody Heights that had been built for the daughter of President Polk. She had servants. It would do her good to be taken down a peg, Celeste decided.

She completed the last part of her journey home from Stewart's. She smelled dinner cooking as she went up the front steps, and called a greeting to Mrs. Bellingstone as she hung her shawl on the peg beside the door.

"It's only the two of us tonight, Celeste," Mrs. Bellingstone shouted from the basement. "The others are out. I thought I'd make us something special; I bought lamb chops at the market this morning. I can't remember the last time I cooked them, way before you arrived."

Celeste went to the top of the basement stairs. "Oh, Mrs. B. I haven't had them since, well, since Willie." Celeste stopped. Willie dead thirteen years now, a lifetime. Part of my life ended then, she thought. But Mrs. B is fixing us a special dinner; that's a good thing.

She went to her room and brushed her hair, removing the hairpins and rat she used to fill out her Gibson Girl hairstyle. Not so blond, anymore, she thought. Maybe this weekend I'll try some peroxide. She had read about the Castle bob, but, as she ran her fingers through her still-thick hair, she knew that she wouldn't submit to the scissors. She had only seen two women with short hair, and she thought that maybe they were a bit funny, a bit off. No, she thought, I just need to be a bit more blond, like I was before.

She had tried some Golden Glint Hair Rinse a few weeks earlier, but that did no good. She had looked at Woodbury's book, *Hair Dressing and Tinting*, the last time she visited the library, and had taken notes. Four parts water to one part peroxide, repeat no more than monthly. Maybe she would try that Sunday. She had seen some women who she knew bleached their hair, but to her they looked too obvious, like floozies. She could not risk that, would not risk her job. She knew that Stewart's would not put up with that. Maybe I should wait, she thought. Maybe I can ask at a few salons. But I must be blond.

Her reverie was broken by Mrs. Bellingstone's call to dinner. She pinned up her hair and bounced down the steps. She always felt like a girl in this house, a girl with a mother who loved her.

The two ate with gusto and Mrs. Bellingstone took empty plates to the dumbwaiter. When she returned to the table she said, "Celeste, there is something that I have to tell you."

Celeste felt a wave of nausea. The lamb sat heavy in her stomach.

"There is no easy way to say this. So." Mrs. Bellingstone paused. "I am going to Philadelphia to live with my sister. We are both getting old, no, we both are old. She is my only family now. We've decided that we will spend our last years together, taking care of one another.

"I'm selling the house. I wanted tell you first, in case you want to buy it. I know that I am probably being silly, wanting you to stay here. But you have brought such happiness to me, such spirit to this house. I thought that I would never laugh after Alfred died, and then you came into my life. So many years we've been together. I can hardly remember life before you came." The older woman reached out to take Celeste's hand.

Celeste's throat was tight; she could not get words out. Finally she said, "Oh, Mrs. B. I can't believe that you are leaving me. What will I do without you? Don't leave; please don't leave." Celeste held onto her landlady's hand, brought it to her cheek, made sure that Mrs. Bellingstone felt her tears.

"It will be terrible for us, leaving each other, my dear," the older woman said. "At first. Then it will be not so bad. We've both been through worse. And I am not leaving just yet. But by the holidays I want to be in Philadelphia. You can understand that. I want to spend the holidays with my sister."

Celeste's mind raced. How could she convince her to stay? "With the war on? Do you think it will be hard to sell the house with the war on?"

"Celeste, let us go on the way we were. You know, life goes on. And we will get through this. But I did want you to know. It will give you time to think, to find a new home. You will always be in my heart, my dear sweet girl."

"Mrs. B., I am thirty-three years old. I am old now, and alone. I don't know how I'll get along without you. I don't."

But this time Celeste didn't cry.

Forty-two

The next morning Celeste dressed and left the house early. She wanted to be in the crisp November air; she wanted time to think. I will just find a new home. That won't be too hard. I have savings; I still have the money from Mr. Strauff. I've saved it all these years. I'll be just fine, she said to herself.

She forced a spring in her step as she walked from the bus stop to the store. They were receiving a new shipment that would need to be inventoried, priced and displayed. She was glad for a busy day ahead of her. After she unpacked the merchandise, dressing gowns, negligees, lingerie sets, chemises, she sat quietly, alone in the storeroom. Even after her years at the store, she still loved to touch the fine cottons, silks, satins, still loved to see lace and ribbons. Yes, she thought, I'll be just fine.

As she entered the items on the inventory sheet, she set two pieces aside, a nainsook nightgown, white, so soft that she closed her eyes when she held it. One of a dozen; they'll never miss it.

The second piece, a set, corset cover, drawers and petticoat, an alabaster white, trimmed in lace, threaded with peach silk ribbons. The only set the manufacturer sent. She put that aside. They'll forget that it was ordered.

At lunchtime, she brought her carpet bag, the same one she had been carrying since her days at Hutzler's, to the storeroom and placed the items in the bottom, underneath her ever-present library books. I deserve a treat, I do, she thought. I'll try them on when I get home.

That afternoon, as she prepared to leave the department, Mr. Price appeared. He asked her to come with him to his office. Once there, he stood in front of his desk; he indicated that she should be seated.

"Mrs. Strauff, today will be your last day with us. I don't think that I need say more. We are most distressed at having to make this decision. You have been one of our most exemplary employees for these years now. The incident will go no further; we will not involve the police. But you must leave now. We will mail you a check for your hours this week. Under the circumstances, you will not be paid for today."

He paused, adjusted his pince-nez. "Also, you are not to enter the store again. Do you understand? We want no scandal, for the store or for you. But you must abide by this directive. And please return the merchandise to the storeroom before you leave. That is an order."

Price turned away and faced the window. Celeste swallowed, started to speak, then stopped. She stood, held herself erect, and left the office. The employee lounge was empty when she got there; she retrieved her bag from her locker and walked to the storeroom. She wrapped the gown, the lingerie set in tissue paper, and placed it on the folding table.

She left the building. On her walk to the trolley stop, she used Clay Street, and walked by the employee entrance to Hutzler's.

Forty-three _____

Dear Mr. Strauff,

First, I want to write and tell you how sorry I am about the death of Mrs. Strauff. I know I am so late in doing this, and I apologize. I will always appreciate her kindness to me, and that she took care of Willie when it was impossible for me to do so.

I am writing you to ask for your help. You have always been so kind and generous to me. I will always remember and appreciate it.

I find myself in the position of looking for both a job and a place to live. I know that you are now living in Hamilton. I think that it would be a good thing for me to have a new start, with a change of jobs and living arrangements. Would it be possible for me to stay with you while I seek work? Or would you know of any work that I could do? I am a very hard, conscientious worker. I have good business skills. I was hoping that a man in your position would know of opportunities. If you could help me do this, I would be forever grateful. I know that Willie is in the Navy now. I have not heard from him in many years. If you could tell me how he is doing, that would be lovely too. I have never forgotten my Willie; I have visited his grave often and stood on that hill in the wind. I also read a lot, books that I think that he would like.

My life has not been easy, Mr. Strauff. If you could find it in your heart to help me one more time,

Your loving daughter-in-law,
Celeste

431

August answered her letter the day after it arrived. He sat at his desk in the front window, staring out at the bare trees lining Catalpha Avenue. He told her of his recent marriage. He did not tell her that his new wife was younger than she. He did not tell her that he lost, that he did not sell, the newspaper. He did not tell her how often he was humiliated by the anti-German sentiment in the neighborhood, what he considered to be a German neighborhood, shop owners turning from him now, he, who had been in this country decades longer than many of those claiming to be American patriots who hate the Huns. He did not ask why she wasn't with her mother. He did write that he knew of a dentist in the area who was looking for a bookkeeper. He would put them in touch if she thought that was the type of position she was interested in. He did not respond to her comments about Willie. He did not share with her his disappointment that his grandson would not be a gentleman.

Then he turned and joined his young wife for a glass of *Underberg*, grateful that he had stockpiled a case before the war.

Forty-four _____

Celeste charmed the dentist, found a room above a store on Harford Road. It had a place for a hot-plate. The dentist, more concerned with Celeste's eyes and derriere than her accounting skills, was surprised at her talent and aptitude. She could complete her job in a half-day, but he liked to have her in the office. His patients liked her as well, especially the men. Celeste was starting to look back, although she kept her eyes lowered when the dentist's wife stopped by, which she did with increasing frequency, suspicious of how this bookkeeper could afford such fine clothes.

Celeste had found a hairdresser and was again a decided blonde. The fashions of the time were less generous to her proportions. She still wore a corset, though others, younger, had thrown theirs off, a stand for freedom even as the war raged on. Many of the young men were overseas. Celeste found the others married, and she would not make that mistake again. But, she realized, time was running out. She had wasted years in that cozy cocoon on Robert Street. She would make up for lost time now.

In May, 1918, she attended a parade sponsored by the Red Cross War Fund Drive. She thought it would be an opportunity to see and be seen by men in the area who were interested in such things. And Celeste was keeping her eye out for men. She noticed someone who looked like a friend of her father. When she caught his eye, he smiled with recognition.

"Are you the Wells girl?" he asked, and when she replied, he responded with a fatherly hug. "Oh, I still remember your father. A good man, George, he was." Celeste told him that she was a widow now, that her mother lived quietly and that Eva lived in New England.

He invited her to attend a reception at the Fifth Regiment Armory following the parade. She could ride with him, if she'd like. He'd see to it that she was returned home safely.

Celeste, happy to be in the comfortable company of someone who knew her father, cheerfully agreed.

At the reception, she was introduced to a tall, young fellow, almost as blond as Celeste now was. He told her that had served in the Navy but had been discharged and worked at Hamburger's Clothing Store at Baltimore and Hanover Streets. He smiled down at her. She thought it nice to be with someone so tall, someone she actually had to raise her chin to speak to.

"I used to work in retail," she said. "How did you come to work at Hamburger's? I hear that it is a fine store." She noted that he wore his clothes almost as handsomely as Willie.

He leaned closer to her; there was something about her eyes, he thought. Beautiful. He laughed, "Well, it is not a very high-toned reason. When my ship docked at the harbor, some of us left the pier looking for something to eat. We saw the sign, H-A-M-B-U-R-G-E-R-S and thought that we'd go there. Once we realized that it wasn't a restaurant, we headed for another place. But I remembered the clothes; they seemed a cut above. It was how I wanted to dress as if I had had the money.

"So, when I was discharged, this is where the ship docked. They gave me a ticket back to Oregon, but I cashed it in and took my chance with the store. I can't believe it, but they hired me on the spot. So, here I am, in Baltimore, at Hamburger's." He laughed, and tried to think of something else to say. He wanted to impress this lovely woman.

"So you were in the Navy," she began. "My s--, my stars," she said, and he laughed at this phrase, so out of character with the beautiful Gibson Girl who stood before him. When he smiled his mouth went over to the left. Celeste noticed, and liked it. She felt happy; then she realized how long it had been since she had felt that way.

He asked if he could escort her home. She told him no, that Mr. Tatum would see to that.

He asked if he could see her again. To that, she answered yes. Later on she told him that she was a widow.

"That must be hard for you," he said. She told him that it had been a long time ago, that they both had been very young. He thought her stoicism admirable.

Karl took her to shows, to movies, to vaudeville. They took the streetcar; she didn't seem to mind. They went to fine restaurants when he could afford it; she seemed to understand. He loved how much she knew about fine food, how much she enjoyed eating, so comfortable in every setting. When she laughed, her eyes crinkled. He was enchanted. As he boarded the streetcar after leaving Celeste at her door, he smiled. *A lady like Celeste is keen on me.*

One evening, over dinner, she asked him where his people were from. He answered, "Portland."

"No, she laughed, your *people*. Where did they come from?" He told her that his father was born in Kansas and moved to Oregon when he left school. "He wanted to be more than a farmer. And I want a life better than my father's." He wanted to be sure that Celeste knew he was ambitious.

Celeste looked over at him and smoothed his hair. "You are such a dear. I meant where in Europe, you know, before they came to this country." She laughed some more. "Now that is something that, if you came from the East, you would have known exactly what I meant. You are such a breath of fresh hair, I mean air," she giggled. "Do you even know?"

Karl blushed. *So much to learn from her, from the Easterners.* He thought. "We never talked about it, and my grandparents are dead. Maybe Germany, or Austria? No one made fun of me during the war, so maybe not."

Celeste put her coffee cup to her lips, and looked deeply into his eyes. "Perhaps you are Dutch? Well, no matter. We are all Americans, especially now." *Yes,* she thought, *he certainly wears his clothes well.*

One evening he told her that he was Catholic and asked if she was. She replied that she had been married in a Catholic Church, St. Alphonsus. He took that as a yes.

The town sponsored an Armistice Day Parade in November. Mr. Tatum invited Celeste to sit in the reviewing stand. She invited Karl. Banners flew, bands played, soldiers and children marched. Harford

Road was packed, and she wanted to be part of the crowd. The couple slipped from their chairs and ran laughing to the sidewalk. They positioned themselves in the second row from the street, standing directly in back of two young girls. Celeste looked down. The blond one, she thought, would be pretty if she'd lose her lemon-faced scowl. Her younger sister, obviously in tow against the older's wishes, was stunning, with long, thick black curls down cascading down her back. A vixen-in-waiting, thought Celeste. As she eyed the pair, she saw the hand of the taller girl grab the dark tresses of the younger.

"Ow," the shorter one shrieked. She turned to her sister. "You did that on purpose. I'm telling Papa."

"Shut up," her sister replied. "Just shut up," and gave the hair another tug.

Jealous, Celeste thought. She knew that look. She had seen it often enough directed toward her. Just as well that I didn't have children. Then she looked up at Karl. She loved the feeling of looking up to a tall man. "Isn't this just wonderful?" she said, and bounced in time with the Souza march playing.

Karl looked at her. Beautiful, he thought. He took her hand and brought it to his lips.

Willie, Celeste thought, just like Willie. Karl leaned down to her ear.

"Marry me, Celeste. Marry me. Please."

Celeste closed her eyes. What took you so long, she thought. She leaned against him, tilted her head, met his eyes. "I thought you'd never ask."

Baltimore Sun
March 9, 1919

Brentano – Strauff

The wedding of Miss Celeste Strauff, daughter of Mrs. Anna E. Wells, of Baltimore, and Mr. Karl C. Brentano, of Portland, Oregon, took place at St. Dominic's Church, Hamilton, at High Nuptial Mass on March 4, 1919. The bride had as her attendant, Miss A. Mildred Brown, of Belair, Md., while

```
Mr. Brentano had for his best man Mr.
Albert Egan, of Bridgeport, Conn. After
a wedding breakfast, the bride and groom
left for a trip north.
```

Annie was there; she sat with August and his new wife. Clara was invited, but did not attend. Eva remained at home, awaiting the birth of her second child. Celeste wore a two-piece dress of taupe silk with lace overlay; she carried violets.

On the train to New York, Celeste looked over at her new husband. "I have something to tell you, Karl."

When she finished, he looked at her. "You have a son in the Navy? How old are you?"

PART IV

One────────────────────────────────

They stopped in Philadelphia to visit Mrs. Bellingstone. Celeste had asked Karl about this before the wedding. He thought it sweet that his sophisticated love was so fond of her former landlady.

The couple was quiet as the train pulled into the Broad Street Station. They spoke little during the cab ride to 13th and Chestnut Streets, to the Hotel Adelphia where they would spend their wedding night. When they reached the entrance, Celeste looked up at the tall brick and stone building. "I wonder who the architect is," she said.

Karl looked over at her, then shook his head. In his mind he heard the words that had been echoing in his thoughts for the past hour. Who is this woman I married? A son in the Navy. Who is this woman? What have I done?

Once in the hotel lobby, Celeste took his hand. She looked at him, waited until he met her gaze. "Karl, I know that I have done a wicked thing, not telling you the truth. I don't know what to say, except that I love you, and that I loved you so much that I was afraid if you knew how old I was, about Billy, that you would not want to be with me. It was wrong, I know that. But I will make up for it, I promise. I will be the best wife you could ever imagine. I will.

"Please forgive me. I promise that I will never lie to you, ever. I promise, Karl, I do."

Karl looked at Celeste, and some of what he had seen before, before she had told him about her son, before he knew how old she was, returned to his eyes. She was thirty-four, eight years older than he. But she was still beautiful, and he loved her clothes and how she wore them, like a real lady. He wanted to be with a real lady. So what if she were older; so what if she had a child. She said that she didn't see the boy, that he was on his own. She promised that he would not be part of their lives, that they could have their own family, if he wanted.

"I know you are provoked with me, Karl. I understand that, I do. But I will make it up to you, I promise. Can we just be together, be newlyweds? I will be a good wife to you. I will do everything to be a good wife to you."

He stared down at Celeste, allowed his hand to remain in hers as they walked to the registration desk. Early on, she had asked him if he were part of the New York bookstore Brentano's. That she would know of a bookstore, that there was a famous bookstore, was news to him. He thought she was the smartest girl he had ever known. He wanted a life different from the one he had known; he wanted to be a gentleman. He needed Celeste.

They rode the elevator to their room in silence. The memory of her elevator ride at the Stafford, with Willie, that wedding night so many years ago, came to her. She bit her lip, squeezed Karl's hand. This is a new life, she thought. I need for us to be happy. I will make us happy.

Karl was quiet, wondering who he had married. This woman he thought so regal, so beautiful, who was she?

Once in their room, Celeste told him almost everything. About Willie, about Stanley, the kidnapping, Willie's death, George's suicide, about Annie, and Mrs. Bellingstone. She omitted Hayley and the reason she left Stewart's. She wanted him to love her.

Karl listened, though his mind was numb. I'm just a simple guy, he thought. All this lying. Is this how these people act, how they live? Who is this woman?

As she talked, he saw that she wasn't quite as beautiful as he had thought. The balance had shifted, though he wouldn't have put it that way.

The wedding night was not what either expected. Karl was business-like. He thought that he would be enraptured once he possessed this beautiful woman, but he realized that she was ordinary, not so different from the other women he had been with. Celeste hoped that Karl would fulfill the fantasies of the years since Willie. Maybe it will get better, she hoped. As did he.

The next morning they took the local to Haverford. Mrs. Bellingstone lived with her sister, Edith, who had worked as a housemother in one of the college's dormitories. When she retired, she had just enough money to purchase a small frame house on a quiet side street, just big enough for the two of them, she said.

The couple walked the eight blocks from the station. Celeste wore her wedding outfit. She wanted Mrs. Bellingstone to see how she looked in her taupe silk and lace. The older woman was waiting at the window and opened the door as they turned in the walkway. "Oh, I am so glad to see you, my dear, dear Celeste."

Celeste gripped Karl's hand when she heard these words, remembering the many evenings spent with this dear woman, the meals they had shared, the music that they had listened to and sung together. It seemed a lifetime ago, a lifetime where she was, if not happy, then content.

She closed her eyes. But all that is behind me. I have the life that I want, and it will be a good life. I will make it a good life for us.

Karl smiled quietly as the women talked. He watched Celeste, who seemed so full of light with this woman whom she loved. Mrs. Bellingstone looked over at him. "You have yourself here a lovely girl," she said, "and you are a handsome consort!"

Karl blushed; Mrs. Bellingstone liked that, and Karl wondered how the landlady could call his wife a girl.

The pair left after an hour's visit. They had a train connection to Boston, where, Celeste said, they would begin their real honeymoon.

When they arrived at Boston's North Union Station, Celeste walked slowly, looking up, taking note of the architecture. "It doesn't have any belvederes, like the old 16th Street Station in Washington or Baltimore's Camden Station," she said.

Karl smiled and shook his head. She was always looking at things he didn't see.

"I think that the waiting rooms are grander, but just one, no ladies or gentlemen's separate rooms. I guess that is a sign of the times, don't you think? Now that women are becoming stronger?" She smiled up at him; he kissed her on the top of the head. Oh, she thought, a man tall enough to kiss me on the top of the head. He makes me feel delicate. It will be all right, she told herself.

Karl took her to Fenway Park, where the Red Sox had won the World Series the year before. They rode the subways, wearing the cotton masks provided by the hotel to guard against the Spanish Influenza epidemic. Everywhere they rode, they saw people wearing them. They had not seen this in Baltimore. They went to movies almost every night, and took in some afternoon vaudeville shows. Celeste had a different outfit for every day, as did Karl.

He loves me, he has forgiven me, she thought, when she looked over and saw him laughing at Harold Lloyd fighting over Bebe Daniels. She held his arm as they watched Eric von Stroheim play the treacherous Hun in *The Heart of Humanity*.

"You know, I thought about becoming a nurse during the war, helping out. But if I had done that, then we would never have met, and that would have been a terrible thing. I am such a lucky girl," Celeste whispered, her eyes fixed on the screen.

Karl looked over at her. You are anything but a girl, he thought. Then he smiled to himself. Yes, she was still beautiful, that he had to admit.

At Celeste's insistence, they visited historical sites. Karl deciphered unwieldy paper maps as they maneuvered their way to Faneuil Hall, to the Old North Church, to Paul Revere's house. Celeste read aloud from the brochures as they walked, trying to remember what Mr. Wilford had tried to teach her, and wishing that she had paid a bit more attention.

Karl watched as she placed her finger on the words to keep her place as she walked. A lady, he thought. This is what they do. He didn't notice the architecture or any of the things that Willie would have been excited to see. Celeste tried not to dwell on that.

They did not visit Eva. Celeste did not want comparisons to Willie. Karl would not fare well in that regard, although he too was handsome. And he was tall. She concentrated on that. And he wore his clothes beautifully.

At the end of the week, they were both glad to return to Baltimore, to the home that Celeste would make for them. There would be no mention of her son.

Two _____

Celeste brought her ivory-handled flatware, her books, her gramophone and her clothes to their second floor apartment on 26ᵗʰ Street. Karl brought his clothes. The landlady, a widow, lived on the first floor. A man and a woman rented two rooms to a on the third floor. The woman was a teacher. Celeste didn't know what the man did for a living. They all worked to respect the other's privacy. They shared one bathroom, which now had an indoor toilet.

"I want this to be a real home for us, Karl," Celeste had said before they were married. "I have a bit of a nest egg put by. I'd like to buy furniture for us, for our home. It will make coming home ever so nice. And I have been studying cooking again. I haven't cooked for ages, but now I will have the time to do it. You must tell me all your favorite dishes, or maybe I'll write to your mother and ask her to send her recipes. Then it will be like we are a family, won't it? Will you like that?"

And so a bedroom suite, a sofa, two chairs and tables and lamps, were delivered from Gomprecht and Benecsh. Buying them took most of Celeste's savings. She wanted them to have a fine start. She would not live with the furniture of others as she had for so long. They could fill in the other pieces later, from Littlepage's on Baltimore Street, she thought, not so expensive.

She borrowed cookbooks from the library, and experimented on two new recipes each week. Karl seemed delighted. Celeste watched him. He has forgiven me, she thought. I have learned; I will not make that mistake again.

She enjoyed playing the role of the housewife. I don't miss working, she told herself. I'm not lonely; it just takes time getting used to being a wife again. We can live on Karl's salary. I'll economize.

She had thought that he made more money than he brought home. She thought that Hamburger's paid their staff more.

Three

Celeste heard the tinkle of the doorbell. She laid the issue of *McClure's Magazine* on her lap, deciding whether to answer. They had few friends, no visitors. A salesman selling brushes, magazine subscriptions, perhaps? She went to the window. No cars on the street. Looking down, she saw the top of a man's head, dark-haired. He stood with his arms at his sides; he wasn't carrying samples.

Tossing the magazine onto the sofa, she walked down the narrow staircase to the door which admitted entry to the second and third floors. She opened it with a wary eye. A young man, tall, stood before her.

"Hello, Celeste. I'm Bill Strauff, your son."

Celeste closed her eyes. She had put his existence out of her mind. Neither she nor Karl had mentioned him since that train ride almost a year ago. She put her hand to her chest, willed herself to speak.

"Oh, Billy, I wouldn't have recognized you. You are so tall, so grown up. And your hair so dark now. How did you find me? You don't look like the same boy, no, that is the truth."

Bill stood, waiting for her to ask him in. Celeste stared at her son. He doesn't look like Willie anymore, not at all, she thought. But he is a handsome fellow, anyone can see that.

Finally she spoke. "Would you like to come in?" Bill nodded. She turned and led the way up the stairs.

Once inside the apartment, Celeste said, "This is just such a surprise, Billy. I thought that you were staying in the Navy. I haven't talked to your grandfather or Clara, well, not since I married. You do know that I am married now, don't you?"

"Yes." He walked toward the chair next to the window.

"Would you care for a cup of tea, some cake? I think that I might have some put away." Celeste moved the few feet from living room to kitchen. "I just can't believe I am seeing you. You are a man, Billy, a man." Almost as tall as Karl, she thought.

She returned to the living room, tea and cake forgotten, grateful that she had fixed her hair that morning, put a dusting of rice powder on her face. "What made you come here today? Is there something that you want?" she said.

Bill tugged at the sleeves of his white shirt, making sure that they did not extend more than an inch below his jacket sleeves. "W-w-well, I am b-back in B-Baltimore n-now." He stopped, closed his eyes, willed himself to speak without the stammer that plagued him whenever he was nervous or in unfamiliar surroundings. "I thought that I would visit you, thought that, now that I am g-grown, we could get to know o-one another. If that is what you would like, of c-course." He raised his left hand to move the hair from his forehead, then put his hands on his knees.

"I have been in the Navy, you know, and j- just arrived back in Baltimore last week. While I was at sea, I thought about you, and thought that now that I was grown, now that you would not have to take care of me, that we could know one another, that perhaps you w-would l-l like to know me." He stopped when Celeste rose from her seat.

"Oh, I did forget all about that tea. Just let me go and put the kettle on for us. You keep talking, Billy. I can hear you."

Bill stopped. He would wait until his mother was in the room to talk to her. He started to walk to the window, then turned. "You have a lovely home, Celeste," he said as he walked to the kitchen. "May I help you with that, help you carry in a tray?" he asked.

She turned toward him. Handsome, she thought. But that stammer, so like Willie. "Why yes, you can help. And I did find some cake. It may be a bit stale, but let's try it anyway. Sometimes it's best that way, don't you think?" And she smiled what she knew was her most beguiling smile.

When they were seated, Bill looked at her, studied her face. "I am looking for a job now. But I don't think that my time in the Navy will help much. I could be a clerk, I think. I have a talent for numbers." He paused. "And how is Grandmother Wells?" he asked.

Celeste put her hand to the back of her head, tucked the few loose strands into the roll at her neck. "Well, Billy, I really don't see her too often. She is a very private person, you know. But I'm sure she would like to see you if you want to visit. She is still in the same house, my house. I mean the house where I was born."

Bill took a deep breath. "May I call you Mother? I would like that very much, but only if it is all right with you. When I was away and thought about you, I always thought of you as Mother."

Celeste put her cup and saucer on the table beside the sofa. "Billy, I think it better, especially now that you are grown, that you continue to call me Celeste. That should make you feel very grown-up, shouldn't it? And we can be friends now. Yes, friends. So it would not do, not do at all, for you to call me Mother. No, Celeste is better, don't you think?"

He did not respond. A mistake, he thought, this whole day has been a mistake. Yet something made him push ahead and put forward the question he had come to the house to ask.

"Actually, I did have a reason to visit you today, Celeste." He knew what her answer would be, knew that his request would be better left unasked, but he continued.

"I was hoping that I could stay with you for a while, just until I get on my feet, just until I find a job and save enough money to find a room. I could stay with C-Clara, but I thought that it would be a chance for us to get to know each other if I could stay here. Just for a w-while, a few w-weeks, maybe a month. I would not be any bother. I could help you around the house if you needed help. And I would like to meet my stepfather. I think that I c-could make him l-like me." Bill hurried with his words, not giving Celeste a chance to respond.

She went to the window, feeling the thump of her heart. She waited for it to slow before she spoke. She knew what he was asking for, to be loved, what she had wanted from her own mother. But not now, Billy, not now. Finally, she spoke.

"Oh, Billy, that would not be possible. It would not be possible. You are better off with Clara. She has that big house, she knows people who could offer you a job, a good job. You are a gentleman, Billy. You must live that life. It would not do for you to live here. No, not at all."

Bill lowered his eyes, concentrated on the tea cup in his hand.

"But you can come for dinner. How about that? You could come for Sunday dinner." She stopped. "Oh, no, not this Sunday. Perhaps you could come another week. I will contact you at Clara's. Yes, that is what we'll do. Another Sunday."

"Yes, of course. I understand." He stood to leave. Celeste extended her hand. Bill shook it. "No need to walk downstairs with me," he said. "And thank you. It was good to see you."

"Yes, it was good to see you too. And I'll be in touch, I will, definitely."

Back on the street Bill considered visiting Annie. He walked to North Avenue, then stopped. I am a man, he thought. I can stand on my own two feet.

His decision was a mistake. Annie thought about him every day.

Four

Celeste's days were quiet; she missed the structure of work. She studied magazines to learn just what a proper wife should do. I didn't feel this way with Willie, but then, she thought, I had Stanley to take care of. She thought of Mrs. Bellingstone, tried to imagine her landlady's days. She wondered how she kept herself busy.

Each morning Celeste rose and dressed before Karl left for work. She wanted him to remember her as beautiful. The housework, with just the two of them, didn't take up as much time as when she was with Willie. She bought a Hoover with the remainder of her savings. She loved the noise and swish on the carpets, delighted in the pathways left there as proof of her efforts. Those afternoons she walked only on the periphery of the living room rug, hoping that Karl would notice the tracks left by the vacuum cleaner when he came home.

She used the laundry tubs in the basement. Karl sent his shirts to the Chinese laundry. It would not do for him to look anything less than perfect at the store.

She marketed most mornings, and developed a nodding acquaintance with the neighbors. She befriended a woman who lived across the alley, both of them hanging clothes in the backyard to the same schedule. Celeste had invited her in for tea some afternoon, but that hadn't taken place.

She continued her trips to the library on Mulberry Street every Tuesday morning, sometimes walking to Howard Street to look in the store windows. She remembered Mr. Price's words, and never revisited Stewart's, though she often found herself studying its columns and carvings. For Willie, she told herself.

Her life wasn't what she had imagined it would be. Karl was still tall, still handsome, but he no longer looked at her as he had done before they were married. He didn't read; he wasn't interested in what she read. He mocked her for being pretentious. "Isn't that one of your words, Celeste? Pretentious?" he parodied.

She struggled to prepare meals that he liked, though they both knew that she would never be a good cook. He didn't criticize; neither did he compliment. Their home was eleven blocks from Annie's. Occasionally Celeste would walk by the house, hoping that her mother would notice and invite her in.

Their bedroom life remained active. Karl was persuasive; Celeste was more than accommodating. She asked that he use a French letter; most nights he did. She liked when he approached her in the early morning hours. He did not always use precautions then, and she chose not to break the spell by asking about them.

When she missed her second period, she knew she had to find someone. She couldn't go to her mother. It had been so long since she had been with her friends from school, she felt couldn't go to them, although she was sure that they would be able to help her. But her desperation prevailed.

On a Monday morning she ventured to the library and asked for the City Directory. Of her four close friends from Eastern, only Margaret still lived in Baltimore. Her hands trembled as she turned the tissue-thin pages of the directory, searching, hoping to find her name. She heard herself laugh aloud when she found it. Margaret has a telephone, Celeste thought, of course she would. She laughed with relief.

As she walked to public telephone in the vestibule to make the call, she practiced what she would say, that she knew that it had been oh so long since they had seen one another, but could she come to visit, perhaps this Thursday? Would it be possible to see her then?

Margaret recognized Celeste's voice as soon as she said hello. Of course, she would love to see her, and Thursday would be perfect. She took notice of the worry behind Celeste's words, and thought back to the blithe, carefree girl she had known, those years ago when they all thought that life could only bring them happiness and adventure.

"Please come," she said, hoping that Celeste would feel warmth in her tone. "I'll be waiting. We can have tea and maybe some scones. How would that do?"

Celeste closed her eyes in gratitude at the kindness in Margaret's voice. A friend in need, she thought, a blessing. She's bound to understand. And she did.

The Monday after their visit Margaret picked Celeste up at her door. Celeste was impressed that her friend had a car, and was more impressed that she actually drove it. They went to a house in Highlandtown and parked in the alley behind. A grey-haired woman met them at the kitchen door. Celeste smelled apples baking as she opened the door.

"Come in, my dear. Would you like a cup of tea?" the woman asked. Celeste shook her head. She felt old. She felt ugly. She felt dirty, though she had dressed in her best outfit and spent extra time on her hair that morning.

Margaret sat with her at the kitchen table. "I'll stay, then I'll drive you home when it's over. You'll see. It won't be bad, really, it won't. Don't think that you are alone in this, Celeste. I'm with you, and this will stay just between us."

Celeste nodded, feeling both older and younger than her thirty-seven years. "Come," the woman said, and led her up the narrow stairway.

Once in the back bedroom, she turned to Celeste. "That will be twenty dollars. It is good to get these financial things taken care of beforehand, don't you think? Then we can just concentrate on making you feel better before you leave." She patted Celeste's hand, as Celeste handed her twenty one-dollar notes, smoothed out, money she had been putting aside each week.

Celeste changed into the cotton gown that lay on the bed. The woman folded her clothes. "Such a beautiful fabric this is. You have an eye for color, don't you?" she asked. Celeste nodded and then closed her eyes.

The woman gave her a handkerchief. "It might be best if you inhaled some of this. It will make you a bit woozy. Yes, best if you keep your eyes closed, or just look up at the ceiling. This won't take

453

long. You will feel a jab, maybe a sting, maybe something sharp. Try not to move. It is best if you keep perfectly still. Perfectly still, do you understand, dear? Do not move."

Celeste followed the woman's advice and placed the cloth over her nose and mouth. Chloroform, she thought, remembering it from Stanley's birth, blessed chloroform.

She was concentrating on the ceiling fixture, counting its carved roses, when she heard, faintly, "All done. You lie there for a while. I'll go downstairs and keep your friend company. I'll be back in an hour. You try to sleep. All went well. It wasn't so bad, was it?"

Celeste shook her head, tried to focus on the woman. She placed the handkerchief against her face and fell asleep.

It was late afternoon when Margaret pulled in front of the house. She looked over at Celeste. "How are you feeling? Up to going home now?" She paused. "Will you tell Karl?"

Celeste shook her head and leaned against the cold glass of the car's window. She wanted to be alone; she wanted to sleep, she wanted this to be over.

"Get yourself a Dutch cap. Much better than relying on a man to look out for you." Margaret reached into her pocketbook and took out a small, blue, leather-bound notebook. She removed the small gold pen from the cover and wrote on a sheet of paper. "Here. Take this. It's the name of my doctor. Tell him that I recommended him, and ask him for a Mensinga diaphragm. Be sure to tell him that I recommended him to you. Do it, Celeste. It will save you worry, believe me."

Celeste looked over toward the driver's seat. "Margaret, how can I thank you?" She pulled herself erect. "Would we ever have imagined when we were girls at Eastern that we would be here, like this?"

Margaret reached for Celeste's hand. "We were raised for a different world. I wouldn't have chosen this one, to be sure. But since this is where we are, we must do what we can to survive. And maybe laugh about it some. Some of us have been luckier than others. And so much of it has been luck, don't you think?"

"Who would have thought we'd be here? You are right about that. I wonder what the world will be like when we're fifty. Not to be imagined; everything so different from what we had supposed. Do you think our mothers thought the same thing? Seems to me that they had the lives they planned.

"Will you call me in a few days, this weekend, maybe Monday, and let me know how you are?"

Celeste picked up her purse from the floor of the car. Her head was bowed. "I don't know how I can thank you, Margaret, truly I don't."

"Think not of it."

Margaret waited as Celeste left the car and made her way up the front steps. Celeste turned before she entered the house, touched her fingers to her lips. Margaret returned the gesture, put the car into gear, and drove away.

Five———————————————————————

Later that year, the couple moved to Maryland Avenue, a first-floor apartment this time, with a yard, a garden, if they wanted it. Karl was delighted to sit on the back porch each morning before he left for work, no matter how chilly the air. "And come spring, I'll be sitting out here enjoying a beer every evening," he said. Celeste smiled. Maybe he would stay home more, come right home from work. Maybe life would be better for them. He was still a salesman at Hamburgers, but had moved up to senior status. Maybe soon he'll be made a manger, Celeste hoped.

She was restless, though she would not have described herself as such. She put the house in order early. She went to the market each day, regardless of the weather. She sometimes walked to the downtown library rather than taking the streetcar because it occupied her time. She spoke to the neighbors when she saw them, but no one had invited her in for coffee. She kept in touch with Margaret, though she knew that the differences in their stations, their lives, precluded further intimacies. She had no one to laugh with.

When she found herself, for the second time, getting off the streetcar with a young woman who lived across the street, Celeste decided to introduce herself. As they parted, she added, "Maybe we could have lunch downtown sometime."

"Oh, that would be delightful. I work on Baltimore Street, near Holiday, but can always ask for a little more time at lunch. Just chose a day and let me know. I'm always ready to try something."

Celeste saw the twinkle in the young woman's eye. How lucky to be so young, she thought, with your life ahead of you.

Celeste and Edith became friends; Karl noticed the difference in his wife in the evenings after they had been together, a lighter step, a more amorous touch. He liked it, a bit of the old Celeste. The two women lunched every week, trying the different restaurants around Pratt and Light Streets. Edith worked for one of the brokers at Alex Brown & Sons. There was not a lot of work for her to do, she told Celeste. When she was busy, she was swamped, but there were many hours that she read magazines. She loved *Modern Screen*, and *Photoplay*, that featured movie stars. *Motion Picture* was her favorite.

"They have the best photographs of hairstyles, close-ups, they're called. My dream is that one day a big producer will spot me and take me to Hollywood. Wouldn't that be super?"

"Yes, that would be super," Celeste replied and wondered if she had ever been so young and full of hope. Such a child, she thought.

On that Thursday, they met for lunch. "I have the rest of the day off. Let's go shopping," Edith said. Celeste agreed. It had been a long time since she had entered into a department store.

"Stewart's. Let's start there. I love the way the first floor is so wide and open. It makes me feel like a real lady to shop there," Edith said. Celeste was silent, considered suggesting another store, then stopped. It's been years, she thought. I deserve to go into any store I please.

When they left Stewart's, the crossed Howard Street. "Hats," Edith said. "This January has just been too grey. Let's look at some spring hats. Don't you think it would be fun to try them on?" She giggled. "Maybe we'll buy, or maybe we won't." She took Celeste's hand as they raced through the intersection, now clogged with automobiles and streetcars vying for space.

Baltimore Sun
January 26, 1923

Two Women Are Arrested On Shoplifting Charge
Alleged Stolen Merchandise Found In Their Homes, Detectives Claim

Two women, accused of stealing merchandise valued at hundreds of dollars from two department stores, were locked up

457

at Central Police Station last night for a hearing before Magistrate J.H.Stanford.

They gave their names as Mrs. Carl Brentano, 29 years old, 2124 Maryland avenue, and Miss Edith Lowman, 25 years old, 2121 Maryland avenue.

Detective Sergeants H.S. Warthen and Frederick Harbourne arrested Mrs. Brentano and Miss Lowman and brought them to the office of Charles H. Burns, captain of detectives. According to Captain Burns, the two women were trailed from one store to the other.

Going to the homes of the women, detectives said, they recovered many silk nether garments, beaded bags, umbrellas, articles of women's finery, a dress valued at $49 and handbags.

Mrs. Brentano is accused of stealing articles valued at $154.50. Miss Lowman, who told the detectives she was a stenographer, is accused of stealing goods valued at $177.

Six ————————————————

August picked up the phone on the second ring. Ida was clearing the dinner dishes. They had no cook, no maid, not this house, not this marriage. He heard the hysterical voice on the other end. Celeste, he thought, it has to be Celeste, though he hadn't seen her since her wedding day. In trouble. I hoped that she would have a simpler life now. So many mistakes that child has made. And now another one, I am sure of that.

"Calm down, girl, take a breath. I cannot understand what you are saying. Please. Regain your composure."

Only the sounds of louder, deeper sobbing came through the receiver. "Celeste," August repeated, this time louder, more authoritatively, "if you want me to listen to you, you must get hold of yourself. What is it? Is it Willie? Has something happened to Willie? Tell me." August fumed and at the same time experienced a sense of foreboding.

Celeste gulped for air, swallowed, fought waves of nausea, closed her mouth and breathed through her nose. Now only shallow sobs came. The pain in her head was so sharp, like electric shocks, that she had to use all her effort to focus, to get the words out.

"It's a mistake. There's been a terrible mistake, Mr. Strauff. It was just a joke and they called the police. The police came and now we are here. I don't know what to do. They are going to put us in jail, in a cell." She put her handkerchief in her mouth and bit down hard.

"This just cannot be happening," she said. "You are the only person I could think of who could make this right. Oh, Mr. Strauff, please fix this, please come and get me. Please tell them that it is all a mistake, a stupid mistake. And I wasn't the one, it was Edith. If anyone should be punished it should be Edith, not me. I haven't told--"

August stopped her. "Be still for a moment. Let me take this in. Let me think. Just be quiet." It wasn't Willie; it was Celeste, in some kind of trouble. She should be calling her husband, he thought. August tried to remember his name. Why had she not called him?

He spoke slowly, hoping that his manner would calm Celeste. "Now, tell me, take your time, speak distinctly, what is the problem? No crying, just speak."

Celeste pulled herself erect, stretched the cord on the phone's earpiece its full length from the wall-mounted phone. "Oh, Mr. Strauff, it was just a joke, an antic, just for fun. And now we are in jail." She paused, told herself to stay calm.

"They said that we would have to spend the night here, in a cell, unless something happened. And I asked them what had to happen, but I couldn't figure out what they meant. That's why I called you. You know the world. You are the only person who can help me. Please don't let them take me to jail. I will pay for the hat, I will. I promise you that. I do." She managed to get to the last sentence when she broke down again.

August sat in the chair beside the telephone. "Let me think. Give me a moment, but you stay on the line. Don't hang up." After a few seconds, he drew his lips together. "I will get the Jew. A German Jew. No one better to handle this kind of thing. There must be no scandal. You must keep quiet. Say nothing; act demure, is that the right word? You know what I am saying. Do nothing to anger anyone there. Be on your best behavior, girl. I will be there, with Hirschlaff. He will be able to do something."

Celeste wiped the tears from her cheeks. "Oh, Mr. Strauff, it was horrible. They put us in a paddy wagon, just like we were criminals. I don't think I'll ever get over it, truly I don't."

August stood. "Celeste, stop caterwauling. You are not a child; stop acting like one. I will be there. It may be a while. It is evening, you know, and not everyone is sitting waiting to rescue you. I'll need to find Hirschlaff and convince him to take you on.

"I will say nothing more about your situation now. There will be time later, but I hope that you have learned a lesson from this. And do not expect me to come to your rescue every time you are in the soup.

"Where is your husband? Why is he not taking this on?"

August waited for a response. Celeste was silent.

"Well, I cannot worry about that now. We will be there as soon as we can. Meanwhile, say nothing and do nothing that would aggravate the police officers. Do you hear me?"

Celeste nodded; no words came. Finally, in a cracked voice she said, "I don't know how to thank you, Mr. Strauff. I would never have troubled you if I had anywhere else to turn. I will never forget this. I won't." Her words caught in her throat.

"Celeste, enough. I will see you as soon as I can fix this."

August replaced the receiver in its holder. Ida stood beside him. "You are a good man, August," she said, and placed her hand on his shoulder.

He looked at his wife. "I have a good woman."

He picked up the phone directory to find Hirschlaff's number. More scandal, he thought. First I must contact Clara, have her keep word of this from Willie. That was the first call he made. The second was to the lawyer.

Thirty minutes after his conversation with Hirschlaff, Ida handed August his walnut walking stick. He returned it to the bamboo rack and picked up the ebony one with the engraved gold handle. Ida smiled. "Be careful, August," she said.

August leaned over to kiss her on the cheek. "I have a gem in you, my dear," he said, and walked into the night.

She stood at the window and watched him enter Hirschlaff's black Hudson Biddle sedan. It would not do to be jealous of Celeste, she thought, though she was.

Seven————————————————————

Hirschlaff and August arrived at Saratoga and St. Paul Streets thirty-five minutes later. As they entered the Central Police Station, Hirschlaff said, "We will present this as a trifling matter, overblown by whoever reported these girls. Just two young women having a bit of fun. They'll pay for what they took and promise not to go into the store for at least a year. I would think being plunked in a jail cell was enough of a warning for them." He laughed.

August wondered if Hirschlaff would be so jolly if it were someone in his family in these circumstances. And he knew that Celeste was no girl. Not for the first time did he draw a breath in thanksgiving that her name was no longer Strauff. He thought about Karl, wondered what this would mean for him, for them.

As he entered the station's lobby August saw him sitting on one of the long wooden benches. Karl sat erect, staring straight ahead. He rose when he saw the two men enter, extended his hand.

"I appreciate your coming here. This is a disaster." His voice was flat, detached. His face was drained of color. August introduced Hirschlaff. Karl nodded, then looked at the floor.

"Anything you can do to avoid scandal. You know that I work at Hamburger's. If this gets out, well, I don't know what could happen, what will happen to my job," he said. Karl felt his bowels loosen. He clenched his muscles tight and the feeling subsided. Shitting in a police station, he thought. That would round out a perfect day. He shook his head and smiled to himself. August saw this and wondered what Karl could possibly have to smile about.

462

August addressed him. "Have you seen her? What happened? What is all this about?" he asked. And why, August asked himself, am I still embroiled in this girl's life?

Karl stood straight, assuming what he had observed as the stance of a gentleman, struggled to sound matter-of-fact, in control. "She was arrested for shoplifting. She and a friend of hers. She says that it was a misunderstanding. She told me that the police went to our home sometime this afternoon. I was at work; I knew nothing about it until she called, just as I was about to leave the store. I went home first to see what they had done and then came here. They say that they found other things that were stolen. She says that is not so, that it was only the hat, and that it was only a prank."

Karl looked down at his hands, adjusted his cuffs so that they showed evenly below the sleeves of his jacket. "They have her in a cell. They only allowed me to see her for a few minutes, told me to wait here. She said that you were coming, that you would help. I've been here in the lobby since then. I don't know what to think. I don't know what will happen if this gets out. It won't get into the papers, will it? That would be the end of me, the end of my job, I know it."

He stumbled as he walked closer the two older men. "I thank you for coming to help. I don't know what I would have done, what she would have done. I don't know what lies ahead for us. Will she go to prison? What will happen?" Karl raked his hand through his hair.

Hirschlaff place his hand on Karl's shoulder; Karl noticed his jacket was from Hamburger's, top of the line. "Let us not think the worst, son. I will talk to the magistrate, see the written report, then go to see her. Mr. Strauff told me that he directed her to say little, and to be calm, not to cause any trouble with the matron. You two just wait here. I should have this in hand soon."

August and Karl sat in silence, each with their own thoughts, each wishing they were somewhere else.

The dim lighting, the stale air, the background noise of reporters going in and out, policemen changing shifts, paddy wagons emptying, lulled the men into a mild stupor. Karl watched a pair of patrolmen walking from the lock-up.

"Just the usual drunks," said the first, as he rebuttoned his uniform, spitting on his handkerchief to polish one of the buttons. "But there's a looker in the back, plus an old one, past her prime, I'd say."

"Too early for the working girls," the second said. "What're they in for?"

"Stealing hats with posies. Plus they found a hoard in the house, I hear. Not a whore, but a hoard." The two laughed.

"Well, I'm off to a hot meal and a warm bed. They'll still be here when I come back. Hope your night is a quiet one," said the first, as he walked down the steps. He didn't notice the two men sitting to his right. They noticed him, though neither commented.

An hour later, Karl looked up to see Hirschlaff approaching, holding Celeste's arm. He saw his wife, bedraggled, tired, frumpy, old. She kept her eyes on the floor.

Hirschlaff said, "It is taken care of for now. She is released on bail. I supplied my name for it. We will appear before the magistrate tomorrow morning."

He looked at Karl. "The police have been to your home, have confiscated certain of your wife's belongings. She tells me that she acquired them lawfully, that they had been purchased over the past several months. I assume that you will corroborate her account."

Karl nodded, sensing that it was best to agree.

Hirschlaff continued. "I do think our city's finest were a bit overzealous in this regard, but it would be best to congratulate them for their thoroughness rather than take them to task. I trust you will agree." He looked knowingly at Karl, who, once again, nodded.

"Now, I think it best if we all went home and got a good night's sleep. Tomorrow will not be pleasant, regardless of the outcome. I think everything will work out, at least from the law's standpoint.

"As for your friend, Miss Lowman, I will have a word with her before I leave. I will not be representing her, but think that Mrs. Brentano's statement, that it was a foolish prank for which she is heartily sorry, should be enough to get us through. And I'm sure that Mr. Strauff will serve as a character witness. Am I correct in that?" The man looked at August. August, feeling trapped, agreed.

Hirschlaff faced Celeste. "Now, you get some rest. For tomorrow's hearing it would be best if you used little or no paint and wore a plain suit and a plain hat, no flowers. Do you have such an outfit?" he asked.

Celeste nodded and swallowed hard, still fighting nausea. In a quiet voice she said, "I don't know how to thank you, sir. Thank you." She looked over at August. "Mr. Strauff, I don't know what to say. I am so embarrassed, and so grateful to you."

August waved his hand, but did not embrace her.

Karl waited for her to say something to him. She did not. She did not meet his eyes.

The older men said goodbye. The couple remained, standing in the wood-paneled room. Celeste moved to a bench near the entrance; Karl followed.

"I don't know what to say," she said.

Karl stood. "Then don't say anything. Let the lawyer figure this out, at least until tomorrow. Then we will talk.

"I don't know what this means, what this will mean for me. Did you ever think that I could lose my job? What would Hamburger's want with a man whose wife is a thief? And if that happens, then what? Did you think of that while you were scampering from store to store stealing hats? Did you?"

Karl's face was red with rage. Celeste sat.

He walked toward the door, then turned to face her. "Come, let's go home. I think we can afford a taxi for this ride."

Their ride to Maryland Avenue was silent. Celeste followed her husband from the cab into the house. The living room and bedroom showed no signs of the police search. Nevertheless, Karl went to the closet, making sure once again that his clothes had not been touched.

Celeste followed him. "Say something, will you? Just say something."

Karl turned, closed his eyes. "I knew that you were a liar, Celeste. I learned that the day I married you. But I didn't know that you were a thief. What do you think will happen when they find out at the store? Do you think they will want a manager whose wife shoplifts? Do you think that will put an extra marker in my file? What do you think will happen if they find out?"

He stopped, inhaled deeply. "At this point, let's figure how, or if, we can keep this quiet. Maybe your Mr. Strauff can help you with that. He seems to be the one you go to when you're in trouble. How often have you gone to him before?"

Karl walked to the bedroom door. "I'm going out for a beer. I think that I deserve that after this night. Do you not agree? Meanwhile, you think, you figure out what you can do to make this right. I don't want to see you. You put your face on for tomorrow, Mrs. Brentano, Miss Lady. You concentrate on that."

Celeste went to him. "Karl, you will be with me tomorrow, won't you? You wouldn't let me go through this alone?" She put her hand in his.

Karl removed her hand. "I will be there. That is what a husband does. I will be there with you. But don't ask anything more of me. Don't."

Karl left the house; Celeste chose her outfit for the next day's hearing. Then she drew a bath and thought about drowning herself in the tub.

*Eight*_____

The hearing was scheduled for 10:30 a.m. Karl decided that they should leave the house no later than nine. They would take the bus. "If we have something to celebrate, we'll take a taxi home; if we have something to mourn, we'll take a taxi home."

At least he is speaking to me, Celeste thought. She fixed coffee for two.

On this cold morning, Karl sat on the back porch, the morning paper in his lap. He stared at the trees in the back yard, studied their bare brown branches. Celeste would know their names, he thought. Of course she would. All that knowledge and no sense. He drew his lips together.

Celeste came onto the porch, her peach kimono wrapped tightly around her. She carried two cups of coffee, his fixed as he liked it, cream poured until a swirl of white reached the top of the coffee, one sugar, stirred in before the cream was added. She walked in front of him, offered the cup. He reached for it without looking at her, took a first sip. It was not hot enough, but he decided to say nothing.

She sat in the chair to Karl's left. When she realized that he would not speak, she left to dress. A few minutes later she returned to the kitchen wearing a beige cotton and silk high-necked blouse, a navy wool suit with a skirt that came well below her knees, white silk stockings, and brown shoes with a French heel. Karl was emptying their coffee cups into the sink. He studied her. She looks stylish, but not too, he thought. She looks like a woman who would not need to steal a hat, a woman who would not need to steal.

Celeste put her hand on top of his. He allowed it to remain.

"Karl, I just don't know what to say. I am so sorry this happened. It was such a childish thing--"

Karl interrupted her. "Let's not talk about it now. Let us just try to get through this day. Then we can figure out what comes next. I asked Howard for the day off. Friday is not a good day to be off." He took his hand away from hers and picked up the newspaper. He moved to the kitchen table, leafed through the pages, glancing at what was written, ignoring the news of the formation of the new Soviet Union, but looking carefully at the picture of Louise Brooks that accompanied the article on her performance at the Lyric. He turned the pages, giving each headline a cursory glance.

Suddenly he stopped, drew the paper closer. "God, could it be worse?" he said. Celeste came to him, tried to see what he was reading. His voice was loud. "My name, oh God, it is my name in the article. 'Carl Brentano, Mrs. Carl Brentano' they've written. Oh my God, how can this be?"

He looked over at Celeste, shook the paper in her face. "See what you have caused. Do you see this? Do you see what everyone in Baltimore will be reading this morning? With my name? What do you think Howard is going to think? What do you think he is going to do? Do you think that he will have the husband of a thief working for him? Do you see what you, what your little prank has done to me? Could you have chosen a better way to humiliate me?" Karl threw down the paper and went into the bedroom. Celeste heard the door slam.

Celeste's hands trembled as she picked up the paper, read the article. She laid it back on the table. I can figure a way out of this, she thought. I have to.

She walked to the bedroom, tapped lightly on the door, then opened it. Karl sat on the bed, his head in his hands. She went to him, but did not touch him.

"My darling," she started, although she had not called him that in many years. "There is nothing that I can say that will make this right. But I will make it right, I promise. I will be the best wife that you could ever imagine. Just stay with me through this. I will figure something out. We will get through this. Mr. Strauff has that lawyer. He will do something for us, I just feel it."

She sat on the bed, close to him but their bodies not touching. "And maybe not everyone will see the article. It is on page twenty-two, after all. And when they asked me my name, I thought it would be better for me if I gave my married name, that they would know that I was a married woman, not just some girl who would steal. I thought it would make it better for me, for us, that's why I did it. I never thought that it would reflect on you, I didn't. That never entered my mind. I would never do anything to hurt you, really I wouldn't."

Karl stared ahead. Celeste willed him to look at her. He didn't.

"I know that I could be a better wife, Karl, and I will. Just please don't let me go through this alone. Please." And now the tears came, this time authentic.

Karl looked over at his wife. She had presence of mind to lie about her age to the police, he thought. Or maybe they just got it wrong. She was no longer the blond beauty he had loved on Armistice Day. Her hair had darkened; her figure had thickened. The sleek, draped fashions of the day did not compliment her curvy, soft figure. But those eyes, when she turned those eyes on you, you forgot everything else.

He would explain to Howard, tell him that he had her in line now, that what happened was a terrible mistake. The Jew will fix that, he thought; he will make everything go away. I will just say what he told me to say. Perhaps it's the truth.

Nine

Clara had just finished her breakfast of tea and toast covered in blackstrap molasses when Willie came into the dining room with his tray. He was surprised to see her. "You're up early this morning," he said. "You must have an early meeting."

She looked over at her nephew, dressed in crisp khakis for his job at the waterfront. He had resisted her attempts to send him to college. She had scolded; she had cajoled; she had pulled strings so that he could have been part of the freshman class at Johns Hopkins.

He had thrown it all away, all that opportunity, all that awaited him. It must be his mother in him, she thought.

He had come home from the Navy and found a job. Not the kind of job that he was meant for, as she pointed out to him, but he could work his way up. She was sure that they would see his intelligence, his bearing, his lineage. He would not be a crane operator at the docks for long. She would see to that.

Clara managed a smile. "I wanted to be sure to see you before you left. We will pick you up at your work this afternoon; the car will be there at four-thirty. Then we'll go for an early dinner at the *Deutches Haus*. We haven't been there in a while and it is a good time to go. The cold weather, some sauerbraten, just what we need. Stanley will join us there," Clara said.

Willie looked at her. "Clara, it would not do to have a car waiting for me at work. How would that look? A toff getting into the car; I'd never live that down. No, I'll take the bus and meet you there."

Clara stood, drawing herself up to her full five feet one inch. "Now, Willie, I want you to do this for me. We can park down the

470

block, east of the pier. But I want you to ride with me. Now, that is a compromise. So, we will, I will, see you at 4:30."

She had discussed her plan with Stanley. They would keep the newspapers away from Willie that day. Clara had taken the morning paper to her bedroom. The maid would take the evening paper there when it was delivered. Willie would be protected from his mother. Once again, Clara thought.

Ten

The day went as Hirschlaff said it would. He and Celeste appeared before the magistrate. Hirschlaff suggested that the police may have been overly rigorous in going to the house, in searching for articles of clothing, for assuming that articles found had been stolen when they had no proof. He asserted that the humiliation of being taken away from the store in a police vehicle, of spending time in a jail cell, was more than enough punishment for two foolish women. The lawyer suggested restitution and a fine if all charges were dropped and the women's records expunged.

The magistrate agreed. August, who attended along with Ida, had not been needed as a character witness. It had all been a misunderstanding. That was how it was presented. That was how it was accepted.

Celeste sat with her eyes lowered. Karl stifled a sob when the decision was presented. He would go to Howard and explain. Perhaps it would all blow over, he thought.

We will go on like this never happened, Celeste thought. Yes, this never happened.

As they left the courtroom, Karl walked over to Hirschlaff. "Please, I will pay you for your service. I am so grateful." He struggled to maintain his composure. His hands trembled as he reached for the lawyer's.

Hirschlaff smiled in an attempt to ease the younger man's nervousness. "Yes. And I will pay the fine and restitution and include that in my statement. I am glad that it worked out for you." He looked over at Celeste. "And you have learned your lesson, no?" She nodded, still not raising her eyes. A pity, he thought. But he knew too much of life to be hopeful.

Karl walked over to August. "And thank you, Mr. Strauff. I don't know what we would have done without you." He shook the older man's hand, and turned to Celeste. "I think it best if I go directly to the store and explain the situation. I don't know if anyone has seen today's paper, but I don't want too much time to go by before they see me and I tell them that there was a mistake."

Hirschlaff struggled into his black cashmere overcoat, bid his farewells, and left the building. August, leaning on his gold-handled walking stick, shook hands with Karl. "It would be well to put this behind you. All of us face setbacks. It is how we recover from them that sets us apart."

"Yes, sir. That is good advice." Karl shook August's hand, then turned to Celeste. "I will see you at home this evening." He turned and left the building. He did not kiss her goodbye.

"Would you care to have lunch with us? August said. "Then you can go home and have a good rest." Celeste nodded; Ida pursed her lips and breathed deeply.

Celeste had dinner on the table when Karl arrived home. He had smelled the aroma from the sidewalk, roast chicken, turnips, carrots, his favorites, and a peach cake from Muhly's Bakery. He ate with gusto, and managed a smile for his wife. Neither spoke of the day.

Later that night Karl reached for Celeste. She was naked. She mounted him, and screamed out as she climaxed when he bit her breast.

Eleven————————————————————

Karl recognized the tall young man crossing Pratt Street. Bill spotted
him at the same time. The two met walked toward each other.

"Nice to see you again," Karl said, shaking Bill's hand while noting
Bill's khaki work pants and shirt. They looked nearly freshly pressed,
though Karl knew was the end of the Bill's shift. "Come round to the
store sometime. Make sure I know you're coming. I'll see to it that
you're treated right."

Bill thanked him. A silence followed that both men found
uncomfortable. Bill was the first to speak.

"You know I'm married now, a girl from Hamilton. Her name is
Hyacinth."

Karl was surprised. "Well, you're a bit young, don't you think? But
maybe not, not if you found the right girl."

"I think I did. And I'm twenty-one now," Bill responded.

After another uncomfortable silence, Karl said, "How about you
and your bride, tell me her name again, come see us on Sunday. I'm
sure your mother would like to meet her. We've moved, you know,
North Avenue, just east of Calvert. We're glad for your news. It is
good that you're getting ahead."

"Hyacinth, her name. What time? What number?" Bill added, a
bit too quickly.

Karl gave him the address, then added, "I think about three. How
does that fit? We've moved. Oh, I said that already." He paused. "Well,
we'll see you then," he said and extended his hand. Yes, we'll see you
Sunday, this Sunday."

Karl told Celeste about the invitation when he arrived home. She was quiet. What's done is done, she thought. Married. Billy married. What does that say about me?

When Bill told Hyacinth about the Sunday date, she was furious. "How dare he come into our lives like that? How dare he think that we would entertain the thought that we would be entertained by them? How dare he?" She looked into the mirror, adjusted a curl by her cheek, then turned back to Bill.

"I hope that you said 'absolutely not.' That is the only suitable answer. She didn't want to have anything to do with you; she gave you away. She is not going to be part of your life now. No. We are not going. Your life is with me now. That is how it is going to be."

She knew that she should stop, but she could not keep still. "Why you would even want to see her? I don't understand why you want me to meet her. She wanted nothing to do with you, she gave you away, she wanted her own life without you. Why would you want to see her?

"Forget all that. You have me now. You don't need anyone else, especially not her. And not Clara either. Nor that old Kraut."

I've gone too far, she thought, then changed her mind. No, I am right. He is mine now. I am his wife. I come first. She stood firm in front of her husband.

Bill faced her, gently placed his hands on her shoulders, pulled his eighteen-year-old bride toward him, spoke quietly in her ear. "Just this one time. Then we'll never have to see her again. I promise."

Hyacinth looked at him. Why am I not enough? How could he possibly love that woman, she wondered. He says that he loves me, and then he wants to see her. I should be enough for him. She stopped. We'll see her. Then he'll know how lucky he is to have me. That will make him love me. And then no more Celeste. She allowed Bill to kiss her, on the mouth.

She dressed with particular care that Sunday, chose her newest outfit. She had seen a picture in a magazine, had asked her mother to make her one just like it. Her mother had a way with a needle. The French-blue silk chemise matched her eyes. Hyacinth liked to think of them as icy-blue. The hem was heavy with embroidery pearls. The long strand of pearls around her neck came from Woolworths.

She wore a grey wool coat trimmed with grey fox, curved at the hem, and closed with a single large mother-of-pearl button, and chose a plain grey felt cloche that covered her blonde shingled hair. She didn't want anything to take away from the effect of the coat. Her stockings were silk, white, and her brown shoes, with low French heels, sported large square rhinestone clips. This will show her I'm a lady, she thought. She'll never be able to match this.

Celeste had studied her collection of outfits from her Stewart's days. Not of the 20's style, she thought, but then neither am I. The sea-green tea dress she chose dipped to her ankles. She liked it that way; her legs weren't what they used to be. She added the garnet earrings that Willie had given her those many years ago.

As she screwed her earrings tight, she closed her eyes and whispered, "Just get me through this day." She counted the hours until the couple would be gone from her house, from her life. It was too complicated, too much, she thought. But she had splurged and ordered tea cakes and petit fours from Fiske's. She would show this girl that she was a lady.

The couple arrived, on time. Celeste complimented Hyacinth's outfit, though not as much as Hyacinth thought it deserved. Hyacinth complimented Celeste's home and the petit fours, though not as much as Celeste thought they deserved.

"You have a very interesting name," Celeste said. "How did you come about it?"

Hyacinth, used to this question, responded, "My mother is a reader, and she saw the name in a book she was reading before I was born. She liked it, and here I am." Hyacinth smiled, liking the attention.

"Oh, yes, Charlotte Braeme. *Shadow of a Sin;* I remember that book," Celeste said. "Interesting that your mother and I read the same books."

Hyacinth pursed her lips and didn't answer. She raised her cup and studied the apartment. Her parents had a house; she made sure that Celeste knew. She talked about her job. She was a businesswoman, she said, and Celeste experienced a twinge of remembrance, a momentary sense of solidarity with this plucky young woman who was using all her wiles to make sure Celeste knew who was boss.

"I am a switchboard operator for the Balfour Candy Company in the Candler Building on Pratt Street. It is very modern to work, you know. Not like in the old days," she added, raising her left eyebrow at Celeste.

"I was a career woman in the old days," Celeste countered, returning a raised eyebrow. Karl watched the interchange and smiled. Bill's eyes remained on the plate in his lap.

Celeste identified jealousy in her daughter-in-law's blue eyes, detected a coldness, and perhaps some underlying sadness, beneath that brittle exterior. She will rule the roost, Celeste thought. She will give Billy a run for his money. Poor boy, he is in for it.

"Well, Celeste," Hyacinth said, "and Karl," she added, "it has been a pleasure meeting you. We will have to reciprocate sometime. In the future." Bill started to speak, but she cut him off. "We need to be going now. We have a lot to do before tomorrow. We will soon have an automobile, so that we will be able to take trips on weekends. So, we will be busy most of the time. If we don't see you again."

Karl had brought Hyacinth's coat to her, saying, "A beautiful piece of material." He helped her into it.

"Yes," she answered.

As she and Bill descended the steps from the second floor apartment, Hyacinth said, "Well, I'm glad that's over with." She's not so beautiful, she said to herself.

Hyacinth's mention of a younger sister evoked a dim recollection for Celeste, who thought that her son's wife could be a beautiful young woman, if only she would change her expression. She looks like she's sucking on a lemon, Celeste thought, and looked in the mirror to practice her smile, the sincere one.

The streetcar pulled up as the couple turned the corner onto Guilford Avenue. Bill was silent on the ride home. Hyacinth criticized everything from the food to the tea to the apartment's steep stairway "We'll have much better than that. I just know it."

First Clara and Celeste, now Hyacinth, Bill thought. Best to keep all these women separate.

Twelve _____

On Celeste's 40th birthday, Annie told her that she was moving to Boston to live with Eva. "The children will give me something to do with myself, and Eva will be there to watch over me. Not that I need watching over. The house, well, the house is really Thomas's. He has taken care of his brother's wife." She smiled. "Isn't there something in the bible about that?" She laughed, and Celeste saw in that moment a glimmer of the mother of her girlhood, when they had been a family.

"He has been so good to watch out for me all these years," Annie continued, "paying the mortgage, the taxes. Such a friend. But it is time to let him have the benefit of his charity." Annie put her hands in her lap.

"I've put a bit of money by, enough to get myself and a few things to Boston. If you want anything from the house, just come and take it. My memories are enough for me. I'll miss being able to visit the cemetery. That's all I have here. I'm sure you understand. You have Karl now, and Stanley is grown, a man. I don't need to worry about you."

Celeste sat with Annie, looked around the front room, remembered herself as a girl, bouncing on George's lap, running into the room with her girlfriends after school, courting with Willie on the sofa where she now sat, standing with baby Stanley at the front window.

She looked into the dining room, remembered teas and dinners served by Meg, Meg who came to their apartment to iron Willie's shirts, Meg who took the blame when Celeste and her girlfriends climbed into the dumbwaiter and tried to haul themselves up from the kitchen to the first floor, snapping the rope. She never told on them. Dear, dear Meg, who loved Stanley and bought him baby clothes she couldn't afford.

478

Celeste closed her eyes and pictured the bedroom where she and Elizabeth stood at the window surveying the house across the street, watching for Willie, trying to work out his schedule so they could be walking in front of his house as he left. My dear, sweet Willie. What would my life, our lives, have been had you not died?

She turned toward her mother. "I will miss you, Mama. When will you leave?"

"I'd like to wait until spring, let the northern winter pass. So sometime in early April," Annie replied.

"I will miss you," Celeste repeated.

Both women remained dry-eyed.

Thirteen ————————————————————————

Times were flush. Baltimore had money, or at least thought that it did. Hamburger's flourished. Suits and hand-sewn underwear sold well. Karl had a large following who took his fashion advice. He and Celeste moved to a larger apartment.

She enjoyed her gramophone. Sometimes they danced. Karl didn't have Willie's grace, but he did a more than passable Charleston. Celeste decried women's fashions, which she described as fabric hanging from shoulders. She emulated "the slouch," but realized that it made her look matronly. When she finally relented and bobbed her hair; she knew immediately that it was a mistake.

In the evenings, they listened to their newly purchased radio. They both loved Rudy Valee, though their favorite program was the Dodge Victory Hour where they laughed to Will Rogers and hummed along with Paul Whiteman and his orchestra.

They went to the movies twice a week. Karl laughed when, one evening after dinner, Celeste produced a cigarette. "I thought I'd enjoy a postprandial smoke," she said.

"And just where did you learn that word?"

Celeste's vocabulary, fueled by her afternoon reading, which now included Edna St. Vincent Millay and a new writer named Fitzgerald, had become a comfortable joke with them.

Every Saturday night they headed to a speakeasy; sometimes they walked to Seymour's on Mulberry Street. On the evenings that they felt like dressing up, they headed to the Owl Bar in the Belvedere Hotel at Charles and Chase Streets. Bootleg whiskey gave Karl blinding headaches. He tried three times before he gave it up. What kind of man can't drink? he asked himself.

He thought it a curse. It proved, more than once, to be a blessing.

Celeste's head gave her no such qualms, and on those evenings out she drank for both of them. She was a woman who could hold her liquor; she was also a woman who knew when to stop.

Some afternoons she thought about her life, the years before Karl, the years with Karl. Maybe this is a good life, she thought. She heard from Annie each year at Christmastime and on her birthday. Billy came to see her on those times as well, without Hyacinth.

"She doesn't want children," Billy replied in answer to Celeste's question. He thought that one day she'd change her mind.

"It doesn't do to dwell on too much," Celeste told him, her way of giving advice.

When the crash came, she didn't worry. People will always need clothes, she thought. She was wrong, though Karl was one of the last salesmen at Hamburger's to lose his job. He had seen it coming, but didn't know what he could do differently.

The restaurant dinners stopped, as did the speakeasy visits and movie nights. The couple found they had little to say to one another. A quiet descended, one that kept them together and apart.

Fourteen

February 17, 1931

Dear Mama,

 I am so sorry that I have taken so long to write to you.
Thank you so much for the Christmas money, and the money
you sent for my birthday. I know that times are hard for
everyone, and I do appreciate every dollar. It went toward our
rent. I hate to say that we have fallen behind, but the landlady
says that she trusts us and knows that we will do our best to
make things right. Honestly I don't think there are many
people who could afford to move in here if we left. We try hard
not to use too much electricity, and she has heat in the house
only from eight in the morning until 4 in the afternoon. It is
dreadful, mama, truly dreadful. There are people with money,
I am sure, but I don't know of any. Even the girls from school,
those I keep in touch with, are poor. They may have their
houses, but there is no money, they admit that. Maybe Clara
has money. I don't know, maybe Eva knows. Does she hear
from her?

 Karl looks for work almost every day, but there is no work.
I just never imagined that life could be so difficult, so hard. The
cold, I am so cold all the time. I try to think of happier times,
but it has been so long since a happy time for me.

 I hope you and Eva and her family are doing better there,
and that you are not having too bad a winter. I hope that the
younger one is getting stronger. And it is lucky that Eva's
husband is still at the Museum. I guess they will always need
a director. But museums, it seems to me, are quite a luxury

482

these days. But maybe with so many people out of work they have time to go to them. Take their minds off their troubles perhaps. Though it would take more than a museum for me to forget my situation.

You have been a good mother to me and I hope that you know how much I love you. If you could spare a few more dollars it would truly help us out. I hate to write and ask you, but our situation is desperate.

I heard that Billy has also lost his job. They are living with her parents now. I think her father is still working. So you see, I can't go to Billy. You are my last resort. I am begging you, if you possibly can, can you help us out. Or maybe ask Eva. She has had a perfect life, it seems, with her husband, and his fancy job, her children, her Boston house.

I am crying as I write these words. Please, Mama, can you help?

Your loving daughter,
Celeste

Fifteen————————————

She heard his tread on the stairway, heavier than usual. He called to her before he reached the top step.

"I've had enough of this, Celeste. We're going back to Portland." Karl stood in the doorway, daring her to respond.

Celeste stayed in the chair by the window, unsure of what he was saying. They had left one another on good terms that morning, but now his eyes were angry. Celeste didn't know how he spent his days; she knew better than to ask.

What Karl did, along with many men in Baltimore in 1932, was sit in the PenMar Diner at Maryland and North Avenues nursing a cup of coffee. Sometimes he sat with the others; most times he sat by himself.

No one needed or wanted a salesman of fine men's wear; no one needed or wanted a salesman. No one was buying anything. Karl had written to his mother, to his sister Wilhelmina, ten days ago. He had received their response that morning. The letter said, "Come home" and had included train fare for him and Celeste. How they managed to get the money Karl didn't know and could not bear to ask.

He stared at the envelope. This was a chance, a new start, back where he belonged. Enough of this East Coast snobbery, he thought, all talk and no money to back it up. He would tell Celeste that afternoon. He was the man of the house; she would do what he said. He rehearsed what he would say to her as he walked up Maryland Avenue. He had already bought the tickets. They would leave in three days.

When Karl left the apartment the next day, Celeste went to her closet. She knew she could not carry the mahogany silver chest.

484

Instead, she placed the knives, forks, spoons, wrapped separately in freshly laundered tea towels, into the red-patterned carpetbag she had carried for so many years.

Celeste walked the eleven blocks and, stepping onto the porch, rang the bell. She tucked her hair under her hat, adjusted her posture, stood erect. The maid, in her black uniform with white collar and cuffs, answered. Seeing her uniform reminded Celeste of her days at Hutzler's, all that black and white. She smiled at the woman, then assumed what she believed to be a pose of entitlement.

"Is Mrs. Gorsuch in? Please tell her that her sister-in-law is here to see her."

The maid glanced down at Celeste's shoes, worn down at the heels, scuffed at the toes. "I'll tell her that you're here. "Is she expecting you?" The woman showed Celeste into the reception room. Celeste sat on the sofa by the front window, the carpetbag on her lap clasped tightly.

Clara came from the back of the house, greeted Celeste warily, then led her into the living room. "Please sit. I've asked Symra to bring us some tea and cakes." Without waiting for a response, she asked, "What can I do for you, Celeste?"

Celeste tried to make small talk, but her words stuck in her throat. She put her carpet bag on the floor, sat straight, clasped her hands in her lap. "Well, Clara, the reason I'm here is that Karl and I are moving to Portland." She stopped, waited while the maid put the tray before them. "You see, Karl has a wonderful opportunity there. A big job. And things are so difficult here. We thought that it would be a great new start for us, this great opportunity he has. So, we are leaving tomorrow. We will have all our possessions shipped out there. Yes, all our belongings will go with us."

She paused again, took a sip of the tea Clara offered. It scalded her tongue and the roof of her mouth. She inhaled sharply, pressed her lips together tightly, waited for the burning to subside. "Yes, all our belongings. But I didn't want to trust the movers with my silver. You remember, Mama gave this to me on my birthday; you were there. It was when we were all living together. So, I was hoping that I could leave this with you. To keep, until we get settled there, or until we come back East. Yes, I am hopeful that we will be able to come back

East to live. After Karl gets on his feet. That is, after this opportunity is good enough to allow us to return."

Celeste smiled at Clara, and Clara, unsmiling, looked directly into Celeste's eyes. Then she returned Celeste's smile, one of the few times she had ever done so. "Of course I will keep it for you. Until you return. Or until you write and tell me to send it to you." She glanced down at the carpetbag.

Celeste tittered. "Oh yes, I brought it in this bag. I didn't want anyone to know that I was carrying something as valuable as this. You can understand that, I'm sure."

Clara nodded. The room was silent; both were aware that the other knew the truth. No need to mention it.

Celeste started to remove the packets of cutlery from her bag. "Clara, thank you so much for helping with this."

"Just a second," Clara said, and left the room. When she returned, Celeste had completed laying the silver on the table in front of the chairs. She stood; she knew that was her signal to leave. The women walked together to the front door.

Before Celeste stepped onto the porch, Clara handed her an envelope. "Here, take this, would you? It is a little gift, to help you, to celebrate your new life."

Celeste looked at Clara, surprised at this unexpected gesture. "Thank you, Clara. Thank you so much." She bent kiss the shorter woman on the cheek.

Clara stepped back, extended her hand. "Best of luck, Celeste. I'll be waiting to hear from you."

She watched as Celeste made her way down St. Paul Street. Always in trouble, that one, she thought. It seems to seek her out. Maybe it was lucky for Willie that he died young. Portland. At least now she will be out of young Willie's life. That is a good thing. She turned the lock with a snap.

Celeste's carpetbag was lighter on the walk home; her step wasn't. When she got to 27th Street, Celeste pulled Clara's envelop from her pocket and opened it. Two twenty-dollar bills. A fortune, Celeste thought. She replaced the money in the envelop. I will keep this. This will be my money.

Sixteen _____

It was their third day on the train, sitting up, the best they could afford. They had arrived in Chicago the day before, Celeste too exhausted to even look around Union Station, to study its architecture, to think of Willie. She and Karl had walked across the long concourse where they boarded the west-bound train for the next leg of their journey. They each carried two suitcases, all that remained of their possessions. Though she tried not to, Celeste could not help thinking of what she had left behind, the blue brocade sofa, the crystal lamps with the ruffled shades, her books, the linens she had purchased set by set.

She replayed her last moments there, walking down the apartment steps, trying to keep the suitcases from banging on the walls, leaving in the middle of the night so that the landlady wouldn't hear, abandoning the furniture, the gramophone, even the radio and the food in the cupboards. Celeste had emptied the ice box. That was the least she could do for Mrs. Duflin, who had been so kind to them, who had been sure that they would pay the past due rent as soon as they were able.

"What could she do, throw us out?" Karl had said. "This way, she'll have the furniture; maybe she can sell it and make up some of back rent. It's the only way, Celeste. I don't like being a deadbeat. But what can we do? She'd call the police for sure if she knew we were leaving owing all that money. She'll find somebody else. Someone who might actually be able to pay her."

Celeste had sat at the window while he spoke. Karl looked at her. "Stop feeling sorry for yourself. We're not the only people who are in this position. At least we have a place to go to. There are jobs in Portland, and we have a place to stay. Buck up and think about me, think about what might be best for me, think about what it's been like for me these years, going hat in hand, begging for work. While you sit here, reading your books. You give that some thought while you're crying about leaving your radio."

Karl had snapped his suitcase closed and gone to the kitchen. He pulled out the bottle of whiskey they kept behind the breadbox, and poured some into the tumbler.

"Your head, Karl. Remember your head," Celeste said, coming into the room and pouring herself the same amount.

"A headache will feel better than this, give me something to complain about."

They had sat in silence that evening, waiting until three a.m. when Karl told her it was time to go. They had walked the five long blocks to the Pennsylvania Station. Celeste always thought of it as the new station, though by now it had been operating more than twenty years. They sat upright on the long, hard wood benches in the station's waiting room. Celeste watched the hands of the clock. It seemed that they barely moved.

When the sun came up they went into the restaurant to have breakfast. "Eat a lot," Karl told her. "From now on, we have to watch every penny." Celeste looked around. Everyone looked as forlorn as they. She reached for Karl's hand. "A new start for us. Yes."

She smiled, and Karl saw the smile he remembered, the smile from Armistice Day.

Seventeen———————————

When the train left Chicago that evening, Karl leaned back in his seat. He looked over at Celeste and was surprised to feel a stab of pity, for her. Dark circles under her eyes, two marked lines between her eyebrows. She wore a dark mauve lipstick. You shouldn't wear that shade, Karl thought, even though he knew that was the style. It makes you look old, hard. Her close-cropped, tightly curled hairstyle accentuated the lines in her face. She had given herself a Richard Hudnut home permanent before they left Baltimore. It had singed the bleached ends of her hair; she had trimmed much of its length, crying as she did so.

He sank deeper into his seat, his knees jutting into the seat in front of him. He leaned toward her, took her hand.

Celeste started at the unexpected gesture. She tried to remember the last time that, aside from their nocturnal encounters, he had reached for her. So much time, she thought, closing her eyes.

"Not quite what we thought our life would be, is it?" Karl asked, looking straight ahead. "Back to Portland, not exactly triumphant."

She didn't answer. She faced him. You are no longer attractive, she thought. His blond hair had faded, his scalp showed at the crown; his face was puffy, whether from lack of sleep, worry, or alcohol she didn't know. He was no longer her handsome sailor, her Beau Brummell. He had missed shaving a patch of whiskers. They were grey.

He took out an apple from the bag of supplies they had picked up during their layover in Chicago, pulled out his penknife and cut a slice, offering it to Celeste.

She took it, though she wasn't hungry, and reached for his hand with her free one. Maybe this will be a new start, she thought. Maybe

I should give it, give him, a chance. She leaned back in her seat; they sat in a companionable silence.

A few minutes later, Karl turned to her. "Tell me why you gave Bill to the Strauffs. All these years, Celeste, and you've never really talked about it. And he is nice young man," Karl laughed, "though he's not so young any more, is he?"

Karl had met Bill only a few times over the last fourteen years. He had expected to dislike him, this boy of Celeste's, this boy who had been to posh schools. But Bill worked on the docks, or at least he had, before the crash had changed everything. Karl thought of him as a regular Joe. If circumstances had been different, Karl thought, they could have been friends.

Celeste stiffened. "I did not give Billy to the Strauffs," she said, louder than she had intended. The woman in the seat across the aisle looked at her, then looked away. Celeste knew that she was listening. She leaned into Karl, said quietly, "Oh, let's not talk about that now. So long ago, it's all water under the dam."

Karl chuckled. Celeste had made a mistake. "It's water over the dam, water under the bridge," he said. Celeste laughed, as gaily as she could manage, pleased to move the subject from Billy. She felt the tension fade. Karl patted her hand. Celeste stared down, concentrating on seeing their hands together.

"Let us try, Celeste, let's try to start again. So much of our life is past." He murmured, "Water under the dam."

He touched her thigh and traced the butterfly pattern of her dress. "Tell me about your life, after Willie died, before we met. Do you ever wish that you hadn't married me? You must. Do you ever miss Willie?"

Celeste looked up, studied the pattern of the car's vaulted roof, working out how to respond, how to make this moment, this rare intimate moment with Karl, last.

"Oh, in the beginning, it was awful. I didn't know what I was going to do. I was so young, so naïve. I was only twenty, with an infant. I couldn't stay with the Strauffs; I couldn't stay in that house. So I moved back with my mother, across the street. But I was, I felt like, a servant there. I had no money. I just worked in the house, helping with the boarders, taking care of Stanley. I couldn't live like that. I was just a girl, and I thought that my life was over.

"Then Clara suggested that they take Stanley and it seemed like a perfect solution. I could get a job. Back then I thought that would be the most glamorous life imaginable, and Stanley would be taken care of, by family. I thought it was perfect."

Celeste didn't mention Stanley's kidnapping; she didn't mention Haley. She didn't tell Karl why she left Stewart's. That never happened, she told herself.

"Then they changed his name to Willie. I understood that, but I thought they should have asked me first. They sent him away to boarding school. He was only five years old. Clara told me that it was better that he thought I went away, so he wouldn't be looking for me, so he wouldn't worry. I thought that was a wise way to handle it. Clara is bossy, but she is also very wise.

Celeste took Karl's hand, rubbed it against her cheek. "And so the years slipped by, and then I heard he had run away and joined the Navy. He was only fourteen. Somehow he convinced them that he was older. Clara was sure that I had something to do with it, that I had signed for him, but I didn't. Really I didn't. And then I met you.

"And now we are an old married couple. We have been though a lot and you have stood by me, Karl. I appreciate that. And I don't look back. If Willie hadn't died, I'd never have met you."

Celeste willed herself not to choke on her words and silently begged Willie to forgive her.

Karl looked at the landscape rushing by. He wondered if it were Nebraska. "A new start for us, Celeste. I'm sure I'll be able to find work in Portland. We can start over, all our cares behind us once I find work. We won't be with Mammy long. And you'll like Willie."

Celeste knew that she could never call Karl's sister Wilhelmina, Willie. She closed her eyes. Oh no, don't ask that of me.

They spent their third night sitting in the Pullman seats. When the sun came up, Celeste said, "I cannot do this any longer. We must either get tickets for a sleeper, or get off this train and spend the night. I can't go on. This is a nightmare."

Karl turned to her, exhaustion in his eyes. "There is no money. We either eat or we sleep lying down. Not much of a choice. Don't hector me. Hector, isn't that another of your words, Celeste? Aren't you impressed that I know your words?"

Celeste felt the sting of his remark. The spell was broken, she thought, but I am just so tired. She pulled herself erect, hoping to soothe her back, her neck. She looked down at her feet. Her ankles had swollen and she worried that she would not be able to put her shoes back on.

"I have a bit of money. Let me pay for the sleeper. Just for tonight. I can't meet your family after sitting up all these nights. Don't ask me to do that." Her voice was louder than she had intended. The woman across the aisle stared unashamedly.

Karl's face flushed with anger. "Where did you get money?" he hissed, trying to keep his voice low. "How do you have money and I don't know about it? Where did you get it? How dare you. Tell me, where did you get it?" He grabbed Celeste's wrist.

Celeste knew that she should fabricate a story, but she was so tired she couldn't think. She told the truth. "Clara gave me a little bit when she learned that we were leaving Baltimore. It is just a bit. I was saving it to surprise you. So that we could have just a little something when we got to your mother's. Really, I was going to tell you about it. Truly."

Karl leaned back in the seat. "I don't need that family to rescue me. I told you not to tell anyone, and you ran to Clara. What kind of woman does that? You want to be the boss? Act like one. You make arrangements for the sleeper." He turned his back toward her and looked out at the grassland, grey in the early morning light. Celeste struggled not to cry.

An hour later, finishing their breakfast in the dining car, Celeste smiled at the conductor and asked about arrangements for a sleeping car.

"That's not so easy to do now," he told her. We're changing lines tonight in Omaha. The cars are the same, but the engines are going to be Union Pacific. And they bring on their own crew." He saw her face fall. "But, I can see if there are any Tourist accommodations available.

It's not a sleeper, not a compartment, but the berths aren't too bad." He smiled. "Certainly more comfortable than those seats you're in."

Celeste nodded, and the conductor moved to the back of the car. A few minutes later a porter came to their table. "I can move your things to the berths, if you'd like. You can make payment when the conductor comes round."

Karl watched his wife, then reached out and touched her fingers. "We are both exhausted. Thank you, Celeste, for doing this. It is wise, the best thing for us. We will meet Mammy rested."

Eighteen————————————————————————

Once in Portland, as he had done in Baltimore, Karl went out every day, looking. There was no work at the docks. There was no work. But he came home to a hot meal, the love of his mother and his sister, and, sometimes, the love of his wife.

Karl's mother, Brigit, found Celeste cold and snobbish, "with all her reading, her books, her walks to the library." Celeste found herself reliving those years with the Strauffs, the ache of not belonging rekindled. She volunteered to cook, to clean, but Brigit shook her head. "You're not meant for cleaning, and I get pleasure from cooking. You don't need to help. Just be part of the family," she said more than once. Celeste had no idea what she meant.

Wilhelmina had been able to keep her job as secretary to a doctor. Her salary had been reduced to almost half of what it had been, but she considered herself lucky to have a job. She now walked the two miles there and back, to save on carfare.

Celeste had expected to dislike this mousy, quiet spinster, but found that she was drawn to her gentle ways. She is sweet, Celeste thought. This must be what sweet is.

Celeste insisted on washing the dishes and cleaning the pots and pans each evening; then the three women sat in the living room and listened the radio. Karl, in all but the bitterest weather, sat on the back porch and stared into the night. Conversation in the household was an infrequent occurrence.

The month that the couple had been there a year, Celeste came downstairs to find a letter, addressed to her, sitting on the table beside the vestibule.

"When did this arrive?" she asked Wilhelmina, surprised to see Eva's handwriting.

"It came with today's mail. I was going to call you, but here you are." She came out of the living room and waited for Celeste to open one of the few pieces of mail she had received in her time there. Wilhelmina looked at her. "Aren't you going to open it?" she asked, with her normal sense of cheerfulness and open curiosity. She pulled at her eyelashes as she waited.

Celeste inhaled. "I never hear from Eva. I hope it's not bad news." She went to the sofa in the living room. Wilhelmina followed, but sat in the chair by the window. She wanted to give Celeste some privacy, but not so much that she wouldn't know what the letter said.

Celeste lifted the pages from the envelop.

April 23, 1933

Dear Celeste,

I am so sorry to have to write to tell you that Mama has died. It was very quick and she did not suffer at all. She was in the garden with Olivia and had what we think was a heart attack. She asked Olivia to help her to a bench, and then when she went to sit with her, Mama leaned on her and closed her eyes. And that was that.

Luckily I was downstairs in the kitchen, and I heard Olivia when she called to me. She is a very calm and very poised young woman. I've written to Uncle Thomas. He is taking care of notifying the cemetery to expect her body.

As you know, Mama was quite the free thinker, so there will be no funeral service. I think that she would be smiling at us knowing that we really did respect her views and wishes. Charles and I will accompany the body to Baltimore. It will be interred sometime next week. I think that she will be happy to be close to Papa again, even if she did not believe.

I know that you and your husband are far away now, and that times for all of us are quite difficult. Please know that I do not expect you to make arrangements to come for the interment. I know that Mama would feel the same way. She had some good years here with us, and I think, all in all, she had a very good life. She was lucky to have had Papa. They had a very loving marriage, I think.

I also wanted you to know that Mama had a small insurance policy, for you and me. She started it when we were children. She paid ten cents every two weeks, and continued it all these years. I'm not sure exactly how much the amount will be, but I did want you to know about it. The money will surely come in handy. I will write to you as soon as the arrangements with that are finalized. It should not be too long after we return from the cemetery.

Celeste, I know that you and I have not been close as sisters. I am sorry for that. But I wish the best for you

Your sister,

Eva

Celeste placed the letter in her lap. She looked straight ahead. Wilhelmina went to her, put her hand on Celeste's shoulder. "Not bad news, I hope," she said, trying to catch Celeste's eye.

"My mother has died." Celeste folded the letter and stood. "Thank you, Willie. Thank you for being here. I do appreciate it, truly I do." She allowed Wilhelmina to take her hand. Then she turned. "I just want to be by myself for now. You understand, don't you?"

Wilhelmina nodded; Celeste went upstairs to her room.

In the weeks following, Karl was uncharacteristically considerate. Wilhelmina had lectured him about what it meant for a woman to lose her mother. As always, he listened to his older sister and tried to take her advice. Celeste sensed it, and was grateful for the easing of tension in the household. Even Karl's mother seemed kind.

Three weeks later a second letter from Eva was delivered. This time it was Celeste who was there when the postman dropped the envelop through the mail slot.

Dear Celeste,

I am enclosing the check from Mama's insurance policy.
She left it for both of us, but after discussing it with Charles,
we both decided that it would be better used if the entire amount
went to you. Please do not take this in any way but the way it
is intended. We know that your life has not been an easy one.
We hope that this will make some difference in that.
    Please take care and do let us know how you are.

Your sister,
Eva

Celeste looked at the check. It was made payable to her alone, in the amount of $150. She folded the check and went to her room. She wanted to think.

Nineteen——————————————————

She had fixed her hair and freshened her make-up before he returned to the house. "We've been here a year, Karl. I want to go home. I want to go back East. This money from Mama, that's a sign. I know it is. We're meant to go back, back to where we belong. This has been a horrible year for us. We tried it here. But things are getting better in the East. Read the papers. They say that things will be better. Maybe you can get one of those Roosevelt jobs. I think Baltimore has them. I read that somewhere.

She walked to their bedroom window, put her right hand on the glass. "I can't stay here. I just can't. And now we have the money to go back. That's what I want to do. I'll pay for the tickets; we can take sleeper cars. We won't have to sit up like we did. I know you've tried your best here. I know that. But it is terrible for us, no privacy, no place of our own." She went to him, took his hand in hers. They stood beside their bed.

"There are just no jobs here. Face it. It is worse here than in Baltimore. No ship building, nothing is here for us. And now we have the money to go back."

Celeste's voice became stronger as she spoke. Karl looked at her, wondering how tough she'd be if she had to go out every day, coming home to everyone looking, waiting, waiting for some good news. How haughty would she be if she had his life?

Coming back to Portland, staying here, had been a dreadful experience for both of them. Celeste stayed in her room most of the time, her offers to help, to share in keeping house, rebuffed by his mother, who openly scoffed at Celeste and her Eastern ways. Only Willie had proved a breath of fresh air, with her gentle demeanor, her calm acceptance of Celeste's need for privacy. Celeste liked her. She called Willie "Portland's saving grace."

Now Celeste had some money. Maybe it wouldn't be such a bad thing to go back, he thought. Mammy and Willie could visit when they got back on their feet. He looked at Celeste, her face set firm. He didn't want to give in to her; he didn't want her to think that she had won, that she was the boss.

"I will think about it. I will give you that. Now I want no more talk of moving, do you hear me? No more talk. I will give you my decision. Then that will be that.

"How much did your mother leave you?" he asked.

"I'll tell you that when you give me your decision," she answered, with a mocking tone delivered on her last word.

Later that evening, Karl mentioned Celeste's idea to his mother. "Don't let her lead you around like a monkey and its organ grinder. You are the man. That money is yours. You can use it however you chose. You tell her that. You tell her that for me, her and her fancy words, flopping about with a book in her hand. You'd think she was the Queen of Moo."

Brigit dried her hands and hung up the cotton dishtowel. She had rewashed some of the dinner plates.

Wilhelmina overheard the conversation and, without being invited, interjected, "Mammy, you are wrong about this. That might have been the old way of living, but no more. Don't you want Karl to have a good life? Don't you want him to get a job, make something of himself? She may be on to something. It may be better back East. Mr. Roosevelt says that it is better. He should know." Her hand went to her face, her right eyelid. She pulled at the few remaining lashes.

Their mother put her hands on her hips. "Your Mr. Roosevelt is over his head. No one knows what is happening, just that no one has a job, no one is working. It's just the work of the Lord that we have enough, blood from a stone, that's what we have. And stone soup." She turned back, giving the plate a final vigorous rub with her thumb.

The next day, Karl gave Celeste his decision. He would allow them to return to Baltimore. She could pay for their passage back.

The train ride east was long, and silent. Celeste had purchased Tourist class. They had separate berths.

Twenty———————————

Once back in Baltimore, Karl found a job more rapidly than he anticipated, though not the job he wanted.

He had visited Hamburger's first, taken the bus downtown to Hanover Street. He entered as a customer, looking for a familiar face, someone he could latch on to. He saw none. He went to the back of the store, to the manager's office. He hoped that some of the old guard would be there. The layout was the same, but it felt different. He was standing in the doorway when a young man, dapper in his Lebow suit, came up to him. "May I help you with something?" he asked.

"I was looking for Mr. Davids," Karl replied.

"Oh," the young man replied, "I'm afraid that he has, ah, retired. Almost two years now. I'm the manager. Is there something that I can do for you?" he asked again, now with some impatience in his tone.

"I used to work here. Perhaps you've heard my name mentioned? Karl Brentano. I worked here for twelve years. Before things got so bad with the economy," he added, unnecessarily. "I was hoping that there would be a position available for me. Now that things seem to be getting better. I have years of experience, you see, and I did have a pretty significant following. In the old days, that is." Karl felt himself stammering, saying too much.

The younger man paused, walked toward his desk. Karl followed.

"Ah, you were here during the good years, I've heard about them." He sat, did not suggest that Karl have a seat. "Unfortunately, we've not been able to keep any of the old staff. We're trying new techniques now, and it seemed that the old timers either didn't agree with the changes, or couldn't modify their style." He straightened some papers on his desk, placed a brass weight atop the stack.

"We've had to revolutionize the way that we do business; that's the only way we can stay afloat. There's no room for the old-world now. I'm sure that you understand."

"Well, could you contact me if anything comes available?" Karl knew that he was begging, knew that it would do no good. He could not stop himself.

"Yes, certainly. We'll give you a call if something comes up."

"I don't have a phone. Let me give you my address." Karl fumbled in his coat for paper and pen.

"No need for that." The younger man walked toward the door, extended his hand. "We'll be in touch if we need you. Best of luck." He turned his back and walked back to his desk.

Karl left the store. He didn't look at any of the clothes on the racks. Another day, he thought. No better in Baltimore.

In that same week, Celeste had found an apartment for rent on North Avenue and had made an appointment for them to meet with the landlord. Edward Coffin had been skeptical at first. Karl had told the truth, that he did not have a job, that he was looking for work. Then Celeste had shown him that they had funds for three month's rent, which, she said, they were happy to pay in advance.

Well, he thought, they are a refined, settled couple. He could tell that from their clothes. Good quality, he saw, though a bit shabby. Then who wasn't a bit shabby these days. And three months' rent. That would come in handy. He looked the tall, light-haired man over. Good posture, wide forehead means a big brain. His wife had told him that.

"My brother-in-law is looking for some help. Distribution. He's in the distribution business. I can tell him that you're a tenant. Go see him. I can't promise anything, but it's worth a try. Things are picking up, more people eating out, more jobs now. Go see him. Tell him I sent you."

Celeste turned her eyes on the landlord. She had lost her looks, that she knew, but she was aware that men still were drawn to her eyes.

"Oh, you are so kind," she said, and reached for Karl's hand. "A good sign; we were meant to come home."

A stroke of luck, perhaps. It's been years, he thought, since luck has visited my life.

The distribution business was soft drinks; Karl's job was driving a truck loaded with cases of glass bottles, delivering them to the restaurants and gas stations on his route. Not a job for someone who wore suits from Hamburger's, but it was a job, and Karl was not the only man who would take anything he could find and be grateful for it.

He told himself that he had agreed to return, but he felt trapped, a decision between some money and no money, his family or his wife. Celeste said that she would not spend one penny of her inheritance in Oregon. He had made his choice, but a resentment never quite left him, a relentless, simmering anger just below the surface. After all I've done for her, he thought, stood by her, lied for her, kept her out of prison. The bitch should be grateful. These words came to him more often than he allowed himself to acknowledge.

Twenty-one _____

Celeste went to the bureau drawer, pulled out the green leather book from beneath her lingerie. She read the first entry. Twenty years ago, she thought, before Karl, before the crash. I thought the world was mine. She moved fingers over the pages, tracing the writing, reliving how she felt when she made those entries. She closed her eyes and saw the red pen, bought just to write in her journal, a Waterman, the violet ink. She thought of Mrs. Bellingstone. Willie, dear Willie, she whispered, why did you leave me?

She walked to the table in the kitchen, uncapped the pen she now carried, the red Waterman long lost, and began to write.

February 2, 1935

> *Today I am fifty years old. I can hardly bear it. Thirty years without Papa, without Willie. On my own. My dreams? I laugh at myself, at who I was, thinking that I would have all that I wanted. A house, I remember now, a house on Mt. Vernon Place. How Willie and I had laughed about that — our honeymoon at the Stafford. We were such children, Billy now older than Willie and I could have ever imagined being.*

> *Fifty years old today. Karl will bring home a cake; we will pretend that it is a celebration. We will pretend. Both of us pretend so much, I think.*

> *Mrs. Bellingham's Robert Street, the first entry I wrote, twenty years ago, thinking myself on a wonderful adventure, a working girl. So much has changed. I must get in touch with Clara to get my silver back.*

The city is the same and not the same. So much sadness and poverty. How could it be what it was? Here we are back on North Avenue, though in another house, two rooms this time, on the third floor. Not Mt. Vernon Place. But with Mama's money we have enough. I just couldn't bear it out there. I needed to be back East, back home, even if there is no one to come back to.

Today I am fifty years old. It feels like my life is over. I wish that it were.

Twenty-two _____

Celeste paced back and forth in the small kitchen; she pinned and repinned her hair back from her forehead. She wanted Karl out of the house.

She had burned the oatmeal, and had spooned what had not stuck to the pan into the bowl. She rummaged through the cabinet looking for brown sugar. Nothing. She peeled a banana and placed thin slices over the cereal, covered that with the sugar and a few sprinkles of cinnamon, hoping it would mask the scorched taste. Hurry up and leave, she thought, walking back and forth from the kitchen to the front window. She pulled the sash of her kimono tighter, rubbed her hands on her sleeves.

Karl came out of the bedroom dressed for work. He had lost only some of his style, though his wardrobe showed much the worse for wear. He planned to update his attire as soon as they had a few dollars set aside. He had his eye on a tweed double-breasted suit he'd seen in the window of Hamburger's. He was thinking about this as he wordlessly ate his breakfast and walked down the stairs to the street. A détente had descended on the household, each going through the motions of marriage, of sharing a house. Conversation between husband and wife had become infrequent; even goodbyes and greetings were rare. Each lived a separate existence, so separate that disagreements were uncommon. Only at night did they come together, though those couplings were silent.

When Celeste returned to the kitchen she inhaled the scent of *Old Spice*, Karl's new cologne. He, almost as fastidious as Willie, she thought. Well, at least that is something.

She had decided to walk to the cemetery. She wanted to be in the spring air; the doctor said that walking was good for her legs, would help the circulation. She wanted to be close to the grey and imposing granite walls of Green Mount Cemetery. They made her feel safe. She wanted to walk by Willie's house, to relive the day they met, she and Elizabeth with their parasols. She wanted to walk by the house where she had grown up, remembering times there, with Eva, with Papa.

Walking proved to be a mistake; the journey was too great. Celeste was tired, hot, her thighs chaffed with perspiration. I am too old for this, she thought, too old for Willie, for all these foolish memories. She reached The Baltimore Cemetery at the end of North Avenue and began to climb the hill to Willie's grave. Thirty years. How old am I that thirty years feels like a minute? How old am I? Older than Papa, than Mama, than the Strauffs had been when Willie and I married.

She had saved on bus fare; she would use that money to buy flowers at the stall at the cemetery's entrance. Not a stuffy wreath with a ribbon that said "Beloved Husband," she said to herself. Willie would have hated that. A bouquet, loose, daffodils, yellow daffodils for Willie, who will always be young, and handsome. You are lucky, Willie, she thought. You are lucky you are dead.

She had to stop midway up the hill to catch her breath. She put down her purse, though she held onto the flowers, brought them to her nose, inhaled, waiting for her breathing to slow. Finally she turned and continued the climb. When she reached the top, she stood and stretched her shoulders. She could see all the way to the harbor. To the west, a grand boulevard stretched as far as the eye could see. It was not as grand as it once was, she realized.

Twenty steps to the right, Willie's grave. She remembered.

The tall granite headstone surprised her. It hadn't been there on her last visit. She tried to remember when that was. She thought that perhaps August had it put up. Before she saw the footstone, *William G. Strauff, Beloved Son*, before she saw the footstone, *Lina Strauff, wife of August*, she saw a third, this one larger, higher than the rest. *August Strauff, 1853 to 1934.*

August was gone. And Celeste, who had not shed tears in many years, who thought that she had no tears left, sobbed. "You were my last hope, Mr. Strauff. I could always count on you. Now there is no one." She unwittingly spoke these words aloud, then bent and placed her hand on the stone, rubbed the carved letters of the name that had once been hers.

Her tears dry, she stood and walked to Willie's grave, laid the bouquet atop it. "Good night, sweet prince," she whispered, and wondered where she had heard that phrase before. She noticed a few pebbles by her feet, stooped and placed one atop the headstone. She had read about that practice somewhere, and liked it.

"Goodbye, Mr. Strauff," she whispered. "Thank you. Tell me what to do now." And more tears came.

She took the bus home, and once there put the kettle to boil for a cup of tea. She sat at the window and watched the boys from Baltimore Polytechnic Institute walk by, laughing and punching one another, their books held by leather straps. How did I get to be this old, she wondered.

Twenty-three —————————————

Karl hated his work, but had resolved to make the best of it, until something better came along. So far it hadn't. One afternoon, when he had been with the company not quite a year, the owner of the Pickwick Diner, Jack Rolston, stood in the alley behind Harford Road as Karl's truck arrived. They spoke of the dust storms in the mid-west, of the new social security program the president was trying to put into place, of the Chicago gangland activities.

"You know we have that right here," Rolston said. "You should be glad you're delivering soft drinks, not beer. It is as bad as when we had Prohibition. Ending that hasn't stopped the, well, you know what I'm talking about. They still come round for their 'protection money.' I'm glad I'm out of it, I can tell you that. No protection from the protectors, that's for sure."

Karl nodded in agreement. All the drivers knew about it. It was not just in Chicago.

Rolston liked Karl. He was impressed by Karl, his posture, his presence, his vocabulary.

A few days later, he was in the alleyway where Karl made his deliveries. "Come by later, after your finish your route. I may have something that would interest you," he said, and clapped Karl on the shoulder.

Two weeks later, Karl was the manager of the Pickwick Diner. He would stay for five years.

Twenty-four _____

That night, he was the last to leave. The floors were swept, the dishes washed and drying in the stands, the glasses upended, ready to be put into the cabinets, the trays lined up on their sides. The trash had been bagged and put in the dumpster in the alley. The cooks, the busboys, the waitresses had clocked out.

Only one light remained on. Karl came from his office. He had counted the day's receipts, prepared the money pouch, ready to deliver it to the depository at the Union Trust branch on Harford Road, the one where Bill's name was on the plaque, a tribute to the Hamilton boys who served in the war. He sat down at a table near the window, rubbed his fingers over the window sash. No dust. He would remember to compliment Johnson the next day.

He placed his hand above the crown of his head, gently lowered it, circled the spot where his hair was, increasingly, thin. He stared out into the night, watched the automobiles, the streetcars, going up and down the street. He wondered about the passengers, where they were going. A metaphor, he thought, one of Celeste's fancy words. They're out there, going somewhere; I'm inside, watching.

He laughed, he joked with the employees at the restaurant. He tried not to think about this life of his. Five years here. At least I have a job. Disappointed, he thought. Maybe that's what I am. Well, who's not disappointed? Certainly Celeste. I see it in her eyes. Quiet she is now, with that bitter set to her mouth, a hard look in her eyes, that Wallis Warfield look.

He closed his eyes and inhaled. Nowhere could he see that beautiful, soft blonde he married. I wish I could get drunk, drown my sorrows, he thought ruefully. God damn it. I can't even get

510

drunk. Fucking headaches come before I even get a buzz on. Fucking headaches, fucking life. He slammed his fist against the table. Enough, he thought. Enough.

That evening he walked to the bank; he walked the three miles to their apartment. He thought that the night air might calm the pounding in his chest. It didn't.

The rooms were dark, Celeste in bed, but not asleep, as he entered the apartment. She heard him in the living room. He made no effort to be quiet. She sensed his anger. It seemed to her that he was always angry now, that she could do nothing to appease it. She had stopped trying. Their evenings, their times together were quiet. She was tired, tired of trying to make a life.

He came into the bedroom and turned on the overhead light. Celeste shielded her eyes. "Turn that off," she said. "Can't you see I'm trying to sleep?"

"Get up," he told her. "Get your fucking ass out of that bed."

Celeste felt her heart tighten. After months of quiet, something had happened. She had seen Karl angry, but this was different. This was serious. She struggled to sit up.

"Karl, what is it? What's wrong? Has something happened at work? Is everything all right there?" She started to pull on her robe, the peach silk kimono.

"I've had enough. Just enough. I'm leaving. I'm going back to Portland. It's where I belong. I want to start over. I want to have some kind of life before I die. I want out. Do you hear me? I've had enough. I want out."

Celeste stared, trying to think of a response, trying to understand what this meant for her, trying to discern if Karl was serious. He turned and left the room before she could respond. She heard the door slam. He did not return.

In the morning she dressed, fixed a cup of tea, and sat at the window, looking down on North Avenue, waiting to see him come down the street. She looked around the apartment. She had fixed it up over the years, made it theirs. They had saved and bought their own furniture. She thought that she had made a life for him. She thought that it was good enough. She was unhappy; he was unhappy, but she thought that it was good enough.

That afternoon, she saw him turn the corner, coming from St. Paul Street. She heard his foot on the stairs, and positioned herself in the chair waiting, sitting erect, waiting for him to come in, to beg her forgiveness, to ask her to forgive him. She had prepared her reply. She would be magnanimous. Yes, that was the word. They would forget it ever happened. No, it never happened.

She watched the door as he entered. He had not shaved; the clothes he had worn the day before, though wrinkled, were neat.

Karl stared at her. His head pounded. One drink, he thought, one drink and this. A wave of nausea came. He lurched into the room.

"You've been drinking," Celeste said.

He struggled to stand straight. "I've been to the bank," he told her. "I closed the account." He walked toward her. "I'll need money to get started. I'll send you what I can when I get on my feet. Don't try to find me. Don't come after me. It is over. I've just had enough, of you, your, your fancy words, your books, your looking down your nose at me. I'm finished with you, with your Baltimore, with this rotten life.

"I want a chance, just a chance." His voice broke. He walked to her and handed her two twenty dollar bills. "The rent is paid through the month. This should tide you over. I'll send you more when I get it. Don't try to find me. Don't."

He walked into the bedroom, pulled his suitcase from under the bed. He went to the closet, folded his four suits and placed them in the valise. He added two pairs of Florsheim shoes. Celeste ran into the bedroom, ran to the bed, threw his suits onto the floor.

Karl grabbed her, held her wrists, pulled them behind her back. "If you touch my things, I'll kill you," he said. He pushed her against the dresser.

"You cannot leave me." Her sobs became screams. "You cannot leave me alone. You cannot do this." She ran toward the dresser, pulled open the top drawer, threw his monogrammed handkerchiefs, his socks, rolled just so, onto the floor.

"Where is the bank book? What have you done with the bank book? You can't have that money. That is my money. That is my money. It belongs to me. What have you done with it?" she screamed.

He turned toward her, pointed his finger close to her face. "Stay away from me. I warn you. Stay away." Karl glared at Celeste; she sobbed, her hands pulled at her hair.

He picked up his Lebow Brothers' suits from the floor, carefully folded them and placed them in the suitcase. He snapped it shut and walked out the door. Celeste was never to see him again.

PART V

One

Celeste stood at the window. On the street below, boys laughed, punched each other cheerfully. A few walked alone, heads lowered. All carried stacks of books, bound with leather straps. Most had them slung over their backs; some swung them freely at their sides, walloping their companions at the knees. Such boisterousness, she thought. She could see their white teeth as they laughed.

"Good for you," she said aloud. "You'll be in for it soon enough."

She walked the few steps to the kitchen. Another cup of tea. She put the kettle to boil and counted the muslin bags remaining. Thirteen. I won't have to leave the apartment until they are gone. Maybe Karl will be back by then, she thought. He would not just leave me like this. This is just to scare me, to punish me. What has gotten into him? What is it I've done? What is it he's found out?

She waited for the kettle to sing. She waited for Karl to return, formulating her responses to whatever charges he would make. He will be back, she said to herself. We will go on as if this never happened. It will be all right; everything will be all right.

She carried her tea to the window. He will come from the east, she determined, like in the bible. She laughed aloud at her thought.

There would be no recriminations. She would welcome him home; they would start over.

She had replaced his socks, the ones she had tossed about, just so, just the way he liked them, rolled, neatly, then placed one in back of the other lined up in exact rows. He didn't take his socks; he didn't take his underwear. His shirts hung, starched and pressed, in the closet. He would never leave without his things. "He will be back," she said aloud. "He would not do this to me."

The next morning she dressed with special care, wore her newest girdle, the silk stockings that didn't show the mended place, brushed her hair so that it looked fuller, applied rice powder to her face, and put just a hint of rouge to her lips. She knew that Karl hated the dark lipsticks that were in style. She returned the cosmetics to the lavender Louis Sherry candy box she used for them. Lifting her face and tapping her chin, she thought, I'll be here when he comes back; he'll see me and he'll love me.

She opened his bureau drawers once again, this time looking for the bank book. She went to the closet, pulled everything out, stood on a kitchen chair and searched the high shelves. Returning to the bureau, she ransacked the same drawers, her hands shaking. The top one held his socks; she threw them to the floor. The middle drawer contained his underwear, neatly ironed and folded. She shook out each piece. She knelt to open the lowest drawer, this one crammed with his out–of-season clothes. All went to the floor. She upended the wicker laundry basket filled with Karl's shirts waiting to be taken to the Chinaman. She found nothing.

When the sun went down at the end of the fourth day, she didn't turn on the lights. She moved from the window to the bedroom, surveyed the piles of clothing strewn around the room. She bent and pushed them all under the bed. She pulled the blanket back, folded down the top sheet. She slowly removed her clothes, hung her dress on the one satin hanger that remained in the house. She removed her make-up, put on a fresh nightgown, and crawled into bed. No book would help her this evening. She pulled the blanket over her head. She wanted darkness. She wanted oblivion.

She woke early the next morning and went to the kitchen. A lone teabag remained in the tin. She had eaten the canned soup, the crackers, the canned vegetables. This was the day that she had to face the world.

Walking to the bookcase, she pulled out the book where she had placed the money Karl had left her. The book had belonged to Willie, one of the few things she had taken from his parents' house when she left. She had carried it with her throughout her moves. It had traveled to Portland and back. She closed her eyes and pictured Willie reading

Emerson on their train ride to Denver. She held the leather-bound volume, ran her fingers over the embossed title, touched the flaking gold leaf. *Self-reliance and Other Essays.* "Oh, Willie," she whispered. "Did you know? Did you know I would come to this?" And, for the first time since Karl left, tears came. She was careful not to get any on the book.

Tea, crackers, sugar and Campbell's Tomato Soup, three cans for ten cents. She gave her order to the grocer at the North Avenue Market. This will do for a while, she decided. Karl will be back before I have to go out again. Then she added a dozen eggs, a stick of butter, and three day-old doughnuts.

When a week had passed, she admitted to herself that her hopes were fantasies. She closed her eyes and imagined a visit with August. He patted her hand, found her a job, gave her money to tide her over, and told her that everything would be all right.

He had always been there for her. Odd, that old German that so many disliked. But he had left her too. Willie, Mrs. Bellingstone, Mama, August, now Karl. Everyone leaves, she thought, and moved to the chair by the window. School would be out soon; she could watch those carefree boys for a bit.

Two———————————

Dear Billy,

I hear that you and Hyacinth have moved into a new house. I am sure that it is lovely and big enough for the two of you. I would like to see it sometime. We do not spend enough time together. I hope that you are doing well. It is a blessing that you found work so quickly. For others it was not so. I'm sure you know that I have had a very hard time of it.

I am writing to you because I am in a bind. If only your grandfather were still here to give me advice. But I have no one, no one anymore. Except you, that is.

I hate to write and tell you this, but Karl has left me. I haven't seen him in more than a week and it appears that he is being true to his word and going back to live in Portland. I have no idea what precipitated this rash move on his part. As you know, we have been married for more than twenty years now.

However, I am now alone, once again. He threatened me if I tried to find him, so I am in fear for my life. He also took all our savings, which you may not know, was really mine. So he is a scoundrel and a thief and I am left here with nothing, living on only crackers and tea.

I am writing to you with a heavy heart, as you can imagine. And there you are, you and Hyacinth, with a big house. I am hoping that you will find it in your heart to let me come and stay with you. After all, I am your mother; I gave you life. And your grandfather was always very good to me. I assume that he left you a substantial inheritance. Perhaps you could share that with me.

I must find work. I know that I can count on no one. There is no one in the world to care about me. Only you. You are my only hope, Billy.

Please come and see me and tell me your answer. I cannot believe that you would allow your mother to live in such abject circumstances. That would not befit the gentleman I know you to be.

Your loving mother,
Celeste

*Three*_____

Celeste heard the bell and ran downstairs to answer the door. Bill stood in the doorway holding two brown paper bags filled with groceries. She stared at her son, seeing an image of Willie at his most frail.

"Billy, I wouldn't have recognized you. What in the world has happened? Here, bring those bags inside."

"I've had a spell of sickness, nothing to worry about."

They walked up the stairs, Celeste leading the way, wondering what significance lay in Billy's bringing groceries. She heard his labored breathing. At the landing she took the bags from him and placed them on the kitchen table.

"Sit, Billy. I can offer you some tea, and," she looked into the bag, "cookies, it looks like."

He nodded; she set the kettle to boil and joined him as he stood by the window. Before she was settled in her chair, he began. "I got your letter, Celeste. Tell me what happened. Where is Karl? When did he leave? He didn't hurt you, did he?"

"He just seemed to go crazy and then he left. He went to the bank and got all the money. So I have nothing. I am living here with nothing. If you hadn't come, well, I don't know what I would have done."

It occurred to her that she should ask about him, find out about his health, his life, but she wanted him to hear her story, her plight. "So that is why I wrote to you. I'm sorry that I haven't been in touch more. I did get your Christmas card, that's how I knew your address, that you have a house now. And the gift, well, I just hadn't gotten around to writing you a thank-you note. It was lovely, really. The scarf was lovely. I have it here, somewhere. I do."

Bill sat across from her, saying nothing. He knew what he had to tell her; he was waiting for her to ask. He picked up his tea cup, looked out at the street below.

Celeste smoothed her hair, twisted the narrow gold band on her finger, rubbed her finger back and forth on her right eyebrow. "So, Billy. So." She inhaled. "You did get my letter. You know how things are. I am desperate. I cannot stay here; I have no money to pay the rent, no money for food. I don't know what will become of me. Which is why I wrote to you. Do you think it would be possible for me to live with you? We could be a family, couldn't we? Don't you think it would be nice? A family, finally, after all these years." She attempted, but could not quite master, a smile. "Yes, a family."

Bill laid the cup on the window sill. He stood, pushed the curtain aside, pressed his forehead against the cool glass. "Celeste," he began, "things aren't so great for me right now. I've spent a time in the hospital. I wasn't able to keep the shop open. Hyacinth and I have fixed up an apartment in the basement of the house."

Celeste's eyes widened. "Oh, that is wonderful news, Billy. You do have a place for me."

Bill turned from the window, knelt at his mother's side. Celeste put her hand on the top of his head. "Your father would kneel like that, Billy, just like that, down on one knee. You look like him today. Not every day, but today you look like him."

"No, Celeste, Hyacinth and I are living there, in the basement. We've rented out the house. We live in an apartment in the basement. Until we get back on our feet. There is just no room." Bill stood, pushed his hair from his forehead.

"And Hyacinth and I, well, we're going through some tough times; we're trying to get along. We've had a bad year. About three months ago I collapsed in the shop. My appendix had burst, and by the time I got to the hospital, blood poisoning had set in. I was there for over a month. I lost a lot of weight. Clara paid the hospital bill for us. I don't know what we would have done without her. I would have been on the charity ward, I guess. But it was very hard on Hyacinth. And what little we had saved, well, that is gone. We couldn't keep the shop open; Hyacinth couldn't run it on her own; she doesn't know antiques.

"You see, we thought that the house would be a way of starting over. Clara loaned us the money for a down payment. We are paying her back, five dollars a week. And then the hospital. That ruined everything.

"So it is just not so g-good for us now. Maybe another time, but n-not n-now. It w-wouldn't w-work with Hyacinth. It wouldn't work if you came there. That's why I brought the groceries." He sat beside her.

"I hate to have to tell you, when things are so bad for you now. I w-wish that it could be d-different, but Hyacinth just will not stand for it." As soon as he heard his words, he knew that he had betrayed his wife. "That is wrong. What I said isn't right, about Hyacinth. It just wouldn't work. Not now, at least."

He stood and reached into his pocket. "I hope that this will tide you over for a while. I wish it could be more." He folded a five-dollar bill and pressed it into her hand.

Celeste looked at the money, then stared at her son. "You don't understand, Billy. What am I to do? I have no one to go to, no one but you. I am fifty-five years old. What am I going to do if you say no? How can you throw your mother out like this? How can you do this?" Her voice became higher, louder as she spoke. Her mind raced.

"Can't you talk to Clara? Can't you get money from her? She would never allow you to live in a basement. You can get money from her, get back in your house. Then I could come."

Celeste put her hands in her lap, smiled. "Yes, you ask Clara." She had solved both their dilemmas.

Bill looked at his mother, swallowed. No stammering, he told himself.

"Celeste, you do know that Stanley, Stanley Gorsuch, is dead, don't you?"

Celeste was startled. "No, I didn't. I didn't see it in any of the papers." She pulled herself erect. "So, now she is a rich widow. All the more reason she should give you money. And what about your grandfather? Didn't he leave an inheritance for his only grandson?" She felt her face flush. He had money. Billy had money, and would not share it with her.

Bill stood. "Celeste, what are you thinking? *Opa*, Clara, do you think that they were not affected by the crash? *Opa* had the house; that is Ida's now. There was very little money left, and what he had is Ida's. She said that I could have anything in the house that I wanted, but they were just things to remember him by. There was, there is, no money.

"And Clara has been nothing but generous to me, to us. But she's turned the house into apartments. The second and third floors. She's not a wealthy woman, Celeste. I don't know what you think, but I cannot, I will not, take any more from her. I need to stand on my own two feet. Surely you can understand that."

He realized that his words were harsh. He went to her. "Maybe you could see Clara yourself. Maybe s-she knows of s-something you could do, somewhere you could go, some place that could take c-care of you." His voice cracked as he spoke. "I could say something to her, if you'd like."

Celeste sat in the chair, her eyes focused on the traffic on North Avenue. "I have nothing. I have no one. And you are leaving me to live on the street."

Bill stood. "Celeste, please. Don't do this. I am doing the b-best I can."

"You won't mind if I don't see you to the door," Celeste said. She stood and walked into the bedroom. She closed the door behind her. She did not turn to see her son leave.

Four————————————————

Celeste decided that she would walk to Clara's. It would give her time to rehearse. She approached the house at St. Paul and 29th Streets from the south. Billy had said that the house was now apartments, though it looked much the same to her. Then she saw the side entrance at the far end of the front porch. Good job, Celeste thought. No one passing by would suspect that the house had been partitioned. Clara could keep her head high.

The hedges and pachysandra were well maintained. Clara has kept the gardener. Not so distressed, Celeste thought. The maid answered the door. Same black uniform, Celeste noted, and smiled, gearing herself up for charming Clara.

"Hello, there, Symra. Is Mrs. Gorsuch in? I hope that she's expecting me. I did write her a note to say that I would be stopping by."

Symra opened the door wider. "I'll tell her you're here," she said, and vanished into the back of the house.

Celeste entered the reception room and sat on the sofa by the window. Symra had closed the pocket doors leading to the living area when she left, and Celeste noted that the room to the right had been closed off. Apartments, she thought, and wondered where Clara was.

She was picturing the new house arrangement when the living room doors opened. She smelled *Molinard de Molinard,* Clara's familiar scent, before she saw her. Clara walked toward Celeste, leaning on a thick cane, her right leg heavily braced. Celeste noted the deep lines in Clara's noticeably powdered face.

"Clara, how are you? Have you had more trouble with your knees?"

"Not to talk about," Clara said, with a wave of her hand. "It is simply a matter of dealing with the life one has been handed, wouldn't you say?" And she looked directly at Celeste.

Celeste was surprised to realize that the look was not meant to intimidate her but rather implied a sense of solidarity. Two women of a certain age dealing with life.

"Oh, yes, Clara. Yes." Celeste followed Clara into the living room. The women walked toward the bay window, sat in the two wing chairs that overlooked the fishpond in the back yard. Celeste noticed that the flowered chintz had worn thin in spots.

"I wanted to say how sorry I was to learn of Stanley's, Dr. Gorsuch's, death. I didn't know. Only when Billy told me. I must have missed it in the newspaper. I would have sent you a note."

"Yes. Well, that is done. We are getting along as best we can, or rather I am getting along as well as I can. Thank God for Symra. She does know how to make my life tolerable." Clara's hand rested on her cane.

"But you did not come here to talk about me. I hear that you are in a fix, Celeste." Clara stopped, waited for Celeste's response.

Celeste searched in her pocketbook, pulled out a lace handkerchief, held it to her nose. She pressed her lips together, then looked up.

"I've shed enough tears," she said. Clara will like that sentiment, she thought. "Yes, I am in a fix. I need a place to live. I'm sure that Billy has told you. It seems that he is too important to have his mother live with him."

Celeste knew that she had made a mistake even before Clara's posture changed. She watched as Clara sat more erect; she noticed Clara's hand tighten on the cane's handle.

"Well, let me change that. I misspoke. I did ask Billy if I could stay with him, with them, just until I got on my feet, and it was not a providential time. So, yes, I was hurt, but I understand.

"He was the one who suggested that I come to you. He thought that you might have some ideas, some suggestions about where I might go." Celeste knew that she was rushing, that she was talking too much, too fast, but could not stop herself.

527

"I do intend to get a job. I was thinking that that might not be such a bad thing. Once I got over the shock, that is. That is what I thought. It is a terrible thing to be abandoned, Clara. A shameful and dreadful thing." Celeste took a deep breath, closed her eyes, forced herself to continue.

"And, so, right now I am quite short of money, as you can imagine. And I will have to move. I cannot afford the rent, I do know that, no matter how soon I find work. Can you believe it? I am fifty-five years old and looking for work. Well, I tell myself, at least it is not the bad years, the crash. So, things are not so bad. There are lots of things that I can do. I was a working girl before I married Karl; I can be that again."

Clara was silent. Celeste obviously hadn't looked in the mirror lately, she thought. She would be no working girl.

"Yes," Clara responded, "It does seem that times are getting better. And the future looks positive, I think. Mr. Roosevelt is gearing up for war, and that will mean jobs. Though not jobs that you would be suitable for. Still, there could be something."

"War, Clara? I haven't heard anything about war here. Europe yes, but not here. Why would we want to get involved? Just let them fight it out over there, leave us alone."

Clara looked at Celeste. So naïve, she thought, still a child, a very old child, and decided against attempting to educate her sister-in-law in the politics of the world.

"Let us get down to business here. Celeste, I know that you need a place to stay. I don't know if Willie told you, but I have bought several houses as an investment. I have converted them to individual rooms and efficiency apartments. Bethlehem Steel has been hiring, and Glenn L. Martin is expanding their plant, more airplanes on order. The workers will need housing, and I think these rooms will suit them. They are temporary workers, at least that is how the jobs are advertised. But I think war is coming. They will stay on for the duration.

"But all this is not your worry. What I wanted to say is that I will let you live in one of the houses, in one of the rooms. You don't have to pay me until you get on your feet, as you put it."

Celeste was silent. This was more than she imagined. She hadn't even had to ask. Clara offered. She closed her eyes. She did not want to be too demonstrative. Clara would not like that. She clasped her hands in her lap, looked down.

"Thank you, Clara. I don't know how to thank you."

"No need. No need. That is just how it is. It is good that circumstances are what they are, or as good as the situation allows.

"Now, I think the best location is right on North Avenue. It is only a few blocks west of where you are now. Willie can arrange to move what pieces you want to take with you. And I would be willing to buy those pieces that you can't take. I can use them to furnish some of the larger apartments."

Clara stood. "Just contact Willie. He can work out the details with you. No need for you to be in touch with me." She stopped, turned. "But do let me know when you get on your feet, as you say. Then we can settle on how you will pay the rent."

Celeste knew that she had been dismissed. She stood, walked to embrace Clara, leaned down. Clara took a step back, extended her hand. "I do wish you luck, Celeste. You have not had an easy life."

Celeste clenched her fists to keep the tears away. It would not do to cry in front of stoic Clara. "I, I will never be able to repay you, Clara. Never. No amount of money. But, I do thank you. And, I hope you will understand this, I think about Willie every day."

"Yes," Clara replied. "I'm sure you do."

Five

Celeste took the bus home. A bit of a celebration, she thought. I have a place to live.

From Clara's, she walked to Charles Street and, while she waited at the stop, studied the architecture of Saints Philip and James Church. All those columns, those domes. Willie would know exactly what they mean. The architect, I think, committed suicide. Willie wouldn't know that. He must be close to me today, she thought. It is Willie I need to thank for Clara's kindness. She didn't think of Karl.

Stepping off the bus at North Avenue, she passed Bickford's Cafeteria. A treat, she said to herself. I deserve a treat, a cup of coffee, maybe a piece of pie. I have a place to live; Billy will handle moving. Maybe he would like Karl's clothes. Wouldn't that be a fateful turn? She smiled at the thought. Irony, that is the word.

She sat by herself. I'm not a bit lonely, she thought. Not a bit. I will be a working girl again, just like it used to be.

As she paid the cashier, she noticed a sign in the window. She hadn't seen it when she entered. When she got the street, she read it. "Hostess Wanted. Apply Within."

She smiled, then closed her lips, remembering not to show her teeth. Once I get a job, I'll see a dentist. This is surely my lucky day.

She walked back into the restaurant, fixed her make-up in the ladies' room, taking care that her lipstick was not too dark and that her rouge was blended well into her cheeks. She pulled her shoulders back, opened the door, went to the cashier and asked if it would be possible to see the manager.

Thirty minutes later, she left. She had a job. Mr. Archer said that she would have to apply for a social security card before she could start work. She walked east, toward home, smiling broadly, not worrying about showing her teeth. Thank you, Mr. Roosevelt, she sang.

Six

She worked from 11 a.m. to 9 p.m. and had her main meal there, part of the package. She made friends with the cooks, the busboys, and the manager. They thought themselves lucky to have such a gracious woman leading the customers to their tables, answering their questions, inquiring about their families.

Clara had been right. The population was growing; people were moving in, up from the South, taking those jobs at Sparrows Point and the shipyards. Celeste observed the neighboring homes being sold, then converted to rooming houses. The character of the neighborhood changed. Pity, she thought. But nothing stays the same. It doesn't do to care too much about a thing, even a neighborhood. She had learned that.

She invested in some new clothes; like Karl, she knew the importance of having a few good pieces, rather than heaps of cheaply made goods. The customers noticed. So did the manager. He thought it gave the cafeteria some class.

Her teeth continued to give her trouble, and she resolved to see a dentist. She bought some new elastic stockings. They were unattractive, but the doctor said that they would help her circulation. Orthopedic shoes had been part of her wardrobe for several years, vanity outstripped by necessity. Getting old, she thought, is ghastly.

Her room in the new house was laid out like the one on Robert Street. She liked that, and considered herself lucky that it was in the front of the house, directly across from Poly, as natives dubbed the Baltimore Polytechnic Institute. I can still watch my boys, she thought. Some of them stopped in at Bickford's after school. They called her Mama Brentano. She smiled, though she always kept her lips closed.

Bill sometimes visited her at the restaurant. She introduced him as her nephew. "It would not be good for them to know I had a son as old as you," she explained. He watched as the boys came in, grabbed Celeste and whirled her around. Her eyes shown. "They are my boys, Billy. Aren't they the thing?" she laughed.

On the last night of the year, the restaurant closed at 9 p.m. No revelers would use Bickford's to ring in the New Year. She walked the three blocks home to her apartment. When she arrived, she pulled the green leather book from the top drawer of the dresser. A good time to write, she thought. My resolutions for 1942.

Celeste uncapped the pen and looked at the page. Finally, she wrote.

> *I am glad that I bought a quality book. After all these years, the cover, the binding, the paper is still in good shape, better than its owner.*

Celeste smiled.

> *For the coming year, my resolutions:*
>
> 1. *Get my teeth fixed*
> 2. *Get my hair fixed*
> 3. *Read a newspaper every day*
> 4. *See Clara and thank her*
> 5. *Start paying Clara rent*

> *It feels like I should write something more profound than just my list of resolutions. If I reviewed my year, it would be interesting. That is not the right word.*
> *Karl gone, left. I thought that I would kill myself. Even Billy said no to me. Then I went to Clara, and a rescue. Just like Mr. Strauff always did. She gave me a home. And then,*

just like magic, a job appeared. So, now I am a working girl again, on my own.

This year I will start paying Clara rent. She will see that I am made of stern stuff. She will have no cause to belittle me. I have pulled myself together. I have started a life.

I thought I would be lonely. I'm not. I thought that I would miss Karl. I don't. It turned out to be a good thing that Billy said that I couldn't live with him. He was here a few days ago. He gave me a check, which I can always use. And a fruitcake. Which I will eat. It is nice to have some treat in the house. I have my hotplate, just like I did at Mrs. Bellingstone's. But I eat at the cafeteria. I don't mind. I like the people there.

There is a war on, just like Clara said. Sometimes I look at my Poly boys and wonder if they will go. I guess I should just wonder when they will go. And if they will come back. It is not like the other war. We are in the soup. Europe and Japan, though I think the Japanese are worse. Doing that terrible bombing. And on a Sunday.

Mr. Archer says that the war has been good for business. Clara seems to know everything about everything.

I will have a glass of whiskey to welcome in the new year. It will be a new start for me. How many new starts have I had? And all written down in this beautiful green book.

Seven _____

Over the next few years, Celeste experienced the war through the soldiers and sailors she seated. She learned to recognize the new recruits, those who had enlisted to keep from being drafted, those who had been drafted, boys with no idea of what war was, and, as the years passed, men who had lived through war first hand.

Rationing didn't impact her; she had her meals at work. She thought it a lucky break. She had enough clothes, though she was sure to take off her shoes as soon as she returned home. Save on shoe leather, she thought. Keep those ration coupons just in case.

The bus took her downtown every week on her day off, to see a movie, to visit the newly built central library on Cathedral Street. Library books were still available, so she was happy and content, personally untouched by the chaos of the world around her.

Her favorite movies were those of the early war years, when Hollywood, and most Americans, were light and full of hope. She heard people at the restaurant talk about *Casablanca*. She saw it, but didn't understand what the fuss was about. That Humphrey Bogart looked like he needed a good scrubbing to her. "Oh, just give me Cary Grant, Walter Pidgeon," she laughed when they talked at work. Secretly, she thought that she looked like Greer Garson playing Mrs. Miniver. Yes, that sweet look, she thought. That's what I have now.

She imagined Willie beside her when she went into the movie theatre, he noticing the architecture, telling her what to pay attention to, identifying different styles, like he did in Denver. Dead almost forty years now, she thought, and he is with me, all the time.

Her favorite movie was the Parkway Theatre, a few blocks west. She walked there, and found that a cane now made life a bit easier.

She would not allow anyone at work to see her use it. That would not do at all, she thought, they might think that I'm too old to do the job. But she grabbed a seat whenever the restaurant wasn't busy. Just for a minute, she told herself, every time.

She smiled now that she had dentures, remembering those weeks waiting for them to be ready, leaving the house only to go to work, and then being so quiet, not talking, and surely not smiling, hoping that no one would notice. Another blow that I withstood, she thought, when she looked in the mirror and smiled, now able to show her teeth, whiter, straighter than they ever were when they were attached to her gums. All that is behind me. I can take it, she said to the image in the mirror.

These days it took more effort for her to walk those blocks to work; she was exhausted when she arrived. She stowed her cane behind the coat rack as she entered, sure that no one knew of it. In fact, everyone knew of it, starting with Mr. Archer.

And, as it would, the day came when, as she entered his office to pick up her paycheck, he asked her to have a seat. A raise, she thought. He's giving me a raise. He's found a way around the wage freeze. She smiled as she eased herself into the chair across from his desk.

Archer fiddled with his pen, not looking at Celeste. She felt her heart drop in her chest. Something was wrong. There was nothing that he could criticize her for. Certainly he wouldn't mind if she sat when things weren't busy. The customers loved her. They said so. She was sure of that. No, she had done nothing wrong.

He opened and closed the middle drawer of his desk twice. Then he looked at her.

"Mrs. Brentano, I've noticed that you seem to have a bit of trouble walking these days. Have you thought that, perhaps, that is, maybe, ah, perhaps, your working here is making your condition worse? That it is not the best thing for you to do this job, so much walking, so much standing on your feet? That perhaps, ah, I'm suggesting, that you might think about retiring, or finding something that is a bit less strenuous? Have you considered that at all?"

Her throat tightened. I cannot be fired, she thought. This cannot be happening. She exhaled, louder than she anticipated. She placed her hands in her lap. "Well, perhaps you are right, Mr. Archer." She stopped, then looked up at him and smiled as she asked, "So, do you think I could be the cashier? That wouldn't entail walking; just sitting at the register. I could do that. I know I could. I am very good with money, very good. And I have been with you so long now, the customers expect to see me."

Archer paused. "Well, you see, we already have a cashier." He looked down.

Celeste felt herself redden. She decided that she would tell him the truth, play on his mercy. "Mr. Archer, may I be honest with you?" He nodded.

"I need this job. It is the only income I have. I must work. If I do not work, I will be out on the street. I am a hard worker, you know that. I will do anything, anything you think I can do. But I need this job. I do." Her voice trembled as she spoke. It was genuine, not staged, although she realized as she spoke, that it might help her case.

"Yes," he said. "I do understand.

"Give me a few days, Mrs. Brentano. I have to be honest with you; I don't think that it is in the cards for you to continue your work here. But let me talk to some people I know. Let me see if I can help you find something, something where you don't have to be on your feet all day.

"You know that you cannot continue as you have been. It has affected your health. Surely you can see that?"

Celeste nodded, closed her eyes, willed herself to be strong. "I would appreciate any help you can give me, Mr. Archer." She rose and, using all her concentration, left the office with as steady a stride as she could manage.

She had to stop and rest her legs twice as she walked home, pulled herself up the steps to her room. Once there, she took off her shoes and looked at her ankles. They were swollen over the tops of the shoes. She removed them and massaged her ankles. Her feet were blue.

Eight————————————————————

The Stanley Theatre's new assistant manager had a reputation as a go-getter. Joseph Liberto started as an usher only a few years ago. He and Archer were fellow Elks. Perhaps, Archer thought, he would be willing to give an old lady a chance. It was Christmastime; people were saying that the war would be over soon. Maybe Liberto had a bit of Christmas spirit in his heart.

Archer called, explained the situation. "She's a wonderful old gal. And what a personality. She can wow them, I'll tell you that. If it weren't for the trouble with her feet, I would keep her forever. The young ones call her Mama Brentano; the men love her, no matter what their ages. Go figure." Archer moved the receiver to his other ear, leaned back in his chair.

"But she needs a job where she can sit. And, Joe, she needs a job. I don't know what her personal circumstances are. She's always chipper when she's here. She lives in one room, I do know that. And I've heard about a nephew. I think that's it. She's never mentioned any other family in all the years she's been here.

"So, if you have anything, if you could give her a break, I'm sure she'd do well for you. She won't let you down. She's in here, rain, hail, snow or sleet, just like the postman."

Liberto hesitated. "I don't know how the patrons would respond to an old face at the ticket booth. I like to have someone, a girl, somebody who's a bit of a flirt, you know. Keeps the guys coming back. I'm not sure this would work."

"Just give her a chance, Joe. Just meet her. You'll see what I'm talking about. She can be a charmer, that's for sure."

Liberto relented, interviewed Celeste, and knew immediately what Archer meant. He worked up a new schedule; he would try Celeste as the cashier at the ticket booth during the week. He still wanted a young face for the weekends.

"And you can stay after the last show begins and see any movie you'd like. Or come on the weekends. That too," he said, as he shook her hand. She was old, but when she turned those eyes on you, something clicked, he thought. He'd kid Archer about it the next time they got together at the lodge.

Nine——————————————————

She worked five, some weeks six, days at the theatre, and was always willing to fill in if one of the other cashiers called in sick at the last minute. Liberto liked her; the customers liked her, and she was a whiz with money. Her ticket sales and cash receipts tallied to the penny.

She soon tired of seeing movies; she preferred the quiet intimacy of her books. Her trips to Central Pratt Library continued uninterrupted. They knew her there, and sometimes the head librarian held books and articles that he thought Celeste would especially like. The staff sometimes commented on this solitary old woman who had been coming there since they could remember, always alone.

One spring Sunday, Celeste realized that her legs felt better. They only bothered her in the evenings, on her four block walk from the bus stop and that final climb to her second floor room. On this day, she looked down and saw her ankle bones. "Hurrah!" she chuckled. "I knew you were there somewhere."

She sat by the window, savoring her tea, a book in her hand, *The Green Years*. When Celeste put in on reserve she was 52nd on the list, but a friendly librarian had bumped her up. She touched his hand when he brought it out for her. "You don't know what these little favors mean to me. Truly you don't," she said. And she meant it.

She read about A.J. Cronin's hero. Poor little orphan boy, she thought. Poor little boy. Not good to read sad books, she decided, and put it on the bottom of the pile by her chair. Looking out at the cloudless blue sky, she heard church bells. So many churches around here, she thought, and wondered which one it was.

She felt a rush of energy. A walk. I'll go for a walk, ankles and all, she decided. She took her cane, just in case.

Forty minutes later she found herself in front of Clara's house. The first floor windows were open. As she stood on 29th Street she heard music. Clara. She stood, listening, remembering those days, those evenings on North Avenue when Clara played and played until Celeste felt like screaming. Today it sounds beautiful, she thought. I should have paid more attention then.

She went to the door, rang the bell. The music stopped. A minute later Clara appeared; she had seen Celeste from the front window. Tell me she's not in trouble, she whispered to herself before she opened the door.

The two women greeted each other, Celeste warmly, Clara warily.

"Well, this is a surprise," Clara said. "Would you like to come in?" she added, after a slight hesitation, which Celeste noticed.

Celeste took a breath, determined not to let anything spoil this beautiful day. "Actually, I walked here. It has been so long since I've been anywhere except for my work and errands, I just decided to take today and do whatever it was I felt like doing. And I found myself here.

"I would like to come in, Clara, just for a little visit. Then I'll take the bus home. I normally have dinner at the cafeteria, even on my days off. It is my second home after all the years I worked there."

Clara looked at her quizzically, not quite trusting that this was a simple visit, that Celeste had not come with some request which only Clara could meet.

"Of course," she answered. "Come in. We can go downstairs to the kitchen. I'll make us some tea. Symra, I'm sure, left some cakes in the cupboard."

Celeste followed Clara into the house, through the living room, the dining room, to the narrow stairway that lead to the basement kitchen. Clara looped her cane on her arm, and, holding tightly to the railing with both hands, maneuvered her way downstairs. Celeste laughed, "Here we are, two old women with our canes. Did you ever think that it would come to this?"

Clara did not answer until she reached the basement hallway. "I always thought it would come to this," she said. Celeste did not respond.

They walked down the dark hallway. The kitchen was at the back of the house and opened to the gardens. Sun flooded the room, blinding the women while their eyes adjusted to the light. Clara switched on the gas for water for the tea, looked into the cupboard above the stove for cake tin. She stretched, but could not quite reach it. Celeste walked over, and, leaning over Clara, lowered it to the counter.

Celeste moved to the kitchen table. "Beautiful light. I've not been down here before. But those stairs, hard for you. How do you manage when Symra is off?" She realized that she was grateful to be able to manage the stairs to her North Avenue room.

"Oh, I manage. One can manage anything if one puts one's mind to it," Clara answered, immediately aware of how pompous she sounded. She smiled, attempting to soften her words, then stopped. Why is this woman here, she asked herself. She must want something, all those smiles and concerned expressions. Haven't I done enough for her? Why can't she stay out of our lives?

She swirled the hot water in the teapot, emptied it and spooned in the loose tea from the caddy. She added more hot water and brought the pot to the table. Celeste watched, thinking that, of course, Clara would not use tea bags. Clara set a plate of thinly sliced fruitcake on the table. Celeste took two pieces.

The two women sat, silently, staring at the pot, willing the tea finish its steep. Finally, Clara poured the hot liquid into the thin china cups.

"It's been a long time since I've had a tea party," Celeste said.

Clara smiled. "I as well."

"You know, Clara, it has been a long time for us. I don't think that there is anyone left who has known me as long as you have." Clara nodded.

"So many gone, don't you think? Now we are the old ones."

Clara did not respond.

Celeste shifted in her seat. "Billy is still quite handsome, don't you think?"

Clara looked up. "When did you see him? I wasn't aware that you saw Willie. How is this?"

Celeste considered her response; she knew that she had entered dangerous territory. She decided to tell the truth. I have nothing to hide, she thought. Why should I feel ashamed?

"Oh, Billy always stops by when he is at the houses to collect the rents for you. When I'm not working, if I'm home, we always have a little visit. Sometimes he takes me out to lunch. So I see him, I'd say, often. Did you not know that? Did he not mention me to you?"

Clara ignored Celeste's question. "Well, he is very busy. It is not a good thing to take up too much of his time. He has the business to worry about, and he does help me out with the collections. And then that child of his. That was a mistake, to be sure."

Celeste felt a delighted shiver. The start of a gossip. "Oh, yes. That was quite a surprise, wasn't it? After being married all those years. Twenty years and then, well, you just never know."

"I'm sure she realized after it was too late to get rid of it. Change of life pregnancy and all that. But he seems happy about it, though she is certainly Hyacinth's child. A pretty little thing, but not much personality. And a burden on Willie, You know he is delicate, like his father, and I don't think that he ever quite recovered from that bout in the '30s. So you should be very careful not to place even more of a burden on him, Celeste. You leave him alone." Clara lowered her cup, for emphasis, she thought.

"Oh, I don't see him that much, really. And you know I have only seen her that one time, right after they married and I've never seen the child. I said to myself the first time I saw her that she would give him a run for his money. Hyacinth, I mean. And I'll bet I was right." Celeste leaned in, closer to Clara.

"He's never said, but I'm sure that she doesn't want him to see me, that he doesn't tell her when he does."

Clara entered the conversation against her better judgment. For so long there had been no one to talk to about this. Now here was Celeste, who understood.

"Oh, she keeps a tight rein on him, you are right. She is the jealous sort. She doesn't even want him to see me, that I know, but she cannot control that. Of course, they spend all their holidays with her family. Once in a while he will drive over on Christmas for an hour or two, but I am not included in any family gathering. But I guess he feels that he cannot rock the boat. She is quite a handful. And now with the child, well, he is trapped."

Celeste looked at Clara. "Well, perhaps. But I don't think that we allow ourselves to be trapped unless we want to be."

Clara pressed her lips together to keep from making an incensed comeback.

Quiet returned to the kitchen, the women silent, each looking into the yard, at the well-tended azaleas in full bloom, some as high as the shoulder-height iron fence.

"They are just beautiful, Clara. I hadn't realized how I missed seeing flowers. My view is only the street. Maybe I'll buy a plant. Yes, a good idea. I'll see if Billy can bring me one." Clara did not respond.

Celeste looked around the kitchen. "Clara, do you ever get lonely, living all by yourself in this big house?"

Clara tilted her head back, looked at the ceiling. Is this what the visit is about? Does Celeste want to move in? She looked Celeste squarely in the face. "No, I am not lonely. Never. This is my home; I have my piano, my music. Symra is a wonderful help. She comes in, does her work, and leaves me alone. I am not lonely. No. that is not a word I would ever use."

Celeste sensed resentment in Clara's tone. "Oh, I didn't mean any offense. I am not lonely, at least I don't think I am, and I live alone, just not in so big a place as you. No, I can see that you are not, that neither of us is, lonely. I guess we are lucky, no?"

The tension in the air softened. The women turned their eyes to the garden.

"Would you care to sit outside?" Clara asked, and the two went to the chairs that were set by the rhododendrons. Clara settled, with some difficulty, into the chair nearer the fence. She knew it would be difficult to get up.

"Well, it is really just the two of us now. Everyone gone," Celeste said. "I think that you are one of the few people who knew me when I was young. I have no more family, all dead. Eva's children have their own lives. I've never even met them, and I never really knew Eva. I think that you knew her better than I."

Clara nodded. "We did keep in touch by letter, more when we were younger, of course. But no, I really didn't know her well." She stopped, then added, "But we have Willie. Perhaps not in the way that we would like, but, yes, I guess we do share that, share him."

"But he chose the wrong woman if he wanted us to be in his life," Celeste said.

"Oh you are right with that. You are certainly right with that," Clara responded.

Celeste sensed that her visit had come to an end. She stood. "I can just leave through the gate in the garden. That will put me right on 29th Street. No need for you to walk me upstairs."

She stopped, looked over at Clara. "I will never be able to thank you for all you have done for me. Please know--"

Clara stopped her. "Yes, the gate is a good choice. It is a beautiful day. I hope that you don't have to wait too long for the bus." She was glad that Celeste would not be there to witness her struggle out of the chair.

Ten

The child danced with cold, her bare legs above the ruffles of her white socks pickled with goosebumps. The two adults stood with her in front of the movie theatre on Howard Street. The trio had just emerged into the frosty night after seeing *The Red Shoes* at The Little Theatre, a movie most unsuitable for a five year-old. Clara had heard that it had dancing in it. The child liked ballet, Willie had told her.

The girl heard her father speaking above her head. "She's working tonight, I think. Should we stop over? She's never seen Sylvie, you know."

Clara leaned on her cane, struggled to pull on the black kidskin gloves with the warm cashmere lining, a recent Christmas gift from Willie. "Absolutely not. There is no reason for the child to be brought into this. Let us simply enjoy this evening, Willie, without complicating it."

The Stanley Theatre stood directly across the street. Bill tried to see into the cashier's window, but the reflections of the streetlights occluded his view. Celeste, however, saw the scene clearly.

Eleven

She had moved the fan beside her bed and was sitting directly in front of it; she had disabled the oscillating motion. She wanted the air directly on her. Even in the early morning hours, the heat in the room was oppressive. She looked forward to the cool of the ticket booth, and had even considered walking down to air-conditioned Bickford's for breakfast.

She heard a light tapping at her door. She had no visitors except for Billy, and this was too early for him. She pulled the neck of the kimono tighter and stood by the door, listening. She opened it a crack, standing directly behind it so that she could slam it shut and lock it if an intruder was outside.

Bill stood in the doorway. "Oh, my, you gave me a fright," she said. "Why in the world are you here this early? Something is wrong, isn't it." She pulled the door wide. She saw that his face was ashen. "Sit here. Let me put a kettle on. Tell me. What has happened? What?"

He started toward the chair, but then stood at the window, looking down at the street, curiously empty this hot July morning. He stared at the high school across the street, quiet these summer months.

"Clara died last night." He stopped, bent his head to look east, toward Guilford Avenue. "I should have been prepared. She was not a young woman, but I didn't think she was quite ready to go. The doctors said that she had a strong will to live. When I left her yesterday afternoon, she smiled and said, 'Tip top.' I had never heard her say that before. 'Tip top,'" he repeated. "Then I leaned down to kiss her goodbye and told her that I'd stop in the next afternoon. She patted my hand, and I left.

"You know, she was the closest thing to a mother that I --" He stopped, aware of what he had been about to say. Celeste did not appear to notice.

"They called from the hospital last night, just before midnight. The nurse said that she had a fine supper and was cheerful, if you can imagine Clara cheerful in a hospital. When they went to check on her, she was dead. They said that she died peacefully in her sleep. I hope they are right."

He inhaled. Celeste put the teacup on the table beside him. He picked it up, then sat. She sat in the chair across from him. Best to just be quiet, she thought, not ask any questions. She wondered if she would have to move.

Bill finished his tea, replaced the cup in the saucer. "I've got to make arrangements now. The funeral will be from Sts. Phillip and James."

He looked over at her. "I didn't know if you would want to attend. The notice should be in tomorrow's paper. You understand that it would be best if you went on your own."

Celeste nodded. "She was always very good to me, Billy. Better than she needed to be, I know that. She and August both."

That Friday Celeste stood at the back of the church. She saw Bill, and Hyacinth, and a few friends of Clara's sitting scattered in the cavernous nave. That is how it is when you get old. No one left to mourn you, she thought. She left before the service ended. She had asked for a few hours off from work. She stood on Charles Street and waited for the bus to take her downtown. She noticed the hearse and limousine waiting on 29th Street.

All gone, she thought. All of us gone. And I'm still here. I suppose I'll be next. And who will be there for me? Who will ride in a limousine? I'd better tell Billy about the plot in Green Mount Cemetery, with Papa, and Mama, and Eva and all those others I used to visit. Who will visit me? How did I get to be this old? Maybe something for that old green book this evening. She closed her eyes and thought about what she would write.

Bill visited the following week. Clara had left a letter to Celeste in her safety deposit box. Bill had read it before he gave it to her.

Celeste opened the envelope. A note, Clara's handwriting. Eight words: *I always meant to give this to you.* A second letter was part of the packet, this one from Willie. Celeste sat and read. Bill watched her.

"Oh, Billy, it's from your father. He wrote it just before he died. How could she have kept it from me? All these years, almost fifty years and now." She put her hands in her lap. "All these memories, Billy. You just don't know. You really don't. Just seeing his handwriting again. This is the only thing I have with his handwriting." Her eyes were filled with tears, real ones.

She picked up the letter and read it again. "He asks me not to let you forget him. He thought of you. He loved you, Billy. He did." Bill nodded.

"You haven't forgotten him, have you? Clara told you about him, didn't she? She did do that, or your grandfather, your grandmother? They told you about him, didn't they? You do know about him."

"I never knew him, Celeste. I never knew you. All I knew was Clara, and *Oma* and *Opa*. I went to boarding school when I was five. The nuns, they were as much my family as anyone. Now I have Hyacinth. You were never there. Neither was my father."

"Oh, Billy, don't be angry with me. I couldn't bear that. I did the best I could. It isn't my fault that your father died."

"I'm not angry, Celeste. I'm just answering your question," his expression belying his words. His heart raced; his mouth was dry. He noticed that he didn't stammer. He drew himself erect.

"There is something else," he said. Celeste looked up, still stung by her son's uncharacteristic treatment.

"Clara left you $15,000 in her will."

Twelve ─────────────────────────

Her Poly boys were back in school when Bill delivered the check. He had knocked at the door with his usual soft tap. She opened it without speaking.

He took four steps into the room. "I'd like to apologize for my behavior the last time we were together. It was uncalled for, and I'm sorry if any of my comments upset you. I was discourteous and disrespectful. I'm sorry that I haven't been to see you until now."

Celeste had moved to the chair in the window; Bill followed her, reaching into the inside pocket of his suit coat. "Here's your check. It was clearly Clara's wish that you have a life without worrying about money.

"You could get a place of your own; you could even buy a little house. I worry about you living here, in this neighborhood, working at the movie. It's no life for a woman of your age, your background. You deserve better. And now you can have it. I can help you if you'd like. You can't stay here. The neighborhood isn't what it was; it's deteriorated badly in the years since the war. It's dangerous. You can't be out walking from the bus at night. Surely you know that it's not safe."

Celeste took the check from him, stared down at it. Until now, she had been reluctant to believe that this windfall was real. "I accept your apology, Billy. I know that you were upset. We all say things sometimes that we regret. You did not act like a gentleman. I never expected such behavior from you. But, that is over."

She continued. "I have been thinking about this inheritance, the best way to use it. And I do have plans for this money. Billy, if you would, I would appreciate it if you would take me to The Savings

Bank of Baltimore. Your father used to talk about it, maybe even your grandfather. And there is where the money will be. Bonds, yes. That will be my nest egg. That will make me happy, not buying a house, not moving, but having a nest egg. It has been a long time since I could even think about having one. And now I do," Celeste laughed.

Bill countered, "But I don't want you to have to work anymore. I can help you. I can afford it now. And I want you to have more than a room. I want you to have a place of your own."

Celeste looked at him. "I appreciate that you care, Billy. I do. But, you know, I like it fine being on my own. I have enough, now that I'll have my nest egg, so that I don't have to worry. And I like working. What else would I do with my time? I can't read all the time."

She paused, sat back in her chair, unconsciously rubbed her left ankle. "All those years I thought that I wanted, that I needed, someone to take care of me, when really, I'm happier by myself, on my own." She smiled and touched Bill's hand. "Your hands, so like your father's, those aristocratic fingers."

She took his hand. "But I wouldn't say no to a gift now and then. And a bigger place. Yes, maybe that. And closer to work. Yes. I'll think about it.

"And what about you? Will you move to Clara's house?"

"No, Hyacinth wants to buy a place in the country. We plan to sell our house and Clara's rental houses. We'll keep the house on St. Paul Street, rent out the apartments, but keep the lower floors for us. We may stay there when we're in town. Clara had a lot of antiques, paintings. I'll take them to the shop; buyers have already contacted me about some of the pieces. Those will probably go to New York or Philadelphia galleries and shops. I'll keep the artwork here, for local buyers."

"So you'll keep the business?" she asked. "I keep meaning to come by and see it. How many years has it been now?"

Bill smiled. "Almost twenty, Celeste, Howard Street, in the heart of Antique Row." Hyacinth is right, he thought. Celeste is concerned only with herself. He shook his head.

"The car's parked outside. Do you want to go to the bank now? Are you working this afternoon?"

Celeste hurriedly finished dressing. Forty minutes later the two entered the bank on Lexington Street. When they emerged Celeste was a lady who, every quarter, ventured to the bank, went to her safe deposit box, and clipped bond coupons. The tellers who cashed them for her always smiled and wished her a pleasant day. They shook their heads after she left. "All that money, you'd think someone would tell her about that make-up."

Thirteen

"You're right. The neighborhood is just too bad for me to stay here, despite my Poly boys. It's dirty, smokehounds in doorways. Even Bickford's has changed. I don't like going in there anymore. There's no one that I know. Everything's changed. And at the market, so many stalls have closed, or moved. No, you were right; it's not the same. So, I will move."

Celeste had struggled with her decision. She was accustomed to her room, used to the neighborhood. She wanted everything to be like it was. Never love anything, she thought. It will be taken away from you.

Bill was relieved, but wondered what had precipitated this unexpected pronouncement. Before he had a chance to ask, Celeste continued.

"And, I know just where I'll go. It's ever more convenient for me, for my work. I can shop at the Lexington Market for those things I need; there's a Bickford's a few blocks away. It's right around the corner from the Stanley. I don't know why I didn't think of it before." She rubbed her knuckles over the arm of the chair.

"The old Kernan Hotel. They're renting rooms, you know, for long-term residents. It's called the Congress Hotel now. I know you know it. Your father loved it, the architecture. You know where I'm talking about, on Franklin Street, just above Howard. It is beautiful, really lovely to look at. And the lobby, well, it is just my style, all marble and--"

She had yet to give Bill a chance to respond. He knew that, like most of downtown Baltimore these days, the Congress Hotel wasn't what it used to be, that Celeste's saying that it was now renting rooms was code for its becoming a hotel for transients. He interrupted her.

"I'm not sure that the Congress will be any safer than where you live now, Celeste. That neighborhood is not good. It's all commercial, not a residential area. And once you get past Eutaw Street, it's slums. I don't think that's such a good move for you."

"Tosh, Billy. Anyway, it's done. I just need your help in moving my furniture there. Of course, the rooms are furnished, but the manager said that he would have no problem if I brought my own. I've paid the rent, six months in advance. So, it is complete. Will you help me?"

He shook his head; he knew there was no use trying to convince his mother that her idea was a mistake. He and his able-bodied assistant moved what furniture she took. He used his new panel truck, dark green, with *Antiquities* painted in gold lettering on the sides.

The day that Celeste moved in, Bill found the manager, asked him to keep an eye on Celeste, gave him phone numbers where he could be reached if he was needed.

"I'll look after her. She'll be our house mother." Louis Fuller laughed, working his toothpick to the right side of his mouth. "There's somebody here nights, Jimmy. He'll look out for her too." Bill shook Fuller's hand, transferring a twenty-dollar bill to seal the deal.

"I'm just a few blocks away, Howard Street, below Read," Bill said, and thanked him again, trusting that his raised eyebrow conveyed that he would make sure Fuller kept his end of the bargain.

He studied the lobby as he left, inhaled the building's particular odor. A combination of disintegrating satin draperies, a disinfectant too strong for the porous marble, and tired lives, he thought. My mother has come to this.

Celeste had chosen a fifth-floor room with a bay window and an alcove; it overlooked Franklin Street. Fuller had told her that the back rooms were larger, away from traffic noise, but Celeste preferred a spot where she could look out at activity. From her window she could see, if she peered around the buildings, almost to the harbor to the south, and to Charles Street to the east. It sat a block west of the Stanley, an easy walk to the cafeteria, and a rigorous walk to Lexington Market.

"Everything, Billy, you see. I have everything here. And it's not so far away from you, from the shop. I will get there one day to see what you have on display. Really I will."

The following day, before she left for her lunch at Bickford's, she came into the empty lobby. A well-read *Morning Sun* lay on the table under the mail boxes. Celeste picked it up and sat in one of the chairs by the fireplace. Nice, she thought, a newspaper waiting for me. She read of the collision of two planes over the Grand Canyon. Dreadful, she thought, and picked up the Women's Pages where she read an article about shampoo.

Fourteen————————————————————————

"What the fuck do you have out there? Good god, we have our own Norma Desmond selling tickets. Jesus Christ, it's *Sunset Boulevard* on Howard Street. Do you think we're running some kind of old age home? Get that old bag out of there and do it now." Liberto heard these words on his second day working for the new owner. He considered arguing, but sensed that it would be a lost cause. Phil Mahon, hired to oversee the upgrading of the theatre was convinced that no one knew better than he how to run a theatre, and was just as sure that Joe knew nothing.

Liberto held his tongue. He knew that Mahon was right. Celeste's appearance had become more bizarre over the past months. That lipstick, rouge, all that black mascara. He regretted not saying something to her; it might have prevented this. Maybe Mahon wouldn't have noticed, or at least not noticed so soon. But he hadn't wanted to hurt her feelings, hadn't wanted to make her feel bad.

He faced his new boss. "I understand. I'd like to give her some notice, or at least a severance. She lives on her own; I'm sure that she needs what she earns here. I'd like to give her some time to make arrangements, other arrangements. She's been with us a long time, and her service is outstanding. There's no one I trust to get the sales and cash receipts to balance like Mrs. Brentano. It will be a loss. I understand that you want a younger face at the ticket booth, but she has been more to us than a cashier."

Mahon folded his arms. "Either you tell her or I do. And I don't think you'd want that."

"No, I'll handle it. And I will give her a severance. Perhaps two weeks pay?" His voice rose with his last sentence. He did not know how far he could push Mahon. Liberto was worried that he could soon be out of a job himself.

The next day Celeste took the news in stride. "Well, it has been a good run, as they say in the movie business. And you have been an outstanding boss. Truly outstanding." She reached out to shake his hand. "You have given me the opportunity to do something I was proud of. And you have been a friend."

She took the envelop he handed her, folded it, and placed it in her black leather purse. She attempted to snap it shut, but the latch was broken. She reached for her cane, and left the theatre.

Once outside, she looked at the sky, not noticing the grey clouds to the west. "Well, Willie," she said as she turned the corner onto Franklin Street, "I wonder what I will do with my time?"

Fifteen

She read, she visited the Lexington Market, she found a small grocery store on Eutaw Street, at the edge of a newly redeveloped area called Seton Hill. Artists and urban pioneers were restoring the dilapidated row houses built in the early 1800s to house workers from the Caribbean brought to Baltimore to service the St. Mary's Seminary on Paca Street. Celeste laughed to herself when she learned about it. George Street had been infamous for its cat houses in the 1930s.

"From seminarians, to whores, to artists, Jimmy," she told the night clerk at the Congress. "Who knows what they'll find there!" But she was glad to rub elbows with some young people on those afternoons when she stopped by for her tea bags and cookies. They referred to the store as Filthy Milton's, but the owner was always kind to her. She patted his hand when he handed her her change.

She walked to the library each week. Bill had offered to buy her a television, but she told him no. "I'd rather read," she said. "And if I want company, or if there is something special, I can just go down to the lobby and watch it with my crew members. They're a good bunch," she added.

Bill, who found it increasingly difficult to find the time to visit her during the day, had stopped by one evening on his way home from the shop. He was less sure of those she called her crew members, and at the end of each visit, cautioned her not to be too trusting. "You can be friendly, but lock your door."

"I wouldn't mind a new radio," she said as he left.

"Next visit," he promised, and was good to his word.

Most evenings she ventured to the lobby for her evening cigarette. The men welcomed her; she was the only female resident there, and kidded her about her "postprandial" smoke, a term they had learned from her. They liked this woman, a bit loony, they thought, but nice. And she doesn't talk too much.

On a cool June morning, Celeste had finished her morning tea and biscuit. She rose later now that she had no work to go to. She found that she went to bed earlier, and some days surrendered to an afternoon nap. Well, she thought to herself, I am getting up there. And a nap is a blessing of fortune.

She came to the lobby to read the newspaper, sitting in the chair that she now thought of as her own. She went to the entrance, looked out at the crisp blue sky. A visit, she thought, too long in coming. I have the address written down somewhere. She returned to her room and stood in front of the row of books atop the radiator, searching until she found the slip of paper, used as a bookmark in one of Willie's old books. *Self-reliance.* "If that's not the truth, Mr. Emerson," she aloud, as she folded the paper and slipped it into her purse. A beautiful day for a walk.

She headed north on Howard Street, past the old City College, past the Fifth Regiment Armory, past the shuttered Richmond Market. So much changed, she thought, remembering the special potato candies she once bought there. All gone. So much gone. She crossed the east side of Howard at Madison Avenue, wanting to look in the windows in the 800 block.

Billy, I'll surprise him, she thought. All these years I've been meaning to stop in, to see this business of his. Antiques. Wouldn't Willie be proud; and wouldn't August be disappointed. "No job for a real man," Celeste could hear him, harrumphing with his never-lost German accent. All gone; so many gone. She shook her head, remembering.

Celeste came to the building she was looking for. The windows were dark, a chain around the door handle. She reached into her purse, checked the address written on the paper. She looked up at the number painted on the transom in gold leaf. She stepped back, working out her bearings. Perhaps she had written it down incorrectly. She went to the shop next door, pushed the door open, the bell announcing the arrival of a customer.

A man, due for a bath the day before and wearing a yellow and maroon argyle-patterned sweater much too heavy for the temperature of the day, came from the back. "Can I help you? Are you looking for something in particular?" he asked, thinking that this old woman would not be a paying customer, and worrying a bit that she would slip a portable object into her purse.

Celeste drew herself up to her full height, placed her cane in front of her, held it with both hands. "Well, yes, perhaps you can help me. I am looking for the shop owned by William Strauff. I seem to have miswritten the address. Can you tell me where it is?"

He leaned on a teak demilune console to the right of the entrance. "Oh, I am sorry. But they've closed the shop. Bill died a few months ago and they decided to close rather than try to sell. It is a loss to the block. We all miss him."

Celeste felt her knees weaken. The proprietor came toward her. "Is there something I can help you with? Were you looking for anything in particular?"

She waved him off, but, noting that she was in some distress, he returned with a chair and a glass of water. She sat, thanking him for his trouble.

After a few minutes she stood, thanked him once again and walked toward the door. She stopped, then turned to him.

"I wonder if I could bother you to call a cab for me."

Celeste returned to her room, sat in the window, drank her tea. She thought about Billy, such a nice young man, so handsome. Now he is gone too. Best not to say anything about that, best not to tell anyone.

And she continued her days as before.

Sixteen

That evening Celeste gave her customary greeting to the men before she went to her chair beside the cracked brown leatherette sofa. Bob sat near her. She pulled the package of Kool Menthols from her pocket. He supplied the light.

She had grown to like, to understand these fellow boarders, her crew. Life had not been kind to them and she appreciated that. They were making do, as was she. Some stayed, some went; those who left did so without goodbyes. Better that way, she thought. All our farewells should be without goodbyes.

The men were quiet about their lives before the Congress. She was as well. They knew she had worked at the Stanley; they knew she had a son.

She allowed herself a favorite, Bob, who seemed younger than his years. They frequently sat late in the lobby, away from the noise of the television, both reading, often not exchanging words beyond a greeting and a goodnight. She learned that he had been in the war, in the Air Force, a tail gunner.

"It took over a year after the war ended for them to get us back to the U.S. I guess we were lowest on the totem pole," he said. "All that time just sitting over there, doing nothing, make-work, while all the jobs here were being taken. Some welcome home. By the time I got back to Baltimore, no one even remembered the war. And no job waiting, either."

He told her about his life, attending McDonough School as a scholarship boy. "I never knew my father," he confided one evening. "He just left. Without a word. My mother worked for Lebow, sewing. She still works there. She's not had an easy life. And I know I disappointed her when I left school. I enlisted in the Army the day I turned eighteen, left all my belongings there. I hated it that much, hated military school. And what did I do? I joined the Army."

He stubbed out his cigarette. "How's that for stupid? Three weeks before I would have graduated. Thought I knew it all.

"So now, here I am, no education, working in a job that I try not to hate, living in a hotel for transients." He realized what he had said and attempted to recover. "Not that this is a bad place. Really, it suits my needs just fine. I'm not one to socialize. I like being able to go to my room, not have to worry about having a house. This, really, this is not bad here."

Celeste looked over at him. Handsome, she thought, very handsome. But all that sadness, it obscures his good looks. Still, any woman would do well to have him.

Seventeen ⸺⸺⸺⸺⸺⸺⸺⸺⸺⸺⸺⸺⸺⸺⸺⸺⸺

"You are the gentleman, Bob. Always," she said. She had spent the damp, drizzly day in her room, looking out at the steady flow of cars on Franklin Street. She liked their mesmerizing effect, hypnotic. Twilight, she thought, my favorite time, when the headlights come on, especially when it rains and the white headlights, the red tail lights merge into long strips of whirling color. Like a painting. If I could paint, that's what my pictures would be. Baltimore in the rain, rush hour. Maybe I'll learn how to paint, take lessons. Why not?

She had come to the lobby this evening to enjoy her cigarette. She never smoked in her room. Too dangerous, she thought, and she liked the company. Just enough. She nodded to the other residents who sat there, staring at the television screen; she wondered how many paid attention to what was on. The sound was low, too low to follow what was being said. Maybe they just like the noise, the company.

One by one the men left, some for their rooms, some into the night, to walk, to be alone with their thoughts, others to a bar, to keep their thoughts at bay. Celeste and Bob were left in the lobby; Jimmy sat behind the desk, reading the racing form.

"You look nice this evening, Mrs. Brentano," Bob said.

Celeste put her hand to her hair. "Oh, Bob, thank you. But I didn't fix up to come down tonight. I had a day to myself upstairs, not feeling quite up to snuff. No, I didn't fix up to come down."

"I like you this way," he said. "More natural. It lets your real beauty show."

Celeste laughed. "Oh, Bob, you should have seen me when. I was a real beauty." She smoothed the hem of her dress, pulled her knees together, sat up a bit straighter.

"Life has a way of wearing you down, you know, of taking beauty away from you, and then you just become old. Like me." She smiled as she said this, and gave a faint laugh. "But it is awfully nice to have you to talk to, to get to know you."

"Do you believe in God?"

"Bob, where in the world did that come from? What a question." She placed her cigarette on the ash tray.

"I hope you don't think me presumptuous. But I am interested. I'm wrestling with it, and you are wise, you've lived a long time, experienced a lot. So I was hoping that you would tell me what you think, what you believe. I've wanted to ask what you thought about it for a long time, but there were always people around. And I thought this best to be a private conversation."

He paused. "I didn't mean to offend you, Mrs. Brentano."

"Oh, Bob, I'm not offended. It's just such an odd question." She took a deep drag on her cigarette, watched the smoke disperse before she answered.

"Do I believe in God? I don't think, no, I know, that no one has ever asked me that before. So it is a good question for me, especially at my age. I need to think about that, since it's likely that I'll be meeting my maker not too far off. If I have a maker, that is.

"You know, I don't think about God, don't think I've ever spent time wondering. I was raised Episcopalian, but it was never really important in our house. My mother, oh, my mother, she was, I guess you'd say she was a free-thinker. She made fun of the priests, the bible, all that, but only when she was with us, and more, much more, after Papa died. She changed after he died; I never really knew why. I never really knew her. Isn't that awful to say, an awful thing to say? That I never really knew my mother. Well, time for truth, right? If not now, when?"

Bob listened, waiting.

"Both my husbands were Catholic, but I don't think that meant much to either of them. Willie, now Willie, he was the thinker. If he were here, your question would be a good one for him. And he would have an answer for you. Yes, an answer that would help you sort out things. But me, no, I don't think I can help you. I was taught that there was a God, that he knew everything, that you had to be good or he would punish you. So maybe I've been bad and I'm being punished. But then there has, most times, I guess every time, there has been someone who has come and helped me out when I didn't know what I would do. Undeserved blessings, perhaps. Or maybe that was God." She leaned back in her chair, the cigarette dangling between the fingers of her left hand.

"But now I am alone, really alone. Well, not really alone. I have you; I have all the men here to talk to in the evening; I have Jimmy to look out for me. I think that is better than if I had a house. I'd really be all by myself then. And maybe I've thought about myself too much, not cared enough about others. Oh, I don't know. Whoever knows these things?"

She shook her head, stubbed out the cigarette that was about to burn her fingers. "But God. I think if you believe that God can help you through life, then it is good to believe. And most people do, right? Most people believe in God, so maybe they're right. What do I know? I'm just an old lady living here." She shrugged.

"And I think that calls for another cigarette, don't you?" She smiled and patted Bob's hand.

I shouldn't have asked, he thought. Best to keep things the way they are. She's a sad old bird. Lonely. All that make-up. People making fun of her behind her back. But she is a good soul.

Eighteen ─────────────────────────

The day was frigid; frost had formed on the inside of the bay window. She walked to it, used her fingernail to scratch her initials into the thin ice crystals, recalling doing the same thing at her house on North Avenue, a little girl, embarrassed that the letters spelled CAW. I am not a crow, she remembered singing, and then calling out the sounds of the crow, caw, caw, caw. Celeste closed her eyes and saw Annie shaking her finger. Meg laughed; she always laughed. Oh, Meg, Celeste thought. How did you end up? How did you spend your days? Probably staring out a window, like I am. Celeste closed her eyes, then went to the closet to get her coat.

Today she would go to the bank and clip her coupons, get her spending money for the next three months. She had planned to walk, but the weather looked so ominous that she asked Fuller to call a cab. She waited at the door, watching the cars splatter the water as it ran, dirty, into the gutter.

Standing in the lobby of the Savings Bank of Baltimore, her coupons redeemed, she asked the manager to call her a cab home. "Certainly, Mrs. Brentano. Not a day to be out in the weather."

"You are right, there," she said. "It would have been best to wait until tomorrow, but I had it in my head to come today, and I would have been at sixes and sevens had I not. You know how it is for old ladies and their plans. We're not too adaptable."

The manager walked Celeste to the sidewalk, helped her into the cab, gave the driver the address. As the cab pulled away from the curb, Celeste leaned forward.

"I say, do you think that you could take me a few places before you drop me of? I won't need to get out; I'd just like to drive by. It shouldn't take too long."

"Where to?" the driver asked, and she gave him the first location, Mt. Vernon Place.

"Just drive slowly around the four squares, no address in particular. I just want to look, to remember.

He shrugged and turned the cab east toward Charles Street. "Tell me when you've seen enough," he said, as he negotiated the steep hills between Charles and St. Paul Streets, then circled around the Washington Monument.

Celeste stared out at the once imposing four-story townhouses, most now needing paint and care. "Willie, which would have been ours?" she whispered. "What colors would we have painted the rooms? Yellow, I think, lots of yellows."

"I didn't catch that, ma'am. What did you say?"

Celeste cleared her throat. "Oh, would you go past the Stafford Hotel?" The cab headed north on Charles Street. She gazed up at the hotel. Not what it once was, she thought. Nothing is.

"Now, will you drive to North Avenue? Turn right when you get there, and stop a block above Greenmount." The old house, she thought. Mama, Papa, Eva. And Willie's house. I want to see it one more time.

The driver followed her directions, watching her from his rear view mirror. An old lady, he thought, visiting old places. Living at the Congress Hotel, not a good place for her. No money, he thought, and the old ones never tip anyway.

Celeste stared out at the grey day. Willie's house looked insignificant, her own even more so. The neighborhood has changed, she thought. That's why the houses no longer seem imposing.

"Now could you take me to Robert Street? Do you know where that is?" she asked. The driver nodded, and the two headed west. She had him stop at 1214. All these houses, so small, shabby. Surely they were better when I lived there. Surely. She started to speak to the driver, but then changed her mind. Best to keep these thoughts to myself, she whispered.

"Did you say something?" the driver asked.

"I should have asked you earlier, when we were there. But could you take me back to North Avenue, to the Baltimore Cemetery? I just want to visit a grave. I'll just step out and take a look and then we can be on our way."

"You're the boss," he said, and turned the cab to return where they had come from. He helped her from the backseat when they arrived at the gravesite, watched her walk the few steps to the high granite stone, stand beside the footstones, saw her reach down to leave something on the headstone.

As he helped her back into the car, she said, "One more cemetery, please. It's on the way back." A few blocks west they turned into the Green Mount Cemetery. Celeste gave him the directions to the plot. She was surprised that she remembered after all these years. Once again, he helped her from the back seat. This time she stood in front of a tall marble obelisk. "My parents, my grandparents, my sister are all buried here," she told him. He nodded and stood quietly, three paces behind her. She looked north, toward the mausoleum that she and Willie had visited that November afternoon. Best not to go there, she thought. Memories are enough.

The driver settled her into the cab. "You have been so kind. Can I ask you to make one more stop, this time downtown again. Stewart's. And if you would wait for me outside, I would much appreciate it." He nodded.

As the cab pulled in front of the store, he said, "Easier if I wait on Howard Street, not so congested. If I'm not here when you come out, it means that the police waved me away. I'll just be driving around the block. So don't worry, just wait and I'll show up."

When they arrived, he jumped from the front seat and helped her to the sidewalk. "Thank you, sir," she said. You are an officer and a gentleman." He saluted.

Celeste walked into the store, trying to remember how long it had been since she had last been there. The layout was the same, the restaurant at the back, notions department in front of it; exquisitely embroidered handkerchiefs, cosmetics, perfumes as you entered. It really is a lovely store, she thought, despite it all. She studied the merchandise, remembering the cab that waited for her. She stopped at the cosmetics counter, examined the tubes of lipstick, picking three up to compare shades. She slipped a fourth, Revlon's Cherries in the Snow, into her bag. She smiled as she returned the three to their slots.

The store detective watched her. Poor old soul, he thought. She's got enough troubles without me turning her in. He turned and walked to the other side of the store.

The cab was waiting for her; the driver helped her into the back seat. "It's been quite a day. I'm ready to go home now," she said. When they arrived at the Congress, the driver helped her up the steps and into the lobby. She gave him a generous tip.

Nineteen

The lights from Franklin Street reflected in the darkened room. Oh, no, this cannot be. Celeste closed her eyes. This just cannot be. She rose from bed, stared down at the soiled sheets. I will handle this, she thought. I will handle this, and then I'll have a cup of tea.

She filled the basin with hot water, sprinkled some flakes of Ivory Snow into it and swirled the mixture until the suds came over the rim. She pulled the sheet from the bed and put the soiled section into the bowl. I will handle this, she said to herself.

When the sheet was scrubbed and rinsed, she moved her books onto the bed and spread the material out over the radiator. Thank goodness it's winter and the heat is on, she thought. That will help it to dry. I will find something to be thankful for.

She cried as she washed her hands, turned on the hotplate, and had her morning bath.

An hour later, teacup in hand, she sat in her chair in the window and stared out, thinking about the condition she had been ignoring. Blood in the toilet, stomach pains, constipation followed by diarrhea, symptoms she could discuss with no one, symptoms she had had for years.

Oh, not this end for me. Please God, don't let this happen to me, she prayed, aware of the rarity of her conversations with God.

She stayed in her room, making sure that no one entered. She broke her own rule and had her evening cigarette there.

By nightfall the sheet was dry enough to put it back on the bed. She smoothed the blankets and spread, fluffed the pillow, bathed again, put on a clean gown and got into bed to read. The day was over. She had managed. This never happened, she told herself.

She woke the next morning, and, convincing herself that she felt renewed, went to lunch at Virginia Dare, walking the few blocks south on Howard Street. She passed the gold-trimmed wood and glass cases filled with pastries on her way to the restaurant at the back.

"I'm treating myself to the veal cutlet this afternoon," she told the waitress who came for her order. Leaving, she purchased a raisin bun for breakfast the following day. That evening she came down to the lobby for her customary cigarette and visit with the crew. It would be her last visit with them.

Twenty

Two weeks later, the maid came to the front desk and waited for Fuller to end his phone call. "There's a problem, I think. Mrs. Brentano has told me not to clean the room. For the past two weeks. When I knocked today she told me to go away, that she was fine and would do the cleaning herself. She didn't come to the door. And there's an odor there; it's bad. I think you need to go up and have a talk with her."

Fuller hadn't seen Celeste in a while. This didn't concern him. She was a private person, though she always spoke when they met. He knew that she spent her days in her room, sometimes leaving for lunch, or shopping. She was, he knew, a favorite with the night crew, coming down most evenings to sit. He decided to leave a note for Jimmy. If there was any unpleasantness, it would be better for Jimmy to handle it. She knew him; his word might carry more weight.

When Jimmy came on duty, he found the note. Later that evening, when Bob came in, Jimmy asked if he had seen Celeste recently.

"I know she's been a bit under the weather. She asked me to go to Milton's and pick up a few things for her, tea bags, some cookies. She told me that she'd come downstairs when she felt better. I tapped on her door this morning before I left for work, but I assumed that she was sleeping. She's not an early riser, I don't think."

They agreed to go to her room to check on her. "Just to see how she's doing," Jimmy said. "The maid said that there might be a problem."

There was no answer when they knocked. Jimmy pulled the passkey from his pocket, and called her name. As he opened the door, he heard a faint voice.

"Don't come in. Just leave me, please. Don't come in."

The room was dark; Bob blanched at the odor.

"Please don't come in. I'll be alright. Just give me some time. I'll come down tomorrow. It will be better tomorrow."

Jimmy went to the window, opened it, hoped that the night air would help ventilate the room. Bob went to the bed, holding his breath. "You need some help, Mrs. Brentano. You can't stay here. Let us get you some help."

"Oh no, please. Don't see me like this. Please leave. Please leave me with some dignity." Celeste pulled the blankets up, tried to sit up. Such humiliation, she thought, I don't think I can bear it. She pulled the blanket over her face. "Oh, please, leave. Please leave me alone."

Jimmy stepped back. "We'll bring you some tea. A cup of tea, yes. That will be just the thing. And I know how you like it, maybe a bit more sugar. That'll do the trick. Don't worry. It will be all right." He stood at the window and took a deep breath.

"Bob, can you help me get tea for Mrs. Brentano? Can you come with me?"

Celeste sank back into the pillows and watched the men leave. They pulled the door closed, the reflections from the automobiles and the streetlights on Franklin Street flashing on the far wall.

She knew that someone had come, men, maybe. She remembered being in the elevator; she had never noticed its ceiling in all the years she had lived there. Gilt, perhaps? Or maybe just gold paint, flaking. Men, yes, it had been men who had come.

Twenty-one

She willed herself to keep her eyes closed. As long as she didn't open them, this would be a dream. She inhaled. An odor that she couldn't quite identify. Not a bad odor, clean.

She listened. Where are my familiar sounds? she wondered. The splash of cars through a rainstorm; the whirr of automobile engines as they geared down for the incline from Howard to Eutaw Street; the shsss of tires on asphalt. These sounds are different, far away. Footsteps, muffled; voices, hushed.

She moved her fingers over the sheet; starched, ironed. Who starches sheets anymore? Not since Meg. Maybe it was Meg. Meg had come back to take care of her. Oh, yes, Meg. I knew you'd never leave me. And when I open my eyes, you will be here.

How she has changed, Celeste thought. I wouldn't have recognized her. And in that white dress, that hat. Most unbecoming. But I won't tell her; she does her best.

"Oh, Mrs. Brentano, you're awake."

Celeste heard the words. Meg would never call her Mrs. Brentano. Who was this, this angel, though an angel who didn't dress to her advantage? She would talk to her about that. Some lipstick would help. And white, no white was not her color. A soft candlelight, perhaps. Or at least a scarf, something to compliment her complexion.

The woman came to the bed. "How are you feeling this morning?" She touched Celeste's face, a gentle touch. "Do you know where you are?"

Celeste shook her head. She couldn't seem to find her voice.

"You're at Maryland General Hospital. You came in last night. You had quite a turn, it looks like. But we're here to take care of you, to help you get your strength back. We need to notify your family. Is there someone you'd like us to call? I'm sure that they're worried about you."

Celeste stared at the angel. "Maryland General Hospital? Fifth Regiment Armory? Howard Street? Antique Row?"

"Yes, Maryland General. Could you tell us who you'd like us to call?"

Celeste closed her eyes. The bed felt soft, clean. Nice here, she thought.

The nurse straightened the bedclothes. "You rest. We can talk later." Poor old soul, she thought.

When the doctor came to check the chart, the nurse gave him the background. The ambulance had brought the woman in last night, barely conscious, soiled, dehydrated, malnourished. They had cleaned her up and brought her to the floor. They hadn't run tests yet; they were waiting for the day shift to come on. The doctor took the chart and headed to her room.

"Looks like you've had a bit of an adventure here," he said. Celeste looked at him, tried to smile, but couldn't keep her eyes open long enough. She didn't notice the IV that was in her left hand. "Well, this afternoon, we're going to run a few tests. See what we can find. Meanwhile, you just rest. And eat whatever they bring you. That's an order. How long has it been since you've had a proper meal?" Not waiting for an answer, he turned to leave. Standing in the doorway, he said, "Mrs. Brentano, do you have your own physician? We can get in touch with him, you know. It would help us out."

Celeste didn't open her eyes. She shook her head.

The doctor wrote on the chart, tossed it to the nurse at the desk. "I'll stop back tomorrow afternoon. We should have enough results by then to figure out where we're going with her. Meanwhile, see what you can find out about family. She can't go back to that fleabag hotel when she leaves here."

The nurse came in to take Celeste's blood pressure. "The chaplains visit today. I could set it up for one of them to come in and talk to you. What denomination are you? Would you like to talk to someone specific? Or do you have your own clergyman? We could contact him for you." Celeste kept her eyes closed. This isn't happening, she thought. This is a dream, a bad one. I'll wake up soon.

"Well, maybe one will just look in on you," the nurse said, and patting the sheet, left the room.

Sometime that day, or the next, Celeste had lost track of time, she felt a presence. It was a priest of some sort; she noticed his black suit and dog collar. Oh, god, she thought. Should I open my eyes? Will he never go away?

"Mrs. Brentano, I'm Father Stockman. Is there anything I can do for you? Would you like me to pray with you?"

Celeste collected her strength, forced herself to open her eyes, forced herself to turn toward this man, whom she knew had a good heart. "Father," her words came out in a croak; it had been days since she had spoken. She cleared her throat. Yes, energy was coming to her. Good, she thought. Maybe his being here isn't so bad. "Father, you are better off spending your time with someone who believes in you. Thank you for seeing me, but I think that I can make this journey on my own." Celeste was surprised at the wisdom of her words. Well, she thought, that must be what I think.

"May I pray over you before I go, say some words of the savior?"

"You can save that too. But thank you for coming. Your presence has rallied me, that I will say." She managed a smile, and the man was struck by the brightness of her eyes.

"Well, that's something, isn't it?" He patted her hand and left the room.

This is what dying feels like, she thought. Just wafting away. Not so bad.

Twenty-two _____

What she felt then was not her death, not yet. And her death, when it came, was neither quick nor painless.

She lay in the hospital bed, ministered to by those she took to calling angels. Undeserved blessings she sang, as the cancer spread throughout her body, tangled her brain.

The social worker, with Jimmy's help, located Hyacinth, who felt put upon and trapped. Yes, she consented; she would help, although she didn't quite know what she had agreed to.

She mentioned it to Sylvie, by this time married and the mother of a newborn infant.

"I'd like to see her," Sylvie told her mother.

"I don't know why. She abandoned your father; she wanted nothing to do with him while he was growing up. She only contacted us when she wanted something. She's not someone to waste your sympathy on."

But Sylvie ventured to Maryland General, found Celeste's room.

Celeste was thinking of her red pen with the purple ink, her green diary when she heard the gentle knock. She did not want to be interrupted. She sensed that someone was there, but kept her eyes closed. She heard a soft voice, kindhearted. It pulled her away from her dream. She opened her eyes.

"Celeste, I'm Sylvie. I'm Bill's daughter, your granddaughter."

Celeste opened her eyes, saw a young woman, tall, blonde. "You look like her."

"Yes, I look like my mother," Sylvie answered.

"Only without the sour puss. Your mother always had such a sour puss, like she was sucking on a lemon. You have a kinder expression, but she was prettier than you. Much."

Sylvie smiled. "I suppose you're right."

Celeste stared at the young woman. "He died and they never told me. They never told me when he died."

"I know. I'm sorry for that."

Celeste closed her eyes. Sylvie sat by the bed, her hands in her lap, looking at Celeste's profile, the Roman nose, the profile of her father. So many secrets, she thought.

Bob stopped in to visit while Sylvie sat. He introduced himself, told her how he knew Celeste. "I didn't know she had a granddaughter," he said.

"This is the first time I've ever met her. And I live only a few blocks away, on George Street, in Seton Hill."

Bob laughed and asked if she ever shopped at Milton's. "Oh, Filthy Milton's. Now I wonder if I was ever there when she was, if I stood right beside her and didn't know it. So much to think about."

Bob nodded.

Sylvie stood. "I need to get back to the baby now. I have a little girl, just three months old." Sylvie looked over at Celeste, whose eyes remained closed.

"Goodbye, Celeste. I'm happy that I got to meet you." Sylvie touched her grandmother's nose.

Celeste opened her eyes, smiled at Bob. "So glad that you came to see me. It won't be much longer. And that's all right with me. But do be sure to return those library books in my room. I know they're overdue."

Twenty-three _____

Hyacinth breathed a sigh of relief when she learned that the new Medicare program would pay for Celeste's hospital bill. She found a nursing home for her, the same one where her own mother lived, and hoped that Celeste would not live too long.

She didn't.

When Celeste was conscious enough to think about death, her death, she hoped that she would close her eyes, exhale and everyone whom she had loved would be waiting for her. Willie, Meg, Annie, George, August, even Clara and Hanne. She didn't think of Eva, or Karl, or Bill.

But when she closed her eyes for the last time, there was only darkness.

There was no funeral. Hyacinth saw that she was buried in the family plot in the Green Mount Cemetery. It was November, and the birch and ginkgo trees stood as silent witnesses.

Twenty-four

The following week Hyacinth called Sylvie. "I cleaned out Celeste's room. Nothing there. She had almost nothing. A ratty old yellow kimono. I think it must have been good at one time, a long time ago. Some old books, an old diary, green, falling apart. I just tossed everything.

"But she did have some silverware. It looks quite nice. Ivory handles. I took that with me."

A few months later an attorney contacted Hyacinth about the bonds. Since Celeste had died without a will, the proceeds would go to her only surviving heir, her granddaughter.

Sylvie put the money into an account for her daughter. She thought that, one day, she would learn Celeste's story.

Acknowledgments

I'd like to thank the staff and volunteers at the Baltimore Streetcar Museum, the Baltimore and Ohio Train Museum, and, the wonderful Enoch Pratt Free Library. Kilduff's.com is a wonderful source of pictures of old Baltimore, and I used them for inspiration throughout my time writing this book. I'd also like to recognize the staff of The Denver Public Library, The Colorado Railroad Museum, The Missouri State Archives, The Missouri Historical Society, The Texas State Historical Society and the Texas Train Museum. Each made me feel that I was living what I wrote.

Thank you too, to Abigail DeWitt, during whose workshop I fell in love with these characters. And, of course, for being there, Sasha and Dick.